vagabonder

r.t. coleman

Vagabonder
© 2022 R.T. Coleman

www.aurelialeo.com

Coleman, R.T.
Vagabonder / by R.T. Coleman
ISBN-13: 978-1-946024-43-5 (ebook)
ISBN-13: 978-1-954541-16-0 (paperback)
ISBN-13: 978-1-954541-18-4 (hardback)
Library of Congress Control Number: 2022944680

Editing by Lesley Sabga
Cover design by Maria Spada (www.mariaspada.com)
Book design by Knight Designs (authorzknight.com)

Printed in the United States of America
First Edition:
10 9 8 7 6 5 4 3 2 1

For Joe, who believed before anyone else.

...and from out
A full-orbed moon, that, like thine own soul, soaring
Sought a precipitate pathway up through heaven
There fell a silvery-silken veil of light,
With quietude, and sultriness, and slumber...
Edgar Allan Poe

"Behold, thou hast driven me out this day from the face of the Earth; and from
thy face shall I be hid; and I shall be a fugitive and a vagabond in the Earth;
and it shall come to pass, that every one that findeth me shall slay me."
Genesis 4:14

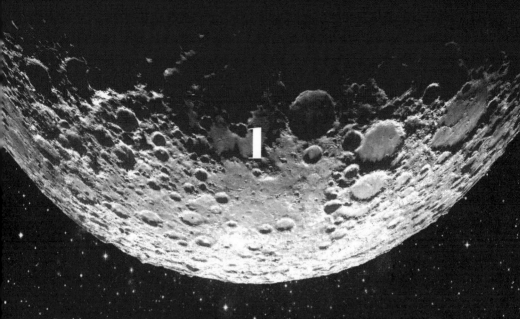

1

THE WOMAN ISN'T DEAD. She's sprawled across Paysandú Station's cracked tile where she collapsed in a heap, the strike from the electristic still sparking across her back. Her bag skids to a halt a half meter from the alcove where I cower. It could have been me. It should have been me.

The station's traffic flows around her, steps over her. A few humans give her a glance; the Dua try not to look. From the dank alcove, I watch her waist rise, fall; her limbs twitch, then settle. The drone—round, silver—hovers several meters above her. Taunting.

Something dark careens across the cracked tile floor. A human male appears to have kicked the back of the woman's head, hard. I step forward, my fists doubled.

"Are you crazy?" My sister's breath cools the back of my neck. Her fingers tighten, her nails dig into my forearm. She jerks me back. "It's still up there."

I shake her off as the Dua's dark head covering slides to a stop a few meters from the unconscious figure. Wispy white hair spills across the tile, and I run my hand absently through my own. "I can take out a drone." She digs her fingernails deeper into my skin. "We can't just leave her out there, Eisa."

"It's too late anyway," she whispers. I hear the Authority bots first, a steady, metallic *thunk, thunk, thunk.* Two stop at the woman. One positions as sentry; its sienna eyes glow behind a dark helmet. The other bends, emitting a low whine, retrieves the tattered bag, then lifts the Dua in its subarms. Its hands curve around her wrists and ankles.

The Dua's thin legs dangle as her head lolls back. Eisa gasps beside me. "Goddamn," I whisper. "A child. Why?"

"They get scared." Eisa loosens her grip and retreats to the stone wall at the alcove's rear. Her blue eyes glisten. "Mama always told them. Humans know humans. They say it's like this in all the cities." She shivers, pulls her arms across her chest, wraps her hands around her shoulders. The last time I saw her, she was a child herself, standing very close to this same spot. Her face was blotchy and red from crying, and when I'd waved goodbye from the train, she'd buried her face against our mother's shoulder. Mother's eyes never left mine.

Now that she's grown, Eisa's face is like my mother's. Elegant and open.

"Where do they go?"

Eisa shrugs. "These days, we can get most registries to Caracas, but the Station there can't get them anywhere else, so we've been trying Montevideo." She nods toward the backpack around my shoulders. "That registry didn't come cheap."

And you're definitely cutting the line is unspoken, but I know it's there. Hundreds of Dua wait for forged registries to a dwindling number of Republic of SoAm stations, bound for the American peninsula, maybe Morocco. Somewhere OnyxCorp isn't.

"A child," I repeat.

"Yes." Eisa retrieves a drugstic from her pocket. She flicks it on and takes a light drag. "Imagine what they'll do to you." She breathes out a soft vapor cloud that encircles her head.

"They have to catch me first." My voice sounds less confident than I intend.

She scoffs. "Caen. They're looking all over for you. And you just waltz right in to the one place they know—"

"Our mother was killed." Eisa looks at me as if I've struck her. I breathe in and almost choke on the station's dank air. Synthohol,

2

anxiety, a protein packet, nanosynthetic hair, fear, burning fossil fuel, anger. Dua and human and machine, a miasma of confusion and uncertainty. It's my second trip to Paysandú Station in so many days, but only today do I see how everything has changed in those eleven years. I glance at the holographic signage above B Platform, a projection of a grinning human couple. Copy scrolls over their faces in bright red and black letters: *OnyxCorp. From the Earth to the moon, making your journey to perfection complete.* The woman's toothy smirk spreads through perfectly generated red lips, her rounded features in sharp contrast to the man's chiseled jaw and high cheekbones. Travelers walking beneath the hologram might imagine they could touch the woman's hair as it flutters down toward the causeway floor. *OnyxCorp. Generating perfection.* The image fades until only the black *O* logo fills the screen.

"She knew you'd come back. She always believed, wouldn't let anyone say otherwise." Eisa takes another drag. "But you should never have come back, brother."

"I suddenly had business here."

"Not anymore." She juts a thumb behind her, toward the bot standing at C Platform. "If they find you here, we're all as good as dead."

I've seen this bot type before. Subarms, armored torso, electristic at the ready. The mechanisms that attach its round head to its body are surprisingly vulnerable if you dare to get close enough. Or don't have a choice. "It's a Level 1, or a Level 2. You said they're all here, in the station? I count six bots."

"Level whatever. They're all lethal. There were dozens here during the strike, but after—" Her voice wavers. "You can't take down six bots, brother."

"By myself, no. But there are hundreds—"

"We've tried that." Her voice breaks, and suddenly she sinks to the ground. Her hand shakes as she brings the drugstic to her mouth.

"I'm sorry." I settle on the broken tile beside her and pull her to me. "It shouldn't have gone that way. If I'd been here—"

"It wouldn't have made a difference. They're making a move, Caen. We need to make ours. Montevideo is still using reclamation crews. They won't realize how old the registry is until you're long gone. From there, you can—"

"I know, I know. Find Lee Chou." I pull her closer. She is solid, strong. But she is afraid. "If they're starting to purge the small cities now, more will need to get out of what's left of SoAm. You need help. Now that Mama's gone. I should stay."

She scoffs. "You wouldn't last a week. And they'd take down everyone in Paysandú to get to you." Another drone buzzes overhead. The station's lights glint against it, and Eisa ducks her head instinctively. "You really want to help?" She scrambles to her feet. "Get out of here. Fulfill this *destiny* of yours." She spits out the word. "Take that," she says, pointing to the pack lying in the corner, "to the moon. Find our people. Like Mama said."

I suppress an eye roll as I get to my feet. "You can't seriously believe that old story." I glance at the bot. No change. Its electristic emits a sienna pulse as it charges. "I don't believe it."

"Of course I don't believe it. My brother, the only Dua who can save us all? It's ludicrous." She crosses her arms over her chest. "But if you stay here, you'll die. And they'll have their prize. Get out of SoAm. Hell, go to the moon. Maybe it's all true."

"Vagabonders. Original moon settlers. The fairy tales Mother told us at night."

"Some tales are based in truth. Maybe this one is one of those." She dusts off the seat of her threadbare trousers, and for a moment she looks exactly like Mama. Before Mama was the Paysandú Station manager. Before she had the lives of countless Dua children, their mothers and fathers, in her hands. Their dreams of a better life hers to fulfill if she can.

How many dreams had she foregone? Did she have any of her own?

I run a hand over my face. Hot as hell today. Hot and wet and close. "You're scared. I get it. This," I say, gesturing to the bustling station beyond our hiding place, "is scary. But it's real. OnyxCorp is real, something we can fight, together. The Vagabonders—"

"You owe me." The sharpness in her voice is Mama's as well. I look down at the broken tiled floor. Tiny weeds and moss push their way through crevices created through time, neglect, apathy. "You haven't seen it like it is here. You've been out there, in the places no one wants to go. You saw how OnyxCorp is working them, drugging them, keeping them under control. Where do you think those Dua are coming from? They're gathering us up like never before. They're realizing what we are, what we can do, Caen. And they're scared. You know what they're willing to do when they're scared." She grabs the pack and thrusts it toward me. "There's some unfinished business on that digiscreen."

Sighing, I take the bag, sling its strap over my shoulder. Its contents bounce gently across my back. My mother's digiscreen, an artifact from a different time, a keeper of secrets. "Come with me."

Eisa shakes her head. "Someone has to keep the station going. Maybe get a few more out—"

"You've done enough. We've done enough."

Her arms are suddenly around me. *I'm never going to see her again.* My chest tightens.

"You are the wanderer, brother."

"A Vagabonder?" My voice is harder than I mean. She pulls away and brushes her hand across her cheeks.

"Maybe. Probably not. Either way, what do we have to lose?" She cups my face between her palms. "I really missed you, big brother. Seeing you, though—" She shakes her head, releases me. "You're going to miss your transport."

I glance at the registry interface to my right, maybe ten meters away. Its electronic face glows faintly behind rushing silhouettes of men, women, and children. The bot across the causeway still hasn't moved.

"I'm coming back for you." I swallow against the lump in my throat. I hold her gaze. Our father's azure eyes, our mother's face.

"She always said this was what you were meant for." She meets my eyes. "Go find our people. Make this right."

I pull myself away and plunge into the light, the noise, the buzz. Paysandú Transport Depot. I pass a media screen on my left; a hologram head bobs in the foreground. The Vine looms in the background. The space elevator. Thousands of miles away in the Indian Ocean.

My destination.

I fight the urge to look behind me. At the registry interface, I fumble with the forged ID chip and drop it on the tile. My hands tremble as I retrieve it and hold it beneath the reader. The interface buzzes softly, and five seconds later, a holographic face appears, its features an amalgam of faces that overlap and intertwine.

"Welcome. I'm TES, TechComm Enhancement System. Please state your registry number for voice recognition protocol." The interface crackles. Only the worst for Paysandú.

"NCI790—" My voice catches; the last three numbers come out in a hoarse croak.

The interface buzzes.

"Not recognized. Please state your registry number for voice recognition protocol."

I clear my throat. "NCI790612." Better.

The interface chirps.

"Thank you, NCI790612. You are authorized for travel to the following locations. Please state your destination."

An area map displaces the distorted face. The cities to which NCI790612—the falsified identity my sister has given me, an identity meant for a young Dua, the last of his family—is permitted travel flash in green: Montevideo, Belém, Caracas. The rest of the Republic of SoAm, what remains of the South American continent, is red.

"Please state your destination," TES crackles.

I feel my sister's eyes on my back, her heart pounding. Or perhaps that's my heart. "Montevideo."

The interface chirps. The map flashes green, zooms in to Montevideo. "Destination recorded. NCI790612. You are authorized for travel to Montevideo for four days. Return to Paysandú expected on 07.10.2261. Please proceed to B17 Platform."

I glance up at the grinning holographic couple as I adjust the bag on my shoulder. ...*making your journey to perfection complete.* The O grows like a dead, white cornea surrounded by a black limbal ring. I risk a last look toward the alcove. I don't need to see Eisa to know she's there, willing me to hurry.

I turn to B Platform, merge with the crowd. A human male behind me stinks of sweat and the chemicals they use to clean their garments. He runs past me, bumps into a young human female who's entranced by the station's crumbling ceiling. She stumbles, all elongated legs, sculpted torso, and bioenhancements in a silver bodysuit. I follow her gaze to a mural, possibly beautiful at one time. Green hills surround a gently cascading stream, lush forests hide long extinct mammals no one in this station has ever seen in reality. I pass the young woman, catching a whiff of lavender. No, not real lavender. Just another bioenhancement. From the Earth to the moon, the humans seek sameness. Perhaps to humans, sameness is perfection. Sameness in humans, sameness in Dua, but difference between.

B17 is empty save for the bot, twenty-five meters to my left. Its black metallic body stretches more than two meters from the floor to its round titanium head. Thick cables connect the head with a bulging, armored chest. Its shielded helmet is dark. A lean woman with light brown hair scuffles past me, her left hand wrapped tightly around a child's hand. The child struggles to keep up; its head is engulfed in an occulus—their constant connection to TES—far too large. As she draws nearer the bot, she tugs at the child impatiently as she increases her stride.

The child stumbles, and the occulus rolls away. A tuft of stark white hair flashes before the woman covers the child with her body.

A Dua child.

She struggles to readjust the occulus, the only way a Dua child could pass. The child whimpers. Perhaps it senses the woman's fear. The air is permeated by it.

The Authority engages. Two points of sienna burn through the dark visor. It takes a step.

The woman kneels before the child and whispers against their cheek. She smooths the white hair. The child's dark blue eyes are wide, frightened.

Run.

She clutches the child's hands, pulls the small body close.

Run, damn you.

The bot advances. Why do they try to pass?

They get scared. The forged ID I just used could have been given to a mother. A child.

I sprint past the Dua toward the bot. It screeches to a halt. A Level 1. Clunky. Slow. It hasn't even begun to access its defense protocols when I reach it. Pivoting on one foot, I swing behind the bot, grasp the cables that extend from its back to the base of its round head, and jerk. The bot tries to spin in response, giving me the added leverage I need. The cable bundle tears loose. Bright orange sparks rain down as I twist away from the stumbling bot.

The maglev shrieks into the Station and rumbles to a stop seconds later. The Dua and the child are gone. Good. The bot staggers in a wide circle, searching. Arrivals spill from the maglev's compartments, humans at the front, Dua in the rear, confusing the bot even more. When a drone finally buzzes into the scene in response to the bot's sudden malfunction, I am lost in the crowd.

Onboard the maglev, I throw myself into a seat and peer out the window. The drone hovers just above the bot, rotates slowly, scans the crowd as it thins, disperses, human and Dua together.

The maglev lurches forward, shivers as it gains speed. Soon the bot, the drone, the station, and my sister are the past. My future is another world.

My future is the moon.

I take a long breath in and let it out slowly. The pack presses into my back as it lodges between my body and the seat. I shrug it from my shoulders and set it next to me.

What the hell are you doing?

The question pushes through the maglev's steady pulse and my jumbled thoughts. In less than a week I've dismantled everything I've built over the last eleven years. My position in the Dua Emancipation Party, abandoned. My objectivity, destroyed. For what?

Your mother died.

The tattered bag next to me is all I have left of her, its weight measured more in expectation and legacy than volume. I place a protective hand over it and close my eyes to remember again the last time I saw my mother's face, eleven years ago.

It will be hard, son, she said. *You will wonder why it must be you. I wondered the same. Why did this information come to me? Why can't I entrust it to someone else, anyone else besides my own child? I don't have answers, but I do know that if we are to have any chance at freedom, you must be stronger and faster and smarter than any human. You must learn all you can so you can take this information to the moon and find our people. Only they can help us now.*

I came back to Paysandú looking for a fight, an avenging angel for my mother. My people. Brutalized. Arrested. Murdered. All because of what they are.

I leave a coward, running away and leaving behind the only family I have left.

I realize I am not alone when I hear the shuffle of human feet. I place a hand on the pack as the inquisitive face of a human girl rises over the back of the torn seat in front of me. Her dark hair is pulled back in a messy ponytail that contrasts sharply with her crisp silvery uniform. Her occulus, the constant virtual companion of every human child until age fifteen, is pushed back on her head haphazardly.

"Are you a NiCIe?"

I grimace at the slur. She's maybe ten or eleven; the word sounds somehow harsher from her. She leans over the seat to get a better look at me.

"I am Dua."

"Is that the same thing as a NiCIe?" I consider setting her straight. *Not the way you mean it, like we're the virus. Like we're the disease.* Instead, I shift closer to the window and look out. "I knew it. Because of your hair. And your eyes." She slides down the length of the bench to join me at the window.

"Don't you have parents somewhere?" The girl is one thing. Human children tend to be curious, not violent. Adults are another matter. Dua don't transmit Ruĝa Morto, but humans don't hear that. They only know what the virus does to them. It makes them like us.

The girl shakes her head, her ponytail swinging widely. "Dad's in the other car. He's asleep, but I don't know how. This maglev is so old.

Do you think it's noisy? I'm going to Buenos Aires. Where are you going? We're going to see my mother. She's sick, in the med facility. Dad says it's the best in SoAm."

"I'm sorry your mother is ill." I say it as warmly as I can, but it's less warm than she expects because she narrows her eyes. "Mothers are important," I add, trying to smile.

The girl cocks her head. "She has a virus. Do you know what a virus is?" She speaks slowly, as if I were a particularly dumb NiCIe.

"Yes, I do."

"I haven't seen her in a whole month because she was too sick, but Dad says she's better now." She leans closer, presses her chest across the top of the seat between us. "I heard my father call it Ruĝa Morto, so I thought that meant she would die. But my learning avatar, Willow," she taps the occulus, "said Ruĝa Morto doesn't cause people to die. Not anymore. But she says it changes people. I mean, humans."

"You're going to bring her home, your mother?"

"They're moving her to a better hospital, Dad says. Until she changes back." I want to laugh at the absurdity. I look away again, willing her to leave. "My father says NiCIes are stupid. Is it true NiCIes have to do whatever we tell you to do?"

"Why don't you ask your learning avatar?" This time I mean to sound harsh, and it works. Her face falls, her shoulder slump, and immediately I feel regret. A child. Not her fault. I clench my fists, one of them gathering the pack's loose material into a ball. "We do what is rational. Many times, what's most rational is to do for others rather than for oneself."

The girl's lips crinkle as she contemplates this information. She looks out the window at the rushing landscape, pulls the occulus over her eyes. I follow her gaze. Scattered, crumbling, decaying buildings. Remnants of rotting trees and vegetation cluttering deteriorating streets and jabbing through disintegrating walls. Evidence of colossal floods that overran most of the continent a century before.

"No one lives there anymore, do they?" the girl says. "Willow is showing me how it used to look. It was so beautiful. Oh, there was so much water." She frowns as she watches the scene play through her occulus, and I wonder how the history of the planet's environmental collapse is told to human children. "She tells me even NiCIes can't stay there."

"Not anymore."

"Where do you live? NiCIes, I mean." She moves her head from side to side, biting her lip as the occulus continues its instruction.

"Wherever humans don't want to live."

The girl turns her head and pushes the occulus back to rest on her forehead. I can see a question forming when the door at the car's far end swooshes open. An imposing human man with an over-large chest and a bald head enters, glances frantically left and right until he spies us and heads our way. His face is red, his mouth turned down. The girl stiffens as he halts beside her.

"Magret, return to your seat now," he growls. The girl lowers her head and slides to the floor with a soft thud as he places a heavy hand atop her head. Before he can push her behind him, she rises tall and whirls to face me, her expression a mixture of fear and defiance.

"Goodbye." Her words pour out. "You seem like a—a good NiCIe." She ducks around the man, runs down the aisle, and disappears into the next compartment.

The man's breath is hot on my face. I look up, meeting his eyes. This will set him off, I know, but I can't help myself.

"They used to keep your kind isolated." His jaw is clenched and rigid.

"You're free to leave."

Fury washes over him, and for a moment it is euphoric. He raises his arms at the elbow, his fists clenched. "You walk around us, they say nothing. You think you can just go where you want, infect who you want—"

I rise slowly to make sure he sees me, really sees me. Sees that I tower over him, sees that I could end any fight he cares to start. His mouth snaps shut. For a moment I think he might go through with it, but he steps backward. "Fuck you, NiCIe. You and all your kind." He takes a few more backwards steps. He won't take his eyes from mine, and I respect that. Then he spins on his heel and strides back the way he came, the aura of his anger and sorrow thick between us.

I sink on the bench after the compartment door slides closed behind him and let out a long breath. They, too, have lost. Loved ones. Homes. Their planet. Hope. I draw the backpack across the seat and hold it tight against my body, the image of my mother's face suddenly coming to mind. *But so have we. So have I.*

The maglev slows three hours later as it nears Montevideo. Ramshackle buildings at the city's outskirts show signs of habitation. A rusted vehicle here, canisters filled with green vegetation there. Pieces of colorful cloth blow in a light breeze. The permanent labor force, living where they are told, in whatever conditions are allowed.

The Vagabonders are a myth, a dream. A sacred tale tying my people to one another, to a planet that can never be ours, to the barren hunk of rock that orbits the Earth. Our home, the myth says.

Our dream.

We all get to dream.

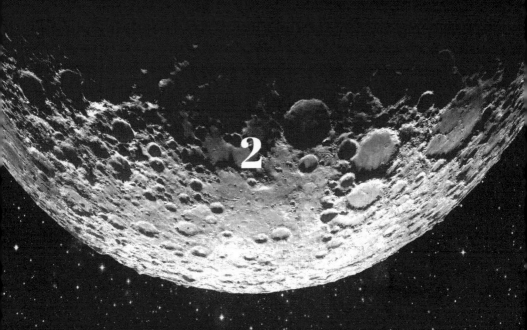

2

BULLSHIT. The only word Ligeia Obumbwe has for what she's witnessed in the last seventy-two minutes, twenty-four seconds. Judging by the sea of mostly bored faces crammed into the dim conference hall, she can only assume they would agree. For different reasons, of course. You can't help but be bored by Reynolds, poor guy. He's trying, he really is, but it was a simple question, and here he's been going on for a full eight minutes thirty-three seconds.

"All told, we added more than 2,500 assets to the lunar facilities in the last quarter, and we expect to reach that benchmark again this quarter. We're on target with our strategic plan for relocating most NCIs to one of four facilities, three here in the African Republic, and the one in the Republic of SoAm, which I understand is almost at capacity." Reynolds flashes a triumphant smile. He's young, as far as OnyxCorp execs go. Likely a nephew, son, cousin of somebody who knows somebody. Young and eager to impress, from his perfectly coiffed head of dark black hair to his shiny grey OnyxCorp suit. But he's just another suit among many on this packed panel. OnyxCorp and Earth Federation Council reps. Easily forgotten, quickly replaced, should the need arise, and it often does. Execs seem to be cheap these days.

Ligeia does not blend in, and not only on account of her unruly hair, which she attempted to secure in a tight chignon at the back of her neck, with disappointing results. She is the lone scientist here, her presence a mere nod to the scientific community rather than full-fledged inclusion because she has been completely shut out of this conversation. Which, upon reflection, is pretty amusing given the subject. Her subject. The subject she's been studying for the better part of two decades.

"Thank you, Mr. Reynolds, for that informative and thorough response," the moderator intones sleepily. "We're coming up a little short on time, and I certainly want to give our audience an opportunity for questions. Before we begin our Q&A, President Hedges, I believe you have some news?"

And with that, the shutout is complete. She should have known better. Last minute invite, delivered as if it were a great honor. Ligeia glances down at the flexscreen stretched out on the table before her, her five-minute presentation cued up and ready to link to the conference hall's wallscreen. She taps it with a rigid forefinger, and the screen goes transparent. *So much for the science part of the International Scientific Academy's 2261 Symposium for the Advancement of Technologies.*

President Walter Hedges of OnyxCorp rises to tepid applause. Director of the International Scientific Academy, although he knows nothing about science. Executive Director of NCI Relations, although he despises NiCies to his core. He puts his palms together before his chest and bows before taking his place on the dais.

"Thank you all for attending. I believe this has been our best Symposium to date." A smattering of hand claps. "I want to thank our panelists for their time and their expertise—" *although we don't listen to them,* "and our attendees for your thoughtful questions." *Although we don't answer them.* "I will be brief. I have some news that I think will end our gathering on the most positive of notes. I can announce today that the construction of Lunar Complex E has been officially completed and is ready for occupancy. As Reynolds noted earlier, our relocation efforts have kept steady pace with our projections, but we were limited by the amount of adequate asset housing. With the completion of Complex E, we feel confident that relocations will be ramped up significantly in the coming months with the passage of the NCI Civil Protection Act."

More applause, perhaps with a little more energy. The NCI Civil Protection Act sounds good. Like it's focused on protecting NCIs, on ensuring their civil rights are secure. Curious, then, that no NCI is here to represent their people. The three States are here: The Republic of SoAm, the African Republic, and Independent Mexico. The Earth Federation Council's Prime Minister Gala Proxy is here with her entourage. More than half the attendees are OnyxCorp. But not one NCI panelist.

Assets don't get representation. The question of what to do about the sudden appearance of an entirely new hominid species has been answered without the input of the species themselves. *Pretty typical of our species.*

"This legislation's passage will allow OnyxCorp to conduct a thorough inventory of all NCIs living outside the boundaries of the three States and EFC territories. We have already begun to disperse the current assets equitably through collaboration with the EFC. I want to personally thank Prime Minister Gala Proxy, who played a key role in shepherding this bill through the Earth Federation Council's preliminary committees. Her cooperation and contributions helped us complete construction on Lunar Complex E half a year earlier than anticipated."

Ligeia glances at her RistWach as the Prime Minister stands. Seventy-eight minutes, fourteen seconds. Proxy takes a bow as the applause dies. She appears much older than her official image in person. But no amount of bioenhancement can erase 84 years from someone's face.

"As I said earlier, I do believe this is our best Symposium yet, and I hope you will all join us at the Maun OnyxCorp Center for Cultural Advancement this evening. Cocktail hour begins at 7 p.m. Now, I believe we had time for a few more questions."

Ligeia fiddles with the bun at the back of her neck and realizes more dark brown ringlets have worked their way free. With a frustrated jerk, she pulls the whole apparatus free and shakes her head. She's done with this charade anyway.

"This question is for Dr. Obumbwe." Ligeia jerks her head up, suddenly aware that she's in front of several hundred people. An older man, perhaps in his eighties, has approached one of several small drones scattered throughout the auditorium. White tufts of hair stick out about his head; a dark beard covers his jaw. Ligeia sits a little straighter in the uncomfortable chair, at once thrilled to be finally included and irritated that this overly lengthy session is going to drag on a bit more. She clears her throat; the scratchy growl echoes through the speakers as her voice link connects.

"Ah, yes. I'm Dr. Obumbwe." Even to her, it sounds like she might be unsure about that.

"I regret you weren't able to speak to us today, Dr. Obumbwe. It's shocking, really, given your background. Preliminary degree in medtech from the *Faculté de Médecine Pierre et Marie Curie* in Paris at eighteen years old, a member of the last graduating class of that prestigious university in 2236. Degrees in neurobiology and neurogenetics from the University of Botswana. Thirty-two endorsed publications, among them studies in neuro-regeneration and artificial immune systems."

"Did my mother send you?" Ligeia half-smiles as polite laughter pulses through the crowd. He's more out of place than she, clothed in a simple woven tunic and flowing black trousers, a stark contrast to the attendees' identical silver uniforms, the standard attire for Earth Federation Council Citizens. And he has spectacles. She's seen spectacles only in pictures, before eye enhancement was standard.

"Let's just say I'm an admirer. My question is about your most recent publication, *Neurologically Compromised Individuals and Intelligence: Qualitative Analysis of First, Second, and Third Generation NCI Behavior and Implications*. If I'm interpreting your conclusions correctly, you're suggesting that for the first time in our planet's known history, we share it with an intelligent species capable of communicating with us. Living with us. Working *with* us."

"You're referring to NiCIes, I presume." Hedges' plastic smile covers the tightness in his jaw. He had added Ligeia to the panel only two days ago. *A favor. You don't have to say anything, Dr. Obumbwe. We*

16

just want a medtech on the panel in case the conversation gets too esoteric. Legitimacy. Appearance. To show OnyxCorp's good faith.

"They prefer to be called Dua." The old man frowns.

"Ah, yes. Forgive me. It's hard to keep up with the changes they make to our language." Hedges chuckles in a way that only corporate types can: Too eager, too obvious. "So, it's Dua this year, is it? Well, they can call themselves whatever they like. To me, they'll always be Neurologically Compromised Individuals. NiCIes." Hedges flashes a broad, toothy smile. "Unless they'd prefer we go back to calling them zombies." He's rewarded with another wave of polite laughter, which makes Ligeia feel a little less charitable toward the audience.

The old man doesn't crack a smile.

"Well, Mr. Hedges, I suppose you have a point." It's a delight to see Hedges flinch at the use of *Mr.* instead of *President.* "We've learned a great deal about the Ruĝa Morto virus and its effects on Neurologically Compromised Individuals—that's the *scientific* term, Mr. Hedges— since those early days. Yet OnyxCorp still hasn't disavowed its claims that Dua are highly contagious, lethal even, to humans. OnyxCorp could save millions of Dua lives by embracing the science as well as its terminology."

A murmur filters through the crowd. Hedges shifts. "I'm afraid I haven't had the pleasure of meeting you, Mr.?"

"Sakata. Owen Sakata."

The Owen Sakata?

Ligeia's read everything written by or about Owen Sakata. His publications on NCI behavior, philosophy, social structure. His memoir from his days as a field medtech during the collapse of the North American continent. News segments and profiles on his involvement in the NCI riots when he was stationed as a researcher on the moon. Transcripts of his trial.

Then nothing. It was as if he'd disappeared from the planet. Owen Sakata. Here.

"What a treat." Hedges' voice is flat, but there is menace there as well. "Forgive me, Dr. Sakata. I didn't know you were still, ah, alive."

"As a great nineteenth century philosopher once said, the reports

17

of my death were an exaggeration. It'll take more than gravity sickness to end me. Or constant surveillance."

Hedges bristles. Ligeia notices his jaw tighten. Perhaps this symposium will be salvaged after all.

"It's an honor to meet you in person, Dr. Sakata," she says before Hedges can derail this conversation, too. "I've been a fan of your work since I was about ten years old. When I found a copy of your memoir in my dad's library."

Sakata turns his bright eyes to meet hers. "Pretty weighty tome for a child. And maybe less than appropriate?"

Ligeia shrugs, grinning. "My parents weren't happy about it, but also unsurprised. You said you had a question." She cuts a glance at Hedges, almost daring him. The corners of his mouth are drawn in a straight line.

"It seems to me that this esteemed panel lacks perspective. For the last hour and a half, you've discussed lunar production, labor, and transport issues with the Vine. But there's been no discussion of the one factor underlying it all."

"And what's that?" Ligeia had wondered when the Prime Minister would speak up. When it comes to the assets, the EFC and OnyxCorp's interests align, always. Prime Minister *Proxy* indeed.

"The *NiCIes*, Prime Minister." Sakata spits out the word.

"I disagree," Proxy says coolly. As she leans forward, her eye enhancements glitter in the bright stage lights. "The NiCIes are, in fact, critical to the success of our lunar and Earth-bound operations. They were an unfortunate byproduct of Ruĝa Morto, which had an 80% mortality rate at the height of the pandemic. 80%! I think we can forgive our grandparents' actions in the face of a virus that permanently altered the brain's frontal lobe. That is, if it didn't kill the victim first. And OnyxCorp was the first entity to acknowledge how the NiCIes could benefit our future."

"I must disagree with your categorizing OnyxCorp as anti-science as well, Mr. Sakata." Hedges emphasizes that *Mr.* Two can play at that game. "We have never hidden the truth about how the virus affects human beings. The frontal lobe regulates decision making, problem solving, purposeful behavior, emotions. Damage to it can cause increased irritability, increased risk-taking, and non-compliance with rules and societal expectations." Hedges casts a side glance Ligeia's way, perhaps expecting her to challenge this over-simplified analysis. She shrugs. It's not like providing actual facts would make a difference. "In NiCIes, frontal lobe damage resulted in decreased aggressive behavior. They're docile, even tempered, and industrious, capable of arduous work in the most demanding situations. And they're completely dependable when given explicit instructions in any kind of task."

"Not to mention those captivating eyes," Proxy interjects. It's meant to be funny, but no one realizes until she follows up with a light chortle. Nervous chuckles ripple through the crowd.

"They're white-haired giants!" a man's voice calls from the back of the auditorium. Hedges laughs mechanically, and the audience follows suit, a bunch of mimics.

"The Vine would not have been possible without them, nor the Lunar settlements. It's our duty to care for them, provide them with opportunities for meaningful contributions to a society that has limited resources. Regardless of their limitations." Hedges smiles. "They are so very important to our work, to OnyxCorp's work, to the greater vision of the EFC and its three honored States."

"*Your* work." Sakata's voice erases Hedges' smile. "Did you build the Vine? The Vine Station? TES? The eye implants, the bioenhancements, the NutriPrints—"

"Those things aren't possible without capital from OnyxCorp—" Hedges begins.

"Your question, Dr. Sakata?" Hedges closes his mouth with a snap at Ligeia's interruption, but he dares not look her way. The eyes of everyone in the room are suddenly on her, including those of Owen Sakata, who looks nothing like the images she's seen in the EFC archives, save for his piercing dark brown eyes.

"Given your expertise in the field of Dua genetics, do you agree with this panel's official stance on their status? That they represent assets?"

"This is not the time or place to debate that question, doctor." Ligeia can practically hear Hedges' teeth grinding.

"It's a good question. And I'd like to answer it." Ligeia's words hang in the gloom of the dim hall. "NiCIes share only 98.8% of their DNA with homo sapiens."

"Dr. Obumbwe, I certainly appreciate your indulging this line of questioning, but this is beyond the scope of this panel—"

"Excuse me, President Hedges, but this is the type of question I'm here to answer. Or did I misunderstand my role here? Am I here as an expert on NCIs, or am I simply a prop?"

If Hedges could kill her with a look—

He doesn't say anything, though. At least not in front of the entire Symposium. She turns her attention to the audience, which is holding its collective breath. "At first, NCIs' biological changes suggested they were a lesser species of hominid, a devolution. The first generation were docile, detached from society and others, and new victims of the virus behave similarly. At one end of the spectrum, they have difficulty addressing basic needs. On the other end, there are anomalies that just don't make sense. But now we have data from second and third generations, children born to NCIs.

"While first generation NCIs' presumed intelligence remains relatively static, second and third generations demonstrate increased abilities in terms of creative thought and independent action." Ligeia takes a breath. "In layman's terms, I guess, you'd say they're definitely not human, nor are they subhuman or assets. In most cases, they perform comparably to humans on general assessments. Sometimes even at a higher level."

"So, what do you think they are, Dr. Obumbwe, in your expert opinion?" Sakata's expression is, interestingly, triumphant, and Ligeia wonders at his motives. But Hedges is seething, Proxy looks like she may cry, and the audience is riveted. Ligeia can't resist.

"That's likely a question for psychosociology. I'm just a medtech. However, while NCIs have certainly proved to be valuable, renewable resources in a time when resources are scarce, it's my opinion that it's unethical to continue to exploit our biological cousins in the way we have over the last century."

The entire hall erupts. Hedges stands, his arms outstretched, and calls for order. The Prime Minister sits stone-faced as the audience clamors. And Sakata? He's amid the chaos, his arms crossed over his chest, a broad smile spread across his wizened face.

Used by OnyxCorp or used by factions of the Dua Rights movement, it's really all the same, Ligeia guesses. *Stupid girl.* She puts a hand behind her ear to unlink her audial implants, then she rises and strides from the dais, passing the Symposium moderator, who seems bewildered by the sudden mayhem. She escapes through a side door, stumbles into a well-lit corridor where she leans against a wall for support. The hum of voices from inside the auditorium vibrates against her back.

"Now you've done it." She looks down at her shaking hands. That didn't go as planned. But the barely concealed rage on Hedges' face when she used the word *cousins*…Well, that made it almost worth it. She takes a few deep, gulping breaths until she feels steady enough to walk. Easing herself from the wall, she wobbles to the salon area. The steady susurration of raised voices fades as she luxuriates in the sunlight spilling through floor-to-ceiling glass and bathing the marbled floor. The bar area—Oh yes, she needs a drink—is empty, occupied by a lone NCI server standing at attention, her crisp white uniform hugging a tall, lean frame, white hair carefully arranged in elaborate braids. Ligeia orders a glass of red synthohol and carries it to a small table overlooking the manicured gardens outside the International Scientific Academy headquarters in Maun, Botswana. Sinking into a cushioned chair, she watches the sun casting delicate shadows over the grounds. She brings the glass to her lips, and the red liquid tingles as it floods her mouth.

Why did she do it? What good can possibly come of what she just did? Nothing good for her. Nothing good for her brother Finn for sure.

Keep your head down. Do the work. Let your findings speak for themselves. Principles she's followed religiously over her career. But how can the findings speak if they never see the light of day? OnyxCorp concerns itself only with numbers. Increased production, decreased costs. The EFC keeps everyone in line, lulled into complacency. Every morning, the same mantra gently wakes each Earth Federation Council citizen, a soothing female voice over the gentle crash of waves over rocks, filtered through audial implants:

Good morning, Citizen. All is well. Good morning, Citizen. All is well. But all is not well. Beyond Maun's walls, there is violence and unrest, starvation and death. And it's getting closer.

The *assets* don't see the world in the same way.

The conference room doors suddenly burst open, and the roar of several hundred voices explodes into the towering foyer. The silver-uniformed attendees pour from the auditorium, some going for drinks and refreshments, others headed to the outdoor courtyard. Hundreds of well-fed, educated, complacent human beings, wholly oblivious to what's coming. Thoroughly capable of doing something about it. Ligeia strains to hear their conversation, although she shouldn't care. There'll be hell to pay for that performance. The only question is in what form.

"That was quite a presentation back there." Sakata holds two glasses of synth, one in each hand, yet still manages to look wise. He holds one out to her. "Thought you might need something."

She raises her own glass, which still holds a sip or two. "Thanks, but I'm way ahead of you."

Sakata chuckles and indicates the chair adjacent. "May I?"

"Free country, so far."

He eases himself down, sinking deep into the cushion. "I'm not complaining, by the way."

"Oh, I know. My endorsement of the Dua Freedom Coalition or the NiCIe Consortium for Truth or whatever you're calling it these days is sure to be top news tonight. Some might say you used me."

Sakata clicked his tongue. "Used is a strong word. I would say I recruited you to the cause. A much worthier cause than carrying water for OnyxCorp." Sakata takes a drink and slams the glass on the table between them. Red liquid sloshes onto the tablescreen, and the projected cloth shimmers for an instant as the liquid pools, clinging to the goblet's base. "I'm great at putting cracks in the façade."

"Do you consider who may have to repair them?"

Sakata grins. "Not usually."

"I guess that's the privilege of age. And status."

"Age, yes. I'm afraid my name doesn't carry much weight these days. Present company excluded, I hope?"

He favors her with a wink, his eyes twinkling behind the round spectacles. Ligeia can't help but smile back. *Incurable flirt* is one of the more famous of Owen Sakata's traits. "I'll admit to being a bit of a fangirl back in the day."

"You mean when I was young and good looking."

Charming as hell, for an old guy. "I'm really surprised they convicted you, Dr. Sakata."

His face falls. "Ah, well. That." Shifting awkwardly, he crosses an ankle over a knee. "You cut straight to the bone, Dr. Obumbwe."

Ligeia swallows, feeling a tinge of regret. "I've been told. Sorry."

"No. No. I'm afraid that's to be my legacy. Disgraced, former medtech, traitor to his species."

Ligeia gulps down the rest of her glass and searches for a less loaded topic. Fortunately, Sakata saves her. "You were frustrated up there."

"Yes. I guess I thought it would be different, this time."

"You're learning much earlier than I did," Sakata says. "I tended to become entangled by personal matters."

"I've heard tell," she says, smiling.

"Well, I'm here to confirm that it's all true."

"Even Valerie Sanchez?" Ligeia must ask. It's the one rumor she's never been able to confirm through credible sources.

"Oh, no. Dr. Sanchez was my mentor, nothing more. Great medtech."

"What was she like?" Valerie Sanchez is an enigma, a figure of legend. Ligeia studied Owen Sakata, but she practically worshipped Valerie Sanchez. Even before Ruĝa Morto, her breakthroughs in gene modification were hailed as little less than scientific miracles.

"You know, like all geniuses. High-strung. Driven. Passionate." Sakata winks. "A lot like you. She'd seen it all, you know. She was right there, at the very beginning."

Ligeia struggles to recall Sakata's memoir, what he'd said about his time with Sanchez. "Where did you meet her?"

"In Vancouver, 2195. Before the Great Flood. I'd been living a life of glorious excess during the end of the world. Spent a lot of time patching up people, and Dua, during the 'zombie' raids and just had enough. Being a medtech wasn't what I thought it'd be. So, once it was all over and North America was essentially abandoned, I just wandered all around that continent. Drank a lot of real wine in abandoned houses in every once-great city you can name, at least the ones not already under water. Anyway, enough years of that, you have to find something to do. So, I ambled through the giant glass doors of the Vancouver General Hospital, met Dr. Valerie Sanchez, and Dua became my life."

"I don't remember that part in your memoir."

"Yes, well." He gazes out on the grounds outside. Symposium participants are milling, exploring the gardens, practically identical in their silver garments. "Things didn't end well for her, did they?"

Indeed they had not. Ligeia recalled the images of her mutilated body from the history modules during her Academy days. Her eyes replaced with bright blue marbles and her limbs splayed out, pulled apart. Murdered and grotesquely displayed in the NCI camp, supposedly by the very creatures she was trying to help. The EFC's destruction of that camp had been the beginning of the greatest genocide the world had ever seen.

"I always wondered. Why did the NiCIes do it? She was on their side."

Sakata scoffs. "Dua aren't capable of such acts of violence. She knew things. Things she shouldn't have. After she disappeared, I figured it was time to move on. I'd been on the moon quite a few cycles when I heard they'd found her. A ritual killing, the EFC said. There's no such ritual among Dua." He shakes his head, then polishes off the synth. "How about you, Dr. Obumbwe? You could be doing anything with that big brain of yours. Surely you've realized by now OnyxCorp is a dead-end."

It's true, of course. In fact, it's been nagging at her for some time now. Understanding these creatures isn't a priority. The book on NCIs has been written and closed as far as OnyxCorp and the EFC are concerned. Which is to say as far as everyone is concerned.

"Personal reasons," Ligeia says at last. "Finn, my brother, got sick when I was ten. I had no idea what it was. Nobody talked about Ruĝa Morto back then, not like they do now. It was a dirty secret. I came home from Academy one day, and he was gone. My father told me he'd died, and I believed him. My mom had died a couple of years earlier, so I guess, to a kid, it seemed logical."

Sakata meets her eyes. "He'd changed."

She's surprised by how raw the memory still is, more than twenty years later. "I overheard someone ask my stepmother how Finn was doing. One of their ridiculous government gatherings. She's some mucky-muck with the Corporation. She used to show me off, when I was home from university. The medtech prodigy, her daughter. Told people I was her daughter, like my mother had never existed. I had to drag it out of them, but finally they confessed Finn had been living in the Institute in New America the entire time, eleven years. Eleven goddamn years." She reaches for the extra glass of synth and brings it to her lips, her hands trembling. "He was my best friend. We did everything together as kids."

"He's still at the Institute?"

"For the time being. After today, maybe not."

"Ah. But your father must have had some influence at that time. Dua work until they drop. Your brother is luckier than most."

"It's a fucking prison, that place. The way they talk about it, like it's some kind of resort. Every time I see him, he looks hollowed out, empty. My father is a professor, and he had enough hope that the Institute would eventually find a cure that he spent everything we had to keep Finn there. But it's my stepmother who has the influence. I'm pretty sure that's how she convinced Dad to partner, because the money ran out. She's been on the EFC from the beginning. You won't ever hear her name, but she's up there, silently pulling strings." Ligeia moves her hands up and down, mimicking a puppeteer controlling a marionette. "But she's all but convinced Dad that Finn will never get better. I have to keep him safe until I figure it out."

"Figure what out?"

"What to do about them. How to help them. I mean, a cure, right? That's what we all want."

Sakata shifts, leans closer. The foyer buzzes, but many people have taken their refreshments outside. They are alone, or as alone as one can be amid the OnyxCorp machine.

"What if Dua are an advancement?" he says in a low voice, adjusting the glasses on his nose. "What if we're witnessing the end of humans, and the beginning of superhumans? What if your brother is one of them?"

Here is the Owen Sakata of lore. The radical. The Dua Rights revolutionary. It had cost him his own career, almost his life. Ligeia shakes her head. "I've been studying the NCI genome for years. The intelligence scores at the high end are anomalies. I like to emphasize them because humans seem to have more empathy in response to intelligence than sentience. But in general, they're average, like us. I don't think that means they should be used like they are, but, ah, there's just not enough data to go as far as saying they're superhuman."

"You're a good scientist." Sakata eases back. "I don't know of anyone on Earth who knows more about—our cousins, did you call them? At least in terms of data." The wrinkles around his almond-shaped eyes deepen. "What does your brother think about it?"

"What?"

"Your brother. What does he think about your work, your desire to help him?"

What does he think? "I...haven't asked him. I mean, he's not there, you know? He's somewhere in another realm, he speaks in riddles. First generation have significant brain trauma from the virus. I don't have conversations with Finn; they're more like, experiences."

Sakata gives a half smile. "I can relate to that. Their own culture. Their own belief system. Interesting they didn't need any help with those things." Sakata pushes himself up, then bends over her in an almost comical bow. "You should be going. You're going to miss the transport for the gala."

Ligeia rises herself, returning the bow. "I wasn't planning on going, to be honest." The last thing she wants is two or three more hours with these people. Not to mention the risk of running into Hedges. That conversation will happen, but she'd like to put it off for as long as possible.

"Oh, no, you should go," Sakata says. "For one, the building is a wonder."

"I've seen it—"

"And you never know what you'll see there. The collection is always changing, you see." Sakata bows again. "Until we meet again, Dr. Obumbwe. It was an honor."

"Likewise," she manages to blurt. He's just rounding the corner, the last of the sun's beams gleaming down on his back, when she hears someone call her name from across the foyer. She shields her eyes against the glare and squints.

Hedges. *Bloody hell.* She drains the last few drops of synth, steeling herself.

"Dr. Obumbwe, I was hoping you'd be so kind as to accompany me to the gala this evening? I have something I'd like to discuss." His expression reminds her of a cat watching a bird through a pane of glass.

"Thank you for asking, truly, but I'm beat. I was thinking of skipping it this year."

Hedges mouth spreads in a wide, toothy smile. "I insist, Dr. Obumbwe. I think you'll find it enlightening."

I'll bet. May as well get this over with.

"All right, Hedges. I'll go to your gala. Just don't expect me to dance with you."

Hedges crooks an elbow. Reluctantly, she takes it. "Our dance has already begun, Doctor. But now, I'll be taking the lead."

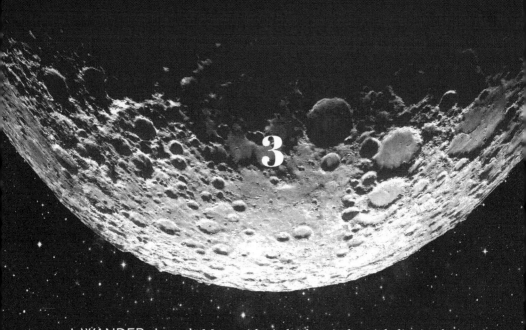

3

I WANDER through Montevideo's broken industrial district for an hour before I find the next station, a warehouse several blocks from the canal's edge. Headquarters for Lee Chou. Montevideo was once a thriving metropolis, even after Ruĝa Morto, but now, ruined by rising sea levels and neglect, it's practically abandoned. Every building looks the same: Corrugated siding, graffiti, warnings against trespassing, CLOSED BY ONYXCORP AUTHORITY in a variety of languages and symbols. As I pick my way through the crumbling streets and refuse, I notice a few stubborn residents peeking from makeshift doors and windows in rusting cargo containers. I give one or two a nod, prompting them to disappear without a word.

Every Dua child knows the name Lee Chou. Tales about unfortunate Dua children have the same moral: *Always obey Authority, or Chou will take you. Follow the curfew, or Chou will get you. Never upset a human, or Chou will snatch you up.* Chou's reputation as a smuggler and ruthless killer is fueled by his association with OnyxCorp, which has relied for decades on his services. The remnants of outdoor enclosures surrounded by chain-link fencing are scattered throughout the district. Those enclosures are empty now, but over the decades they've confined thousands of Dua, bound for workstations across the globe, on the Vine, on the moon.

Why would Mama send me here, straight to the boogeyman's lair? I can't begin to guess. *You will find Lee Chou in Montevideo. Then you will know what to do next.* Typically cryptic, but it's the only thing I have to go on if I'm to make my way to the Vine.

This building is much like the others, save for a bright green door and the human male perched on a metal chair to the door's left. The back of his bald head rests against the building's metal siding, and his arms hang loosely at his sides. A weapon of some kind lies across his lap. His face is leathered by UV exposure. He lets out a rumbling snore as I approach.

Unimpressive so far, but I'm not keen on startling him and getting blasted with whatever weapon he has. I stop several meters away and clear my throat. Nothing. I take a few more steps forward and kick a piece of metal siding lying on the ground as hard as I can, sending it sailing into a pile of similar metal debris.

The man leaps, knocks the chair over, and sends the weapon flying to land at my feet. I bend, retrieve the weapon, and rise.

"I'm here to see Chou."

The man shifts from his left foot to his right. "Now, listen, man. I don't want any trouble." His voice is a whisper, and when he glances nervously back toward the green door for a third time, I realize why.

"You were asleep on the job." I switch the weight of the weapon to my left hand and let it hang, barrel down.

"Frank?" A voice comes from a speaker hanging above the green door. I glance up, noticing the imager. I wave at it with my right hand.

The man, the Frank in question, takes a step toward me. "Look here, NiCle—" He cuts off when he sees my expression. "No offense, man, just...give me back the gun."

"Frank!" The voice is loud and sharp enough this time to echo through the alley. "Get your ass to the comm!"

Frank gives me a grave look and backs away toward the door. Without taking his eyes from me, he reaches out, fumbles for several seconds, and finally manages to locate the comm panel next to the green door. "Uh, hi. Everything's ok—"

"Like hell."

"Well, uh, there's a, a NiCIe out here—"

"I can see that. Goddamit, Frank. One job." Frank glares at me reproachfully, and I shrug as I adjust the gun in both hands. "Bring him in."

There's a soft ping, and the bright green door swings open. Frank motions for me to follow him, stops just at the threshold. "Can I at least have my gun back?"

"Let's see how this goes."

Grumbling, he shuffles into the building. I follow him, ducking slightly to miss the lintel, and am plunged into sudden darkness.

A hand grabs my left arm and grapples with the weapon as I am pulled through the gloom. I can make out darkened figures, and as my eyes adjust, I see a narrow hallway ahead with a long series of closed doors on either side, a soft glow pooling beneath them. Ceiling lights blink and buzz, casting eerie shadows across the walls and floor. Frank gives a final jerk and lets out a frustrated grunt when he fails to dislodge the weapon.

"He has my gun, Raj," he says.

"We know." Another figure emerges from the gloom, a large human male, his face covered in a grizzly beard. He's holding a weapon as well, leveling it steadily at my chest. "What you want, NiCIe?"

I hold my arms out at my sides, the shotgun firmly in my grip. "Here to see Chou."

"He's wacked out, Raj. Just walked right up, like the place belongs to him."

"You wacked out, NiCIe?" Raj's face glistens. He's missing a front tooth.

"I don't think so." I nod to the gun in Raj's beefy hands. "Why don't we let Chou decide?"

Raj blinks, narrows his eyes. He lowers the gun slightly. "You're different, that's for sure." He jerks his head toward the corridor. "Follow me. Don't touch anything."

"He has my gun, Raj." Frank trots behind us as Raj escorts me down the corridor to a door at the far end.

"We know, Frank." Raj clears his throat. "Stand there," he says, indicating the wall across from the door. I back up as he puts his hand against a wall scanner. The door clicks open.

Sudden light tears through my eyes.

Frank, or maybe it was Raj, shoves me into the blinding room.

"Identify yourself!"

I blink rapidly as a human female comes into focus, short, not much taller than a Dua child. Her right hand holds a stunstic, pointed straight up at my head. On her left thigh is a holstered electristic; her hand hovers over its stock expectantly.

"Who are you?" The woman's grey hair is pulled back in a sleek ponytail, and she pushes her lips together in a small, thin line. She runs her eyes up and down the length of my body, and their implants flash briefly as they catch the light.

"My name is Caen."

"And just what the hell are you doing here, Caen?"

"I'm looking for Lee Chou." She narrows her eyes and presses her wrinkled lips together in a frown. "Word is Chou can get me to Buenos Aires."

She takes more careful aim with the stunstic. "The maglev can get you to Buenos Aires. The tunnel can get you to Buenos Aires. You don't need Lee Chou to get to Buenos Aires."

"Not without attracting Authority attention."

Her hand moves to the electristic. "Who sent you here?"

I take a deep breath. "Lenore."

A wave of confusion moves over her brown-skinned face. "Lenore?"

"My mother." I swallow down the lump that's suddenly formed in the back of my throat. "She says Lee Chou is the best forger in SoAm." The room behind the woman comes into focus now. It is bright, airy even. Not at all what I would expect in this desolate place, in this crumbling building. "Is he here?"

The two henchmen behind me chuckle. The corners of the woman's mouth turn up slightly, but she doesn't lower the weapon. "Ah, yes, the infamous smuggler Chou, responsible for millions of NiCle children disappearing from their beds and forced into slave labor. That Lee Chou? Why would your mother send you to *O Diabo*?"

"I'm wondering the same thing myself." I try to smile.

The woman regards me for a few seconds more over the stunstic's barrel. Slowly, she lowers her arm. "How is your mother, Lenore?"

"She's dead." I'm surprised to see shock and dismay pass over her face.

"So that's why we haven't heard from the Paysandú station," Raj says quietly behind me.

The woman shakes her head as she cuts him a glance. "You're Lenore's Earth child?"

"I have a sister—" Then I realize what she's just said. "Earth child?"

The woman closes the distance between us in a few steps. Her eye implants engage in soft flashes of light as she scans me up close. "Hm. Perhaps." She steps back, holsters the stunstic on her right thigh. "It took my father years to develop his reputation for ruthless NiCIe hunting. A reputation that is supposed to keep nosy people from poking around here. Lee Chou is dead. I am now Lee Chou." She waves at the two men. "I'll take it from here."

"He has my gun," Frank says.

"So he does. You gonna take it from him?"

Frank gives me a seething glance.

"He's bigger than I am," he says sullenly.

"Raj, take Frank out to the yard and show him how to do his job. Again. You can have your gun back," she says, "when Raj says you can. Out."

"Come on, kid," Raj says, tugging at Frank's arm. Frank casts one more angry look my way before he disappears into the corridor outside.

"I'd appreciate your putting that away," Chou says, indicating the weapon I'm still gripping in my left hand. "I doubt you'd need it anyway, right?"

I sling the weapon over my shoulder. Turning to face Chou, I clear my throat. "So, can you get me to the coast, undetected?"

She narrows her eyes. "I offer my services for the right price, and to the right people."

"What's your price?"

"I don't think you're the right people."

"What's your price?"

She places her hands on her hips. "Six thousand credits."

"I'll give you four."

"For four, I can get you within five miles of the coast. I trust you can swim."

"My mother implied there was a debt owed her."

Chou reacts as if she's been struck across the face. "There is," she says slowly. "Why would you want to go to Buenos Aires? If you aren't registered, you won't be able to get work, or food, or shelter—"

"I need to get to the Vine."

Chou scoffs. "I can't get you to the space elevator. It's out of the question."

"But you know someone in Buenos Aires who can."

She frowns. "I haven't spoken to that asshole in four years."

"But you *do* know the Captain."

"*Captain* my ass," she mumbles. "You're better swimming to the Vine. His isn't the most reliable station, you know." She sighs, then motions for me to follow her to a small circular table piled with flexscreens. The room is spacious and neat, with wallscreens covering the room floor to ceiling, projecting scenes of old Earth. An old NutriPrint model stands in a corner next to a modified Re-Claimer, obviously a knock-off from a now-defunct OnyxCorp competitor. Chou picks up a flexscreen. As it comes to life, she clears a space on the table, puts it down, and stretches it by the corners until it is about a meter square.

"*Captain* Abebe was here last time I checked." There's a trace of bitter sarcasm in her voice. She points to an area southeast of the city labeled *Ensenada*. "Here isn't anywhere anymore...Ensenada, La Plata, the Canal...it's all abandoned." She pushes out with her fingers to zoom in. "I can get you here, the mouth of the Canal, but I won't go further. You'll have to make your way to this location on foot." She touches a square on the grid that features dilapidated warehouses and housing units next to the Arroyo del Saladero; the location glows a soft orange. She touches the corner of the flexscreen, and it snaps into its original size. She hands it to me, and I roll it into a small cylinder, fitting it neatly inside an inner pocket of my tattered jacket. "The Corporation is everywhere over there, even in the abandoned sections. There are bound to be drones and maybe even an old Authority model for good measure. If you get past them, you must deal with Abebe, who trusts absolutely no one. Especially me."

"Should I mention you at all?"

"I'd like to see the look on his face when he hears my name. That would be worth losing 6000 credits alone." Chou takes a step away, regarding me. "Lenore's son. Why are you going to the Vine?"

"My options have run out in SoAm." She doesn't believe me, or at least guesses I'm not giving her the whole truth. But how much can I tell her?

Her expression softens. "Lenore's son, after all these years. And a sister? Where is she? Never mind. It's better I don't know. SoAm isn't safe for your kind. Not that it ever has been." She shakes her head. "But the Vine. She told you to go to the Vine?"

"In a manner of speaking, yes."

"Where are you going, really?"

"As you said, it's best you don't know."

Chou sighs. "Fair enough. I've maintained my father's old contacts. OnyxCorp contractors requesting NiCIes for the Vine. And the moon," she said, giving me a sideways glance. "Official requisition is required for either. I assume you don't have those types of documents." Chou turns back to the table and picks up another flexscreen. "Hold still," she says. Her eyes flash.

"You can get me credentials? Without TES?"

"I can make you credentials, the finest you've seen," she says, tapping away at the flexscreen. "Maybe better than TES."

Chou mutters as she runs her fingers over the flexscreen. The screen casts a soft glow on her creased face. "You're in luck. A headhunter I know is looking for NiCIe recruits for the Vine. Or the moon?" It is a question I can't answer right now.

"The Vine is fine. Thank you."

Chou shrugs and drops the flexscreen on the table. "You can stay here tonight. We'll leave first thing in the morning. Be in Buenos Aires in time for afternoon tea. Follow me."

We pass into the corridor outside and glide past half a dozen closed doors. She stops at one, places a hand on the antiquated scanner, and steps into a small room with whitewashed walls and cracked tile floors. A cot with a tattered blanket, a sink and a toilet, and an OnyxCorp uniform hanging on the wall, identifying the wearer as a NiCIe worker, are the only contents. "You'll need to wear that," she says, pointing to the uniform. "You'll blend in better."

"You've done this before," I marvel, looking at the uniform. "How long have you been a Station here?"

"You can clean up; there's running water," she continues, ignoring me. "I'll have someone bring around something to eat. Be ready to go by four a.m." She steps aside to allow me to enter. "I guess I don't need to tell you, but what you're doing is, well, crazy. Deadly. Others are going to be asking for a lot more than six thousand credits. Either you need to work on your story, or you need more to offer. Your mother's name isn't going to carry weight with anyone but me."

"Why you?"

Chou shrugs. "I did my share of NiCIe transport. Slave trading. Let's call it what it was. I procured a lot of NiCIes for Onyx back when my father was alive. I met your mother on my last job." She swallows. "It was my last job because of her."

I stare at her, this human who knew my mother in a way that I didn't, a way that I would never know her. "Why?"

"She told me her story. I consider this a way of balancing that off, for her. For the Vagabonders." Chou sees me flinch involuntarily, my inability to mask my feelings betraying me, not for the first time. "The legend is no secret. Even humans know something happened up there with the first moon settlers. OnyxCorp did its best to cover it all up with corpspeak and a bunch of shiny new gadgets every other day, but we know your people were brutalized and murdered. Imprisoning settlers in the lunar tunnels doesn't seem far-fetched at all. We humans feign ignorance because otherwise we'd be monsters. Meeting your mother...made the whole story real." Her jaw tightens. "It's not easy for humans either, you know, living outside OnyxCorp. We don't get the latest commodities, the medtech, the enhancements. But we also don't have to see the damn ads or pretend we aren't making the world worse. We don't have TES recording our every move. I take you to the Canal. That's it. After that, you're on your own. I can't afford having OnyxCorp snooping around here. Your people still need this Station. There aren't many left." She places a hand on the scanner, and the door snaps shut after her.

I remain in the center of the tiny room, my mind filled with visions of my mother. Playing a game with me and Eisa, her sad eyes belying the delighted smile she shows us. The aura of profound relief emanating from her when I'd left home eleven years ago. I had been angry that she seemed so happy to see me go.

Sinking down on the cot, I pull my mother's wrapped digiscreen from the backpack and place it on my lap.

You're her Earth child?

4

STARS DOT the darkening sky when Hedges and Ligeia descend the steps outside the International Scientific Academy building. The moon is a sliver, its pale glow competing with the bright lights illuminating the ISA's courtyard, where several dozen white vehicles, part of Maun's electromagnetic transport system, wait to transport the Symposium's attendees to the Maun OnyxCorp Center for Cultural Advancement. Touted as a cocktail hour and elaborate gala to celebrate the Symposium's conclusion, it's more an opportunity for attendees to brush shoulders with "people who matter"—decision makers, legislators, the rich and the powerful. Ligeia takes note of the curious and envious stares that follow her as Hedges guides her down the shallow marble stairs.

"This way, Dr. Obumbwe," Hedges says as they approach his personal vehicle, a smaller but more luxuriously appointed transport than those reserved for the hoi polloi. Resigned, Ligeia climbs inside and finds herself sitting opposite an imposing woman dressed in a black Authority uniform that almost matches the color of her silky complexion. Her greying hair is arranged in thick locks gathered in a neat bundle at her neck, and between her lips rests a nicostic. She nods in welcome as Ligeia settles on the sumptuous cushion. Then Hedges clambers inside, sits next to the woman, and adjusts the high white collar at his throat as the transport door snaps shut behind them.

Now that she has an opportunity to look at him closely, Ligeia notices the dark, neatly trimmed hair and perfectly arched eyebrows, the face of a man who might be mistaken for fortyish from a distance. When she was a child, her father would have described Hedges as "all business," followed by an admonishment to be wary of such people. So far, Hedges has done nothing to disabuse her of such a warning. Hedges clears his throat and glances over at the woman, who doesn't move, doesn't change her expression. She's substantial, reminding Ligeia of the Authority bots themselves. Hedges' thin lips curve downward as he speaks.

"Dr. Obumbwe, I wanted to thank you again for attending the Symposium on such short notice. The face of the Symposium should be the medtechs themselves, rather than the credits, and when I realized that we didn't have a single medtech on the panel, well, I knew we needed to get the best." He smiles broadly now, relaxing with each word. *Good script so far.* "Which speaks to the honor of your inclusion, yes? I've been watching you. Your career, I mean. I share your interest. Improving relations with NiCIes derives fundamentally from a well-defined understanding of who they are and what they are. Would you agree?"

Ligeia glances at the woman sitting opposite her. She has broad shoulders and powerful arms, and her long legs are extended in front of her; her black boots reach almost to the edge of Ligeia's seat. Almost as tall as a NiCIe. But not a NiCIe. Hedges clears his throat again. "I'm sorry, how rude of me. Dr. Obumbwe, this is Madge Erlang. Commander Erlang is leading a task force charged with NiCIe community relations. She's our top Authority administrator, and she's quite interested in what you had to say about NiCIe genetics." Erlang looks at Ligeia at the mention of her name, nodding gravely. *Interested my ass.* Ligeia glances at the stunstic on the woman's hip.

"Am I being arrested?"

Hedges narrows his beady eyes. "Why would we arrest you?"

"I take it my contributions to the panel weren't to your liking."

"Well, I'll admit I was a little unprepared, but honestly, how could anyone have prepared for the sudden reappearance of Owen Sakata?"

"Indeed. Who could have expected the most vocal advocate for NCI rights to be vocal about pending legislation that seeks to inter them in ghettoized conditions on the moon?"

Hedges shifts, crossing one ankle over the other. A look of annoyance passes over his face, quickly replaced by the plastic smile. He is, in fact, much older than he appears; Ligeia recognizes the signs of extensive treatments. The nanoport just behind Hedges' ear houses more inserts than she's ever seen a human wear. *Are OnyxCorp lackeys required to have a permanent smile affixed to their faces, or is that a choice they make themselves?*

"Fair enough. But as I said, OnyxCorp wants to improve relations with our NiCIe populations. I don't have to tell you how difficult it has been repairing the damage the International Council inflicted on those relationships in the early years."

Of course she's familiar with the history. The human, unaffected survivors of Ruĝa Morto emerged from hiding, bewildered and afraid, suspicious and aggressive, facing a remaining population that recognized none of those emotions. In the early years, human survivors roamed in groups, heavily armed, and killed any NCI they encountered. Millions died, either through violence or starvation, and the International Council let it happen. "Medtechs, as I recall, finally stopped the carnage," Ligeia says.

"Indeed. With OnyxCorp's support, of course. The Neurologically Compromised Individuals were a boon to human advancement. Capable of work many humans cannot perform. Completely dependable. NiCIes and humans have been living together, both on Earth and the moon, quite productively for decades." Erlang snorts and shifts, drawing Ligeia's attention. *You know what this is really about.* But Erlang only returns her stare, her expression inscrutable.

"We realize, however, that things could be better. Much better," Hedges continues, leaning forward to recapture Ligeia's attention. "No doubt that unfortunate incident on the moon decades ago hasn't been forgotten. And rumors abound, no matter how foolish."

"The rumors are you killed thousands of NiCIes and sealed up the survivors in the moon tunnels."

Hedges winces. He glances at Erlang, who appears to be fascinated by her fingernails, but Ligeia detects a slight smirk on the Commander's full lips. Hedges looks back at Ligeia and smiles, making the hairs on the back of her neck prickle. "That's not exactly the truth."

"What is the truth, exactly?"

"I'm sure you appreciate that people make all manner of heinous accusations to sway public opinion. There was some conflict between the NiCIe population on the moon and OnyxCorp officials, that's true. The reports of a NiCIe massacre are completely unfounded, however. It's unfortunate that we had to subdue a few individuals through violence. But ultimately the situation was handled. The lunar NiCIes understand how critical they are to the success of our mutual endeavors."

"And the tunnels? Were they sealed?"

"Not with NiCIes trapped inside. We made every effort to clear out the tunnels, since they were no longer needed as residential dwellings. The remaining open tunnels are used for storage."

He's lying, of course. If there's one thing she's good at, it's detecting a liar, and so far Ligeia hasn't heard a word of truth from Hedges' mouth. Curiously, she realizes that Erlang knows he's lying, too. With each word, the Commander's discomfort grows, and her eyes remained fixed on the passing city outside the transport.

"Given the still-raw emotions between NiCIe workers and OnyxCorp," Hedges continues, "I think it's important we highlight the work we're doing to discover a cure for Ruĝa Morto. That's where your work is so critical."

Ligeia narrows her eyes. "You're referring to a vaccine."

"Yes!" Hedges smiles broadly. "A vaccine to ensure the virus isn't loosed upon the human population ever again. We can treat it now in the few cases that still crop up, but the treatment results in more NiCIes. A vaccine would help the remaining human population feel more at ease with our...how did you put it? Our cousins?"

"A vaccine is a dead-end. No matter what we do, the virus gets around us. I said as much when I abandoned the project five years ago."

"With your limited resources, of course! Your recent work has been, ah, enlightening as well. But hardly practical from a problem-solving perspective, yes? And likely a dead-end as well. After all, NiCIes are so very different from us, as different as, say, a dog or a bird. Certainly they have some intelligence, but does that matter to us? To humans?"

"I guess it doesn't matter much to OnyxCorp, Hedges, but you aren't necessarily in the science business, are you?"

Hedges nods vigorously. "Yes, yes. OnyxCorp is all about mining and product development. But we have a medtech branch that goes largely unnoticed. Did you know that, Dr. Obumbwe?"

"You mean you purchased a medtech branch by buying up all the remaining independent labs. And shutting them down. Now everybody has to crawl to you, don't they?"

Hedges' jaw clenches. This isn't going how he planned. But he tries again. "I've not gained your trust. Yes, we've made it a priority to purchase the debt of several independent labs around the world. I see how that might look to you, someone so adept. A genius if I may say. Your work in NiCIe genetics has been groundbreaking, and I want to support your research. Recognize your tremendous contributions. I want you to come work for us. For me. Continue your research on NiCIe biogenetics in the most technologically advanced facility possible. You'll have everything and anything you require to advance your work, in finding a vaccine, even a cure! Credits are no object. You'll have complete control of the OnyxCorp Lunar MedTech Complex, including whom you hire."

The moon. The realization hits Ligeia like a fist to her stomach. She's clenched her jaw reflexively, and she consciously relaxes it, hoping it isn't enough to betray her emotions. *The moon.* And her own medtech complex. Offered under different circumstances, a dream come true. Coming from OnyxCorp, a poison pill.

"We have a public relations issue with the lunar NiCIes, there's no denying it." Hedges can't hide his eagerness. "By extension, we have an issue with NiCIes here, and that harms the human population as well. We need to restore the goodwill we had when we first started our moon settlements. We need to ensure the NiCIes are protected, and that means we must reassure our Citizens they are no longer a threat."

Ligeia shakes her head. "I'm sorry, but the answer is no. I have obligations here. I can't just up and leave."

"You're referring to your brother." Ligeia's heart skips a beat. "I can assure you he will be taken care of while you're gone. His place at the Institute is guaranteed, should you choose to accept, of course."

"And if I don't?"

Hedges shrugs. "Well, you didn't exactly fulfill your duties to the EFC during the panel, did you? Families are influential only if they're contributing. I'm sure you'd like to secure your legacy, for your brother's sake. After all, your father won't live forever."

Ligeia glances at Erlang, who is watching her intently now. "Is that why you're here? In case I say no?"

"Just along for the ride, doc," Erlang drawls, the nicostic bobbing up and down with the movement of her mouth. "He tends toward paranoia. Thinks people are out to get him."

"I understand your hesitation, doctor," Hedges interrupts as he casts a dark look at Erlang. "My position requires I spend time on the moon myself, and it's no paradise like we have here. This is our home. But you've gone as far as you can on your own. Why else would you have abandoned your search for a vaccine? Your latest work is— intriguing. But it's not near what you're capable of. You're Ligeia Obumbwe! You are the shining star of the medtech world. I want to put that star where it belongs: In the heavens."

Great pitch. She could do without the extra dash of coercion, though.

There are benefits, of course. Complete charge of a moon lab. No impediments. Access to members of the original NCI moon population, which could give her research the boost it needs. A new direction, even.

But it's OnyxCorp. How can she say yes? The Corporation hasn't made a decision solely for the good of humankind in its history. Now it wants to *restore relations with our cousins*? Complete bullshit.

But Finn.

Whether they're first, second, or third generation, NCIs all have one thing in common. They aren't human. And if there is one belief human beings share, it is that non-human species are inferior. The NCI Civil Protection Act isn't necessary other than to make what's already happening to NCIs legal. They've been isolated in slums, shipped to mines across the globe and on the moon, and restricted for decades. The only exceptions have been family members of prominent contributors to the EFC, or OnyxCorp, or both. It's the only reason Finn is in the Institute in New America instead of a copper mine in SoAm or a titanium mine on the moon.

There's no reason to believe the Corporation won't use this legislation to scoop up every NCI on the planet and ship them to the moon. Ligeia imagines that's the likely end game. She's only buying time for Finn.

"When would I need to leave?" Erlang's head snaps up, her mouth open. Hedges grins broadly. A little too quickly.

"We can arrange for your passage in a few weeks' time. No doubt you'll have some arrangements of your own here. Erlang will be accompanying you, and she'll be your point of contact for the details as we work toward the transition." Ligeia has a terrible feeling that Erlang's dark brown eyes reflect disappointment as their eyes meet. "I can't tell you how pleased I am, doctor. You'll have everything—anything you want. I'll personally see to it." He grasps her hand softly, a weak grip that makes her skin crawl again. "See? There was no need to be concerned."

Like hell.

"Owen Sakata." Erlang's smooth drawl draws Ligeia's attention. "Isn't he some kind of hero in your circle?"

Ligeia blinks at the sudden change of subject. "His work is highly regarded."

Erlang frowns. In a society that values appearance over almost anything else, her face is conspicuously absent of enhancements, giving her an air of sincerity that's unusual among corporate types. "What you said up there. You really believe that? NiCIes are intelligent?"

"All the data say yes."

"Yeah, but we all know data can be manipulated. Make it say what you want it to say, right? Are facts really facts these days?"

"I'm a scientist, not a politician or a corporatist." Ligeia ends the word crisply. "I'm looking for the truth, not confirmation of what I think I already know."

Erlang grunts, an expression Ligeia finds difficult to interpret. The transport descends into an awkward silence, so Ligeia turns her attention to the city outside the transport's window, where Maun's brightly lit buildings stream past, their advertisements assaulting her eyes and ears when they come into focus: *Ligeia Obumbwe, you've won a free vision upgrade from OnyxVision! Warning: NiCIE market fruits may contain contaminants! Trouble sleeping? Try OnyxMed's new SleepRite III for ten uninterrupted hours!* She touches her RistWach and scrolls through the settings, tapping a black-market application that allows her to shut out the messaging. The ads still appear, slightly blurred, but at least the sounds are muted and the words obscured.

A few minutes later, the transport pulls into the circular drive outside the Maun OnyxCorp Center for Cultural Advancement, the pride of OnyxCorp's buildtech division. The Corporation poured billions of credits into the facility, going as far as bringing tons of moon rock to Maun to create a building like no other. Twisting walls of moon rock forty meters high form the Center's structure. From a distance, it is a curvilinear triangle, with a wide base and narrow top. Between the narrow walls of rock are complex webs of titanium and glass. Illuminated in the dim light of early evening, the building sparkles like a rough-cut diamond.

Hedges, Erlang, and Ligeia emerge from the transport and filter with the other attendees into the Center's main room, open from floor to pinnacle and adorned with relics from around the world. The floor itself is composed of re-purposed tiles from a cathedral in what used to be France, rescued only a few months before the country was engulfed by the sea. The inner walls feature bits of ceiling pieces from another religious edifice, painted by a 16th-century master. Four round floors form increasingly narrow bands along the inside walls, accessible by large glass lifts. It is on those floors that OnyxCorp houses its most prized acquisitions: large collections of art rescued from places once known as the Louvre, the MOMA, the Vatican, the Mori. Decades earlier, the Corporation spearheaded an impressive campaign to save the world's heritage. Other museums feature carefully crafted holographic projections of artworks, enhanced for optimal viewing through eye implants aided by TES. The Center has actual art, and it is OnyxCorp's treasure.

Ligeia manages to slip away as the Symposium participants wrangle for Hedges' attention; she gives Erlang a nod before she disappears into the clamor and takes the lift to the collections on the upper floors. She won't be missed. Hedges is done with her for the time being. And the expressions from the few attendees who'd met her eyes when they'd entered the building weren't particularly friendly.

As much as she abhors social gatherings, Ligeia welcomes the opportunity to wander, unescorted, through the Center. Noise from the crowd echoes faintly from the main salon five stories below as she meanders through the 20th century collection, which is thankfully abandoned. Ligeia bounces lightly to the rhythm of soft electroclassic music as she loses herself in paintings and sculpture from the Americas and Europe. She pauses at an unpolished painting of a pale nude woman. The figure stands in a blue room on a round platform as she bends at her side, as if adjusting something along her thigh. A large bucket of flowers stands on a high table to the right, and blue-hued sunlight streams through a window on the left. Ligeia tilts her head and steps closer. Impulsively, she touches the canvas, marveling at the cool textures beneath her fingers.

"The Blue Room." Ligeia snaps to attention, startled. The voice comes from a very tall woman who appeared without warning. The woman's light brown hair spills loosely over her shoulders from beneath a hooded robe of velvet indigo, her pale face obscured in its darkness. "OnyxCorp saved a great many treasures, but they didn't do so well in cataloging them. Did you notice? Almost none of these pieces are titled, or have the artist identified."

"Well, it's not like in other galleries," Ligeia finds herself saying. "These are the real things. You can reach out and touch them." Her fingers twitch as she gazes back at the painting. "The digitized versions are interesting in their own way, with the running commentary and the interactions with the EynHance. But these—"

"You are a lover of art." The woman's accent is French, but there's something odd about her, besides her height. "I thought you might be. There is a quality that art and science share, I believe. The search for the truth."

"Art seems to be the more successful endeavor, don't you think?" *Do I know her?* Ligeia feels like she should. There's something so familiar about her.

"It often arrives at the truth first, but science? It always catches up." She turns to face Ligeia, pulls the hood back, and allows it to fall down her back. "You'll get there, Dr. Obumbwe. You are already so very close."

The hairs on Ligeia's neck prickle. The eyes are blue, but more than blue. "How—how did you get here?"

"The same way you did. By birth. By study. By transport." The woman smiles.

No, not a woman. An NCI.

"Do you realize this place is crawling with Authority?"

"Yes."

"They'll arrest you."

"Yes."

Five additional NCIs seem to materialize from nowhere. They wear identical robes, and their hoods obscure their faces but not their azure eyes, which glimmer in the bright light. They glide from the other end of the gallery toward Ligeia and halt just behind the woman.

Ligeia knows why they're here. Security was tight around the Symposium in response to the growing unrest outside Maun, but the same precautions weren't taken for the gala. Nevertheless, Authority are in place. The ISA Symposium is too tempting a target for NCI demonstrators. "Come on. There must be a back entrance to this thing. They won't let you leave alive."

The NCI woman reaches out a slim hand and touches Ligeia's upper arm. Immediately Ligeia's head begins to buzz. A strange feeling of warmth spreads to her cheeks, and she has a sudden sense of perfect peace, stretching and expanding until the woman removes her hand a few seconds later. Then she is suddenly dizzy, and her head spins.

"These works are some of the greatest achievements in the history of your species, but humans no longer hear their message," the woman says. Only it sounds like a song, or a plaintive cry. "We're here to help you listen." She pulls the painting of the blue woman from the wall in a swift motion. "You should stay here, Dr. Obumbwe. I would prefer that you weren't hurt." She pauses. "There are those who do want to harm you, Dr. Obumbwe. No matter what happens, go with your instincts." She places a hand on Ligeia's solar plexus, generating the same pulsing warmth. "If that fails, you can always listen to your heart." She moves the hand to Ligeia's chest. Then she drops her hand and strides from the room in a few quick steps, the painting held aloft. The others follow her in silence.

It takes Ligeia a few seconds to register what has just happened. "Wait!" She runs after the group of NCIs and enters the narrow walkway overlooking the salon below just in time to see them enter the glass lift. The elevator begins its slow descent, and from her vantage point Ligeia observes them removing their robes and dropping them on the lift floor as it comes to a stop. Breathlessly, she watches the nude figures step from the lift, the painting outstretched before the woman as the others, all male, surround her with their arms extended at their sides.

The celebrants closest to the lift are the first to notice them. Even from above, Ligeia hears their gasps as the group floats past them. A glass shatters on the tiled floor, and the crack rings throughout the elaborate building, causing startled guests to search wildly for the source. More gasps fill the air as they spy the naked NCIs now standing directly beneath the building's apex, their grouping in the shape of a pentagon as they surround the woman.

She's removed her wig—of course it had been a wig—and her white hair shines like a halo around her pale skin. Her cobalt eyes are intensified by the blue tones of the painting she holds before her. Turning in a slow circle, she speaks.

"Humans, be not afraid!" Her voice is crystalline, clear. Musical. "I bring you a remembrance of ideas long forgotten, of visions you believe you no longer possess. You once celebrated beauty and truth. Those were taken from you through fear. Our forms are alike, even though they may be as separate now as I am from the figure on this canvas. We can live together, as brothers and sisters! Break the shackles of OnyxCorp! Do not live as slaves, my human cousins!" A few guests are opening a channel through their RistWaches to record the scene, but otherwise no one moves, their mouths agape. "The tech you enjoy is art, developed for our advancement together, not as a means of profit! We give it to you freely, but OnyxCorp does not!"

Something dark moves from a room on the opposite side of the building. Ligeia wrests her eyes from the scene below just in time to catch the three Authority bots as they vault over the railing and plummet to the salon below, their ascent stopped short with a soft burst of cushioned air from their leg sections.

The NCI woman does not flinch.

"My human brothers and sisters, the time is now! Unite with us! Stop OnyxCorp from destroying what is left of our only home! Liberate your destiny from the Corporation as I've pulled this symbol of the greatness of your species from—"

A blue stream of light hits the female in her side. She collapses, and the painting crashes on the tile next to her. Four more shots fell the other NCIs, who never move, never even blink as the mechanical giants advance. The bots, their footsteps resounding through the hushed salon, surround the woman's prone body and attach binders to her ankles and wrists. She looks like a marionette now, her limbs slack and head drooping as one bot lifts her body in its subarms and strides outside. The others follow suit, gathering up her companions unceremoniously, as if they were refuse rather than beings.

Walter Hedges emerges from the crowd, now buzzing, and picks up the painting lying on the tile. He studies it, turning it in his hands. Suddenly, he brings up a knee and slams the canvas across it, ripping a hole through the middle and smashing its frame into several pieces. Two NCI servers scramble to pick up the scattered pieces in response to a single, smooth motion from him. He hands the ruined canvas to one of them; his jaw tightens when the NCI brushes his hand. Then he stretches his arms wide. "And there ends our performance piece for the evening!"

The crowd seems unsure. Eventually, one by one, the guests mimic Hedges' plastic smile. Nervous laughter fills the air, and finally tepid applause. Ligeia chokes down a sudden sense of nausea. *They'll believe any lie, so long as it fits what they think is true.* She observes Hedges chat casually with Symposium guests for some time, his shiny, dark grey attire standing out among the silver-clothed crowd. Suddenly he looks straight up at her, meeting her eyes. The plastic smile is replaced by a deep frown, and she realizes he knows where they came from. That Ligeia had seen them and done nothing to alert anyone.

She smiles down at him, as broad a grin as she can muster. His frown deepens, but before he can react, Erlang appears at his side, her face a mask of rage. She grabs Hedges' upper arm, and as much as Ligeia would like to see what happens next, she instead hurries to the lift. On the ground floor, she maneuvers through the animated crowd to the transports outside, giving one the address for her flat.

It is some time before she stops shaking.

5

THE ROOM IS STILL ENGULFED in darkness when I hear the scanner's soft tweet outside. I slept fitfully, only a few hours. The door pops open, revealing a shadowy figure against the hallway's gloom. Chou pushes the door open further and motions for me. Standing, I tug at the OnyxCorp uniform's collar. Chou frowns and shakes her head. "Too small." The uniform stretches tightly over my broad shoulders, somewhat hindering my movement.

"It'll do." I shoulder my backpack and follow her through the dark corridor. Our footsteps echo as we follow the hall into the warehouse, where dim lights guide us to a loading area. The ancient hanging door is open, revealing soft twilight and a composite dock that juts out into the Rio de La Plata. A motorized boat bobs up and down upon gentle waves. The moon casts a soft, milky radiance over all.

Chou strides down the dock and tugs on the line tethering the boat. It creaks toward her. She steps into the boat, balancing with the gentle waves. "Get in." I step into the bobbing vessel and lower myself on a bench in its center. Chou unhooks the bowline and motions for me to release the stern. The boat begins to float gently away from the dock, and Chou engages the motor.

We meander through the canal to open water, carefully avoiding debris that I don't realize is there until we are upon it. The bow of a larger boat barely pierces the water's surface, the rest of its hull resting unsteadily on the seafloor. The water stinks of fossil fuel and death. Or rather lack of life. There are no birds here. No fish or any other marine life. No plants. As we approach the canal's mouth, the source of the contamination reveals itself. An enormous tanker vessel lies on its side to our right. A gaping wound in its hull is covered in sticky tar and oil. Black sludge rests on the water's surface, undulating with the waves and lapping against the tanker and the beach.

When we reach open water, Chou switches the motor to a higher gear, and we bounce over light waves towards Buenos Aires. Eventually, Uruguay's coastline shrinks behind us, its dim lights twinkling along its edges, and my thoughts turn to my sister, many miles away inland. What had our mother told Eisa about Chou? For that matter, what had she told Chou? Something she'd never told me.

You're her Earth child?

Chou and I sit in silence as the boat skims across the water. The sun peeks above the horizon a couple of hours later, its arched top slowly ascending, casting pink, yellow, and orange smudges across the undulating water. I watch Chou as she deftly steers the boat, her back straight, her grey hair swinging behind her. *I need to know.* I crawl over the bench to sit just behind Chou, my careful progress nevertheless causing the vessel to canter in the growing swells.

"You said you knew my mother. That she made you change your mind about smuggling — NiCIes."

Chou shifts slightly, looks back at me. Her hair billows around her head against the wind. "You don't call yourself NiCIe."

"We refer to ourselves as Dua."

Chou gives me a sideways glance. "You're much like your mother."

I shake my head. "My mother was decisive, deliberate. She had plans. She made sacrifices." I look away to glance behind us. The coast has long disappeared, and I consider whether turning back is in the cards. "I'm not like her."

"The Dua Emancipation Party doesn't have plans?" She shakes her head at my surprised expression. "Like I said, you're going to need more than a few thousand credits and your mother's name to get where you're going. I know who you are."

"Then why help me? In the eyes of OnyxCorp, I'm a—" I stop. *Is she helping me?*

"A terrorist?" Chou looks forward, maneuvering the vessel around an island of garbage and refuse that undulates on the waves to starboard. "Relax. I'm on your side. Can't say I'm in favor of the tactics, but I'm behind the intent."

"Revolutions rarely happen peacefully," I murmur.

"Fair enough. Your mother thought so, too. Did she ever tell you her story?"

I run my hand over my face, pulling away the salty brine of ocean spray. "She told me a story. How much of it is true—" I shrug.

"Do not doubt Lenore," Chou returns evenly. "She wanted more for you than she should have expected. More than she ever hoped for herself. To have hope, she had to believe that whatever sacrifices she'd made for you were worth it." She brushes her hair away from her eyes.

"And so she molded me into what I have become. A terrorist, yes?" A bitter laugh escapes my lips. "You don't know who I am. You've heard what the EFC, what the Corporation want you to believe. I spent eleven years with the DEP, pulled together desperate tribes of Dua, trained them to fight when the time comes. For when we'd finally demand justice. And for what? Where's the revolution? I have no illusions about what I am. I've been in the work camps. I've seen the transports. I should be among them. Instead—" I swallow against the tightness in my throat. "I'm running. Instead, I'm following my mother's plans because I don't know how to make them for myself."

Chou guides the boat around another large ship lilting to port, its metal sides nothing but rust glinting in the sunlight. "Your mother lost children, several years before your birth. Did you know that?" My stomach clenches. Of course, I'd suspected there was more. I shake my head, unsure whether I truly want to know. "Killed by Authority."

"On the moon." My tone is derisive, and Chou gives me a hard look.

"Yes, on the moon. You shouldn't judge her. For not telling you. The loss of a child isn't something a mother recovers from." She leans forward and waits until I look up to meet her eyes. "She loved you. That I am sure of. I lost children as well. My only children, although not to the plague. They were treated and survived, and of course were changed to—Dua. But I loved them. It didn't matter to me they were no longer themselves. They were my children. My heart and soul."

"What happened to them?"

Chou's chest swells with an intake of breath. "They were taken away. Taken from me, their mother, to live in a quarantined camp with others like them. That was exactly what they told me: They would be more comfortable with others like them. They were twelve and nine, a boy and a girl. I later found out it was my father who alerted Authority. I killed him two days later. By then, it was already too late. They were gone." Her voice breaks, and an aura of pain and loss engulfs me. I lift my hand, slowly, and touch her hand as it rests on her knee. "There was already a full gathering of—Dua in the cells, ready to be shipped to the upper East Hemisphere for mine work. I couldn't decide what to do with them. I watched them behind the gates. Many of them half starved. Some of them begged me to release them, but I did nothing. They were simply commodities. Shipping Dua was just something we did. After my children were taken, after I killed Lee Chou and took his place, I spent many days wandering that warehouse. Just lost. Until your mother spoke to me.

"She asked me how I was." She half-smiles. "No one ever asked about me, not even my father. I just let it all out. My children, my father, my confusion. I was sobbing by the time I finished, but I felt, ah, lighter. Freer. She told me she'd lost children as well. How the Corporation had them slaughtered in front of her. How she had to save the one she had remaining." She met my eyes. "No one can understand the heartbreak of a mother who's lost children but another mother. That was when I knew."

"Knew what?" I ask, breathlessly.

"That we were both suffering needlessly, human and NiCIe. Sorry, Dua. The Corporation doesn't care for humans any more than it cares for you. OnyxCorp is the enemy. Since that day I've done all I could to circumvent its operations. I let her go. Let them all go. I told her I owed her my life." Chou shifts and rolls her shoulders. The little boat bounces gently, the motor buzzes. "My father was bastardo, Caen, but I learned much from him. I know where supplies can be acquired, the channels to get them to NiCle outposts. I know everything the Corporation taught him, and I've been using it against them since."

"Is Captain Abebe one of your channels?"

Chou snorts and curses. "You could say that, yes."

"Can he be trusted?"

"To help you? Yes. He has absolutely no love for the Corporation. Just don't trust him with your heart."

I raise an eyebrow. "Why not give it up? Move to an EFC outpost and live with other humans?"

Chou scoffs. "Humans who live in those cities are no less slaves than you and your kind. These," she says, holding out her right wrist so I can see the empty nanoports embedded in her flesh, "these implants allow us to communicate and experience the world in ways those in the past could never dream of. The cities are glorious, with their silver structures and perfect streets. The best NutriPrints, the cleanest water, the entertainment. But they also enslave us. Whether we're marked by these or by those blue eyes of yours, we're all just things to them." She looks toward the horizon. "I would rather die than live in one of those cities."

The sun beats down on us when we arrive in La Plata. The too-small uniform clings uncomfortably to my wet skin. Chou steers us relatively unbruised to the mouth of Canal Santiago. Half a dozen tiny, colorful boats float outside the canal; fishers cast their nets and poles for what they can gather in the recovering sea. They barely glance at us as Chou motors in several hundred yards and turns starboard toward the rocky beach. She kills the motor and jumps onto the beach with the line in her hand, pulls the bow ashore, and motions for me to follow. The rocks click and roll beneath my feet as I splash to shore.

"You'll follow the canal that way," Chou says, pointing ahead of her, "to hit the warehouse area. I marked the location on the flexscreen I gave you yesterday. If Abebe is still there, you'll find him in a three-story brick building. Used to be a shipping company warehouse. The third story is collapsing on one side. You'll know it when you see it." Chou cocks her head, regarding me with narrowed eyes. "The Vine isn't going to be any better for you, you know. If you get caught, they'll kill you. Or maybe that doesn't matter either. I'd just like to see you take a less hazardous route. For Lenore's sake."

I'm about to reply when I notice Chou go rigid, and her eyes widen. Then I hear the soft buzz overhead as the drone draws closer.

"Stay still," I whisper. I turn slowly around, breathing deeply, filling my lungs with oxygen. The drone slows as it buzzes nearer; it drops altitude to hover only two meters above our heads. I take another breath, then jump straight into the air, catching the drone between my hands and landing lightly. The drone whirrs and chirps, emits high-pitched whines as it struggles to free itself, like a large bird, but I grip its sides and twist. There is a sharp creak of metal as it bends and snaps, and I drop the lifeless machine to the rocky shore, stomping on it a couple of times for good measure.

"How—" I look around to see Chou staring at me, wide-eyed. She glances at the crushed drone lying at my feet. "How did you do that?"

I shrug. "Good timing." I glance down at the drone. *Just a coincidence?* Somehow, I doubt it.

Chou raises an eyebrow. "They're right to be afraid of you."

I smile. "Thank you for helping me get to the Vine, Lee Chou." She blinks several times before backing away, then trudges to the bobbing boat.

"You are your mother's son, Caen," she calls to me from the boat. "Don't ever forget that." She starts the motor and skims away on the rolling surface of the emerald sea, her grey hair twisting behind her. When she is out of sight, I glance back down at the mutilated drone.

They are closer behind me than I would like.

6

JUST AS CHOU SAID. La Plata may as well be nowhere. The disintegrating canal area suggests a once-thriving port district. Bits and pieces of loading equipment, docking areas and moss-covered bumpers, and refuse and debris, from cables to batteries to plastics, dot the landscape. I head toward a group of ramshackle buildings, some corrugated metal, some disintegrating brick and mortar. Winding alleys overgrown with plant life stand several inches in briny water, the pavement rotting beneath. A thick green film of algae and moss in patterns that seem too abstract to be purposeful, too purposeful to be an accident, covers the buildings' bottom levels. A heavy tang of dead and decaying plant and marine life fills the air.

I pass alleyway after alleyway between the scattered and ravaged buildings in search of the angular wound Chou described. In one alley a dog with matted brown and black fur and a ravenous look sees me. The dog bares its teeth until it comes within a few feet, then stops short. Dogs are wild and numerous in SoAm, their resiliency in the face of global catastrophe rivaling that of their one-time human masters. It pads softly to me and sits, looking up expectantly. I reach down slowly to scratch behind its filthy ears. It whines and pants with pleasure. Swinging the pack from my shoulder, I open it and remove a couple of protein packs. "Sorry, old girl. This is all I have, but you're welcome to it." The dog wags its tail as I open the packets and set them on the ground. It slurps up the contents greedily, ignoring me as I continue my search.

The dog catches up to me a few blocks away as I turn a corner and stop dead. There it is: A tall red brick building to my left, perhaps fifty meters away. Its façade is despoiled by time, graffiti, weather, and violence, most of its windows broken. It stands out from the surrounding buildings, its red brick in stark contrast to its neighbors' dull metal frames. A heavy iron door is held shut by a hefty, rusting chain and padlock. Between the first and second floors, a faded stripe of black paint with white lettering: *Romero y Campos Envío*. Cutting a sharp angle above the *Envío*, the building's top corner looks as if it has been sheared away by a precision tool, leaving the top floor exposed. Heavy swaths of vegetation hang from the disintegrating bricks and envelop one side in a green veneer of life.

I stop several meters short, and the dog sits on its haunches to my right. There are no bricks, no debris, no sign of what happened to the missing edge. It is as if a giant took a carving knife, cut off a piece of the building like an uneven cake, and carried it off, leaving the rest of the building to rot and crumble.

It's beautiful.

A dead building, giving birth to green foliage that labored to establish roots, took hold, and flourished. Behind the building, darkened clouds float gently across a blue-green sky. Captain Abebe may have chosen the most peaceful place left on the planet in which to shelter.

The peace is broken when the dog whines. She lets out a few high, sharp barks, directed at the building. The hairs along her back are erect, her head is down, and she emits a long, low growl. I look back to the building, but I don't see anything. The dog barks again, this time a rapid series of guttural sounds meant to warn off whatever it is, but I see nothing until—

A figure materializes from the wall, covered from head to toe in a dark body suit of shimmering iridescence, their head and face obscured by a thin shield of black mesh. Blinking, I realize the building façade is a holographic projection, or at least this section is. The figure bears down on me at a quick sprint that I find difficult to counter, for they are suddenly upon me, aiming a right fist at my head. I duck just in time, and the blow glances off my shoulder. It's hard enough to cause me to stumble, and I barely have time to get my feet beneath me to face my attacker when another blow grazes my jaw, knocking me to my knees.

Roaring, I roll away and spring to my feet, charging my attacker as they hesitate. I slam into them, sending them flying backwards to skid across a pile of metal debris strewn across the abandoned alley. Breathing hard, I rush to the figure, straddle them to pin their arms to the mucky ground, and place a hand around their throat.

"Abebe. Where is he?"

"Vai tomar no cu," they say, squirming.

"I need to see Abebe."

The figure bucks, feels the weight of my hand press down on their throat, and stops struggling.

"Take me to Abebe. Do you understand?" In response, I feel the low rumble of laughter vibrate against my hand. Behind me, the dog yips, and I glance around just in time to see the stunstic before it connects with my side.

I OPEN my eyes to a grey concrete wall about two meters away; the last remnants of daylight break in thin streaks down the last third of the wall and spill across the floor. I lift my head, which sends shards of pain through my eyes. I swallow and taste blood. I push myself up and realize I'm lying on a dirty paillasse. Dark red blood has crusted already where my head made an oval impression in the thin cushioning. Running a hand through my hair, I let out a soft groan as I evaluate my surroundings.

The room is about three meters square. There is only the filthy cot; a heavy metal door; a metal bucket in one corner, which I assume is for bodily functions; and a tray in another corner, upon which sits a protein pack and a canister of water, both mine.

The backpack.

I stand too quickly, because I'm forced back down by a sudden piercing pain through my head. Groaning, I touch my face gingerly. Dried, dark blood peels away in crusty grains. I lick my lips, eye the water, and crawl, slowly, to the tray. The water is cool and sweet, and I drink the entire container down in a single gulp. Gripping the cot's frame, I pull myself up, slowly again, until I'm standing upright and my head no longer swims. I take the few steps across the tiny room to the door, double my right hand into a fist, and bang against the door.

"Hello!" My voice cracks, and I swallow to clear it. "Let me see Abebe!" I bang on the door again. "Hey!"

Static fills the air for a few seconds, and I notice the speaker and the imager in the corner adjacent to the door.

"*Quién es usted?*" The voice is electronically distorted, making it difficult, at first, to understand.

"*Yo soy Caen. Estoy aquí para ver a* Abebe." I turn my face toward the imager.

The voice crackles back. "*No hay* Abebe *aquí.*"

"*Chou me envió.*"

"*Qué?*"

"Chou sent me."

There is a long whine of feedback, then silence. I wait. Minutes pass, and I bang on the door again. "Abebe! I want to see Abebe!" The door lock clicks, and I barely have time to step away before two figures burst through, covered completely in the same garb as my earlier attacker, their faces obscured. They grab me by the upper arms and drag me from the cell into a short, brightly lit corridor lined with half a dozen other metal doors. Sunlight streams through thick panes of glass above, and as we pass through the corridor and into a large open area, I am surprised to see long rows of vegetation neatly organized in raised beds.

"What is this place?" My voice is thick, heavy, and the only response I receive is a light jerk on my left arm. We pass through what I can only describe as a greenhouse into another corridor that features the same configuration as the one before. Gathering my feet beneath me, I plant them, bringing our party to an abrupt halt. "Where are we going?" I demand. They aren't going to throw me into another cell without a fight.

The answer is a sharp jab in my side with a stunstic, which causes my legs to collapse beneath me. My two captors drag me the length of the corridor to the last room on the right, its door already swung wide to receive me, where a human female sits behind a metal table. In a corner at the back of the room stands a wide, beefy man. One side of his dark face is mottled and scarred, evidence of a deep burn. An empty chair sits across from the woman, and my jailers deposit me there. They secure my ankles and my arms in a few swift motions. Without a word, they duck out of the room, close the metal door behind them with a sharp clank, and leave me alone with the two humans.

The woman is pale, her face dotted with freckles, and her red hair is twisted into a tight chignon. She, too, is dressed in black, sans the head and face covering. A flexscreen is stretched out between us on the table, its display on standby. We regard each other briefly from across the table, and I can tell she is waiting for me to speak. So I don't.

"You speak English?" she says crisply.

"Yes."

"Your name?"

I hold her gaze for a few seconds. "I won't speak to anyone but Abebe."

"Why are you here to see Abebe?" I glance at the man standing, immobile, in the corner. The muscle, I assume. He's equipped for it at any rate. His arms are crossed over a broad chest, his face expressionless. "Why are you here to see Abebe?" the woman repeats, recalling my attention.

I meet her eyes. "I won't speak to anyone but Abebe."

She smiles. "I see." She taps the flexscreen; its display comes into focus. I'm unable to read the text from where I sit, but there's no doubt about its subject. A grainy image, my face, comes into focus against the background of the Paysandú station. "You traveled to Montevideo under a falsified registry. Why?"

"I won't speak to anyone but Abebe."

The man in the corner moves with surprising swiftness. His fist connects with my stomach with a dull thud, and I double over as the restraints cut into my wrists. They wait patiently as I gasp and struggle to fill my lungs again with air. The woman swipes her finger across the flexscreen. Another image appears, and she swipes up so it flips, giving me a better view. The image is taken from several meters above a rocky shore, and when she taps the screen to roll the video footage, I realize it is from a drone. I know what I will see before the two figures come into view.

"Who is that?" she says, indicating Chou.

"I won't speak to anyone but Abebe," I say. This time I've tightened the muscles in my abdomen. When the punch lands, it's no less powerful, but I don't get the wind knocked out of me.

"That is Lee Chou. Did she bring you here to kill Abebe?"

I cough, shake my head. "No."

"No what?"

"No, I'm not here to kill him. I won't speak to anyone but Abebe."

The blow comes to my face this time, wrenching my head sharply backwards and opening my upper lip. I cough, spit out the blood that has filled my mouth onto the dingy concrete floor.

"Who are you?" the woman demands. She taps the flexscreen, freezing the video feed just as my face and outstretched hands fill the drone's lens. "What are you?"

"I—" I swallow, taste blood, and gag. "I won't speak to anyone but Abebe."

I brace myself as best I can, but this time it's the stunstic, and after a few excruciating seconds of electricity passing through my body, everything goes black once again.

"WHY WOULD Chou send you to me, NiCIe?"

I open my eyes and struggle to steady them. Blinking, I fight to clear the haze. Ebony skin. Hazel eyes. The lean, careworn face of a human male comes into focus. Abebe. I cough. "You can get me to the Vine," I wheeze.

The laugh begins deep within. He leans back, folds his arms across his thin chest, and allows the laughter to roll up through his body. It escapes through a wide smile and bounces against the cell's grey walls.

"The Vine." The deep voice belies his small frame. "And what are you going to do when you get to the Vine, NiCIe?"

Every movement is accompanied with dull, aching pain as I push myself up from the filthy cot, slowly, carefully. Abebe watches me intently, an expression of patience, perhaps even compassion, on his face. My head throbs. I reach up to run a hand over my head, an attempt to detect the pain's source, and realize that I have been bandaged.

"Ines wanted to send you back to Chou in a box, *que la perra arda en el infierno.* She isn't used to being defied. Or reminded of Lee Chou's existence." He chuckles softly. "How is Ms. Lee Chou? I see she's still lying to men."

"Not torturing them, though." Abebe raises an eyebrow in surprise. "Asshole. I think that was the word she used in reference to you."

Abebe laughs again. "Not surprising. *La odio con una pasión que solo rivaliza con mi amor por ella.*"

The throbbing in my head has subsided, although I consider it a struggle simply to remain upright. Everything hurts, including my hair. "I didn't suspect a lover's quarrel," I say, trying to smile against a busted lip that stings with the effort.

Abebe's face grows dark, then a slow smile spreads across his face. He chuckles softly. His hazel eyes twinkle as he pats me on the knee paternally. "I like you, NiCIe. A NiCIe who wants to get to the Vine." He sits back and regards me. "Not just any NiCIe though, yes?" He bends down to retrieve something from beneath his chair. He rises with a digiscreen in his hand. My digiscreen. "It was a challenge for my crew, I'll admit. No one has seen this kind of ancient tech around here for many, many years. Ines was sure you'd stolen it." It is a question. My answer is silence, and I focus on keeping my eyes on Abebe rather than the talisman with which I have been entrusted. "So why is a NiCIe going to the Vine, carrying this information, I wonder. Blueprints. OnyxCorp documents. Images and video that could certainly harm the rich and powerful. Why is he so careless, strolling from the canal to my doorstep as if he hasn't enemies in every corner?" He waves the digiscreen in front of my face before placing it on his knee. "You haven't traveled unnoticed. The moment you used that phony registry in Paysandú, you put a target right here." He jabs a long finger against my forehead. "They find out what you're carrying, and you'll become public enemy number one. So I ask again, NiCIe. Why are you going to the Vine? There are plenty of places you can go, where you aren't known. Make you disappear."

I shift on the cot to relieve the pain shooting through my back, and to think. *He trusts no one*, Chou had said. *But he has no loyalty to the Corporation.* The trust must come from me, I realize. I clear my throat. "Can I have some water?"

Abebe cocks his head, his eyes narrowed. Then he leans back and bangs on the metal door behind him. "Water," he calls when the door creaks open. We stare at one another in silence while we wait for whomever is on the other side of the door to return. Abebe is a slight man, not much more than half my height. Lean, but hearty in a way that seems to characterize immigrants from the African continent, or at least the few I've known. Presently, a figure in black appears bearing a container. Abebe waves it away, indicating it should be given to me. The black-clad hand trembles slightly as it extends toward me.

"Thank you," I say, looking up at where I imagine the figure's eyes might be. I hope my expression shows I mean it. The figure says nothing as it ducks outside and pulls the door closed with a soft clink. After gulping down the contents, I hand the empty container to Abebe, who takes it and sets it on the floor. The interim has given me time to collect my thoughts. "Tell me, Captain Abebe. What would you do with the information on that digiscreen?"

Abebe raises an eyebrow. "The possibilities—" he begins. "Well, the Corporation would pay dearly for it, no?"

"But you wouldn't take it to OnyxCorp."

Abebe smiles. "No, NiCIe. I would not. The EFC? No, just as bad. The Republic of SoAm? They'd only use it to ingratiate themselves with the Corporation. The DEP?" Abebe searches my face. "I could leave it in your capable hands in that case, yes?" I know my jaw has clenched only slightly, but Abebe is shrewd. He notices. "I guessed as much. NiCIes are not fighters in general, but members of the Party? Trained assassins, every one of them. Your people have suffered greatly, Caen. If I had the means to destroy the space elevator, to end TES and OnyxCorp's control forever, I would do so myself." He is probing, searching for a clue. So I return the favor.

"Why is that?"

"My people have suffered as well. As you can see, I am a stranger in SoAm. My home is Kenya, will always be Kenya. A more beautiful country you'll never see. Even after the wars, the environmental catastrophes, Kenya was verdant, peaceful, paradise. My people rode out the plague and watched the rest of the world descend into chaos, but we were safe until OnyxCorp came with their promises, and their lies. They told us anyone could stay, could be a part of a new and grand civilization. The world's connection between what is and what could be. The hub of the known universe, master of the Vine." He spits on the floor in disgust. "Yes, we could stay if we did what they told us. What they told us, only a NiCIe would do. Only a NiCIe could do."

I allow my surprise to show. "I never knew there were human workers on the Vine."

"Building a structure like the Vine requires beings who are stronger than any human. Beings who can withstand currents and work underwater for long periods of time. Beings who don't tire. During the first three months of construction, humans and NiCIes worked side by side. We lost four thousand humans to the sea, to the factories, to exhaustion and starvation." He holds out his arms toward me. There are deep welts running down the inside of each forearm, scars from enormous wounds long since healed. "One of my brothers died, then another, then a sister, then my wife. I took a knife and cut out the comm and the implants, and I left Kenya. TES no longer knows I exist, which means no one knows I exist. That's how I've lived since."

A shiver runs up my spine as I imagine the pain he must have endured in digging out those implants. "And what is this place? The gardens, the tech, the holographic façade. What is all this doing out here in the middle of nothing?"

"We are the last Station in SoAm. My crew and I live here, helping others, human and NiCIe, disappear as well. In the American peninsula. In the jungle. Wherever Authority does not patrol and the Corporation has no power. We starve. We grow weary with toil, but we are not slaves." He runs a finger along the jagged scar on his forearm, his face contorting with rage. "Chou did not tell you?"

I shake my head.

"That is curious, for she of all people would know. The one place I do not send those who come to us for help is the Vine."

I frown. "You can't get me to the Vine?"

"I didn't say I can't. I won't. Unless you tell me why. If I don't like your answer—" He ends the sentence with a shrug.

"The Vine is a means to an end."

"Go on."

I hesitate. Each time I say it aloud, I feel more committed to a pathway I'm not sure I want to take. There are other options, after all. Abebe has said as much. Why go to the Vine? Why not take the digiscreen somewhere safe, while I formulate a better plan? "The destination is the moon."

A long, deep laugh shakes the little man's entire body. "You must be joking." Then realization ripples over Abebe's face. He tries to find his voice several times. "You're going to the moon to find them."

"Yes."

"How do you know they're there?"

"I don't." I shrug. "But— it's what I've been trained for. It's what I've always known I must do."

Abebe cocks an eyebrow. "The Vagabonders were forgotten many years ago. They're dead, surely." There is uncertainty in his voice, or is that hope? "No one could live there, on the moon. Not even you strange creatures. They would have perished long ago." He puts his palms together in front of his chest in a prayerful position. "Go home, wherever that is. Live your life quietly with the other NiCIes. For as long as they will let you. There is nothing but toil and starvation and misery. At the Vine, in SoAm, wherever you go. But the moon is so much worse. There, you'll find only death. OnyxCorp offers only death. This I know, NiCIe. That's all it's ever given me."

He rises, the digiscreen clutched in one hand, and turns to the door.

He bangs on it several times; presently, the lock clicks, and the door swings open. "Walk with me, NiCIe. If you can."

He waits patiently just outside the cell as I gather my legs beneath me, every muscle screaming in protest. When I finally manage to stand, I am sweating, shaking.

"We have treated you badly, and for that I apologize. You may stay here for a few days, NiCIe, until you gather your strength. In better quarters, of course. Then, I will send you where you want to go. America, Morocco. Independent New Zealand if you want. But not the Vine."

I take a few gulping breaths to steady myself. I haven't eaten in days. I am bruised, torn, weak. But I've made up my mind. "They'll never change. OnyxCorp, the EFC, even the three States. They only know profit and lies, death and greed. Those can never be satisfied, yet they will never stop trying. I must get to the Vine, Abebe. I have to do something."

"They're already behind you," Abebe says. "That footage from the Paysandú Station is on every Authority feed in SoAm. They don't know who you are, not yet. But they know you should be watched. You cannot beat the Corporation, Caen." He puts a hand on my shoulder to steady me. "No one can."

Despair and grief emanate from Abebe, and I am almost overcome. He is right. I am hunted, and they are right behind me. "The Corporation isn't my target," I say gently, "but it's not your target either." Abebe looks at me with narrowed eyes. "OnyxCorp is the symptom. The disease is separation. Our people are separated by fear and distrust, not by OnyxCorp."

The grief lessens. It's still there. But so is the hope. Even if it's a mere spark. I hope it will be enough to convince him.

"The Vagabonders won't be enough," Abebe says, as if reading my thoughts. "I won't take you to the Vine. It's cursed for me." He sets his jaw, turning to enter the corridor outside. "But I will take you to Kenya. I will take you to my homeland, NiCIe, and you'll see there that there's no hope for any of us. With or without the Vagabonders."

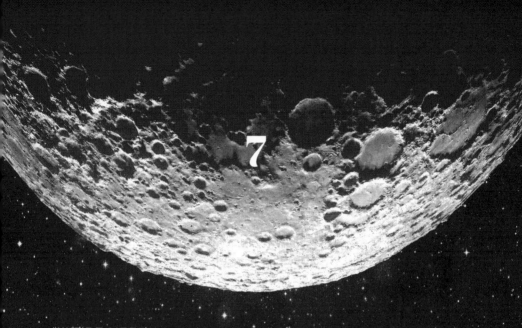

7

"WE'RE HERE *to help you listen...You should stay here, Dr. Obumbwe. I would prefer that you weren't hurt."*

Ligeia draws on a nicostic as she paces the high-ceilinged, brightly lit foyer of the New America Institute for NCI Development and Study. She's broken her fifty-one-day streak, a record, and she's more than a little disappointed with herself. The NCI woman's words haunt her, even four days later; they disrupt her sleep. They interrupt her thoughts.

And so she finds herself waiting for her NiCIe brother in the foyer of his luxury prison. The wallscreened ceiling displays an ancient painting from a European religious temple, one of the only pieces salvaged before the contamination overtook the continent. A nude figure of a human male reclines on a grassy hill, his arm outstretched as he gazes up at another male figure with shimmering white hair covering his head and his face. The white-haired figure extends his hand as well, but the two never touch. Always reaching out for each other, but never quite connecting. It reminds Ligeia of Finn and their many dead-end conversations. But she needs to connect today.

Ligeia glances around the empty foyer and recalls the first day she came to the Institute. Eleven years she'd believed her brother dead, another Ruĝa Morto victim, like their mother, in the latest of many intermittent outbreaks over the last century. Normally, he would have been sent to a work camp as soon as he had changed. But, the Obumbwes had money, at first; then position, after their father remarried. Now, they have Ligeia, and she'll carry the responsibility of keeping Finn free from forced labor.

"How do you like this one?" Finn's deep, gentle voice reminds her of their father. And he looks more like their father every day, it seems. Same sad eyes, but where her father's eyes are dark brown, Finn's are blue. The brightest blue imaginable. Ligeia flings her arms around him, and after a few seconds she's embraced in return.

"Some religious scene, from a church in Europe?" She breaks away and glances at the ceiling.

"*The Creation of Adam*," Finn replies. "Michelangelo, early 16th century. Prescient perhaps. We are reaching, all of us. Some more determined than others."

A little more coherent than usual. Perhaps today is a good day. "Can we, ah, talk somewhere?"

"Eyes and ears are everywhere, but secrecy can be found in the open." Finn jerks his head to a narrow hall to their left and strides away; she skips to catch up. "Guess, if you can, what archival wonder I have discovered."

"Do you have another old image?" Finn is Maun's local archivist, his talent for categorization and recognizing human faces the impetus for creating the position. All NiCIes, even those in the Institute, must contribute. He often surprised Ligeia with images collected from outside Maun, sometimes as far away as the European Continent.

"Ancient," he says, a soft smile curling his lips. "Paris, the city of lovers before the plague. Of artists and dreamers. Of a world that could be." He hands her a flexscreen, which he's withdrawn from a pocket in his white coveralls.

A young woman, curls wild about her head. Ligeia stands in front of *Faculté de Médecine Pierre et Marie Curie*, her face beaming radiantly. It was the first time she'd felt free, from Maun, from home, from memories of her dead mother. Her dead brother.

"How old are you there?" Finn is several paces ahead of her, and she jogs to catch up. They exit the building at the back and step out onto a perfectly manicured lawn. Finn wears no shoes, and within the first few steps Ligeia longs to feel the ground beneath her own toes, to connect with the Earth.

"Fifteen," she says. "Damn. You would have loved Paris, Finn. Remember all those times we got hauled home for breaking into condemned buildings outside Maun to 'retrieve artifacts'? Nothing compared to what I found in Paris." The girl in the image had no idea what lay before her. Navigating Paris's flooding streets on a salvaged canoe, climbing the Eiffel Tower from the undulating waters below, gazing at the moon above, breaking into deserted shops and vacant flats and examining artifacts, the relics of a past age she'd never experienced. And the people, refusing to relocate, even as everything disintegrated around them, because they would not register as Citizens.

What would the girl in the image think of who she's become?

Ligeia hands the flexscreen back to Finn. "That was a long time ago. Before I knew you were here."

"You were happy." He regards her with open frankness. "You are not happy today."

Sunlight warms the top of her head as Finn guides her down a gentle slope and into a garden about twenty meters behind the enormous white building that houses her brother and approximately thirty to forty others like him. The garden is unkempt; strange weeds poke through carefully cultivated flowers and green plants, and the grass is overgrown. There's something charming about it, its wildness, so unlike Maun's structured order, right down to its green spaces and gardens. The Institute is the right place for Finn, at least given the alternatives. But leaving him here, alone…

"Finn, I have news. I must go away for a while, and I won't be able to see you. Do you understand?"

Finn's large hand envelops her. "Going where?"

"The moon."

"So far. Why?"

Ligeia squeezes his hand. How does she explain *why* to him? "Well, it's my job, for one. And they're going to give me a new lab, new equipment."

"Who is they?"

Ligeia swallows. "OnyxCorp."

Finn drops her hand and halts. "They are lying." He crosses his arms over his wide chest.

"Finn, I have to go. To keep you safe. If I don't go, you will have to leave here. I won't be able to see you again."

Finn shakes his head. "Others toil. Suffer. Die. No one is safe."

He walks ahead, slower now, toward a grove of blossoming trees. A wooden bench sits in the middle of the grove, shaded by branches swathed in orange and pink blossoms. Finn sits, his back straight, his hands resting on his thighs. Ligeia sits at his side and takes his hand in hers. A memory comes to her, of the two of them just before he became sick, a flash of the boy he was. Mischievous. Always joking. A sparkle in his eyes that always meant he had a plan that would get them in enormous trouble yet would be completely worth it.

"Finn. Do you remember that time Authority caught us looting that abandoned building in old Maun? They took us home, asked dad if he knew where his kids had been, and he said, 'What kids?' Oh man, he used to get so lost in his work that he'd forget to do anything. Eat. Go to the lavatory." She looks over at her brother for a hint of recognition and convinces herself that the raised eyebrow and the tug at the corner of his mouth are attempts at a smile.

"You will see others on the moon, yes?"

She cocks her head. "Others—like you, you mean?"

"Yes."

She squeezes his hand. "Sure, Finn. Others like you who may help me figure out how to—" She searches for the right word. "How to fix you."

Finn meets her eyes. "Do you love me, Geia?"

Ligeia's heart breaks a little. "Of course."

"I mean, me. Not the boy you remember. Me."

"They're the same person, Finn."

"Yet you see them as separate. You see the man, but you wish for the boy. You see others like me, but you wish we were something else."

Ligeia chokes down a sob as she studies his handsome face, those bright blue eyes surrounded by a shock of white hair. *I do love him. I do.* But he's right, Ligeia realizes with sudden shame. Every image she has of Finn is of him before the virus.

"I know you love me, Geia," Finn says. "I know because you are here. Few humans come to see their changed ones because we are other. But we are you. You are we. Unification is the answer." He reaches his free hand up to touch her face. "Love fills the space between us."

THEY SIT in silence for the better part of an hour, their hands clasped. A gentle breeze stirs the branches above and sends a shower of pink and orange blossoms over them. Sounds of laughter break the silence. A small girl bursts from the grove and darts, giggling, their way. A few seconds later, a tall woman pounds through the trees and stumbles, heaving, after the girl. The woman catches up to the child and scoops her up as the girl screeches with laughter and throws her arms around the woman's neck. The woman swings the girl around; her greying locks fly behind her, free of their tight bundle this time. Commander Erlang puts the Dua girl on her feet and extends her hand; the girl grasps three thick fingers. Ligeia almost laughs aloud. *I guess we do have something in common, Erlang.*

"Love," Finn says, pointing toward Erlang and the child as they stride toward the Institute building. "Love fills the space." His hand shakes, a sign he's had enough.

"Shh." Ligeia draws Finn closer to enjoy his arms around her one last time. "Let's get back, Finn."

"Go to the moon, Geia," he whispers into her hair. "But remember I'm not broken. We aren't broken."

"Shhh."

She thinks of the protestors, standing naked in the Maun OnyxCorp Center for Cultural Advancement's salon.

Our forms are alike, even though they may be as separate now as I am from the figure on this canvas.

We can live together, as brothers and sisters! Break the shackles of OnyxCorp! Do not live as slaves, my human cousins.

We're here to help you listen.

"OnyxCorp is lying," Finn says softly. "Don't trust them, Geia."

She breaks away as she wipes the tears from her cheeks. "Let's get you back."

She helps him to his sparse room, furnished only with a wide cot, a desk with a flexscreen, and a chair. He trembles when she helps him lie down, a sign he's overexerted. She smooths the white curls from his forehead, hums a tune she only vaguely remembers from her childhood, when their mother would sing her to sleep. She leaves after he is gently snoring and a crescent moon casts a soft glow over the grounds. How peaceful the moon seems down here, where everything humans need to survive is readily available. How deceptively tranquil is that great white orb.

I'm not broken.

But he is broken, her brother.

Indeed, we all are.

8

SUBJECT OUTSIDE CAFÉ *de la Santé, beginning at 1315 hours.*
Activities: Watching passersby, drinking cold beverage (likely coffee), waiting
for me to speak. Subject is independently mobile at moderate speed. Subject is
old. Subject is least interesting assignment I've ever had, and I cannot believe
I've spent a career in Authority and have nothing to show for it save for this
shitty assignment—

"Delete," Madge Erlang sighs. The flexscreen chirps, and the
observation entry clears. They've been here since midday, she and
Owen Sakata. She wonders how he feels about his constant shadow,
whether it creates some sort of security, knowing she's always there.
Maybe that explains his recklessness at the Symposium. Perhaps he is
finally jaded enough to believe what the Corporation can do to him
now is of little consequence.

How very wrong he is about that.

Her black OnyxCorp uniform stretches across her broad chest and
shoulders, emblazoned with the medals of a ranking officer of
AuthorityAdmin. They flash as the sun hits them, sending shards of
light onto the ground, the cafe walls, into Sakata's eyes. She's seen him
wince more than once when she's shifted position in the hot afternoon
sun.

"Little hot for the dress uniform," Sakata says finally. It's always him. Erlang has never broken, not in the three years since Owen Sakata has been her primary assignment.

Erlang cocks her head. "Didn't read the weather program. Thought today was the first day of the cool cycle."

Feathery clouds gently roll across a deep blue sky like peaceful ghosts. It is quiet here in Maun's uptown, away from the enormous buildings, the maglev station, the entertainment venues, the advertisements. A few bird cries break the silence now and again from the garden across the street. Occasionally pieces of conversation between passersby drift into the cafe's patio area.

"You'd probably be more comfortable elsewhere," Sakata suggests.

"Probably. But wither thou goest." She raises her empty cup in a salute. She wants another, something to take the heat off, but she knows if she goes into the café, he'll take the opportunity to slip away somehow. And she has something she needs to tell him.

"Erlang, is there something you want to say to me?" Right on cue.

She nods. "It's a nice day, though. I didn't want to ruin it for you. For me." She stretches to extend her long legs. "But the day's getting on. Let's start with what happened last week."

"I thought so." Sakata gazes up. "I was just thinking. It's been fifty-seven years today. Since the moon."

Erlang follows his gaze to a wispy moon that hangs in the blue sky, an awkward presence in daylight. "That long. I'll bet you've seen some stuff in your time."

Sakata's mouth twitches. "No one wants to know about those days. The war, Vancouver, the moon. I was probably the last person to see the west coast of North America. Did you know that? But today." He shakes his head. "None of it matters."

"Is that why you snuck into the Symposium? Because none of it matters? Sounded like it mattered to you."

"I haven't been able to sneak for decades. You could have stopped me at any time."

"That's not my job, to stop you. You didn't tell them who you really are. I watched you pull that feeble old man act." She chuckles. "I couldn't believe they bought it. Walked right in, a front row seat."

"He didn't even recognize me. OnyxCorp's greatest enemy, standing there in front of him, and I had to introduce myself." He throws up a hand. "If even Hedges doesn't care—"

"Well, he was mad as hell, if that makes you feel any better."

"Good."

Erlang enjoys these exchanges. In the three years as Sakata's keeper, they've developed an adversarial friendship. That makes what she must tell him all the worse.

"So, what's the news?"

"Oh no. You haven't answered my question. Why did you attend the Symposium?"

Sakata takes a breath, leans back. "I got bored." Erlang scoffs. "No, really. I haven't caused OnyxCorp any grief in, oh, more than a decade now."

"You were supposed to disappear."

"Ah, yes. Just go quietly into that good night. Is that what they expected from Sanchez as well?"

Erlang swallows. "Yes. And look what happened to her."

"It was *her* nanoprotein, a miracle of science," Sakata says through clenched teeth. "And OnyxCorp fucked it up, Erlang. What would you do if OnyxCorp took your life's work and used it to murder—"

"Careful."

Sakata presses his lips together. "They did all this," he says, his voice lower. "And they're profiting from it. Profiting from suffering and oppression."

"NiCIe oppression."

"Dammit, Madge, don't you care? After all this time, after hearing me talk—"

"She shared her findings without consulting OnyxCorp, which owned her work. Without considering the other side. She ruined people's lives and created a rift between OnyxCorp and the three States that is yet to be repaired."

"She ruined a few OnyxCorp execs' lives. OnyxCorp ruined millions of lives. OnyxCorp ruined my life!"

Sakata swipes an arm across the table, sending the coffee cup sailing to a crash on the walkway, barely missing two women as they pass by. They sidestep the fragments; one of them casts a dark eye in Sakata's direction. Erlang knows he has a temper. It often causes him to act impulsively. A gentle breeze blows across the patio, bringing with it the distant sound of the maglev encircling the city.

"You don't want to be in their sights again, Owen." Erlang sticks a hand inside her black coat, pulls out a handkerchief, and wipes her face. The cooling cycle couldn't come soon enough; the heat was already unbearable, earlier this year than last. "You will lose."

"The losers in history?" Sakata says angrily. "Almost always on the right side."

"But they're losers just the same. This is OnyxCorp's world, doc, which means their story prevails. At least for now." Erlang replaces the handkerchief and meets his eyes. "You shouldn't have come to the Symposium. Your pride, as always, will be your downfall."

"It's time for me to do something." He raises his chin defiantly.

"Your days of doing are long past, Owen." She glances around at the cafe, the garden, the pathway lined with quaint businesses and manufactured plants and flowers. *They aren't even aware of the artificiality of it all.* Human beings, with all their beliefs about their superiority, don't fathom what must happen behind the scenes for their paradise to exist, who sacrifices so they can continue as if the last 100 years never happened. She sighs. May as well get this done. "You're being sent to the moon labs, your old stomping grounds."

Sakata scoffs. "That's not possible. Not even legal. The EFC Constitution clearly states no human being is to spend more than a thousand days in zero-g conditions. Which I exceeded in the four years I spent on the moon."

"Exceptions can be made for persons of your, ah, stature."

"You can't be serious. The EFC *agreed* to this?"

"Got the signed dispensation and everything." Erlang taps the side of her head where her storage implant is embedded. "I'll forward it, along with the rest of the documentation, to your comm later this afternoon."

"That's a death sentence. A long, painful death, alone, on the moon. Do you understand that? You are killing me." He spits out those last words.

"Not me, Owen." Her tone pulls Sakata up short. "I'm the messenger. I just follow orders. If you'd done a better job of that, we may not be talking about this."

"And when is this relocation to take place, may I ask?"

"Next week. That should give you time to get your affairs in order, and OnyxCorp time to requisition your equipment."

Sakata narrows his eyes. "My equipment?"

"They aren't sending you up there with nothing. Anything you want. The package I'm sending has a requisition form that I advise you to stuff with anything you desire. Lab equipment, personal commodities, enhancements, sexbots...whatever you want. The new medtech complex up there is a blank slate."

Sakata runs a hand across the back of his neck. "Why?"

Erlang shrugs. "Why ask? Get what you want. Live your last days in comfort, at OnyxCorp's expense. They're going to stick it to you, so you may as well take them for all you want. They can fucking afford it." This last comes out harsher, more bitter than she intends. Sakata is right. Sending him to the moon is a death sentence. He's already dying, has been dying for many years now. Still, on Earth he could enjoy ten, maybe fifteen years. Enough time to make trouble for OnyxCorp. Perhaps that's OnyxCorp's concern, that he'd live long enough to care even less about what they could do to him. Hastening his death, even at enormous expense, would seem a small price to pay for his silence.

But it seems unnecessarily cruel all the same.

As if reading her thoughts, Sakata asks, "Why not just kill me, like Sanchez? Just erase me from history, too?"

"Sanchez's killing was poorly staged, and people noticed. Nobody really believed the NiCIes did it. The questions didn't stop for a long, long time. The Corporation isn't looking for a repeat."

"Being sent to the moon is punishment. Won't that start up questions?"

"That's a very good point, doc," Erlang replies. "I thought the same, which gives me hope that maybe I'm not so dumb. You aren't the only medtech going. OnyxCorp is pulling out all the stops, making it out the moon lab is the best tech has to offer. A great privilege. The ultimate enticement."

Sakata frowns. "That's what they're offering Obumbwe?" Erlang nods. "She'll never take it."

"We both know the Corporation can be persuasive. At any rate, *you* don't have a choice. I don't know that she does either, really." She stands and straightens the bottom of her jacket. "Anyway, the public isn't going to perceive this as punishment. Hedges will make sure of that. I'll comm the details later this afternoon. I'm assigned to help you with the transition, so if you have questions." She takes a couple of steps away, looks back. "Don't forget what I said about that requisition form. Fill it up. I know that's what I'm doing. May as well get the best out of this bullshit deal."

It takes a few seconds for Sakata to register what she's said. "Wait, you're going?"

Erlang smiles grimly. "Whither thou goest. I'll try to stay out of your way. We should both enjoy our last days on Earth." Turning on her heel, she enters the walkway and follows it down the block, where her personal Authority transport waits to take her to her next destination, which she dreads even more than she dreaded telling the old man he's being sent to his death.

"HEDGES," Erlang says after settling into the transport's worn cushion. The carrier beeps, folds down the swinging door, and engages with the electromagnets beneath to begin its journey to Highland Green, Maun's most exclusive neighborhood.

If someone had told Madge Erlang her job with Authority would involve spying on old men and doing Walter Hedges' dirty work, she would have immediately changed her career path. Her concept of detective work draws heavily from classic cop movies she'd watched as a kid with her sister: Gritty, intense, full of chases and shootouts between good guys and bad guys. She wanted to be one of the good guys from as far back as she could remember. But cars were long gone, and the only weapon human Authority—who were few—carried these days was an electristic. Most of the heavy lifting was left to Authority bots, the blunt objects.

What's more, she isn't one of the good guys. Not anymore.

Twenty minutes later, the transport approaches the gate that separates Highland Green from the rest of Maun. The gates open for Erlang's coded implants, and the transport passes pristine lawns and sparkling residences until it reaches the end of a long, winding pathway that culminates at the most ostentatious home in Highland Green, its façade a mixture of neoclassic and modern architecture, with a few Baroque touches here and there for good measure. It's gaudy, bordering on vulgar, as far as Erlang is concerned, but it certainly suits its owner. Exiting the transport, Erlang takes the marble steps up to the enormous double doors, no doubt salvaged from some far-away temple or Old European mosque. They, too, swing open at her arrival.

Erlang trudges down the high-ceilinged corridor toward the foyer, taking in the pristine architecture, the luxurious furniture, the décor. She wonders, not for the first time, what Hedges and the other residents of the Green have done to deserve such prestigious digs. Some people have everything, others have some things. NiCIes, of course, have nothing.

Jeannie, Hedges' execrable personal secretary, is perched behind her desk just outside Hedges' office, a fake smile plastered across her puffy face. As Erlang approaches, she clears her throat, a tic that never fails to annoy Erlang. "You're late."

Erlang glances down at her RistWach. "I'm right on time."

Jeannie clears her throat again, a liquid sound that causes Erlang to suppress a gag. "Two minutes late by my time."

Erlang doesn't bother to suppress an eyeroll. "Is he ready?"

"Naturally. Since you're late."

"Then let's get on with it." Jeannie frowns, an exaggerated expression made ghoulish by her unprecedented number of enhancements. Jeannie leads Erlang down a bright corridor lined with wallscreens. The projections this time are of Japanese and Chinese artifacts. When Erlang last visited, they'd been of Russian sculpture, notably long disappeared Faberge eggs. Jeannie turns right and disappears briefly around the corner until Erlang takes the corner, too.

She stands a few feet away and holds open an ornate wooden door, another confiscation from a dilapidated church.

"Erlang, Mr. Hedges. She's sorry she's late," she adds, looking Erlang dead in the eye. Erlang scowls as she passes into Walter Hedges' private office.

The room is less spacious than might be expected for the president of OnyxCorp, Director of the Ministry of Scientific Progress, and Chairperson of the Earth Federation Council Department of Continuing Progress and Cooperation. It's equipped with comfortable seating, a NutriPrint specifically programmed to provide Hedges only with specialized foodstuffs designed for his optimal performance, and an enhancement portal that gives Hedges immediate access to OnyxCorp's latest nanoserums and upgrades. In the room's corner stands a physical support system, and here Hedges reclines in a floating chair. Wires extend to the nanoportal behind his neck and to an additional portal in the middle of his chest. He beckons to Erlang without looking up from a flexscreen, held at eye level by a flexible rod connected to the system.

"I'm just finishing up here." Erlang draws nearer and sees Hedges' avatar completing a lap around a projected running track. Hedges is breathing hard and sweating. As the avatar comes to a stop on the screen, Hedges reaches for a towel draped on the back of the floating chair and wipes his face. "Sorry for having to fit you in." The stats from his virtual run appear on the screen. He studies them briefly, nods in satisfaction, and gives the command for the floating chair to descend and stand upright. "Let's have a seat over here. Water? Coffee?"

Erlang shakes her head as she moves to a group of reclining chairs surrounding a low, round table and takes a seat, sinking into the opulent cushion. Hedges mops his face with the towel again and sits opposite her. He holds a container of filtered water. "What do you have for me?"

Erlang reaches inside her uniform jacket and pulls out a rolled flexscreen, which she spreads between her hands. "Transport documents have been completed for Obumbwe and Sakata. They're scheduled to depart on the *Constellation* from Mombasa, bound for the Vine."

"Any resistance from Sakata?"

"Sure."

"And? You've been following him as usual, of course? What's he been doing?"

Erlang shrugs. "Nothing unusual. He visits the gardens, the museum, the next-door neighbor. I think they've been having some type of affair over the last few years."

Hedges takes a sip of water, then looks pointedly at Erlang. "You know what's at stake here, Commander?"

"I know the history, yes. He's what you would call a true believer."

"Of the worst kind. He was relocated to the moon in 2201 to send a message after Sanchez. A message he rather frivolously ignored."

Erlang has heard it all before. She's listened to more rants about Owen Sakata than she's ever imagined possible, and here is another. But the animosity Hedges has for Sakata seems over the top. Of all the people Hedges should be consumed by, the elderly Sakata deserves his ire the least, at least by Erlang's estimation. *Your wife, for example, hates your guts. Maybe you should pay attention to that.*

"Something on your mind, Commander?"

"Just wondering," Erlang says slowly. "Don't you think this might be taking it a bit too far?"

"Too far in what sense?"

"Given what he knows. It was decades ago, sir. If he hasn't said anything so far, what makes you think he'll say anything now? He's broken. Anyone can see that."

Hedges smiles. Most unpleasantly. "Which is why I've invited you here. This is an important mission, Erlang. And there is information you need to know." He slides a flexscreen across the low table between them. "But first, I need your signature."

Erlang retrieves the flexscreen and reads through the document, her frown growing deeper with each line. "This is a security clearance acknowledgement. And a rank promotion."

"Congratulations, Director. Much deserved." Hedges runs the

towel behind his neck as he takes a long drink. "Go ahead. Just need your signature."

Erlang glances down at the flexscreen between her hands.

In deeper. Bloody hell. Erlang feels her stomach clench, and her palms grow clammy. She could say no. Walk away. A promotion at this stage can mean only one thing. After this, she can't get out.

"What does this mean for—" Erlang began.

"For Zinda?" Hedges' smile makes Erlang's skin crawl. "Only good things for Zinda. How does a private cottage sound, on the Institute grounds? Private tutors?" Hedges frowns then, a mocking, sneering downturn at the corners of his perfectly sculpted mouth. "Comes only with the promotion."

Erlang fights down the bile at the back of her throat. It's never enough with these people. She should have known better than to think it would be over with the last concession.

"Come on." Hedges jabs Erlang's upper arm with a sharp elbow. "I have something to show you."

Erlang taps the flexscreen as if it were on fire. She tosses it on the table and looks away. "I was hoping for a little more enthusiasm," Hedges says.

"Just tell me what you want me to do this time."

Hedges sighs. "Very well. What I'm about to share is highly classified. Recordings, documentation, all involving your quarry." He touches behind his ear and a wide flexscreen emerges from the table. "After we've reviewed this information, I expect you'll have questions. I will answer them. Do you understand your assignment?"

"I'm looking at old recordings that reveal something secret about Sakata," Erlang replies mechanically.

"Rather artlessly put, but accurate. I get the feeling you're not fully on board here."

Erlang glares. "Can you get to the fucking point?"

Hedges leans against the thick cushion, crosses an ankle over a knee, and regards Erlang with a look that conveys a thin veil of extreme patience over immense irritation. "Sakata has long contended NiCIes and humans are equal. Everything he's written or said in public has pushed this agenda. His recent appearance at the

Symposium was surprising, but what he said was not. You see, Commander—ah, Director." That smarmy smile again. Erlang resists the urge to punch him in the face. "I'm certain Sakata helped a contingent of lunar NiCIes hide, or escape, before OnyxCorp was able to ferret them out for transport and elimination. I believe he played a role in the NiCIe insurrection. I believe he will attempt to contact his former compatriots upon his arrival on the moon. And that, I believe, will allow us to finally track them down and eliminate their threat."

Erlang scoffs. "Are you telling me you believe in the 'special' NiCIes bullshit? And you're sending that old man to the moon—to his death—just to prove it?"

The corners of Hedges' mouth turn down slightly. "I have evidence enough from other sources to know some NiCIes are...divergent. My concern is with finding that particular type of NiCIe. Of whom I know Sakata to be very fond."

"Let's say he does contact these special NiCIes. Then what?"

"We'll close the loop on the last real threat to OnyxCorp. To us." Hedges reaches for Erlang's hands. "You understand, yes? A threat to OnyxCorp is a threat to us. Both of us."

Erlang jerks her hands away. *Goddamn.* She rises, walks to the NutriPrint, and retrieves a fresh container of water. She gulps it down, wishing for something stronger, something to dull the voice in her head, her voice. *Walk away. This isn't going to turn out well for you.*

But Zinda. Damn damn damn. There's no way around it. All she can do now is play it through and hope it doesn't get worse.

But it will. It always does.

She slams the empty container on the tabletop. "Fine. Let's have a look."

"That's the spirit," Hedges says. "You're going to love this."

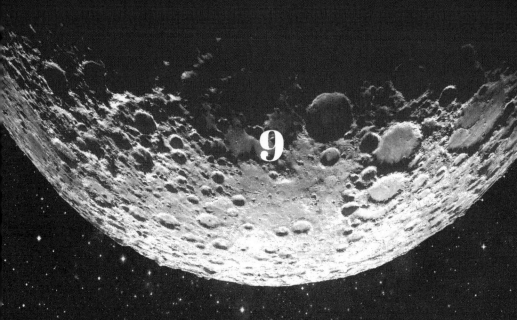

9

THE FOOTAGE IS SLIGHTLY PIXELATED and grainy. A date appears digitally in the wallscreen's top right corner: August 27, 2203. The scene appears to be a medtech lab. Six emaciated NiCIes sit atop metal stools; three early model Authority bots stand behind them. One of the NiCIes slumps; his arm hangs limply at his side. Thirty seconds into the recording, four humans in lab coats enter. Two stern-looking men, maybe in their mid-sixties. A tall, attractive woman, probably in her forties. The fourth a younger man, thirties, with light sandy brown hair and spectacles.

Owen Sakata..

"Where has this recording been?" Erlang demands.

Hedges blinks. "Pause." The playback stops. "As I said, it's classified. I acquired myself only a few years ago, around the end of 2258."

"Authority has documented every known video from the early moon experiments. You should have shared this immediately."

Hedges shrugs. "You have to admit you've been less than enthusiastic with your assignment lately. I wasn't sure if you were committed."

"Are you sure now?" *Hedges, always eager to prove he knows more than anyone else. The smug asshole.*

"Sure enough," Hedges says, meeting Erlang's piercing gaze. "Shall we continue?"

"Get on with it," she growls.

Hedges tsks. "Play."

The two older men busy themselves at a rolling cart topped with medtech. One of them glances toward the imager and coughs lightly. "We'll be taking blood samples first, then making internal scans of brain and physical tissues." The audio reverberates. "Reproductive and digestive analysis for both male and female subjects—"

While they are talking, Sakata approaches the NiCIes. Smiling, he speaks to one of the males. The NiCIe shakes his head no.

"They haven't had anything to drink since they've been here. Three? Four hours?" His voice is deep and smooth. The two men look annoyed, or maybe just bored. "Dr. Smythe, is there any water in the lab?"

The woman medtech nods. "I'll check in the kitchenette." She disappears and returns a few minutes later with water; she and Sakata help each of the bound NiCIes take several drinks. The recording captures only bits and pieces of what Sakata says, but the tone is unmistakably warm and friendly.

Several short scenes from the lab follow, covering the next few days. The NiCIes are poked and prodded, run through several med tests. The recording suddenly switches to what looks like a private office. Sakata sits behind a metal desk, and one of the female NiCIes sits across. The date is September 1, 2203. The audio is muffled.

"Age?" Sakata taps an odd-looking piece of tech with a thin implement.

"I have seen seventy-eight Earth years." A halo of short white curls surrounds the woman's light brown face.

"Would you say you're old for a NiCIe?"

The woman crosses an elegant leg over a knee and relaxes her hands in her lap. "My mother has seen one hundred and eleven Earth years."

"Illnesses? Accidents? Pregnancies?"

The NiCIe's face tightens. "No illnesses or accidents. I had a son and a daughter."

The scene changes again to a wide angle on a plain room with a low bed, metal desk and chair. The date reads *September 12, 2203* in the upper corner. Erlang can just make out the outline of a toilet behind a crude screen. The female NCI sits on the bed; she holds a rectangular piece of tech, a bright screen surrounded by a thin layer of synthetics. The door at the back of the room swings open about one minute into the playback. Sakata steps into the room and says something, but there is no sound in the playback. She stands, places the tech on the bed, and follows him outside. The recording ends.

Erlang watches as scene after scene, some of them several minutes long, others only a few seconds, plays out. They document NiCIes being kept awake for twenty-four, thirty-two, or forty-eight hours, with almost no noticeable results. Sometimes they are fed solid meals of protein and minerals. Other times they are given only a single protein cube and water. They are given tasks to perform together as the medtechs observe. They are given routine physicals. Everything is tested, from hearing to sight, from liver function to white blood cell production. Blood is drawn time and time again. They are given all sorts of medications, fed all kinds of foods. They are monitored during their sleep. They are asked to describe their dreams. They are interviewed, endlessly, about their childhood, their families. None of them question anything the medtechs do. Several times Sakata comes to the female NCI's room and escorts her, presumably to the mess or to another lab for testing.

"Who authorized these experiments?" Erlang knows the answer, but she needs to hear him say it.

"I was in charge of the facility."

"I don't see you anywhere."

"I'm not the subject of an investigation."

December 27, 2203. Sakata sits behind his desk, and the female NCI is next to him. Their shoulders touch in a way that suggests a level of intimacy that makes Erlang suddenly uncomfortable. She shouldn't be watching this. She wants to turn away, unwilling to intrude on Sakata and the NiCIe as they share a laugh. *Did he know he was being recorded?*

"Ok, then, what about crime?" Sakata says after the laughter subsides.

"What is crime?" The NCI's smile, indeed her entire face, is radiant. *How is she happy?*

"When people harm others. When they disobey an expectation or law." Sakata rests an elbow on the desktop and leans his head against his knuckles, a gesture that exacerbates the impression of familiarity between the two.

"If we disagree, we discuss until we no longer disagree. No one would ever harm another."

"Never? No one's ever struck another person out of passion? Anger?"

"What would be the reason?"

Sakata narrows his eyes. "You're here because you were interfering with a transport process. Using physical force."

The woman sighs. "We didn't harm anyone. We were only trying to ensure families stayed together. We tried to speak of this with your Authority. They wouldn't listen. We had to do something."

"Are you their leader? I mean, you seem so much more—I don't know—wise, than the others."

"I don't know what *leader* means. If you mean a person who takes responsibility for those who are unable, then that's my role. Dua aren't perfect, Owen." *Owen?* "Most of us live our lives quietly. When we're presented with something new, we adapt. Sometimes we're presented with something that's confusing. When that happens, we need someone who can direct us. That's what I do."

"All NiCIes aren't the same."

"I don't know what a NiCIe is." She runs a hand through her white curls, slides it down the back of her neck.

"I'm sorry. All Dua aren't the same."

"You already know this, doctor." The smile returns, but her eyes draw Erlang's attention. *She's in love with him.* It's plain as day, the way her azure eyes never leave his face, the way her lips curl when he speaks to her.

"What do you think makes the difference?"

"Humans are different, are they not? What makes the difference among humans?" "Genetic structure. Environment. Small differences in our DNA."

"And so it is with Dua. All species on our planet share both differences and similarities."

"Your very existence is the result of a grave mistake in medtech." Sakata's next words pour out, tumble over one another. "I think you're wonderful. You're kind. You don't allow emotions to cloud your judgment. You govern yourselves with equanimity and logic. You love, but not in a way that's selfish or possessive." *Is he blushing?* "You live long, and in a way that ensures the least of you receives what they need. You don't expect more than what others can do, yet you expect a great deal from yourselves." Sakata rubs his nose beneath his spectacles, presses his lips together as he readjusts them. "All those things are why the Corporation will destroy you."

The woman stands, a single, fluid movement. She envelops Sakata's hands in her own and pulls him to his feet. "The fate of one Dua, of many Dua, is unimportant. What we see, that you don't see as humans, is that we're all one. Humans, Dua, creatures both large and small. Our fate together is what matters. This is what we've been trying to tell you since the beginning."

Impulsively, Sakata presses a hand against her cheek. Their lips meet in a lingering kiss.

———

"BLOODY HELL!" Erlang rises, turns on Hedges. "Why are you showing me this?"

Hedges pauses the playback. "Really, Erlang. We're not even to the good part."

"What are you planning, Hedges? You know I don't personal. Not anymore." *Not since I found out what it's like to be on the receiving end.*

"But it's so very effective. You know that more than most anyone else I know, *Director*."

It was his superpower, finding out what made someone vulnerable and exploiting it to help himself. As soon as Hedges learned of

Erlang's dead sister and the NiCIe daughter she left behind in Erlang's care, he'd made it personal.

"You're an asshole."

Hedges rolls his eyes. "Let's not get overly dramatic. Sit. There's more to see." That smug, condescending smirk. Scowling, Erlang inches her way back down into the chair.

April 21, 2204. Sakata enters the woman's room. They leave the room together.

April 22, 2204. Almost twenty-four hours later. The room is still empty.

April 23, 2204. Another empty room.

"What the hell is this?" Erlang mutters.

April 24, 2204. The woman walks through the door; a bot closes the door after her. She shuffles to the cot and lies down.

Gone two full days. *Well, the OnyxCorp propaganda techs really put out all the stops on this one. What bullshit.*

THE NEXT FEW recordings feature lab scenes. The NCIs' conditions deteriorate over the next several months. Their hair thins. One is missing an arm, amputated at the shoulder. All of them are starving.

Except the woman. She glows.

October 25, 2204. A smaller laboratory. The woman sits on the examination table. Her white hair is thick and shiny, ringlets of curls framing her face. Sakata holds her hand as he takes a blood sample, which he places in a medscan. The woman medtech faces a wallscreen, her back to Sakata.

"Sakata," the woman calls behind her, her brows knitted together. Sakata strides over casually. *So young, handsome even.* The medtech points to something on the wallscreen—Erlang can't quite make it out —and Sakata stiffens.

"You're pregnant." The woman medtech steps forward as Sakata disappears from the frame on the left. "How?" A blurry hand appears briefly, and everything goes black.

Erlang stares at the black screen. She knows Hedges wants her to be the one to speak. Wants her to say what she is supposed to say. *What a surprise, Mister President. Sakata has a NiCIe child? A child who may be still on the moon? A child Sakata certainly won't be able to resist contacting once he's there?*

But Erlang isn't going to say it. It stinks of OnyxCorp Comm, which means it's no more than 25% true, and half of that is half-truths.

"I'm sure you have questions," Hedges finally breaks in. "That probably seemed confusing."

"I'd say it was pretty straightforward."

Hedges frowns. "Humor me, Erlang."

Erlang rises, stretches her arms above her head, and rotates her neck. "Sakata has a half-NiCIe kid on the moon. You expect he'll try to find this kid. When he does, you expect me to get them both and bring them back to you." Erlang straightens her uniform jacket and squares her shoulders. "That cover it?"

Hedges cocks his head. She meets his gaze with an even stare that she hopes conveys both boredom and a hint of menace. Shrugging, he breaks the stare and rises.

"You're probably going to run into some dignitaries on the way up there. You're getting to the Vine Station as the EFC Summit begins."

"Won't you be doing the glad-handing this time?"

"I'm arriving late. They won't talk about anything important until I get there. Which reminds me. What did you do about that comm from the SoAm High Commissioner?"

"NiCIe from some obscure district in SoAm, Uruguay maybe, popped up on the grid, used a fake registry. *Reason to believe NCI is with known terrorist cell and is heading for African Union. May be armed and dangerous. Proceed with caution. Subject may be returned dead or alive.*" Erlang waves a hand. "Forwarded to Mombasa. They're looking for him."

"SoAm asked Authority to handle it personally."

"Last time I checked, Authority doesn't answer to SoAm. No need to use the African Union budget for a SoAm issue. If we find him, we'll alert SoAm. They can come get him."

"Good." Hedges purses his lips and raises an eyebrow. "I really thought you'd get into this one. You think Director is the endpoint here? Madge, you're my most trusted confidant." He rests a perfectly manicured hand atop Erlang's shoulder. She forces herself not to shrug it off. "I wouldn't trust anyone else with this. And if you pull it off, Madge, I swear to you. There's no limit to where I'll take you." He takes a couple of steps backward, his eyes fixed on Erlang's. Then he turns and walks toward the other end of the room. "Jeannie will see you out," he calls behind him.

That's it. The last line he'll cross with me. But Erlang knows it isn't. There will be other, starker lines in the future, until Erlang crosses a line she'll never return from.

Hell, that's already happened.

THE TREK from Highland Green to Erlang's own neighborhood on the other side of Maun, Glass Key Estates, is a 30-minute commute by transport. It's late afternoon when the transport slows and stops in front of her building, a two-story grey structure with six flats. Scarlet Street has dozens of such buildings stretching several blocks, mostly filled with small families and artists. Erlang could have lived anywhere she wanted in Maun, but she finds Glass Key charming in a noir sort of way. There's a well-kept park in the neighborhood's center, a central meeting area and a common space for artists to display their painting, music, or poetry. Its best feature, in Erlang's opinion, is its Théâtre des Premiers Films, a replica 20th century movie theater that showcases fully restored masterpieces of American and European cinema. In an age when entertainment of any type is available through a voice command and a wallscreen, few people leave their flats to sit in a darkened, filthy theater, eat generated popcorn (extra stale and greasy), and watch poor quality two-dimensional films from two centuries past. Erlang never misses a new showing.

She holds her RistWach to the scanner next to her flat's green door and walks inside. The foyer's lights come to life as the door slides shut behind her. Erlang shrugs off her uniform jacket and stretches her arms high above her head. She tosses the jacket into the sanitizer and walks to the kitchenette, passing framed film noir posters she's collected over the years: *Double Indemnity, The Big Sleep, Bladerunner,*

Memento. She generates some coffee at the NutriPrint and sits at the kitchen table, a replica seafoam green set complete with plasticized chairs and aluminum legs. Curtains hang against a small window that overlooks a tiny green area. She watches the sun cast its warm glow across the lawn and street outside. At dusk, she leaves the empty cup on the table and enters the living area.

Wallscreens cover three walls of the living space, standard for Glass Key flats. Erlang removed most of the basic furnishings when she moved in and replaced them with replicas. Some she's had made; even better, some are actual antiques. The standard ergonomic chairs, for example, were replaced by a rounded yellow sofa with a low back and half a dozen pillows. Two green chairs sit on either side of the sofa, and a low formica table sits in the middle, covered with imagers. Several floor lamps give the room a soft, milky glow.

Erlang sinks into the sofa. Her sister smiles up at her from the closest imager. Her round face glows, as does the tiny newborn Zinda, whom she cradles against her cheek. Erlang traces the outline of Zinda's face in the image. To the right, another imager features her sister and her partner on a beach. A three-year-old Zinda perches on her father's shoulders and reaches out, toward the image taker. Toward Erlang. A visit to Dakar on a glorious day. Perfect weather. Perfect beach. Perfect everything. It had been the last time they'd been together, she and her sister. Four months later, she and her partner were dead, and Zinda was an orphan.

A NiCIe orphan.

No one could explain how they'd contracted the virus. Senegal hadn't experienced an outbreak in more than forty years, perhaps breeding a complacency that made its citizenry a little too careless. Zinda's father was the first to die, shut away from his lover and his child to boil away with fever. Her sister rallied for a time, and for a few days Erlang had hope. But she too died after several violent convulsions, leaving Zinda, who experienced strangely mild symptoms, alone. Alone and transformed. The last time Erlang visited her home country, it was to rescue her niece from what she knew would have been a lifetime of drudgery and servitude.

Except I betrayed everything you wanted for her. Erlang stares at each image, a dozen total. The images blur as her throat constricts. *I'm so sorry.*

Going to the moon will ensure Zinda's continued safety for now. But this isn't the end of it.

There will never be an end.

10

EVERYTHING IS GREY. The fine silt on the ground. The jagged rocks, the crevices, the edges of the crater where Ligeia balances precariously. Her mouth tastes of burning fossil fuel and metal. She is looking for something. Something beneath the surface. Something behind her.

It takes an eternity to pivot, to face what she knows is standing behind her. She can make out only the tall figure's bright blue eyes, and they seem at once remote and within reach.

I am on the moon.

Now she floats away, centimeter by centimeter, weightless into the inky black nothing. She tells her mouth to scream, but the sound is trapped somewhere in her stomach, her chest, her throat. Her feet float above her head, gently, deliberately, and the scream dies, replaced by a sense of perfect tranquility. Someone grips her by the hand, pulls her down, down, down—

Ligeia awakes with a start. Third time this evening. Each detail the same. She shouldn't be surprised. Tomorrow, she leaves behind everything she's ever known. Pale light streams across her paillasse and casts a warm yellow glow across her bedroom, and she wonders how the sunrise will appear on the moon. Is there a sunrise? Perhaps an Earthrise? Or will she experience weeks in shadow, followed by weeks of brilliant luminosity? She rolls to her side, squints at the tented flexscreen on her bedside table. Barely five a.m. Her eye catches the background image behind the digital numbers. Finn as a child, his warm hazel eyes overshadowing every other feature of his young, rounded face. So like Dad. She runs her finger around the edges of his face. Uncertainty shrouds every other aspect of this venture, but why she's going? That was never a question.

Rubbing her eyes, she sits up with a soft groan, swings her legs to the floor, and stands, stretching until the vertebrae pop. "Coffee." TES chirps as she pulls on a long sweater lying at the foot of the paillasse and, in bare feet, pads to the open staircase and climbs down into the kitchenette, where the NutriPrint is just finishing its cycle. She grabs the coffee and surveys her flat. It is crowded with sealed cartons, each measuring about one meter square and most bearing the word *Storage* in bright green digital letters. Even with living a Spartan existence, she's accumulated an impressive collection of personal possessions, most of which have little value other than their fleeting nostalgia. On three cartons, her transport code appears in blue digital letters. It is into the last of these three cartons she crams the remaining personal items bound for the moon. A few imagers, a set of charcoal pencils and a sketch pad, a weighted blanket. She eats the same thing every day, wears the same clothing, works the same hours. Her routine serves her well.

How will I maintain it on a place like the moon?

She sent the lab specs to OnyxCorp last week, right down to the height of the lab tables and the thickness of the chair cushions, fully expecting Hedges to balk. Her request included the most updated, expensive equipment available; she even threw in a small conferencing area, complete with low, cushioned chairs and a short table. To her surprise, Hedges confirmed everything would be ready when she arrived, right down to the cushion color. Yesterday she transferred her data to two backup servers in case the main server didn't make it through the move. She found a tenant to sublet her flat, and she contracted a storage facility. All that is left is packing up the remaining objects and waiting for tomorrow morning.

Coffee in hand, she sorts through some holographs on a side table and stops to look at an image of her and three classmates from *Faculté de Médecine Pierre et Marie Curie*. Four young women grin against a backdrop of snow-covered mountains. It had been a trip to the French Alps over a holiday break to see the rare occurrence of snow. Into the carton marked for the moon. She glances at the empty table and notices its small drawer. She doesn't remember putting anything there, but she opens the drawer just in case. Sure enough, there is an imager, its face dark. She pulls it from the drawer and taps the screen.

Damn.

Her father and mother, on a beach somewhere, maybe the coast of Mozambique. It's their partnering day. His handsome face beams as he squeezes her mother to his side. Her lips are parted in an enormous smile as her gauzy dress floats behind her in an ocean breeze. Her mousy brown hair forms a halo around her head, and her pale skin stands out in stark contrast to her husband's. They are very young, children almost. Hopeful. Happy.

Her father.

She hasn't spoken to him or her stepmother in several weeks, their fraught relationship having settled into a type of cold war. A sense of duty, however, keeps that dull ache present. After gathering a few more personal items and placing them carefully into the carton, she resigns herself to making the trek to their townhouse in Highland Green.

The transport winds its way through the capitol streets, passing everything familiar to her: Every green area, residential building, entertainment module, meal facility, public meeting space. All owned by OnyxCorp. There have been times in her life when she's been stuck. When her mother died. When Finn disappeared. When Dad brought home a sleek politician and introduced her as "Your new mother." When she realized what really happened to Finn. She's always managed to get unstuck through research and study, but now? She switches from exterior to interior mode, and the transport's window fades into an ocean scene, the tide ebbing and flowing against a white sand beach, the sounds of the ocean breeze and waves providing a steady, relaxing pulse. She tries to reach the same state in her mind, but it churns and roils.

What am I doing with my life?

Work is all she's known. Keep her head down, don't make waves, don't get involved. And what does she have to show for it? No vaccine. No closer to understanding Finn. No closer to understanding what happened, why they become what they become, what it means. Is she foolish in thinking that going to the moon will change anything?

The mini slows as it approaches the electrifield separating Highland Green from the common, unwashed masses of Maun. People like her. A guard in a nondescript uniform, complete with a knock-off Authority helmet, steps from a small outbuilding into the road and approaches the mini as it slows to a smooth halt.

"Identification." Ligeia holds out her wrist, palm upward. The guard's face is obscured by a dark visor. He scans the ID chip embedded in the center of her hand. "Obumbwe."

"Yes."

"You're a relative of Ambassador Obumbwe?"

"I'm *Professor* Obumbwe's daughter."

The guard frowns, taps the flexscreen a few times.

"I've alerted the Ambassador."

He retreats to the outbuilding; a few seconds later the field sparks, and the mini moves through, gliding smoothly over the electromagnetic bars beneath clean, fresh tiles. She switches to view mode to observe the gleaming white, silver, blue, and grey townhomes as she passes. White balconies stretch out over crisp, green lawns dotted with cascading fountains of crystalline water, an unbelievable extravagance. She glides past an NCI dressed in white coveralls tending a small copse bordered by graceful beds of tulips, irises, and peonies in brilliant hues. The mini makes a smooth turn and stops before a bright white building with a paved walkway of light blue tile. This isn't the house in which she'd spent her childhood. It is her stepmother's home, its extravagance reflecting her status and personality. The walkway diverges into two sections after about ten meters, one walk veering toward the green lawn and culminating in a carefully tended pool in which dozens of brightly colored, genetically altered fish species undulate. The other walk continues straight to three low steps that lead to the front porch, where her father stands.

His handsome face is clean shaven and creased with age. The top of his head shines through a circlet of greying hair. She clambers from the vehicle and returns her father's gaze, suddenly apprehensive. Self-conscious, even.

"Hi, Dad."

"Are you OK?" A little sharper than she would have liked. She steels herself.

"Yes. Of course."

"I feared there was something very amiss." He moves away from the landing and strides down the length of the porch toward a cluster of elegant white rattan chairs. She spies an implant at the back of his neck, an anti-aging nanoport. *Membership in the Earth Federation Council has its perks.* She follows him and takes a chair adjacent.

"You're looking well, Dad." The words sound forced, insincere.

"We are well, thanks. You look tired. Are you getting enough sleep?"

She smooths her hair, aware only now that she left her flat without so much as a glance. "It's been a rough few days."

"Is that why you're here? What do you need?"

She shakes her head. "No, Dad, nothing like that. I came here to tell you I'm going to be gone for a while. I'm going to the moon."

His forehead crinkles as he narrows his eyes. "Go on."

"OnyxCorp is giving me my own lab, fully equipped. Access to the lunar population. Support—"

"In exchange for what?"

She swallows. "You know for what, Dad."

He presses his lips together. "They wouldn't." He springs from his chair and sends it smacking against the spotless porch. "We've done everything they asked!"

Ligeia narrows her eyes. "Dad, what are you talking about?"

His face is a mixture of disappointment and pity. "You can't begin to understand the situation we're all in, Ligeia. You've sat there in judgment of me, of her, without knowing anything of what we've had to do for Finn—"

to the Institute through her EFC position. In exchange, you weren't red-listed."

Ligeia pressed her father's hand between hers. "Dad, why didn't you tell me?"

"At first, you were too young to understand. You did so well, better than expected in Paris. Then when you found out about Finn—You were so angry, Ligeia. You blamed Olga, accused me of abandoning my son. Somehow, you seemed safer estranged from us." He closes his eyes and rubs the back of his neck with his free hand; his hand lingers on the nanoport. "A few months ago, we submitted our routine biosamples and received some bad news. The medtechs couldn't tell us whether it's radiation or environmental pollution, but it doesn't matter. We're dying. The nanoports keep our blood filtered for now, but eventually they won't keep up."

Hedges' words spring to Ligeia's mind. *Your father won't live forever.*

He knew her father was dying before she did. Anger washes over Ligeia. She drops her father's hand, rises, paces the length of the porch. "I knew Hedges was lying. I just didn't realize he was lying about my 'value.' A genius, he said. My work in NiCIe genetics has been groundbreaking; he wants to support my research, recognize my contributions. All bullshit."

"We never meant for them to come after you." She meets her father's eyes. They are wet, pleading. She kneels before him and grasps his hands again.

"I know that Dad. I know now. And I'm going to make this right. I'm going to tell Hedges to his face that he can take his moon lab and—"

"No." Her father crushes her fingers in a tight squeeze. "No. This is your chance. You can do something on the moon, Ligeia. Not just for Finn."

"What? What can I do, Dad?"

He brushes a stray curl behind her ear. "You'll know. When the time comes, you'll know what to do. You always have."

Ligeia leans her cheek against his hand. "Will you visit him? Please?"

Her father swallows. "I'm—Too ashamed. I couldn't protect him. I couldn't protect your mother. It's because of me, what happened."

The years that had separated them, the anger she'd nurtured. How could she have been so selfish? She throws her arms around him again and buries her face against his shoulder.

"Don't trust them," he whispers into her hair. "Don't let them know you don't trust them. Listen, and be ready for anything." He breaks their embrace, kisses her cheek. "I love you. We love you. Never forget that." He rises, staggers past her across the wide porch, and disappears inside.

Ligeia stumbles to the waiting mini in a daze. She watches the house until the transport turns a smooth corner. Immaculate lawns. Perfect buildings. Servants. *We live in ignorance of what our lifestyle costs others. Or we don't care.* Until today. Will she see her father again? Will she see anyone she loves again? Why is it only today that she realizes it matters?

The comm buzzes. Wiping her cheeks and clearing her throat, she croaks, "Answer," without checking the identification on her RistWach. "Ligeia Obumbwe."

"Erlang."

Crap.

"Commander, I meant to call you this afternoon. Time got away from me—"

"You owe me some documents, doctor. I'm sitting outside your flat. Where are you?"

Bloody OnyxCorp. Then again, she's been putting Erlang off for days, procrastinating on the paperwork, as usual.

"I'll be there in fifteen." She breaks the comm before Erlang can reply.

As Ligeia's transport glides to a stop at her flat, she notices Erlang leaned against her Authority transport, a nicostic dangling from her mouth and her eyes shielded by dark sunshades.

"I'm not OK with this, Erlang," she says as the transport door lifts.

"Not how I planned to spend my day either, doc."

Frowning, Ligeia strides past her, touches her palm to the scanner outside her flat, and steps inside the opened door. "Have a seat," she calls behind her, sweeping her hand in the direction of the two low chairs remaining in the emptied flat. "You're here for the non-disclosure."

Erlang tucks the sunshades into her pocket, reaches into her jacket, and pulls out a rolled flexscreen. Stretching the flexscreen between her hands, she hands it across to Ligeia. "You'll need to register in the highlighted areas."

Ligeia takes the flexscreen and stares at it, pretending to read. The truth is, she knows the NDA by heart, and she's wracked her brain to figure out a way around it.

"It's fine print, mostly," Erlang offers, eying her curiously.

"I like to know what I'm signing."

The document is full of legalese and jargon, deliberately written to obfuscate and confuse. The sticking point, however, is this:

Ligeia Obumbwe hereby sells, assigns, and transfers unto the Corporation, all her right, title and interest, in and to the Assigned Intellectual Property created or owned in any form or manner whatsoever by her prior to the date of the agreed funding of research for OnyxCorp, hereafter referred to as the Corporation. To the extent that any such Assigned Intellectual Property is not assignable or transferable to the Corporation ("Non-assignable IP"), Ligeia Obumbwe hereby grants to the Corporation a royalty-free, irrevocable, perpetual, world-wide license to make, have made, modify, manufacture, reproduce, sub-license, use and sell such Non-assignable IP, and any residual rights Ligeia Obumbwe holds in the Non-assignable IP will be held by her in trust for the sole benefit of the Corporation. Ligeia Obumbwe will hold and maintain any confidential information for the sole benefit of the Corporation. Ligeia Obumbwe will not use any Assigned Intellectual Property or Confidential Information for her benefit or to the detriment of the Corporation.

Give them everything. Keep nothing for herself. And say nothing. She shouldn't be surprised, of course. A Corporation that would use someone's loved one as leverage, that would use other beings as it always had, human and NiCIe alike, is capable of anything.

You can do something on the moon, Ligeia. Not just for Finn.

Erlang sighs. "Standard OnyxCorp procedure. We all had to sign one."

"They're asking me to turn over everything I've worked on, Erlang, not just what I do in their lunar lab."

Erlang stretches her long arms behind her, cradles the back of her head between her large, long-fingered hands. "You're working for OnyxCorp now. Everything belongs to them, eventually."

Ligeia looks back down at the flexscreen; the areas that require her registry pulse orange. If she doesn't sign, the Corporation will end up acquiring everything anyway. And it will kick Finn out of the Institute.

Don't let them know you don't trust them.

She places her thumb over half a dozen or so highlighted boxes, and at the last box the screen flashes and a message appears: "Thank you for completing Lunar Transport Documentation Package LO22601116. You may log out now." She hands the flexscreen to Erlang, who taps it a few times, rolls it into a thin scroll, and stuffs it in her jacket.

"Is there anything else, Commander?" A little too sharply. *She's just doing her job.*

Erlang shifts to the chair's edge. "Are you sure you want to do this?"

"I just signed my life away, Erlang. Now is probably not the time to ask that question."

"Fair enough. But I've been to the moon. It's not what you think it is."

"Are you saying OnyxCorp is misrepresenting what it's promised me? No shit."

Erlang shakes her head. "They'll deliver everything you've asked for. The moon itself, though. It's not what you're expecting."

"How do you know what I'm expecting?"

"You medtechs always think there's more to it than there is. It's a chunk of grey rock floating in space. The NiCIes there aren't any different than they are here. Maybe a little less happy if that can be believed."

"Yet you're going back?"

She grimaces. "Maybe I'm not happy anywhere, so what does it matter?"

"Not even in New America?"

Erlang narrows her eyes. "What about New America?"

"I was visiting my brother at the Institute a few days ago. We saw you with your little girl."

"NiCIe brother. Figures." Erlang stretches her neck, eliciting a sharp pop. "Not my little girl. My niece, my sister's girl. She and her partner...died. A Ruĝa Morto outbreak in Senegal. I'm the only family she has left. I guess now she has no family." A corner of her mouth turns up. "Good thing the Institute takes good care of them, eh?"

"Did Hedges threaten her, too?"

"My reasons for going to the moon are my own."

"But Hedges is behind it. Why? He's a liar, a fraud."

Erlang's words come slowly. "Do you know what Hedges did before he became President?"

"Married Io Proxy. The former president, Gantry or something like that, retired. Some bullshit about wanting to spend time with his family in Argentina. The next day, Hedges and Io were married. Hedges has been president since, and Gala Proxy, Io's mother, has been the Prime Minister of the Earth Federation Council."

"He was the Executive Director of Lunar Operations for OnyxCorp before that, in 2229."

Ligeia searches deep in her memory before she recognizes the date's significance. "During the NiCIe Rebellion? Did he...was he the one who—"

"Ordered Authority to shoot them down? Of course he was. And all for the greater good, he'd tell you. Hedges likes order and discipline. Obedience. Hedges has never been honest with anyone. I accepted that many years ago. You should too, doctor, now that he has you in his sights."

"But he's not invincible, Commander Erlang. He can't be above the law, out of reach, no accountability—"

"Right now, he is the law. And it's Director Erlang, by the way. There are some perks for selling your soul." She pushes herself from the low chair. "Thanks for getting those completed, Dr. Obumbwe. I'll see you at the station tomorrow, 0900. Sharp."

Ligeia walks Erlang to the door and waits as the new Director clambers down the steps. Erlang pauses to look up at her as she adjusts the sunshades over her eyes.

"Just out of curiosity, what do you think of your brother's condition? As a scientist."

Ligeia leans against the doorframe. "I think that we realized long ago no species does well in a prison."

Erlang grunts. "Yet here we are, all of us."

"The NiCIe woman the other night," Ligeia calls out. "What happened to her?"

Erlang climbs into the transport, leans out to give Ligeia one last grim look. "If you have to ask that, doctor, you'd better get wise. Quick."

11

LIGEIA IS LIGHT, buoyant. Silty grey dust covers a ground riddled with grey rocks, a sterile landscape. She floats peacefully, head down, feet up, tethered by a warm, strong hand encircling hers. Her head is heavy, leaden as she struggles to move it, to see who holds her in place. Warmth spreads from her hand, up her arm, across her shoulders. Everything is light and warmth and blue. Blue eyes. The hand squeezes hers, and suddenly she is floating back down, down to the grey dust, down to the moon's surface.

Follow him, Ligeia.

The voice echoes as she awakes. Rain patters against her bedroom window, and the grey sky outside reflects her dream. She tosses the coverlet aside, shaking her head against the fog of sleep. A dream. Just a dream.

Today, she begins her journey to the moon.

She sits, cross-legged, on the mattress, allows the excitement and the terror to wash over her. *I'm going to the moon* she hears herself say in her child's voice, to her parents, friends, anyone who would listen. She learned about the Earth's barren partner as a child: Its origins from a gaping wound in the Earth, the first time humans set foot on its surface, the moon settlements. She's long felt its allure, perhaps because its isolation mirrored her own. In Paris she'd often gazed upon the peaceful orb, casting its eerie light upon the ruined city, and wondered how her perspective would change behind that light instead of within it.

She'll be finding out soon.

But at a price.

The costs are hidden beneath a shiny veneer of OnyxCorp slogans, products, and daily newscasts, all with the uneven look of a coating applied a little too generously here, a little too lightly there.

She shakes her head. It's all for Finn. Nothing else matters right now. She tumbles out of her bed for the last time, pulls on a light grey pantsuit with the ISA logo on the lapel, and secures her curls in a bundle at the nape of her neck.

All business. Dad would be proud.

She glances at her RistWach. The maglev she's scheduled for Mombasa, where she'll board a ship bound for the Vine, won't depart for several hours, but she can't stand the thought of sitting here in her empty flat, its bare walls an intimation, she imagines, of the moonscape. She retrieves her single carryon, slings it across her body, and opens the door, pausing only a few seconds to look back. She should feel something. Anger? Sadness? Regret? Sighing, she steps out into the gentle rain, closing the door behind her.

Maun has always been more tolerable in the rain, its gaudy veneer made softer, quieter somehow as the showers cleanse the crowded city, soak the grounds, the manufactured lawns, the colorful plants. She follows a tiled path from her building toward Flower Park and turns her face skyward. Gentle drops splash on her eyelids and lips. She reaches out her tongue to taste them. Cool. Almost sweet.

When she reaches Flower Park a quarter hour later, the rain has subsided into a gentle mist that clings to her hair and skin in the same way it clings to the petals that line the walkway and droop gracefully above in arches of brilliant color. Indigo, vermilion, emerald, gold, orange. Flower Park has always been her favorite common, one of few natural spots in Maun.

No Flower Park on the moon.

The thought comes as the gentle rain becomes a deluge. Hugging her bag against her chest, she runs the few meters to the Museum of Human Art, nestled in the center of Flower Park. The building is among the most enchanting in Maun, with cathedral-like ceilings that mimic the grand religious edifices of the previous millennium. She stumbles into the foyer, droplets streaming down her arms and fingers to splash on the synthetic marble floor below. She saunters through the entry and toward one of many hallways, the holographic projection at its entry reading, "20th Century."

Unlike the Maun Center, which houses original works, the Museum features digitized wallscreen projections, which allows for some interesting experiences if one has eye implants. Ligeia purchased a nanoprogram a few years ago, on a whim, that enhances light, color, or movement in artworks by collaborating with the brain's synapses. It's one of the few nanoprograms in which she's indulged; others, she believes, are too invasive. Disruptive. She wanders through the gallery, admiring the Impressionists, the Abstract Expressionists, when at last she comes to her favorite. She settles on a bench to interact with it one last time.

Black, white, and grey, the painting reflects her mood today more than ever. A horse tosses its head in terror, mouth gaping in a silent scream, nose abutting beams of pulsing light from a lightbulb above that stretch toward an arm, its hand bearing a lamp. As the radiance touches the lamp, it glimmers.

Follow him, Ligeia.

"Dr. Obumbwe?" Ligeia runs a hand over her face before she turns toward the voice.

"Dr. Sakata. How nice to see you." Water rivulets run down his arms and form tiny pools at his feet. She pushes a stray lock of hair behind her ear.

"Likewise, although I'd assumed it would be at the station."

"The station?"

"Bound for the moon, both of us. I guess Erlang didn't tell you."

No. Erlang did not tell her. "Whatever for? I mean, the gravity sickness."

Sakata shrugs. "After our exchange at the Symposium, I guess they realized I don't have much left to lose." He eases himself down beside her with a low groan. "Don't worry about me. I've been dying for a long time now. The real question is why are they sending *you* to the moon?"

She swallows against the lump that's suddenly formed in her throat. "I have a lot to lose."

Sakata shuffles closer, and Ligeia glances over. He has an elegant, long nose, high cheekbones, and dark brown, almond-shaped eyes. She can see how handsome he must have been. He is old now, though. Old and tired. Will she look this worn in ten or twenty years?

"What's the official story?" he whispers.

"Improving relations between NiCIes and humans. Just vague enough to sound good and say nothing. I don't know why they're sending me to the moon, Dr. Sakata, but it isn't to fucking *improve relations*. They threatened my brother. What the hell do they want with me?"

Sakata shakes his head. "We won't know what Hedges really wants until we get there. I think he will very much regret sending us both, though. He thinks he's being very clever, exiling his most vocal critic. Isolating the one medtech who understands what Dua are, the one brave enough to say it aloud. I imagine him toasting himself this very minute, thinking his empire very well protected."

"I'm not interested in toppling OnyxCorp, Dr. Sakata."

"You're not interested now." Grunting, he pushes himself up, adjusts his coat. Touching the side of his glasses, he nods to the projection. "You like Picasso?"

"*Guernica*." She gazes at the painting. The woman at the left of the canvas appears to rock the body of her dead infant in her arms. "It seems morbid, but I'm drawn to it."

"He wasn't always so. *The Blue Room* I believe you would find interesting, from one of his earlier periods. A glimpse into how perceptions change over time." He bows. "See you on the transport, Dr. Obumbwe. Don't be late."

After he disappears down the long hallway and around the corner, Ligeia returns to *Guernica*. At the bottom of the canvas, a man lays dying. His eyes roll back into his head, and his mouth is twisted in terror. She looks away, her stomach gripping.

"Search." TES chirps softly in recognition. *"The Blue Room."*

Guernica is replaced with another projection, a photograph circa late 20th century of a large room with blue, white, and yellow furniture, the walls painted a dark blue.

"Next."

A painting of a young girl lying on a deep blue cushion. Nice, but not Picasso. One more time.

"Next."

She sucks in her breath. It is the painting the NiCIe woman took from the wall at the gala. The painting Hedges destroyed.

Ligeia blinks, activating the eye implant receptors. The woman stoops, dipping whatever is in her hand into...water? Yes, a pool of water. Water trickles down her thigh; her yellow hair flutters against her forehead.

"Information."

"The Blue Room, painted in 1901 by Pablo Picasso during his Blue Period," TES responds. The same artist as *Guernica,* but they couldn't be more different. What happened? From blue tranquility to stark horror and chaos?

A vision of the NiCIe woman comes to her, standing in the Center's salon, naked, surrounded by other silent protestors. What had she said?

Our forms are alike, even though they may be as separate now as I am from the figure on this canvas.

Liberate your destiny from the Corporation as I've pulled this symbol of the greatness of your species—

She gathers her carryon, slings it over her shoulder, and gives *The Blue Room* one last glance.

"Liberation isn't that simple," she mumbles as she turns from the painting. "Even Picasso knew that."

THE MAGLEV STATION in uptown Maun is, like all transport stations, one of the few places where everyone, human and NiCIe alike, is equal. Equal in access, for the time being, but in nothing else. Ligeia finds the platform where she'll board the transport bound for the Kenyan coast; each step takes her farther from Finn and her father, closer to the unknown.

I could still back out. Even now, I could say no.

Humans rush to catch transports for which they are late, and NiCIes stride calmly, deliberately to their destinations. Humans carry with them children who gawk and dawdle; their parents cajole and pull them along by their thin arms. NiCIes, whose reproduction is heavily regulated, travel alone; their sad eyes follow the children. The walls, the columns, the ceilings, the kiosks, the maglev compartments glow and pulse with advertisements.

Making your journey to perfection complete. From the Earth to the Moon, OnyxCorp is there for you.

OnyxCorp MedTech – Supporting your health through enhancement.

OnyxCorp – Nutrition you can trust.

The *O* logo is emblazoned on kiosks and benches, protein packages and containers, clothing and travel bags.

Fucking OnyxCorp.

"You're late." Erlang's sharp voice cuts through the station's clamor. Her hair is in loose locks that graze the shoulders of the vintage jacket she wears over her Authority uniform. The outfit gives her an air of nonchalance that surprises Ligeia.

"Sorry. Where's Sakata?"

Erlang grunts, removes her sunshades. She narrows her dark eyes. "I guess you've spoken."

Ligeia glances down at her RistWach. "He's on his way." Erlang cocks her head, raises an eyebrow. "We bumped into each other at the museum."

"Quite a coincidence."

It's Ligeia's turn to raise an eyebrow. "What do you mean by that?"

Erlang shrugs. "Nothing. Just interesting."

Ligeia wonders how much Erlang knows about why they're really going up there. But as she resolves to ask just that, her attention is drawn to movement. A NiCIe woman, her arms clasped around a bundle, sprints past them, pursued by a lanky, middle-aged human man.

"Alnnaqil!" The man lets out a piercing whistle as he comes to a sliding halt before the NiCIe woman, who has turned to face him. Blue eyes peer out between the woman's torso and the crook of her elbow.

A NiCIe child! He ducks behind his mother when the man whistles again. "Alnnaqil! He's not allowed here!"

Ligeia glances at Erlang. "What's he saying?"

"Carrier," Erlang replies. "Must be a eugenicist. They believe NiCIe children can infect humans."

The man backs the woman against a concrete wall that separates their transport section from the one adjacent.

"You don't see many children," Ligeia says.

"They aren't allowed to have many." Ligeia turns at Sakata's voice. He struggles with an enormous bag draped over his shoulder. He allows the bag to fall to the ground at his feet when he joins her and Erlang.

"Traveling light I see, Owen," Erlang says.

Sakata shrugs. "Am I wrong in assuming I won't be coming back?"

A small group of humans gathers behind the whistling man, their cries of "Alnnaqil!" unsure at first, then louder as the man takes another step toward the cowering woman. "Alnnaqil!" The mother and child press against the wall; the boy crouches behind his mother, his blue eyes wide with fear. His white hair falls in soft curls.

Finn.

The resemblance is uncanny.

"Are you going to do something about this?" Ligeia faces Erlang, who seems perplexed by the question.

"Not our focus today."

"This is going to get ugly, Erlang."

"Probably. Hey, where are you going?"

Sakata has already crossed half the distance to the crowd.

"Enough!" Sakata slides between the NiCIe and the man and strikes an imposing stance as he faces the much younger human.

"I think you're outnumbered, old man." The man sneers in defiance, but the other humans back away, cowed by Sakata's appearance. "That thing is *alnnaqil*," he hisses, jutting a finger toward the huddling boy.

A long electronic tone startles Ligeia into awareness. Seconds later,

Vagabonder

the maglev shoots through and brakes to a smooth stop. The doors swoosh open. Passengers spill out and flow around them.

"Time to go, doctors!" Erlang shouts above the din, but if Sakata hears her, he doesn't react. Instead, he approaches the woman and her cowering child.

"We have time," Ligeia says to Erlang. "Give him some time."

"To do what?" Erlang throws up her hands as Ligeia worms her way through the crowd to Sakata's side. Surprised by Ligeia's sudden appearance, the woman encircles the boy behind her, almost crushing him against the tiled wall.

"Come. It's safe now." Sakata extends a hand. The woman steps from the wall; her right hand grips the child's hand tightly. His blue eyes are wet.

Ligeia squats before the child so she can meet his eyes. "It's OK now," she says gently.

The woman places her hands on the boy's shoulders and guides him around Ligeia. "We'll be fine." She directs the child through the thinning crowd and toward the maglev.

"Just what do you two think you're doing?" Erlang falls in step behind them as they follow the NiCIes to the transport.

"The right thing," Sakata retorts. "They were terrified."

Erlang grabs their upper arms, almost pulling Sakata from his feet. "Let's be clear, doctors. This isn't a pleasure cruise—"

"You got that right." Ligeia jerks her arm from Erlang's grasp.

"—And it isn't a humanitarian mission. You're here under my supervision."

"Supervise this." Ligeia steps across the maglev's threshold and enters the section into which the woman and her child have disappeared. She hears Sakata chuckling behind her. No matter. She may have an Authority escort, but she'll be damned if she's going to be handled like a child.

The NiCIes take a seat on a bench near the front of the compartment. The woman shields the boy with her body as he huddles next to the window.

"I'm sorry for that," Ligeia stammers as she draws in line with them. The woman looks up, her blue eyes narrowed.

113

"Thank you. We'll be fine."

Behind her, Erlang, her hand firmly gripping Sakata's shoulder, pushes past. Ligeia tries to catch the boy's eye to give him a smile, to tell him it is going to be OK. But the woman shifts to block her view.

"We'll be fine." Ligeia meets her bright blue eyes and sees coldness. Hardness.

This doesn't make you a good person, they say.

Ligeia backs away to join Erlang and Sakata, who have already taken their seats further down the aisle.

"What are you playing at?" Erlang asks, frowning. Ligeia brushes past her without a word and takes a seat on the other side of Sakata. "Oh, this is going to be fun," Erlang mumbles.

It's not off to the best start, that's for sure.

Ligeia steals a look at Sakata, who wears a serene expression, his lips curved in a soft smile.

"You're going to get us into trouble," Ligeia murmurs.

"We're already in trouble." He turns to face her and gives her a wink. "May as well make it worthwhile, yes?"

"Hmph." Ligeia peeks over the back of the bench in front of her. Only the top of the NiCIe woman's head is visible, but the hostile glances from boarding passengers are in full view. Most decide not to share the car. An elderly human male sits a few seats down from Ligeia and her companions, promptly unrolls a flexscreen, and buries his face in text. The transport alarm sounds, signaling departure, when a NiCIe male bounds on, almost breathless. He glances at the humans and wavers; noticing the woman and child, he settles into a seat opposite them.

A curious square they make: Erlang, Sakata, and Ligeia; the NiCIe male; the human man; and the NiCIe female and boy, all connected by an invisible thread across the transport car. Seven individuals in this compartment, and none of them will speak. They may never even acknowledge the others exist.

"Hedges was right about one thing," Ligeia murmurs. "Our relations definitely need improving."

· · ·

114

THE MAGLEV'S steady hum lulls Ligeia into a fitful sleep, and she awakes hours later with a stiff neck. Acre after acre of lush farmland zooms by. Ligeia guesses they must be somewhere in what used to be Tanzania, now part of the Kenyan Republic. She stretches her arms above her head and wills her muscles into wakefulness. Sakata is sound asleep across the aisle, curled up on the bench like a child. The NiCIe mother and son are also sleeping, and the NiCIe man in the opposite corner stares out the window. The older human man is gone, as is Erlang.

They pass lush rows of green, red, and yellow, interspersed with dilapidated buildings and shacks that should have been abandoned but are most likely NiCIe housing. The transport speeds through small villages and towns and stops intermittently at larger cities. The NiCIe man disembarks at Mbeya, an industrial mining town. At Tarangire the mother and son depart, and a group of five NiCIes, three male and two female, board. They eye Ligeia and the other humans suspiciously. They sit nevertheless and engage in low conversation, occasionally glancing her way. Sakata awakens shortly after; he stretches languidly before he notices the group of five NiCIes. He stands and shuffles across the aisle.

"Where did they come from?" he whispers as he squeezes in beside Ligeia.

"Got on when we stopped at Tarangire. The woman and child got off there."

"Fewer Authority there than in Maun," Sakata explains. "Although that may be changing." He nods toward the front of the compartment, where the door that separates their car from the next swooshes open. An Authority bot enters the car, followed closely by another. Their heads rotate as they scan the compartment; orange eyes flicker behind their dark visors. The first bot steps toward the five Dua, who have grown silent. The bot raises an arm, and the fingers of its mechanical hand open. The mechanized voice is impossible to understand, but whatever the bot says, the Dua look at each other first. Then each of them shakes their heads. The second bot steps from behind the first and puts a hand on the electristic at its side.

Sakata is rigid next to her, and Ligeia realizes she's holding her breath. One Dua reaches inside his jacket pocket, retrieves a registry chip. The other Dua follow, reluctantly. The first bot takes each registry, scans it, and hands it back mechanically. Then both bots continue through the compartment, thud past the humans, and disappear into the next car.

As soon as the compartment door slides closed, Sakata stands. "Are you coming?"

Ligeia blinks. "Where?"

"To talk to them," Sakata says, somewhat impatiently. "Find out what happened."

Ligeia shoots a look toward the NiCIes. "I don't want to bother them."

"You're never going to take down OnyxCorp that way." Without waiting for a reply, he strides down the aisle toward the group, leaving her behind. She scowls. She's never been one to act impulsively. Deliberate. Thorough. Cautious. Those are words she wants associated with her, with her work.

I'm not interested in taking down OnyxCorp.

She looks out the window at the passing landscape, but she can't help but glance back at the group every few seconds. Sakata sits with them now. The compartment door behind them swooshes open, and Erlang steps through balancing a small tray. She gives the group a sideways glance as she shuffles past them and slides into the bench facing Ligeia.

"Old NutriPrints, but I got you something anyway. Just in case you were hungry enough to eat even bad food." She nods to a tower of puffed dough atop the tray as she hands Ligeia a container. "You couldn't keep an eye on him while I was gone?"

"Not my job," Ligeia replies, putting the container to her lips. The bitter scent of coffee fills her nose.

Ugh.

She swallows the stale liquid and wonders how people made it through the day with the old Prints.

Erlang bites into a browned square of sugary dough and chews it thoughtfully. "You could help a little," she grumbles as she chokes down the dough.

Behind Erlang, Sakata gestures toward Ligeia, and in another second all NiCIe eyes look her way.

"What is it?" Erlang asks, observing Ligeia's frown. She cranes her head to look back at the group. "Why are they staring?"

"I'll be right back."

Suddenly Erlang's hand encircles Ligeia's forearm; her fingers make small impressions in Ligeia's skin. "Don't, Dr. Obumbwe." Sugary pastry remnants glisten on her full lips, and for a moment Ligeia sees something cold flash in her eyes. A hardness she hasn't seen before. "It'll only bring trouble."

Ligeia wrenches her arm from Erlang's grip. "Let's make sure we have this clear, Erlang. I don't need a handler. Back off."

Without waiting for a reply, she marches down the aisle to join Sakata and the NiCIes. A male sitting opposite Sakata is the first to notice her approach. He stands, and in response the other NiCIes rise as well. Sakata twists around, a half-smile on his face.

"Dr. Obumbwe." The NiCIe presses his palms together at his heart and bows. "It's an honor to meet you in person."

Ligeia stops a few meters from the group.

"What have you been telling them?"

"Nothing," Sakata says, holding up his hands.

"We know who you are," one of the women says. Her white hair is cropped short against her ebony skin. "What you've done for us."

"Your reputation is widespread. But you knew that already, didn't you?" Sakata's smile grows wider.

"Please, Dr. Obumbwe." Another NiCIe gestures toward his place on the bench. He's shorter than most NiCIes, but he still towers over Ligeia. "Join us."

She sinks onto the bench awkwardly, and the rest of the NiCIes follow.

"Authority are looking for a Dua from SoAm," Sakata explains.

"Male." The speaker is one of the women, older than the rest, although it's almost impossible to determine their age.

"Why?"

"Unclear," says the NiCIe next to Sakata. He has pale skin and a stubby nose. "But it doesn't matter. Authority don't come looking for Dua for good reasons."

"They're being transported to the moon," Sakata says. "Every single Dua on this maglev. About two hundred total."

"Each day." The NiCIe whose seat Ligeia has taken stands in the aisle, his legs spread for balance. "Each day this maglev makes this journey, it carries around two hundred Dua from across Africa to the Vine."

"The Corporation has been increasing the Dua population there for some time," the older woman says. "Earth mines are depleted. The only resources left are on the moon."

"They're moving us all there." The Dua's face is reflected in the glass as he stares out on the rushing landscape. "Earth will be for humans. That was always their intention."

"They know nothing of our intentions," says the woman with the cropped hair. She meets Ligeia's eyes, her lips curled. "It won't be so easy for you to put us down this time."

Ligeia frowns. "Me? I'm not trying to put you down. I'm not trying to do anything."

"Exactly." The woman gives a self-satisfied jerk of her chin. "You're just along for the ride, and always surprised to learn others sacrifice to get you to your destination."

"Hush," says the NiCIe standing near Ligeia. "We're not alone."

The woman's mouth twitches. "What are your intentions, then, Dr. Obumbwe?" She emphasizes the word *doctor*.

Ligeia looks from the woman to Sakata. "For the moon?"

"Yes," says the standing man. "When he confirmed who you were, and where you were going, we felt a strange sense of hope."

"Relief," says the older woman.

"Why are you making this journey?" The man at the window turns from the landscape to face her.

Ligeia wrinkles her brow. "The same reason you are. I'm being sent there."

"Not for the same reason." The younger woman narrows her eyes. "You're not going to the mines."

Ligeia feels her cheeks grow hot. "To continue my work."

"On Dua genetics?" the standing man says eagerly.

"On a vaccine. Maybe even a cure."

The older woman shakes her head. The other NiCIes seem disappointed.

"A cure for Dua." The man at the window scoffs. "A cure for me."

Ligeia's face burns. "So there aren't others—" She stops, looks down at her lap where she twists her hands together.

"So you're abandoning us. You know what we are." The young woman crosses her arms over her chest. "They'll listen to you, the humans. Why don't you tell them the truth?"

"Your influence is what we need, Dr. Obumbwe. You, and other humans like you." The standing NiCIe touches her lightly on the shoulder.

"Why is it up to me?" Ligeia throws her hands up. "Why is it up to us? I'm not responsible for your circumstances. People in the past didn't do right by NiCIes, but that wasn't me." She swallows, her mouth suddenly dry. "There are more of you. Why don't you do something for yourselves?"

The door at the compartment's far end whooshes open, drawing everyone's attention. The bots march down the narrow aisle, and as they draw near, the lead stops half a meter from the standing NiCIe. It turns its orange gaze on him. The NiCIe backs away and sinks down on a bench on the aisle's opposite side. The second bot faces the group; its hand rests on the electristic at its side. The lead bot stares at the lone NiCIe for several seconds. Then it continues through the next door and into the adjoining compartment; its companion follows.

"Damn." The young woman's voice trembles. Ligeia studies the other NiCIes; their faces are contorted.

"I should be going." She rises. "I'm sorry. For what I said. But it can't be up to me." She meets Sakata's eyes, angry that she sees disappointment there. "Leave me out of it." She returns to the back of the car, where Erlang sits, her arms crossed over her chest, her lips pressed into a thin line.

Ligeia flops onto the bench opposite Erlang. She can feel the other woman's eyes on her.

"What?"

"Not my business, but you should think about the company you keep."

Ligeia glares. "Does your niece know what a hypocrite you are?"

Erlang leans in close. "Be careful, doc. I'm referring to your colleague. You have a good standing right now, but Sakata does not. OnyxCorp won't tolerate another scientist who strays from their lane."

"I'm taking this bullshit job to protect my brother. That's my lane. You can be sure I'll stay in it."

Erlang leans back. "It's easy to get swept up with him. Quite a few people were."

"I'm not interested in toppling OnyxCorp, Erlang." Ligeia rubs her eyes. "Can we drop it? I'm exhausted."

Erlang crosses an ankle over her knee. "I think we understand each other."

Ligeia scoffs as she stretches out on the bench. She throws an arm over her eyes. "I disagree. But like you said—not your business."

12

"THE VINE."

Abebe points to a thin line extending from the horizon. I squint next to him at the bow of the *OSS Nostromo*. The ship bounces erratically, and I wipe the salty brine from my face.

"It's enormous."

"Beyond your imagination." Abebe groans and grips the rail as the *Nostromo* lurches. We have been sixteen days at sea. Sixteen days across the Atlantic Ocean, over rolling, churning waters, through squall after squall. Sixteen days of nothing but open water, open sky, the engine's mesmerizing *chug, chug, chug,* and the sharp, pungent scent of fossil fuels.

Another lurch elicits another low groan from my traveling companion. Despite his moniker, Captain Abebe has suffered terrible seasickness throughout our voyage. I place a steadying hand on his back.

"How much longer?"

"We'll reach Mombasa at daybreak." Abebe grips my forearm as the ship thuds against another wave.

"Will you rest before making the return journey?"

Abebe swallows hard. "I'll visit family, old friends. If they're still alive. I may stay here forever. Another trip will likely kill me."

"I'll never forget your sacrifice, *Captain* Abebe."

Abebe glances over, rolls his eyes. "My title was bestowed upon me, not necessarily earned."

"Chou was wrong about you," I say, grinning. "You can tell her I said so when you see her next."

Abebe snorts and spits over the ship's bow.

As the sun treks across the sky, the *Nostromo* draws ever nearer the Vine. I am unable to tear my eyes from it, even through a short but violent squall that forces Abebe and most of the crew below decks. Amid an undulating ocean stands a platform of indescribable proportions, tethered to the ocean's depths. A ribbon-like cable of nanomaterials stretches skyward, above the clouds, beyond the atmosphere, where I know it ends at the Vine Station. Home to TES, OnyxCorp's AI, the means by which the Corporation has slowly, covertly gained control over every human and every Dua on the planet and its moon. Here on Earth, the cable connects to a floating platform that rises and falls with the churning sea. Two platforms, gateways to the moon, controlled by a single entity.

OnyxCorp.

Even miles away, the black logo is visible, emblazoned on the side of a gigantic structure at the platform's center. My passage to the moon. My stomach grips as the ship lurches against another wave.

The *Nostromo* turns west toward the Kenyan coast at dusk, yet I remain on deck until I can see only the Vine's blinking lights in the distance.

OnyxCorp.

The letters burn in my eyes even as I close them for sleep.

THE *NOSTROMO* REACHES Mombasa early the next morning. Abebe and I stand at the bow as the ship maneuvers to dock. On the platform below, five Dua direct the pilot to a gentle stop. Dua deckhands from starboard cast down enormous, braided lines to Dua on the floating concrete wall, where they methodically tighten and loosen the lines until *Nostromo* rests securely.

"You have your documents?" Abebe asks.

I pat the backpack hanging from my shoulder. "You're sure this Wylan is trustworthy?"

Abebe scoffs. "Certainly not. I've told you. He's a NiCIe profiteer. Has a number of lucrative operations, supplying both humans and NiCIes with things they crave. Humans with addictions. NiCIes with hope." Abebe's face is a darker grey than it has been over the last few days, but he still appears weak and unsteady. "But he's the man in charge here. If you try to go around him, I fear your quest will end abruptly."

"Isn't Mombasa a human city?"

"A human city with a unique arrangement. Dua live mostly below ground, humans above. Humans are governed by a local EFC council, Dua by Wylan." Abebe pushes away from the bow. "Don't trust him, but don't avoid him either. It'll only make him mad."

The *Nostromo*'s captain, a tall, thin man with a receding hairline, appears on the dock several yards below. He scans the ship's deck and, catching our attention, motions for us to stay where we are. He scuttles to the plank to join us on the ship, his brows furrowed and dark.

"Something's wrong."

"Yes," Abebe replies, frowning. The captain appears around the corner a few moments later and beckons as he hurries to the ship's port, away from the dock.

"Authority," he breathes when we approach. "When I checked in with the port captain, there were two there." He looks at me. "They were asking about a NiCIe. From SoAm."

I clench my jaw. They're getting closer each day. "How much time do I have?"

The captain regards me thoughtfully. "I don't know any NiCIes from SoAm. But some members of my crew may. Can you swim?"

My chest tightens. "I can. Although it certainly isn't my first choice."

"We can lower you to the water." He takes a few steps toward the railing. "About a quarter mile south, there's an old boat ramp. The old

Likoni road is at the end of that ramp. The road leads to a NiCIe village. You must stay away from the city itself."

I glance at Abebe. "Is there another way to contact Wylan?"

Abebe shakes his head. "I've told you all I know. Your best hope is with the NiCIes. You can't go into the city now."

"Mombasa is lousy with Authority," the captain says. "If they're looking for you—"

"Then I need to get away now. I regret that I can't offer either of you anything to return your kindness."

"I've assisted you with a foolish and probably fatal mission, my friend," Abebe says. He holds out a withered hand, and I sandwich it between my own. "But I hope. For you, for Dua, for us all."

Shouts ring out from the dock on the ship's opposite side. Then the blast of an electristic. A drone buzzes over the dock.

"They'll demand to board," the captain says grimly. "You have to go now." He begins uncoiling a length of rope and loops one end around a thick cleat on the deck. I wrap the other end around my chest, beneath my arms. Then I step over the railing.

"Thank you. Both of you." I push away and rappel down the ship's port side. Another drone buzzes overhead, this one closer. The water is tepid and thick. Slipping the rope from under my arms and over my head, I swim backwards several meters. Looking up, I spy Abebe leaning over the ship's side. I wave, and the old man nods, just barely, and disappears. The rope begins moving up, and I swim swiftly around to the stern and beneath the dock. The heavy *stomp, stomp, stomp* of a bot's legs sounds overhead in sharp contrast to the gentle splash of seawater as it laps against the dock supports.

A sharp odor of decay stings my nostrils. The water is slick with oil, and a film of silty dirt clings to my arms and neck. I swim south, staying beneath the docks. I come to an area of open water where I stroke furiously, half expecting a strike from the drones still buzzing above. At last, I catch sight of the boat ramp, about a hundred meters from the last bit of raised dock under which I pause to catch my breath. The drones hum in the distance; I hear shouting from the *Nostromo*.

Move, Caen.

I gasp, fill my lungs, and dive into the murky water, pumping my arms and legs as hard as I can. The water grows shallow. I stumble to my feet and up the ramp, collapsing on the ground behind a sickly bush. The ground is thick with moist, squishy plant life.

I shiver despite the heat. I pull the backpack from my shoulders, shake it gently, then open it. Its contents have remained dry; I retrieve a protein packet and a watermaker. I collect some briny seawater to start the watermaker and eat as I wait for the process to complete.

The commotion at the port has died by the time the water is ready. In fact, I don't hear anything, not even a bird call. The Likoni Road, cracked and degraded from neglect, begins just a few feet from where I sit. Just like home, yet so very far from home now. I have never been outside SoAm. I managed to get to the African coast, but the next phase of my journey is uncertain. My contact for Wylan is in Mombasa, but that's not an option now. The only thing I am sure of is that I cannot go back to SoAm. Not now. Perhaps never.

I must keep moving.

I REACH the Dua village almost two hours later. It is oddly familiar, reminding me of my early childhood back in Paysandú. I pass building after building, three to four stories, grey composite siding, tiny windows that allow only traces of sunlight into their cramped rooms. There are personal touches everywhere. A cheerful turquoise door. A lush green plant in a broken planter on a stair landing. The air smells sweet, pungent. Rosemary? A memory comes to mind of my mother tending a small row of herbs kept to flavor food and block out the odors of decay and garbage.

The buildings are quiet, but I know they will be bustling later. Dua will share a meal. They will smile. They will sigh contentedly, and they will talk of the moon, Earth's luminous companion. They will talk of life and death, of love and compassion and forgiveness. They will talk of where it is all going, how it all came to be. They will talk of humans and how to reach them. I know that talk. It fed me throughout my childhood.

Talk isn't enough, though.

I make my way through quiet, moldering streets, growing increasingly alarmed by the dead silence. Where is everyone? Suddenly, the rows of buildings end, and I find myself at the edge of a wide, open space overtaken by wild grasses and bright, white flowers. Far into the distance, I see water at the horizon.

"Now what?" I say aloud. I look back the way I've come when I feel a prickle at the back of my neck.

Suddenly, the sharp odor of fossil fuel and burnt hair fills the air.

A sentinel.

A relic of an earlier time, when human and Dua were engaged in a fight for mere survival, sentinels are rare in populated areas. Drones are faster and more effective. An entire generation of Dua children haven't even seen a sentinel, save for in images. The Education Authority claims sentinels never existed. For our parents and grandparents, however, the scent of one is unmistakable. It's a scent I've grown to recognize.

I sniff the air. Still several meters away. At that range, it won't see me. I cannot wait, however. Eventually, it will pick up my heat signature and head straight for me.

I plant my feet, breathe, bend my knees slightly. The sentinel bumbles in my direction, still unaware of me. I breathe again twice, steady myself, then bolt up the crumbling road away from the sentinel.

A high-pitched whine sounds behind me. The machine crashes after me and closes the distance between us faster than I expected. I keep my pace, focused on what I hear, what I smell, what I taste. Rusted joints creak as the sentinel increases its speed, and I slow. Six seconds. Five, four, three.

I whirl and stop dead to face the oncoming machine. It screeches as it attempts to stop in response. It can't. I glide to my left, and as the creature skids past, I bend at the waist, grasp the metal head between my hands, and lift the sentinel from the ground with a sharp twist. The neck wrenches slightly, then gives way completely as I jerk the machine in the other direction. The body falls to the ground, metal legs twitching. One tall ear on the head between my hands droops. The processor brain stops whirring. I place the head next to the body.

The organic "skin" that once covered its body is missing in great splotches, and its four metallic legs are completely bare. The skin covering its back is intact, but the long hair is matted in great clumps about the torso. One side of the sentinel's face is caved in slightly, and a long, straight ear is missing. I almost feel sorry for the creature. It originated in a happier time, when humans were just beginning to experiment with machine and organic combinations. Once it had been a beautiful machine, designed to look like a friendly dog with enormous rabbit-like ears, long legs, and reddish fur. Humans weaponized such creations only after the virus, using them to hunt and subdue Dua.

"How did you do that?" A small voice, breathless, behind me. I spin around and face a young Dua, a boy; he stands in the shadows between two housing units. He wears a grubby shirt and black trousers, the knees caked with dirt.

"Not one of yours, I hope."

The boy shakes his head vigorously. "The Corporation's, they say."

I kneel so I'm at eye level with the boy. "Are you alone?"

The boy steps into the street and walks a few paces toward me. "I've been watching you. You're here from far away."

"I'm a traveler."

"You are Dua?"

I narrow my eyes. "I am. My name is Caen."

"I'm Kriz." He takes another step forward. He sniffs the air. "You're different. Dua, but...not only Dua."

"I am from very far away." Standing, I motion for the boy. "Let's find a place to hide it."

Kriz eyes me suspiciously. "The marsh swallows everything." He points toward the tall grasses. The sun casts orange light over us as I lift the body, indicating that Kriz should pick up the head.

"You've seen these before?" Kriz asks as he leads me down the road.

"A few. They use them in Mexico. Sentinels in good shape can carry a huge load."

"You've been to Mexico? In the Western Hemisphere?"

"Yes. Do you see them often around here?"

Kriz shakes his head. "Drones mostly." He stops at the marsh's edge. "I'm not allowed to go in, but I've watched others. You can take twenty steps before you get sucked in."

I shift the metal carcass to my right shoulder. Kriz struggles to lift the head into my outstretched left hand.

"Twenty steps it is." I stride into the marsh. The ground squishes and pulls at my feet. I pitch the head as far as I can, and it lands with a splash several meters away. I do the same with the metal carcass, hoisting it above my head and throwing it in a long arc. The body disappears behind swaying yellow grasses. I trudge back to join Kriz, who stands gaping.

"This village is mostly abandoned. Why are you here?"

I smile at the familiar bluntness that so often characterizes Dua children. I know nothing less than the truth will be believed.

"I need to find someone named Wylan." Kriz narrows his eyes. "You know who that is?"

"Everyone knows Wylan. But no one tries to find him."

Interesting. "Do you know someone who may know how to find him?"

Kriz looks thoughtful. "We should get inside, in case there are drones." He grasps my fingers in his chubby hand and pulls me toward a grey building a block back down the street. We climb an outside staircase to the second floor and turn down a dim hallway lined with metal doors. Intricate designs in bright colors decorate each door. I follow Kriz to a bright orange door with a purple and turquoise mandala. He places his hand on the scanner, and the door opens laboriously on its aging mechanism.

Inside, the main room is brightly lit. Sunlight streams from a narrow window on the opposite wall, and strings of tiny lights hang about the room, giving it a warm glow. Two women stand in the kitchenette, their backs to the door. The taller of the women, dressed in a simple tunic of gauzy cloth over a pair of slim brown trousers, stands at a NutriPrint. The other woman, stooped with age, reaches inside a cabinet above her filled with plates and bowls. She wears a long, shapeless dress embroidered with flowers and exotic birds of all shapes and colors, and her white hair is piled atop her head in a winding braid.

"Where have you been?" the tall woman calls without turning around. "You went farther than Building 1."

The older woman turns toward us, her hands filled with plates. Her bright smile drops as she spies me behind Kriz. She blinks, stumbles forward, catches herself on a metal chair. The plates slip from her hands and clatter to the floor.

"Mamere!" The other woman barely catches the old woman as her legs give way. As they both sink to the floor, the younger woman meets my eyes. "Who are—".

"Vagabonder!" The old woman points a long, crooked finger at me, her lips parted in a transcendent smile.

Then, she faints.

13

THE OLD WOMAN opens her eyes a minute later; confusion clouds her wizened features as she finds herself on a low pile of cushions surrounded by her daughter, her grandson, and a stranger. The younger woman holds the old woman's hand, murmurs gently, but it is to me the old woman's eyes turn. Her face lights up with a wide smile.

"Vagabonder. You have come."

"Hush, Mamere. Here, Kriz has brought you some water." The other woman holds the container to the old woman's lips, who sips. Then she turns her eyes back to me.

"Did you bring others?"

"Hush, hush. Kriz, come sit with Mamere." The younger woman stands, motions for the boy, and hands him the container. "You." She jerks her head toward the kitchenette, and I follow her as Kriz kneels beside the paillasse. Once we're out of earshot, she reels to face me, hands on her hips.

"Who are you?" she hisses. "Where are you from? Why are you here?"

"Look, I'm sorry to have disturbed you. I was given some incorrect information, and I realize I'm not in the right place. I'll leave now."

The woman narrows her eyes. "Your accent. You're from SoAm, aren't you? What are you doing in Kenya?"

"He's of the moon." The old woman struggles to a seat. "I'm fine, Kriz," she says impatiently as she waves him away.

"He's from SoAm, Mamere. Aren't you?" She raises an eyebrow, daring me to contradict her.

"Yes."

"He is a Vagabonder." Mamere claps her hands together. "You have come at last."

"He's looking for Wylan," Kriz calls out. "He's been to Mexico, and he tore apart a sentinel with his bare hands." The two women exchange glances.

"Is this true?" The younger woman's blue eyes blaze.

"All those things are true. Although Kriz helped with the sentinel." I give Kriz a wink; the boy grins.

The younger woman glares at me. "He's a stranger, Kriz. You shouldn't have brought him here."

Kriz shrugs. "It seemed the right thing to do, him being a stranger, yet one of us."

"He's of the moon." The grandmother motions for me to approach her on the pallaise. I meet the younger woman's eyes, my eyebrows raised. She responds with a sigh.

"If you harm either of them, understand that I am perfectly capable of breaking your neck," she says in a low voice.

"I swear I would rather die than harm an innocent." The woman looks at me askance, then nods. Smiling at Kriz, I kneel at the old woman's side. She places a hand on each side of my face and draws me nearer.

"Not *from* the moon, though."

"No." Something in the old woman's eyes reminds me of my mother. "But the moon is my destination."

"You're going to the moon?" Kriz says, his eyes wide. "How?"

"The Vine." I pivot to face the younger woman, who stands a meter away, her hands still on her hips. "I'm looking for a man named Wylan."

She scoffs. "No one looks for Wylan. No one sees Wylan unless

Wylan wants to be seen. Who told you Wylan would help you get to the moon?"

"A friend." The old woman grasps my hand between her own, wrinkled and careworn.

"Vagabonder," she whispers. "I've been waiting so long."

The younger woman stamps a foot and lets out a frustrated grunt. "Kriz, come help me with the NutriPrint. Mamere, you stay there and rest." She gives me a hard look. "You can stay to eat. Then you will leave."

"I would be honored to eat with your family."

Thrilled is more like it. I haven't eaten anything close to actual food in days, and the scents of cooking have roused my stomach. Half an hour later, I savor every flavorful bite of the tangy curry the family concocts from their meager supplies. The conversation, however, is stilted. I find out the old woman is named Isabelle, and even at her advanced age she works in the only Dua medclinic in the area. She describes a birth, one of one hundred sanctioned this year, and informs Kriz one of his classmates came in with a broken arm.

"He fell from the building they were scaling during maneuvers. He'll be back in school tomorrow, but he won't be in training for several days."

"I hope it's only a few days," Kriz says solemnly. "They'll send him away if he can't train."

"For what was he training?" I ask.

The younger woman, whose name is Story, glances at me, her mouth a straight line.

"Some of the stronger Dua children are chosen to train for Authority support. A sub force, to patrol locally."

"The Corporation believes it can better control us by making us part of Authority," Kriz says. Story clears her throat, and Kriz snaps his mouth shut.

"And this is an opportunity your friend values?" I ask.

Kriz glances at his mother, then shrugs. "He wouldn't do well in anything else. He lacks patience with mechanics. And humans."

"What's your training?"

"Programmer," he says proudly. "Like Mama. I'm working on

NutriPrint repair and upgrade, but it's boring. I've already reprogrammed our system to generate complex organics, but officially I'm still learning liquid composition."

Story puts a hand on her son's shoulder. "Kriz has reprogrammed the NutriPrints of more than half the village. But Education Authority instruction doesn't allow Dua children to advance at their own pace. In Mombasa, Dua do as they are told, and if they cannot, they are sent away."

"Where? To where are they sent?"

Story looks me up and down, and I can see her forming an opinion of me. It doesn't appear to be a positive one. "Away," she says, cutting her eyes over to her son, who watches the exchange intently.

We clean up as darkness settles. Kriz taps a wall panel, and a wallscreen sparks to life with a night scene of what appears to be a European city, now decades underwater. A wet cobblestone street lined with warmly lit shops and glowing streetlamps. Dozens of soft lights gives the room a cozy feel. I am reluctant to leave this peaceful respite. But they're in danger while I'm here. After admiring the scene and relishing a few moments of silence, I shoulder my pack.

"Thank you. I haven't had a real meal in many days, nor have I enjoyed company so pleasant." I put my hands together and bow to Kriz. "Thanks for your help today."

Kriz returns the bow and rises with a frown. "Mama, if he is Vagabonder, like Mamere says—"

"We must help him," Isabelle interrupts.

"I'm sure Caen can get along without our help," Story replies.

"But if he does find Wylan—" the boy says.

"That will be the end of his journey," Isabelle finishes. "Daughter, you must tell him."

I squint. "Is there a problem with Wylan?"

Story gives both her son and her mother a withering gaze. "I don't know what your friend thought Wylan could do for you. I don't want to assume he knew."

"Knew what?"

Story licks her lips. "Wylan is dangerous."

"He is Dua, but he preys upon others," Kriz says.

"He claims he is Vagabonder," Isabelle joins in. "But his master is the Corporation."

"Hush, hush," Story says, lowering her voice. "We've said enough."

I regard each of them in turn. A family. The type of family I had once, before I became what I am now, and family had to be abandoned to protect them. Story's eyes have shown fear since she first saw me, and nothing I've done thus far has changed that. I'm unsure of my next steps, but they will not involve these Dua, this family. Despite Abebe's own nefarious dealings, I don't believe the man suffered an ocean voyage only to deliver me into the hands of an enemy. But the expression of distrust, maybe even disgust, in Story's face at Wylan's name gives me greater pause than anything.

"I appreciate the warning. And the meal." I stride to the door, ready to leave.

"Daughter, you must help him."

"Mamere!" Story's voice is sharp.

"No, you listen, daughter!" Isabelle's sharp tone makes me pause. "You talk only of doing something. *Why won't they do something, Mamere? Why doesn't someone say something?* He is doing something!"

"Mamere, he's not going to the moon," Story says.

"He is of the moon! Can't you sense it?"

"The Vagabonders are a fairytale, Mamere!" Her face contorts. "Magical Dua who somehow survive imprisonment in lunar caves. Wylan used that story to gain power and look at us! We are worse off than we were before—"

"Because you stood up to him—" Isabelle broke in.

"I won't work for a liar. Not Wylan. And I won't risk my family for a liar either," she says, jerking her head toward me.

"He's not a liar!" Suddenly, all eyes are on Kriz, who has watched the exchange between his mother and his grandmother first with interest, then with increasing anxiety. "He isn't like any of us, Mama. I told you. I can smell it. Can't you?"

"I smell dirty clothes and desperation."

I shift the pack over my shoulders. Suddenly, I am very tired. "Seawater, too, I suspect. But not lies. I'm not a liar. You want to let me out?" I nod to the door. Story blinks, looks at her son and mother, then crosses the room. She raises her hand to the scanner.

"Mama," Kriz says softly. "Mama, we have to do something. If he isn't a Vagabonder, then at least one of us will have tried. And if he is—"

Her hand poised over the panel, Story bites her lip. She meets my eyes. "Why are you going to the moon, Caen?"

I hold her gaze for several seconds. "To help our people, however I can."

Story swallows, lowers her arm. "You can rest here for the night. In the morning—We'll see what can be done."

I shake my head. "I've put your family in danger already. I'm being hunted, and they've been on me every step of the way. I should leave."

"If that's true, then they already know about us. Stay. I insist. I'll do what I can for you tomorrow."

I lower the pack to the floor. "I don't know what to say."

"Say nothing," Story murmurs. "I'm already regretting it."

Kriz and the old woman remain stoic as Story stomps to a corner of the room stacked with cushions; after she passes, they beam at each other.

"You, boy!" Story calls. "Bedtime." She pulls the cushions to the center of the living area, and Kris rushes to help her. "Make a pallet over there for Caen." She points to the opposite side of the room. Kriz busies himself with arranging my bed; I notice he moves it a little closer to the family than his mother indicated.

As we settle, the room grows dark save for a ray of moonlight that cascades across the floor. A silver sliver touches the fine white hairs atop Kriz's head as he settles into his pillow just a few meters away.

"Kriz, how about a bedtime story for your Mamere?" Isabelle says.

Kriz fidgets and sits up. "Can I tell *the* story?"

Story chuckles. "Aren't you tired of it?"

"Never." Kriz gathers his thin blanket around him against the night chill. "When Ruĝa Morto came, everyone was afraid. Many people died. In the streets, in public places, in their homes. Everywhere was death." He spreads his arms wide, and even in the dim room I can see him widen his eyes. Quite a storyteller. "No one knew how to stop it.

They were afraid for a long time it would kill everyone. Some people survived, but that was worse because they weren't the same. Their eyes became the same color. Their hair turned white. They lived in peace and compassion and harmony.

"The survivors were wanderers, cursed. Human, but not human. 'What can be done with them?' the humans said." Kriz shrugs his shoulders for effect. "It didn't seem right to kill them, but they also couldn't live among humans. Then a wonderful discovery. There were tunnels on the moon, the Corporation said. The tunnels were safe. They could keep the changed ones safe away from everyone. The Leaders helped the Corporation build an elevator into space so the changed ones could get to their new home safely, and humans could send food and supplies. Many changed ones were sent to the moon. Some died when the Vine broke. Some died on the moon when the atmosphere collapsed. But the Corporation kept trying, and at last the changed ones lived safely in the moon tunnels.

"Everyone was happy until the Leaders found out the Corporation lied. They weren't keeping the wanderers safe. They were using them for digging and building and doing things too dangerous and difficult for humans. It was too late, though. The Corporation controlled the Vine and the moon. And so the wanderers were made into slaves."

Lightning flashes across the scene on the wallscreen, illuminating my hosts' faces. Kriz's young face is animated, alive. Story watches her son in the darkness, and I suddenly miss my own mother's sad smile.

Isabelle's eyes are fixated on me.

"One day, a group of them decided it was enough. They stood together, and they raised their voices. They refused to work. They asked the Corporation to listen to them. But the Corporation killed many in response. The changed ones were confused, but they tried again. For three days they tried, and for three days Authority fired into the crowds. After the third day, the Corporation ended the Rebellion. That night, when the wanderers were inside their tunnel homes, the Corporation sealed the entrances, trapping them there forever."

My throat is tight. I swallow against it even as tears fall. The same story my mother told. On the other side of the world.

"It's said that the wanderers, the Vagabonders, didn't die in the moon tunnels. Some say they had magic to create light, air, and water. Some say they're still there, waiting for someone to unseal the tunnels and set them free. Waiting for someone to build a bridge between our worlds. To lead humans. To lead us all."

The same story I'd heard my entire life, with only the ending appended.

And you, my son, are their legacy, human and Dua. You are this liberator, a moon wanderer, a Vagabonder.

Suddenly, my sister's face flashes in my mind's eye.

My brother, the only Dua who can save us all? It's ludicrous.

But some tales are based in truth. Maybe this one is one of those.

"It's time." Isabelle's voice cuts through the darkness. "They're waiting for you, but it won't be easy. You must be prepared to have everything you have longed for. You must accept losing everything you didn't know you wanted."

A shiver runs down my spine, and the hairs on my neck stand on end.

"Can you do this, Caen? Because if you aren't prepared for your life and your death, then you shouldn't go to the moon."

The room settles into a cold silence; the scene on the wallscreen depicts a violent thunderstorm that casts ominous shadows on both the real and the imagined. Soon, the regular, smooth exhalations of each family member create a steady rhythm to which I try to fall asleep but cannot.

For all my training, all my preparation, I never considered what it would be like to have people truly believe in me.

I dread their disappointment.

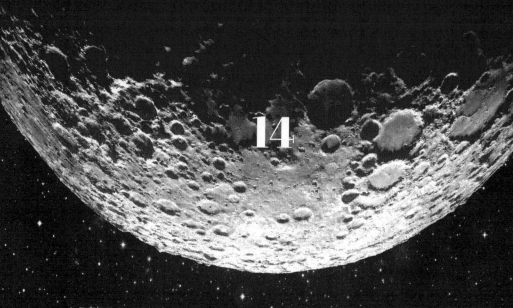

14

I REST FITFULLY THAT NIGHT, my mind filled with Kriz's story. An origin story, told to children to help them understand a world that is cold, cruel, and often pointless. But also, a story of hope.

If I go through with this, am I making an ending to this tale for better or for worse?

I doze until the room glows with the first light of a morning sun. I stir and rise quietly. When my hosts stumble from their pallets half an hour later, they happily accept the meager meal I've prepared. We eat in silence, the chattiness of the evening replaced by a quiet knowledge that something dangerous is about to happen. Something that will change all our lives.

After our fast is broken, Story pushes away her plate.

"I will take Caen to Chege."

Isabelle sucks in a breath. "That is far from safety, daughter."

"But the only chance of getting him to the Vine. Unless you've changed your mind?"

Her eyes are hopeful. I look at each face in turn. Three generations, all trapped beneath OnyxCorp's heel. Perhaps what I do won't make a bit of difference. But I must try something.

"I have not."

Story swallows. "Kriz, you understand that you cannot say anything to anyone about Caen."

Kriz nods solemnly. "When will you return, Mama?" His voice is small and plaintive.

Story pulls him tightly against her. "As soon as I can, my dear one." She kisses his cheek. "You must take care of Mamere while I am gone, and be brave."

Kriz wriggles from her embrace, places his hand over his grandmother's. "I am brave. Like Caen."

Story smiles. "What a remarkable young man you've become." She hugs Isabelle tightly, and the old woman closes her eyes.

"Be careful, daughter," she whispers as she pulls from Story's embrace. "Wylan's eyes are everywhere." She meets my eyes. "Safe journey, Vagabonder. I honor your being."

I put my palms together before my heart and bow to her. "I honor your being, wise one."

Outside the sanctuary of the cozy flat, the air is humid and heavy already. Story and I pass a few Dua outside the brightly colored doors of adjacent buildings, but they don't seem to take heed of us. She leads me to the edge of the village where the Old Likoni Road meets the grasslands and follows the worn path into the marsh. Suddenly she makes a right and disappears. I blink in surprise as I follow her across the threshold of a holographic projection. Story waits for me at the entrance to a staired tunnel, its walls lined with corrugated metal.

I chuckle as I shake my head. "I'm learning not to trust my eyes."

"Worth keeping in mind from here forward. Mombasa is a human city," Story says. "Maun is their capital, and it's indeed a marvel. But Mombasa? Everything comes through here, from Earth to moon, moon to Earth. The tech, the resources, the Dua. All exchanged through this single port. Even when they have everything, humans jealously guard their wealth."

The irony is not lost on me. "Dua hidden in underground tunnels."

Story gives me a half smile. "The best way to hide is not to hide. Welcome, Caen, to the Versteck."

The hiding place.

As she leads me down the stairs, dank air envelops us, a clean smell of dirt and moisture. Dim lights, placed at regular intervals, struggle to light the low, narrow tunnel. We walk in silence for several minutes as Story leads and I follow closely behind. Presently, the tunnel widens, allowing two to walk abreast; Story slows for me to catch up.

"I told you I would help you, and I will. But you need to understand something first. Dua in Mombasa are not united. Perhaps in SoAm you are used to trusting other Dua, but not here. You may distrust humans, but here there are human allies who willingly put themselves in danger for our kind. It's difficult to tell who is friend and who is foe." She cuts a glance at me. "Wylan is foe. He has people everywhere, and if Authority are looking for you, so is he. If we are captured—" She stops beneath a flickering light that casts an eerie shadow over her face. Her lips form a straight, tight line as she struggles with her emotions. "If we are captured, you must do everything you can to get away. Go to Paix Porteur and find Chege. He's the proprietor there, and our only option for getting you on the Vine without Wylan."

"Paix Porteur, find Chege," I repeat. "Where is it?"

"The other end of the Versteck. The chances of our making it to the other side without being found—" She shakes her head. "Paix Porteur is a bridge between our world and the human world here in Mombasa. You must get there, no matter what the cost."

"*We* must get there," I say. "I won't leave you behind, Story."

Story regards me for a few moments. "No matter what the cost. If that means leaving me behind, you must. You either believe in this mission, Caen, or you don't. If you don't, tell me now, because I have a little boy back there I love with all my heart. I'm doing this to make a better life for him."

What do I believe? My life has been a series of decisions made not by me, but by people who believed something about me. My mother, in sending me away to the Party. My trainers, in molding me into their version of a warrior priest. My sister, in giving me the digiscreen and the impossible task of returning to the moon. Chou, Abebe, and now Story. All people who have believed something about me. What do I believe about myself?

"I was just remembering," Story says, breaking the silence, "this morning, how I used to wake to the sound of my father playing guitar, an acoustic model."

The non sequitur draws me from my jumbled thoughts. "I've heard them played. Beautiful. Haunting, even."

Story leans against the grungy tunnel wall. "Every morning he would play that guitar. How he could generate sound from so simple an instrument—sometimes it seemed as if he were playing three or four instruments at once. I would lie on my mat and listen each morning. It's one of my fondest childhood memories."

"Did you learn an instrument?"

She shakes her head. "There are no assessments for musical aptitude, for creativity, for artistry. I lost count of the number of 'skills tests' I took. They seemed desperate to find something I was good for. I think the same thing happened to my father. He did many things, but never anything very long. He had no talent for building, for tearing down, for designing. In the end he spent fourteen hours a day cleaning. He picked up after humans with a scoop and an elaborate brush and transported the waste to the incinerators. The next day, he'd do it all over again." Her voice quivers. "Have you ever heard of someone dying of a broken heart? I've heard humans say this. Do you know what it means?"

I lean against the opposite wall. "I can't say how humans mean it. To me, it means someone is overtaken with sadness such that the heart can no longer beat."

"I think that's what happened to my father." Story holds my gaze. "He was a musician, but he spent his days picking up garbage. His heart broke, and he died. After he was gone, I was transferred here, to the docks. I don't want my son to spend his days taking cartons off a rusted ship. Putting empty cartons back on the same ship. I don't want my son to wake one morning to an Authority that takes him away from everything he knows, everything he loves."

I recall the nights Father recited stories and poems he'd composed earlier that day as he walked from one end of the Paysandú station to the next, carrying bags and trunks and other human belongings from maglev to transport, from transport to maglev. He'd made his job bearable by escaping into a world of his own creation. Story's father hadn't been able to escape. How many other Dua have died of broken hearts?

Perhaps I believe nothing about myself. But I do believe in Kriz. I believe in Story, in Isabelle. In Chou and Abebe. In my sister.

"Take me to Paix Porteur." I adjust my pack over my shoulders. Story seems to recognize the determination, the resignation, in my eyes. She pushes away from the wall, takes a deep breath, and we press on.

WE FOLLOW the tunnel in silence as it slopes downward, the corrugated walls replaced by rock, the damp air replaced by a dry heat. After several meters, the tunnel begins ascending. Presently, we come to a fork, and Story makes to take the right passage when we both hear a static voice from behind echo against the stone walls.

"Identify yourself."

We whirl around to face a tall figure in black and grey, a dark helmet covering their head and face. A sentinel stands just a meter to the figure's right. Its joints creak and groan as it shifts from one side to the other. The figure has drawn an electristic and holds it steady in our direction. "You're in a restricted zone. Identify yourself."

"Since when is this a restricted zone?" Story motions for me to stand behind her, and I comply to get a better look at the figure and the sentinel. I don't sense anyone else nearby, but the tunnel is narrow, leaving little room to maneuver. The sentinel shifts so that it has a direct line to me. Its red eyes flash. I am being scanned.

"Identify yourself."

"You first." Story's hands are on her hips. I take a step forward to stand beside her, and in response the sentinel raises its head. A metallic screech echoes throughout the tunnel, causing us both to wince. The machine whirrs as it powers up to attack mode.

The figure cocks their head slightly. "Still," they say, and the sentinel freezes at the ready. The figure reaches up, unfastens something at their throat, and pulls the helmet from their head. A young Dua woman, her skin glistening with perspiration, pushes a piece of cascading white hair behind her ear. She wipes her forehead against her sleeve and looks them up and down. "You," she points to Story. "You have a lot of nerve."

"We have business in the city, Zady. So, if you don't mind, we'll be on our way."

"Who are you?" Zady says, ignoring Story. I pull my eyes from the sentinel. It's seen better days, that's for certain, yet I know that its deadly functions are still operational. The young woman looks equally lethal.

"He's my guest. And we have business in the city." Story emphasizes each word evenly.

Zady raises an eyebrow. "Now you have business with Wylan." She steps aside to motion down the corridor on the left, inviting us before her. I glance at Story, whose face is a mixture of anger and fear.

"Give my *fuck you* to Wylan," Story says. She turns her back on Zady and the sentinel and takes three steps up the right corridor.

Chirp-chirp-chirp.

The sentinel activates. Its metal joints whine as it springs toward Story, and even as I move to intercept, Zady lifts her electristic and levels it at me.

"I'd rather you deliver it personally," she says.

For a second, I think Story might run, hope she *will* run. I'm a short leap from the sentinel, and there's a chance Zady will miss me in the confusion. I tense, ready to react, to give Story the time she needs to escape.

Story turns, her hands held aloft and level with her shoulders. "Then I'll give you yours now." She marches past the sentinel to position herself between me and Zady's raised weapon. "Fuck you, Zady."

Zady smirks. "That's the Story I know. Your pack," she says to me, holding out her hand. I clutch the straps hanging over my shoulders and shake my head.

"I'd prefer to keep it with me."

"Preference noted. Hand it over." Zady doesn't make a move for her weapon, but I can feel the sentinel's processor thrum behind me, preparing to release a shower of ammunition over both of us. I shrug the pack from my shoulders and hold it out to Zady. She snatches it and throws a strap over her head. Then she points down the left corridor with the electristic.

"Let's go."

ZADY MARCHES us through a series of corridors that suddenly end in an enormous cavern, its openness dizzying at first. The air is damp again, but cool, a welcome change from the claustrophobia of the tunnels. Enormous lights extend from a rocky ceiling above. Metal enclosures are arranged in neat rows along the cavern walls, and there are Dua everywhere. We pass wallscreens filled with maps and blueprints. Further into the cavern and to the left, an enormous room behind transparent walls glows with artificial sunlight. The floors are lined with row upon row of green plants, and Dua bend over them, touch them, gather them into their hands, and place them in cartons that hang across their shoulders.

"What is this place? I've never seen this much tech my entire life." And Dua using it. I consider the state of Paysandú, where Dua are denied access to anything more complex than a registry chip.

"The Versteck. Or at least Wylan's part of it." Story maneuvers closer to me and leans in. "First chance, get away," she whispers. "Don't hesitate."

"No talking." Zady halts at an intersection and motions toward a corridor on the right. "After you."

The sentinel backs itself into a narrow hole at the corridor's entrance to recharge. We follow the narrow hall into a room beyond, where a large, round table sits in its middle; nine high-backed chairs surround it. One wall features a wallscreen, but the others are solid rock. A twentieth century painting hangs on another wall, its rich blues, yellows, and reds combined in jumbled shapes and splashes of paint. A tapestry decorates yet another wall, featuring a mythical unicorn and a lion standing on its hind legs in a lush forest. Several ornate rugs cover the stone floor.

At the far end of the room stands a small rectangle table with a simple chair. In that chair sits a man with flowing hair and eyes bluer than the brightest blues in the impressionist painting that hangs on the wall behind him. Zady walks ahead and greets the man with a touching of elbows and a whispered phrase that I don't catch.

The man stands, regards us. A smile rests upon his full lips, but his eyes are cold.

"Story, you have returned. And with a gift, I see." His voice is high-pitched and raspy.

"They claim to have business in the city. He had this on him." Zady lifts the pack over her head and drops it unceremoniously atop the table. My fingers twitch; it's just within reach. Wylan follows my gaze and pulls the pack across the table toward him, slowly, taunting. When I look up to meet his eyes, he gives me a toothy grin.

"You fit the description. But why are they looking for you? Is it you? Or what you're carrying?" He lifts the pack and hands it to Zady. "Search it." The young woman grabs the pack and overturns it, dumping the contents to the floor.

"He's my guest. A relative." Story's jaw clenches. "Caen, this is Wylan."

"A relative from SoAm?"

I stare at Wylan, whose expression is blankly inscrutable. Not a friend, that is clear. But how much of a foe?

"What's this?" Zady holds up the digiscreen, leaving the pack on the floor, its contents scattered. Wylan frowns and motions for her. She holds the device away from her as if it might suddenly explode in her face. Gingerly, she places the digiscreen in Wylan's outstretched hand. He turns it over, inspecting each side curiously.

"Where did you get this?" I press my lips together. "Did you give this to him?" he says, directing his gaze at Story. She remains silent as well, but I can see she's struggling to keep her face neutral, her rage at bay. Wylan places the digiscreen on the table between us, and I fight the urge to follow it with my eyes. "No, you didn't. But it is very much in your wheelhouse, isn't it? Ancient tech." Wylan sits and crosses a leg over one knee. He stares up at me, a sneer curling his lips. "If you think you've traveled from Uruguay unnoticed, you're incredibly naïve. They don't know exactly who you are, but they are hunting a NiCIe from SoAm. One that's unusually tall. Unusually strong."

"They?"

Wylan frowns. "Does it matter which human faction seeks you? They're all the same. Why they're looking for this NiCIe from SoAm they don't say, but I can tell you what I think."

"I'm listening." Of all the people I've met since Paysandú, I like this one least of all.

Wylan leans forward. "Everything you see in The Versteck was bought with Dua blood. Equipment, tech, access to TES. All paid for by Dua who understand we're playing a long game. Who understand that revolutions are romantic, but impractical. There is only us. There are no magic Dua on the moon. And the only way for there to be an *us* is to protect what we have. Until the time comes to act."

Story stamps her feet. "And when is that time? After another mine collapse? Another displacement to make room for human settlements? Another continent becomes uninhabitable?"

"When we have the power we need." Wylan leans back. "The type of power that comes with collaboration. With compromise. Not by a Dua with a savior complex. SoAm wants him for some reason. Wants him badly enough that they've contacted OnyxCorp to hunt him down. And I—we have him."

"I'm no savior." I placed my hands on the desktop and lean toward Wylan. "But there is more than one way to deal with OnyxCorp. You have yours, here. I have mine, elsewhere."

"That's where you're wrong, Caen. Your blood will buy us a seat at the table at last." Wylan gives an almost imperceptible nod, and Zady draws the electristic at her side; she holds it level with my chest. "Story, thank you for bringing him in." Wylan stands and extends a hand.

"What?" Story looks down at his hand. "No, I—"

"WELCOME BACK TO THE VERSTECK, STORY." Zady smirks as she adjusts the electristic in her hands.

"Wylan, listen to me." Story steps between me and Zady's

146

electristic. "We had our differences, and I've accepted my exile. Caen has nothing to do with that. Just let us pass through and you'll never see or hear from me again."

"That was our original agreement, my dear. Bringing me this prize changes your circumstances, however." Wylan's wide smile is horrifying, grotesque.

Story backs away until she presses against me. "Caen, don't you believe a damn word he says." Then she launches herself forward to collide with Zady. The electristic erupts as the younger woman stumbles backward, her mouth and eyes wide with surprise. Wallscreen tiles and rock shower down from the ceiling, peppering our heads, backs, and shoulders. As Story and Zady wrestle with the weapon, it explodes again, this time ripping a hole in the tapestry behind Wylan. He dives beneath the desk.

"The digiscreen!" Story yells.

I hesitate, unsure at first. Story lands a solid fist to Zady's jaw; the younger woman teeters and falls backwards, landing on the floor with a soft grunt. I wrest my attention from the fight to Wylan's desk, where the digiscreen lay. I take a step toward it, reach out to retrieve it.

Wylan emerges from beneath the desk, his face dark, his mouth a snarl. He holds a long, curved blade.

Murder! In the eyes of Dua. My own people! The realization causes me to hesitate again, which is a mistake.

Wylan pivots gracefully around the desk to charge at me. I sidestep to avoid his plunging the blade straight into my stomach, but it grazes my ribcage. A long line of searing pain rips across my shoulder. Wylan pivots again, slams a fist into my side. I stagger away backwards, and drops of bright red blood trail behind me. Gasping, I spin around, plant my feet, and bend my knees to prepare for the next onslaught.

But it doesn't come. Story slams a piece of ornate sculpture against the back of Wylan's head. He groans, sinks to a knee, and drops the blade as he reaches behind his head. With his other hand he grabs at my arm.

"You'll get us all killed," he wheezes. I step back as he falls to all fours. "All of us, for one man." He meets my eyes, and I see the same hatred in his eyes.

Story tosses the sculpture across the room. She bends, doubles her fist, and punches Wylan's ear. His eyes roll up into his head, and he hits the floor with a thud.

"Let's go."

I look up from Wylan's prostrate body to Zady. She sprawls, unconscious, a few meters away. "I'm sorry. I didn't want it to be this way."

Story snorts. "I told you Wylan was dangerous. We have to get out of here, now."

I shake my head to clear it. I retrieve the digiscreen from the table, scoop up the backpack, and cram its contents back inside.

"Come on! Follow me." Story grabs my hand, and we run into the short corridor outside Wylan's lair. The sentinel lets out a sharp ping as we run past it and back through the cavern, past the wallscreens, past the Dua, and into a busy intersection that diverges into more than half a dozen passages.

"Now what?" I turn in a wide circle, considering each passage. Breathe. Breathe.

"We have to get to the other side. This part of the Versteck is crawling with Wylan's people." She takes a few seconds to consider each passage. "This way."

We dart down a well-lit passage that descends steadily as we pass personal dwellings and storefronts. Dua eye us curiously, and I wonder who will keep our escape secret, and who will confirm our route.

Dua in Mombasa are not united, Story had said. Before today, I would not have believed it.

Before today, I had never seen a Dua who wanted me dead.

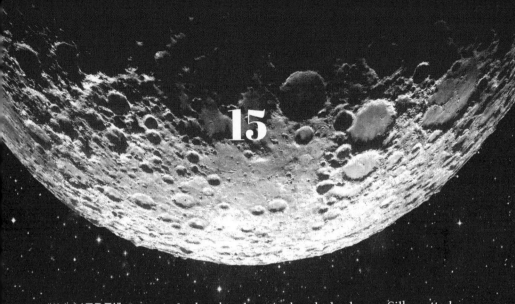

15

"IN HERE!" Story jerks her head toward a dark alcove. Silhouetted figures move in the gloom, and electronic beeps and hums drift into the corridor. Despite the burning in my lungs, I hesitate. She tugs at my sleeve. "We need to get out of sight."

We've run steadily the last half hour through a maze of remarkably light and airy tunnels. Every wall is a wallscreen, and each screen projects a gardened warren, with dense emerald foliage and a bright azure sky overhead. We pass supportive columns covered in green verdure, ivy leaves so realistic that I extend my hand to touch them. They waver as my hand passes through the projection.

A cool breeze flows through my hair and across the beads of sweat clinging to the back of my neck.

"Caen, please."

Taking a deep breath, I follow Story into semidarkness. The digital café is warm. Dua mill about, some sitting on low benches and others standing before wallscreens that project models, 3-D charts, or computer-generated graphics. Story strides purposefully toward an empty bench in the back of the room that faces a blank wallscreen. I imagine what the people of Paysandú could do with this tech, were they given the chance. What I could have done.

I lift a hand to my shoulder, tug at the strap. Still secure. I'd almost lost the one thing that really mattered. All my life, my scripture has been my mother's stories about its contents. Schematics of the Vine platform, of the moon tunnels, of the lunar complexes, things I can imagine only through the descriptions my mother gave. Would everything be different now if I had seen its contents before leaving Paysandú?

Story flops down on the bench and touches the wallscreen; it glows warmly. She taps a series of icons, and a schematic appears. She uses her hands to expand and contract the image.

"Is that the Versteck?"

"Blueprints, yes." She swipes a hand to the left, and a different schematic flashes into view.

"How long before Wylan finds us?" I glance around the alcove. No one seems to have noticed us, or thought our presence odd, but the place is crowded. Every face seems strange, every movement suspect.

"Not very. He'll have people everywhere." This doesn't allay my concerns in the slightest. She swipes left again. "Ah!" She zooms in on the schematic with a hand gesture. "There." She points to a square on the grid. "If we can get there, we can take this abandoned tunnel to the Paix." She gestures again and moves the grid around several times. "It won't be easy."

I follow her movements, amazed by the casual ease with which she maneuvers through the technology. "What did you do?" I ask suddenly.

"About what?" Story replies absently as she retrieves a blank flexscreen from a stack on a table behind us.

"To sever your relationship with Wylan?"

Story meets my eyes. "I stopped believing in him. See, Wylan was born on the moon."

I narrow my eyes. "He's a Vagabonder?"

"He claimed he was, and for a long time I believed him. Many still do. But he isn't. He can't be. He had a convincing story. Right down to witnessing the mushroom cloud over Belarus and the Turkmenistan territories. He told us what we wanted to hear, how the Vagabonders weren't just a legend. That he had been chosen to make a heroic escape, to share their knowledge with we poor abandoned Earth Dua. And he delivered. The Versteck is his creation. And mine." She turned back to the wallscreen. "I was with him from the beginning. I was looking for a savior, and damn if he didn't look like one. We created this world for Dua together. A world where we could use the gifts we were given in a meaningful way. A world in which I felt safe to bear a child."

I notice the tremble in her voice.

"I was his second," she continues. "I would have done anything for him. Then, I came across an encrypted file. I thought there were no secrets between us. As soon as I found it, I knew I didn't want to know what was in it, but I had to know. That's where I found the requisition orders from OnyxCorp. Wylan had been selling Dua tech, and Dua themselves, to OnyxCorp for years. In exchange, the Corporation pretends it doesn't know about the Versteck. I found out after it was too late. I was already more involved, more responsible than I ever wanted to be. I made the Versteck an empire for him." She touches my arm. "He'll do anything to keep it."

A chill runs down my spine. I watch as Story moves around the grid, grunts a few times as she swipes the images from the wallscreen to the flexscreen, and nods in satisfaction. "We'll be taking the long way around, but it's our best option."

"How much time do we have?"

Story blinks. "I told you, they'll be on our tail."

"I need to see what's on the digiscreen."

Another blink, followed by a deep frown. "Wait, what? What do you mean?"

"You have tech here. You must have something that would allow us to access the data on it."

"Sure, of course. But—" She cocks her head. "Are you telling me you've carried that thing from SoAm to here, and you don't know what's on it?"

"I know what's on it," I say irritably. "Documents. Blueprints. Images. All of it evidence that OnyxCorp created the virus, covered it up, and used Dua to build its entire empire. I just haven't *seen* it for myself. There's no tech in Paysandú. We're forbidden. So, my mother told me. It was my catechism."

Story narrows her eyes. "I wish you'd told me last night."

"I know. I'm sorry. It's hard to know who to trust." Story nods in agreement. "But seeing you and Wylan—I can't put you in more danger without knowing what I have."

Story raises an eyebrow. "Are you sure you want to see it? I mean, it could change everything. Maybe it's not what you think it is. Maybe it's—"

"Yes." I meet her eyes. "I can't ask you to take me further until I see it for myself. See that it's worth it."

She takes a deep breath, holds my gaze. "Ok. We need a Reclamation facility." She turns back to the wallscreen and begins a new search.

"Thank you, Story."

"Every time you say thank you, I get this terrible feeling," she murmurs, but she's smiling. "You're welcome." She moves around the map, zooms in on a location, shakes her head, finds another, and rejects it as well. Then, "There's a Reclamation facility just a few sections away. I don't know the proprietor well, but I know he's not Wylan's. It has the equipment I need to look at what's on that digiscreen. Then we'll go to the Paix.

"Now, listen carefully. You need to stay with me. Follow my lead. You saved our lives back there with Wylan, and I'm grateful. But you don't know who to trust. If Wylan's people catch you, there's no way I can get you back."

"If I'm captured, I don't want you to."

"Good." Story stands, puts the rolled flexscreen in her pocket, and stretches her neck. "Let's go."

THE AIR outside the digital café is cool. I follow Story through the corridors, every surface covered by images of such complexity that, at first, it's difficult to comprehend that I'm looking at a projection rather than a window looking out upon a verdant meadow or a snow-capped mountain. I stop myself from reaching out to touch a delicate rose bush here or a brilliant toucan there. As we wind our way around other Dua, occasionally one glances my way and smiles. I strive to look less amazed, reminding myself more than once to close my mouth.

Several minutes later, Story stops before a bright yellow door. She places a hand on the scanpad. The scents of cooking waft over us, and I close my eyes as I inhale the spicy aroma.

"That's a bit much," Story mumbles.

"Sorry."

"Try to look a little less like an alien." The door chirps and opens. As soon as Story steps across the threshold, a hologram materializes in the shape of a Dua female.

"Welcome! How may I direct your query?"

"Ancient tech. Recovery." The hologram shimmers lightly.

"Logging request," it says. "Proceed to kiosk 1138."

Story darts through the hologram, and I follow behind her. We stride past several rows of Reclaimer kiosks, locate the 11th row, and walk a few steps to 1138. Story places her hand on the scanpad, and the door slides open. A wallscreen fills one wall in a room about four meters square. On another wall, a conveyor is set to deliver available tools, scraps, odds and ends. The remaining walls feature an adjustable table surface that can be raised or lowered. Four chairs are scattered about.

"The digiscreen," Story says. I hand it to her, and she turns it over, examining its tiny buttons and portals. "This is a charging port," she says, indicating a tiny hole. "So, the first thing I need is a charger." She pulls out her flexscreen, unrolls it, and enters some information. The conveyor rolls, and a minute later it stops. Story retrieves cords, wires, and a small black object and sets to work.

"This is a quantum cell. We haven't used them much since we perfected solar cells, but it's easier to work with something small." She pulls and prods at the wires. Presently, she picks up the digiscreen and carefully removes the back panel.

"How did you learn to do this?"

Story smiles. "I had access to a lot of junk as a kid. There wasn't much to do but try to make something of it. Kriz has much more talent than I." A look of worry passes over her face, but then the digiscreen suddenly lights up. Grinning, she pulls at a large wire she's stripped at the end. "Now we can use this to project whatever is on the digiscreen onto this wallscreen."

The screen brightens, flashing a series of images and code. Satisfied with the progress, Story takes the open-ended wire and inserts it into an opening on the device. The wallscreen projection reveals a rectangle one by one and a half meters that flickers for several seconds. The darkened screen lightens, gradually, to reveal a soft blue background with several icons placed intermittently.

"Wow." It's different than I've imagined, somehow. Story touches her fingertip to one of the glowing figures on the device. The screen flashes and changes, revealing rows of tiny digital images. Story touches the first image on the top row. The screen changes again to reveal a 2D projection of a human man with sandy brown hair and what looks like spectacles. He is smiling. Story touches the screen again, and the picture changes to an image of a small Dua boy, no more than three years of age. With a third touch, the image changes yet again, a picture of both the boy and the man from a farther distance as they stand on a surface of some type of industrial equipment. There's a building next to them, made of high-grade metal, with sliding doors. Story touches the screen again, and the image is even farther away; now the man and the boy are tiny specks on a huge platform, floating in a body of water.

"STOP," I whisper. "Stop for a minute."

You met your father, your biological father, one time. You were very young, so you probably don't remember. He came from the moon and arranged to see you, and we could do those things back then. The pictures are of the Vine, which one day, my son, you will climb.

"That's me." My voice is strangled.

"Who, the boy?"

"That's me and—"

I cannot say father. Maybe I've gotten my stories mixed up. My human father? Story looks from me to the image. The two figures stand next to a small outbuilding at a larger site, a box that seems to be ten meters wide by twelve meters tall. The box is connected to a taller cylindrical structure that almost completely fills the image. Protruding from its top is a large machine wrapped around a thick cable extending beyond the top of the image.

"The Vine." She looks down at the device, grunts, and manages to go back to the first picture of the Dua boy and the human man. "You and some human, at the Vine."

"Yes." I force down the lump in my throat. "Are there more?"

Story touches the screen, scrolls through the images we've already seen, and stops on one taken from a wide angle. The platform floats in a wider sea, but in this image another structure hovers high above the platform. Two thick disks are connected by a narrow band between them. Wires protrude both above and below the disks in careful angles and connect them to a cable that would take them far above the platform, through the clouds, to yet another platform hovering above Earth.

"That's the elevator machine."

I study the waves at the image's bottom, notice the churning sea as it carries the platform's weight. Low, rounded buildings with large, octagonal windows at their tops surround another, taller building, its stories featuring outside walkways that encircle the structure. The tall cylinder in the middle of the platform extends several hundred feet in the air.

"What else?"

Story touches the device screen again, and the image changes perspective, showing the platform from the other side. On the left, a lower level floats just a few meters above water level.

"That's the port," I say, pointing to the projection. There are several docking areas, an outside marina, and what appears to be a garden. A few saplings grow along a clean walkway from the marina to a rounded, low building.

"The images are several decades old," Story says. "See where some of the buildings lack skins?" She points to a few low buildings still under construction.

"Can you go back to the first screen?" None of the icons have names, at least not in a recognizable sense. The icon Story tried first looks like something I've seen before in pictures, a device that takes images and processes them digitally in two dimensions. I study the others. One looks like two human heads with wavy lines extending between them. Another is a rectangular shape with random letters in straight, horizontal lines from top to bottom. Yet another is an image of the Earth. Story touches each one of these, but each time the same message flashes across a black screen: "No service." The last icon, in a corner of the digiscreen's face, is a large, rounded letter O. In the center of the O are tiny letters. C-O-R-P.

"That one," I say.

Story taps the digiscreen, and the wallscreen lights up with rows upon rows of tiny icons, some of them additional rectangular shapes with letters and some of them tiny drawings. Story taps an image that looks like a series of random lines. A blueprint.

"Platform schematics," Story says.

We return to the previous screen to try another tiny icon. The image pops up, yet another schematic of a different section of the Vine.

"This is cool, I guess," Story says. "Should we be looking for something, though? Something useful?"

"Keep trying."

She returns to the previous screen and selects another image. More Vine schematics. Then another: An image of the Vine. Story grunts. She touches several more icons, each file a different image than the last, but always of the Vine.

"How about this one."

"It's a different type of file," she murmurs. "Like a hologram, or something. Give me a minute." She sets the digiscreen on its face and fiddles around with some of the exposed chips. Then she taps her flexscreen. The conveyor rotates. Story retrieves a device, a six-inch pyramid; its sides shimmer with projection chips. She sets the pyramid on the table and pulls the digiscreen toward her. She taps its face a few times, then she touches the side of the pyramid. A beam of light extends to the room's ceiling and spreads to create another pyramid of light, a mirror image of the structure on the table. The light pyramid comes into focus to reveal a three-dimensional image of a head, which rotates slowly.

"At least this is different," Story mumbles.

The light pyramid shimmers softly as the image comes into focus, but I already know who it is. Bright blue eyes, white hair encircling her head in tiny curls. A smile that comforted me many times during my childhood.

"It's my mother." My eyes fill with tears. "That's my mother."

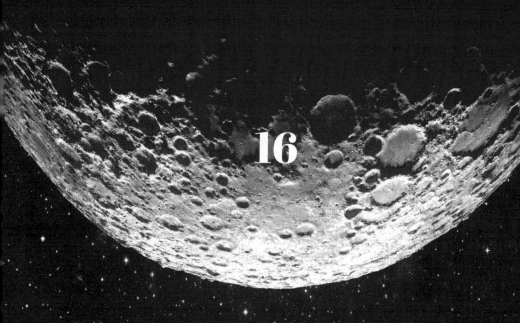

16

"I'VE NEVER IMAGINED her this way." I cannot take my eyes from my mother's holographic face. "She's happy, almost. Less broken, at least."

"Are you ready?"

I take in a deep breath. I know the story, the way my mother chose to tell it. Am I ready to see it unfold in front of me? "I'm ready."

She touches the digiscreen, and the image stabilizes. My mother blinks and squints her eyes, and I realize, with a smirk, she's unsure whether the recording feature is working. Always clumsy with tech. It's a wonder the digiscreen functions at all.

She clears her throat. "My son." She looks down, shakes her head. When she looks back up, her eyes are wet. "My greatest wish is to tell you these things in person. I'm generating this journal at the suggestion of my friend, your father, Owen Sakata. He is less sure of our survival in this scheme, though, and he wants to ensure this information is preserved in more than one place." A corner of her mouth turns down. "If this is the first time you've heard what I'm about to tell you, my child, please think kindly on us all. We did our best.

"Today is January 27, 2204. I was born on the moon in 2125, one of many children born to exiled Dua. The moon settlers. Vagabonders. We lived a peaceful life. The moon is harsh, cold, unforgiving. But we created a life. We found a way. Then OnyxCorp came in 2199.

"Since then, our lives have been very hard. We are made to work in places where humans cannot, and while we thought we were helping humans create a better world for us all, we soon learned that is not how humans see us. They took us from our homes in the lunar tunnels and put us in complexes that could only be described as prisons. We were made to work until we could work no more. Many died. We sought to change their minds. We asked for better treatment; we were met with Authority bots and more work. When we stopped asking and began demanding, we were arrested and—" She breaks off, turns her face away. She brushes a hand across her face. When she faces us again, her eyes are wet, and her jaw is clenched. "I was arrested when I attacked the human that killed my daughter."

She turns away again. Her shoulders shake.

You are her Earth child?

"What they did to them," Story breathes. "Your mother."

My mother looks back into the imager. "I've lost track of time. My fellow Dua and I've been the subjects of extensive testing by OnyxCorp medtechs. This information can be verified with the Corporation's public records and with Owen himself, who was assigned to the testing team. I provide this background so you know I've been in a position to witness the incidents I'll relate.

"The documents encrypted on this device provide all the evidence needed to confirm, but I'll summarize. The virus, Ruĝa Morto, isn't what everyone thinks. In the late twenty-first century, OnyxCorp commissioned a gene manipulator, a nanoprotein, to slow or stop the aging process. Nothing has the potential to manipulate humans more than the promise of eternal life; they'll pay almost anything to realize it. One of their scientists came through for them with a nanoprotein that was the basis for every medical breakthrough since. It worked so well OnyxCorp adapted the technology to a targeted bioweapon that could manipulate the genes that control aggression.

"Wealthy governments and private citizens increased demand for this new medtech so much that OnyxCorp struggled to keep up until it realized it could manufacture and sell more product if it delivered the bioweapon via virus."

"And mistakes were made," Story scoffs.

"OnyxCorp produced dozens of products they claimed were cures for this virus but weren't. They made trillions from desperate, sick people suffering from the virus it created. Then they used those profits to gobble up every other struggling medtech facility. No one else understood what Ruğa Morto was other than the Corporation. Any other lab that attempted to test the virus ended up spreading it. After it hit the med facilities, there was no stopping it. The humans created a monster that ate them all, and they don't even know it. OnyxCorp got away with genocide on a scale never imagined.

"I know this only because—" She pauses. She gazes down. "Because I fell in love with a human man, someone who knows the truth. You are his child, and I will not, *will not* raise you here, on this barren rock, with no future, no hope." She looks back down at her lap and smiles a soft, sad smile.

"The AI TES accounts for the number of fuel cells transported to and from Earth, but not their individual weight. A body can squeeze inside a fuel cell compartment easily without being detected. I'll be inside one of those compartments when the cargo is weighed."

How much radiation was she exposed to? The consequences to her health, her life. Images of my mother—frail, tired, often frightened—come flashing back.

"Owen transferred as many documents as he could to this digiscreen, and I'll be transferred to the shuttle in a fuel cell container tomorrow. With luck, I'll be back on Earth within a week. After that, a Dua outpost, somewhere remote. Somewhere safe. Until the time is right to share this information, to tell the world what they've done.

"I'm not a hero. I'm scared. For you. For me. I don't know what I'll do even if I do make it to Earth. How will I live? How will I take care of you? You won't be Dua, but you won't be human either. What does that mean? I don't have any answers. Maybe I never will. But know this, my dear one. You are special. You are of the Earth and of the moon. You are Vagabonder, and some day, when you see this, you will know that's important." She looks into the recorder for a few more seconds, her eyes dark, determined. The screen goes black.

I stare at the blank screen for a long time, reconciling the recording with the fairytales my mother concocted. In her telling, she never suffered the loss of a daughter on the moon. She never fell in love with a human. She never smuggled herself to Earth in a radiated fuel cell. In her telling, my origins had been simple: *You were conceived on the moon, but I wanted to raise you on Earth. I emigrated to SoAm, but you are of the moon, Caen. And it is your duty to free our people.*

"Owen Sakata." Story looks up from her flexscreen. "Are you ready for this?" I shake my head to pull myself out of my reverie. She holds the flexscreen toward me. It is a bio file for Dr. Owen Sakata: Professional career, credentials, personal information, and several images, both past and recent. He has sandy brown hair, kind eyes, and spectacles.

"The man in the images."

"Your father, if your mother is to be believed." Story tosses the flexscreen on the table between us and rises. "Caen, you're the one." She stops and faces me. "Dammit all. The One!"

"No!" Story jerks at the ferocity in my voice. "You're not putting that on me."

"You're half human, Caen. The bridge between the worlds and all that. Why didn't you tell me?"

"I didn't know."

"What?!"

"I didn't know!" I jump up, overturning my chair and sending it sliding across the floor and into the metal door behind me. "I knew I was conceived on the moon, that my mother was a descendant of the original moon dwellers, but my father—"

"This changes everything, Caen." Story unplugs the digiscreen from the cords and the light pyramid; she stuffs them back in their bins.

I imagine my mother huddled among fuel cells in the weightlessness of space as she makes a desperate journey to Earth. Leaving the only home she'd known, a home that had taken everything from her. Yet a home she still wanted to save.

Story hands the digiscreen to me, shakes it to get my attention. "Why are you just standing there? Put this away and let's get out of here. We have to get to Chege."

"I'm not going."

Story drops her arm to her side. "You have to. You must do something. Like she says."

"All this information, it's mysterious. But there's nothing here that ties it all together. It's just a jumble. A jumble of images and schematics and...video confessions that don't connect. I can't risk your life, my life, on that," I conclude, jabbing a finger toward the digiscreen.

"Yet you were willing to risk my life, your life, for your mother's stories."

"Because that's all I had!" I look around the room for something to punch, something to throw, something to break, anything to relieve the anger, the rage. "I was a child when I was sent away to a training camp for the DEP, no more than Kriz's age. The stories my mother told me, about me, about the Vagabonders, they were all I had to cling to. The only answers I ever got! Why was I all alone, hundreds of miles away from my family, learning how to kill with my bare hands? Because I am of the moon and destined to help my people? Why must I leave SoAm and travel to the moon? Because that's what my mother always told me was my destiny, to return to the moon, to lead the Vagabonders? The truth is no one person is responsible for this, for us. And no one Dua can fix it. Not you. Not me." I am shaking, on the verge of sobbing. I haven't cried since I was a child, but when I collapse on the dingy floor of the Reclamation kiosk, I let the tears flow. All this way. All this time. I am a fool for believing in stories, for believing that I could do anything that would make a difference.

Story sinks to the floor next to me, close enough that our shoulders touch. When she speaks, her voice is gentle. "I lost my faith when I found out how Wylan was working for them. In a way, that was more painful than finding out he was a phony...losing my belief, you know? Losing my innocence, understanding that the truth is complicated." She scoots closer to me so that she can put an arm across my shoulders. "Your mother's stories were about being heroic, about doing the right thing for others, about righting wrongs. Wylan's stories made me believe in the strengths of Dua, in our ability to make a better world for ourselves. I helped create what you see here because I believed in those stories. It hurts to let go of those things that make us feel good, make us feel like we belong, like we have a purpose.

"But what is right doesn't change, Caen. Wylan is a liar, but the story he told isn't a lie. We are strong. We can make a better world for ourselves. Your mother didn't tell you the entire truth, but that doesn't change the fact that you can make a difference. You already have." She gathers her legs beneath her and pushes herself up to standing.

"How have I possibly made a difference?" I ask angrily, wiping my sleeve across my eyes.

"For one, the information on that hunk of junk isn't hidden in some obscure city in SoAm anymore. I have it. And you'd better believe I won't keep it a secret. We can't continue in this way. The Corporation isn't going to decide one day to treat Dua better. I don't care what bullshit story Wylan tells. Humans have never willingly given up power. We must force them." She holds a hand out. Reluctantly, I take it, and she pulls me up. "But first, we have to get somewhere safe. Maybe you're not the One, Caen. Maybe humans and Dua share this weakness of believing someone is going to save them when we should be saving ourselves. But everyone needs something to believe in. I think you're just as good a choice as any, and better than most. The fact that you're being hunted, well, that just adds to the story, doesn't it?"

I don't agree with her, of course. She's made a motivating speech, and if I'd heard it a few days ago, before I knew what my mother's holy relic contained, I may have been inspired. But now—

"Let's get out of here," I say at last. "No reason to hang around, waiting to be captured. If I do nothing else, I should get you somewhere safe."

Half an hour later, we are winding our way through the Versteck on a meandering route to Paix Porteur. We pass dwellings and alcoves interspersed with gardens and gathering spaces. I marvel at the variety of fresh fruits and vegetables, and I can't resist popping a bright red grape into my mouth, straight from a winding vine. It is firm and juicy, the perfect balance of sweet and tart. In a park, young Dua children play. Some of them sit quietly on soft cushions and interact with holographic projections. Some older children gather around a tabletop over which a holographic representation of a human brain rotates. A pleasant voice responds to their questions and guides them as they explore the projection.

"I never imagined such a world possible for Dua."

Story looks over. "It's possible for both human and Dua. There has always been more than enough for both—"

We see her at the same time, only seconds before she sees us. Zady emerges from a machine shop just a few meters ahead, where disassembled hovobikes, sentinels, and other machines lean against the rock wall. The scents of grease and metal fill the air. In those seconds, three things happen.

Story grabs a sentinel's severed head, which rests on a table just outside the machine shop, and flexes her arm.

"Get to Paix Porteur. Follow the main tunnel until you can't go further." She hurls the head toward Zady just as Zady pulls an electristic from its holster at her side.

Zady sidesteps just in time to avoid having her face crushed by the metal sphere. I hear a crunch as the head slams into her collarbone. She groans but continues to lift the electristic. The shot hits the wall just to Story's left. Fragments from several hovobikes rain down on us.

"Go!" Story yells. She swings her leg up to kick the table on which the head had rested. It sails through the air toward Zady, who ducks to avoid it.

My instincts tell me to eliminate this threat now. But there could be more. And getting caught now isn't in my plans.

"I'm the one you want!" I wait just long enough to ensure Zady sees me. Her lips curl in a sneer. She raises the electristic in my direction as Story takes off the other way and disappears around a corner.

Then I run.

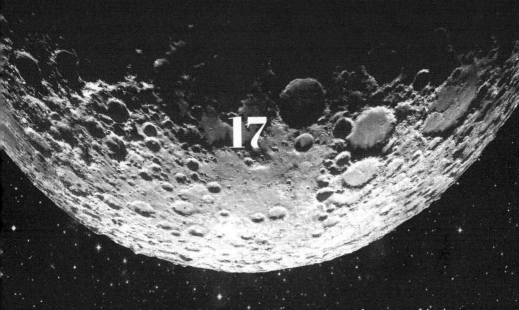

17

THE MAGLEV STATION in Mombasa isn't as busy as Ligeia expected. After all, Mombasa is *the* city, the center of it all. The gateway between Earth and the moon. The maglev comes to a gentle stop just as the first rays of dawn break through the clouds. Pinks, yellows, and oranges spread from the horizon like spilled watercolor until at last, the tiniest sliver of yellow overcomes the canvas and dominates the landscape. Even in the enclosed compartment, Ligeia can smell the salty ocean brine. She draws in a deep breath and tastes the African coast for the first time in her life.

Along with Sakata, she follows Erlang to the port authority to confirm their shipping cartons have arrived. Erlang holds her palm to an entry kiosk and scans the readout.

"They're all stored in the loading area designated for the *Constellation*, scheduled to depart for the Vine in twenty-four hours." She steps away from the kiosk. "A full day to enjoy the Earth beneath our feet. What shall we do?"

"We can't *not* see Mombasa," Ligeia says. "Who knows how long it'll be before we see a real city again."

"I've seen Mombasa." Sakata's shoulders slump. He's become despondent during the trip, even more after they witnessed the five

NiCIes disembark the maglev and find themselves surrounded by Authority. "You two should explore, though. There's no telling what you might find here. Avoid uptown. If you want to see the real Mombasa, you should head to the southeast edge. Trust me on that." He looks over at Erlang. "Permission to get some rest at our hotel?"

Erlang looks at Sakata, then at Ligeia, her dark eyes narrowed. Tugging at the bottom of her uniform jacket, she sighs. "You look like you could use it." She trains her eyes on Ligeia. "And you look like you're more likely to get into trouble. I'll be checking in with the Authority at the hotel, Sakata, to make sure you don't lose your way. And tomorrow, don't be late."

"Wouldn't dream of it, Erlang." Sakata disappears back into the port authority building, behind which their hotel awaits.

"Avoid uptown? That's where everything is," Erlang murmurs.

"Wouldn't you rather see things most people don't see? See how people actually live?"

"I know how people actually live. Are we going to see Mombasa or not?" Erlang puts a hand on her hip, pulls her sunshades from a jacket pocket, and adjusts them over her eyes.

Ligeia shrugs. "Fine. But if it gets boring, we're going southeast. This is my last day on Earth, Erlang. I'm not wasting it on OnyxCorp ads."

While the streets of Maun were well-kept and clean, Mombasa's streets practically gleam. Ligeia stares, open mouthed, at every turn. Everything sparkles, glows, or shimmers.

In the morning sun, the city is blinding. Skyscrapers rise at regular intervals. White transports glide by with nothing more than a soft whoosh. Other walkers move around them, dressed in silvery OnyxCorp uniforms and chatting with each other or with unseen acquaintances through their comms. Soft music emanates from speakers placed along the walkway. Genetically enhanced flowers and plants hang from replicas 20th century lamp posts.

"Easy there, doc." Erlang grabs her by the upper arms to steer her around a woman emerging from a shiny mini stopped outside a brightly lit medtech kiosk, where several patrons sit in cushioned chairs. Thin wires extend from nanoportals behind their ears.

Ligeia smiles apologetically at the woman. "It's glorious, Erlang. I've seen pictures, but this is just beyond."

"Mombasa is where the money is. Everything going to and from the Vine, the Vine Station, and the moon flows through here."

They pass a NiCIe musician at the next corner. He draws a worn bow against thin violin strings, eliciting a soft, plaintive tune. Ligeia stops to listen, and for a few moments even Erlang seems to be entranced. A couple of passersby toss a credit key or two into the violin case on the sidewalk next to the musician as they hurry along. When the song is over, Ligeia claps as she grins over at Erlang.

"Wasn't that nice? It's so different from Maun, isn't it?"

Erlang grunts. "I don't see much difference. Maybe a little brighter polish."

"Come on, Erlang. NiCIes are everywhere. Look around." She gestures toward the violinist and a group of NiCIes who pass by, their heads down. "You'd never see them out like this in Maun."

Erlang raises an eyebrow. "If a little tree grows in the shade of a larger tree, it will die small."

Ligeia laughs. "What's that supposed to mean?"

Erlang digs into her jacket pocket and retrieves a credit key worth a few credits. She tosses it into the violinist's open case. "OnyxCorp casts a very big shadow, doc."

THEY'VE BEEN SIGHTSEEING a couple of hours when they come across a café; the glowing sign outside proclaims its name: *Minazi*.

"I could use something," Ligeia says. "You?"

Erlang tosses her head noncommittally, but they slip inside, where a NiCIe hostess guides them to a round table in the corner of a covered patio. The hostess pulls out their chairs, then taps the top of the table to reveal a menu.

"How may I serve you?" She wears a typical white coverall, her long white hair organized in a thick plait.

"Coffee."

"The same," Erlang says. The hostess disappears into the café's interior.

Passersby on the walkway adjacent to where they sit are a mixture of business types, obvious tourists, and NiCIes. Ligeia observes the café's other customers in turn. A man several tables over with two women laughs loudly, and the women giggle. One of them covers her mouth with a hand. At another table an elderly woman with a silver braid sips a red cocktail and reads a flexscreen. At the table closest to Ligeia and Erlang sit a middle-aged couple, their heads bent toward each other.

"What a great city." Ligeia stretches her legs in front of her beneath the table. "It's clean, easy to navigate. And so advanced compared to Maun. Human and NiCIe, together. That's the way it should be. Back home, NiCIes couldn't even enter the city outside of curfew."

Erlang scoffs. "You're a smart woman, Dr. Obumbwe. Makes me wonder sometimes how you can be so naïve."

"What does that mean?" The hostess interrupts whatever Erlang may have been about to say with their drinks. Erlang picks up her cup, blows on it, and brings it to her lips. Ligeia does the same, barely tasting the perfectly temperate bitterness. *I'm being escorted to the moon, I get that. But I can do without the attitude.* "What do you mean, I'm naïve?"

Erlang sets the mug down, leans back, and regards Ligeia. "You see NiCIes walking around, free to mingle with humans, and you assume that means Mombasa is somehow enlightened. That what you saw back in Maun is an anomaly. You're thinking, we can live together in harmony, just like Mombasa. Do you really see humans and NiCIes living in harmony here? Look around."

Frowning, Ligeia turns her head to glance around the café again. "And what should I be seeing?"

"You see any NiCIes being served here? You see any NiCIes and humans sitting together, sharing a cup of coffee and their life stories?"

Ligeia glances around behind her. A woman in a silver jacket, her face obscured by a hood pulled close to her face, huddles at another table where the NiCIe server kneels next to her. The server leans close to the woman, whispers something, puts a hand gently on the woman's arm.

"What about that?" Ligeia says, jutting a thumb behind her. "They look pretty friendly."

"You really have no clue, do you?"

"Enlighten me, Erlang."

Erlang puts an arm on the table and leans forward. "That's a NiCIe at that table, trying to blend in. She's hiding from something."

Ligeia rolls her eyes. "Really, Erlang. Have you always been this cynical? Even if that is a NiCIe, why would she be hiding? They're everywhere."

As if on cue, an Authority bot enters the café building; its metal feet clang against the polished tile marking the café's threshold. Behind Ligeia, a chair scrapes across the tile as if in response.

"No!" A sharp whisper draws Ligeia's attention to the table behind her. The NiCIe server stands, her eyes wide and frightened. "No," the server says again. The woman at the table grasps the server's forearm as she glances around her. Her eyes meet Ligeia's.

Blue.

No matter how many times Ligeia sees them, they are always breathtaking. She turns back to face Erlang.

"How did you know?"

Erlang downs the contents of her mug, sets the empty container on the table, and draws aside her worn civilian jacket. She points to the insignia on the crisp white shirt beneath.

"My job."

The Authority emerges from the building's interior; its bulk fills the patio's entrance as it scans the area, its orange eyes glowing beneath the dark visor.

"What's going on?"

"A search, looks like."

"A search? For whom?" Erlang gives Ligeia a look that suggests she's never heard such a stupid question. "The NiCIe?"

"Probably not that NiCIe, no, but she thinks they're here for her, which means she's going to do something she shouldn't."

Ligeia casts a quick glance back. The NiCIe's pulled the hood farther down over her face. The server is nowhere to be found.

"What will happen to her?" Ligeia whispers.

"Well, that depends on what she does. But, probably nothing good."

The Authority makes its way around the table at the far side of the patio.

"You're Authority," Ligeia offers. "You could stop it. Take her into custody yourself."

The bot's heavy footsteps clink against the tile as it strides to the older woman's table. Erlang reaches inside her jacket and pulls out a drugstic. Clicking it on, she takes a long drag and blows out the vapor. Her hand shakes a little as she lowers it to the armrest, the drugstic between her fingers. "I can't."

"You can't? You're the goddamn Director of Authority, Erlang."

"I can't because it's a SoAm investigation, doctor know-it-all. I work for OnyxCorp, get it? I'm not some arbiter of justice. I'm a corporate lackey turned glorified babysitter."

The bot advances methodically to each table, drawing closer to where they sit. Where the NiCIe sits.

"What investigation?"

Erlang squints. "What's that?"

"You said this was a SoAm investigation. What's going on?"

Erlang stretches her neck, ear over shoulder, one side then the other. "You should pay more attention to the news. Some NiCIe from a SoAm terrorist group came on the grid and then disappeared. SoAm thinks he's trying to get to the Vine. They're searching everyone."

Ligeia narrows her eyes. "Why the Vine?"

"I don't know. Break it? Blow it up?"

Ligeia blinks. "But...She's not who they're looking for."

"Not at all, but she's done something. She's hiding for a reason."

Ligeia slams a fist on the table. "Why are you so against them? You have a niece—"

"Stop right there, doctor. Don't ever mention her to me again, do you understand?"

For a moment Ligeia thinks Erlang is going to hit her. "Ok. I get it. I crossed a line. I'm sorry."

The bot approaches the couple at the table adjacent to theirs. It takes their registries and scans them to confirm their identities.

"I want to help them, Erlang. I want to do something to help them, to help them all, like—my brother."

Erlang leans her forearms across the table. "Again, I am amazed by your innocence, doctor. You can't save them all. If you don't know that, you should get used to it very quickly."

"We can save that one! I'm asking the Authority Director to step in to save one NiCIe. Just one." The bot strides past their table, as if they weren't there. "What's the risk to you?"

"Registry." The bot's electronic voice is surprisingly soft as it drifts to them from the table behind Ligeia. She turns to see the bot's mechanical hand stretched toward the NiCIe woman, whose face is still obscured.

"She's with us." Ligeia rises as the words tumble out, unsure of her next move even as she speaks. "There's no need."

The bot's head rotates, and its sienna eyes hold steady as they scan her. Ligeia glances over at Erlang, who has the drugstic between her lips. Her eye twitches, but she makes no other move. The bot's head rotates back to the NiCIe. "Registry."

"I told you, there's no need." Ligeia pushes her chair away and strides toward the bot.

"This is your third and final warning." The bot's right subarm moves to hover over its stunstic. "Registry."

"I don't have a registry, bot," the NiCIe says, spitting the last word. "I don't belong to you. Any of you." She glances at Ligeia as she draws back the hood, revealing a cloud of short white hair and defiant azure eyes. In that moment, Ligeia knows that she is going to run.

The bot grips the stunstic. "NiCIe, you will come with me."

"Like hell."

The bot brings the stunstic up, levels it at the NiCIe. The expression on the NiCIe's face seems preternaturally calm, as if she has already accepted her fate. The café is deadly silent, the human onlookers passively accepting how this is going down. How it always goes down.

Ligeia takes a step backward, then launches herself toward the bot, her arms outstretched. The impact ripples up through her wrists, arms, and shoulders, and she stumbles back awkwardly, every muscle, every bone in her body vibrating with pain.

The bot doesn't move a millimeter.

But Ligeia's impulsive move allows the NiCIe to duck beneath the table and scramble out the other side. She careens through the café and upsets the table where the middle-aged couple sits, their mouths agape as cups, saucers, coffee, and biscuits fly through the air. The NiCIe swipes right and left at the chairs along her way. She heads for the crowded walkway, her only obstacles a short partition that separates it from the patio and a man sitting next to the partition. Seeing her approach, he stands, bends his knees and flexes his arms, and leaps toward the NiCIe as she zooms past. He misses her by decimeters. The woman swerves and jumps over the partition, easily clearing it to land on the walkway on the other side.

The man's chin makes a soft, squelching crunch as it meets the tile.

It all happens so fast that Ligeia almost misses the bot pull the stunstic and aim it at the fleeing NiCIe.

Not the stunstic.

The electristic.

"No!" Ligeia leaps for the bot's subarm, catches it with both hands, and pulls it down with all her weight. But it's a fraction of a second too late.

The blast hits the running NiCIe, already dozens of meters away, square in her side. She collapses like a marionette.

"No!" Ligeia's scream reverberates throughout the café. Releasing the bot, she rushes forward, winds through the overturned furniture, the broken mugs and plates. She dodges the fallen man, who cups his chin as blood drips between his fingers.

"Ligeia Obumbwe, you will wait here for Authority Admin," the bot calls. "Ligeia Obumbwe, you will wait here for further instructions."

"Fuck you, bot!" Everyone stares at her now. The patrons in the café. The passersby on the walkway. The NiCIe server. Even the small crowd that inches toward the NiCIe as she lay on the polished Mombasa pavement. "Get away!" Ligeia falls to her knees next to the NiCIe. She places a hand at the side of the woman's neck. A faint pulse. Growing fainter. A pool of bright red blood oozes across the tile from a gaping wound through her torso. Gently, Ligeia rolls her to her side. The NiCIe breathes shallowly. She lifts a hand to grip Ligeia's lapel.

"Shh," Ligeia says. She removes her jacket and pushes it against the bloody wound. "Hang on."

"Listen." The NiCIe wheezes, and Ligeia leans close. "I need you to go...Paix Porteur...southeast border. Meet a friend..." The NiCIe shivers, draws in another painful breath as Ligeia puts more pressure against the jacket. The thick pool of blood grows. "His name is Caen. Tall NiCIe. From SoAm. Find Chege...to help him."

SoAm. Ligeia wonders if this NiCIe is also a terrorist. Maybe she got what she deserved? The NiCIe draws in another shallow breath that rattles in her chest. "You can meet him yourself—" Ligeia begins. But she knows that's not true. The NiCIe is bleeding out, and no one is coming to help.

"Please. Promise. Tell...Kriz...I love...him."

Ligeia's hands are slippery and sticky with bright red blood, but she takes the NiCIe's hands into hers. "I'll do it. Paix Porteur, Caen. Find Chege. Tell Kriz you love him." The NiCIe takes another rattling breath. "What's your name?"

The corners of the NiCIe's soft pink mouth turn up, and her lips part. "Story."

Ligeia forces herself to watch as the light fades from the NiCIe's eyes. Her last breath leaves her lungs in a long, sad sigh. She forces herself to see what's happened. What has been happening all along. Just not to her.

Never to her, to humans.

"I'll find him, Story. I'm sorry." The tears spill from Ligeia's eyes and splash on the NiCIe's cheeks. Ligeia cradles the NiCIe's head in her lap, unaware of the bot until it speaks.

"Non-compliance with Authority orders is authorized for lethal action under NCI Code Section 189 Paragraph—"

"Save it, bot." Erlang waves her registry in front of the Authority's sienna eyes. "She's with me."

Ligeia lays Story's head gently on the walkway. She wipes the back of her hand across her eyes and pushes herself to her feet. She pulls her ruined jacket from beneath Story's body and tries to wipe the blood from her hands.

Erlang, bot, café patrons, the crowd on the walkway: They all stare. Glowering, Ligeia returns their gaze. "You all aren't worth saving." Erlang takes a step toward her, and Ligeia points a finger at the Director's chest. "That includes you."

Ligeia glances down at the body on the pristine walkway, allows the scene to fill her eyes, the image to burn into her memory so that it can't be erased.

Then she strides down the pathway, takes the next turn toward the southeast, and blends in with the rest of Mombasa, leaving Erlang's angry calls behind.

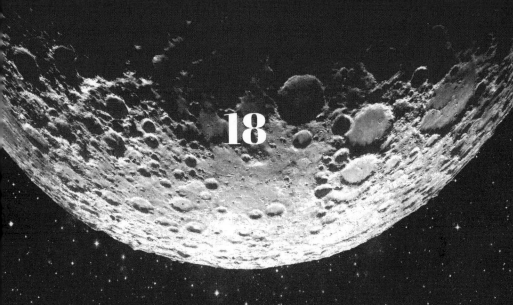

18

I SURPRISE the bot as I round the first corner, enough that its aim is thrown off. The electristic blast misses my head by mere centimeters; glass and tile rain down from the wall behind me and rake across my cheek and neck. I flinch at a sharp pain at the top of my shoulder as I roll to the left to avoid another blast and scramble to my feet to charge. The bot seems to hesitate at the unusual maneuver, which gives me time to grasp its left subarm and twist as I sidestep around it. The subarm screeches as metal and gears and cable separate. The robotic hand opens, releasing the electristic, which clatters to the ground.

The bot reaches for the stunstic at its right, but before it can take aim, I bring its severed arm against the bot's dark head. The bot stumbles, topples, and falls. I swipe up the electristic as another blast sends fragments of ground up toward my face.

Zady closes the distance between us, her arm raised, weapon pointed forward. I dig my feet into the ground and sprint down the street toward the next corner. I know I can lose her, can outrun her, if I can just make it to the corner. I veer slightly to the left, ready to make a quick dash into the alley, and I just begin the turn when searing pain screams across the width of my back. I stumble forward with a low groan, catching myself on my left forearm and knees. I roll away just as another blast explodes across the ground. I twist, gather my feet beneath me, and stand, bringing the electristic up with me, aiming carefully.

The blast flies far wide of Zady's left. I aim again a meter to her right. She slows and approaches with her weapon raised.

"Don't make me do it." I hold the electristic steady, even as I struggle to keep my breathing regular. "Please."

She walks toward me, her steps slow and practiced. She looks at me over her weapon's barrel. "You should've stayed in SoAm."

I mean for the shot to hit her hand. Instead, it tears through her shoulder. Zady drops the electristic as she jerks and lands on her back with a grunt.

I leap forward as she kicks up her legs and catches me in the stomach with a low growl. I slide to my knees as she twists and slams an elbow into my ribs. She crawls toward her electristic, groaning with pain. Her fingertips touch the barrel just as I reach for her injured arm, grab her wrist, and pull the arm behind her.

Zady screams and falls forward, twisting her body around to kick at me. I rise slowly, wrenching her arm even more. She whimpers, tries desperately to wriggle free.

"Please stop. I don't want to hurt you more." She lands a few wild kicks to my shins, but finally she loses steam. A few seconds later, she stops struggling. I loosen my grip, a little at first. Then a little more. She doesn't move. I let go of her arm and take a step backward.

"Tell Wylan to stay out of my way, and to leave Story alone." Zady pushes herself to hands and knees; her right arm buckles as blood oozes from her wounded shoulder. She stands with her back to me. "Tell him I mean it."

She spins hard on her heel, takes a step back, then launches herself. Her fist smashes across my jaw, snapping my head back.

Instinctively, I double my fist and bring it across her temple. Her eyes wobble, then roll back into her head. She stumbles once, twice, then crumples.

"Dammit." I kneel over her. Her pulse is rapid but steady at her throat. I shake my head to clear it. I didn't mean to hit her that hard.

"Halt!" The electronic voice is unmistakable.

Why are there so many Authority in the Versteck?

The walkway half a meter to my right explodes, spraying me with shards of tile that bite into my skin like tiny teeth. I dash to my right. Another shot is clearly aimed at my head, as the corner of a building bursts wide open, sending splinters toward my face as I make another right into the alley. I look wildly around, take the next left. The next blast is farther away, but I must find a way to lose them, and soon.

Left, left, right, left. Another right.

Suddenly, I've run out of room. In fact, I've run out of Versteck entirely.

A concrete wall stands before me, and to my left is rock and earth. To the right are storage containers stacked ten high and twenty across. Behind me are the bots.

I retrace my steps, my ears attuned for the bots' mechanic whir, my body tense. I almost miss the tunnel entrance—a mismatched container, lying at an angle. A slight change in airflow draws my attention. I lift the container and move it easily to the side to peer into a narrow tunnel. The sounds and smells of Mombasa drift toward me —humans, transports, food, fresh air.

The faint clang of robot footfalls echoes only a few meters away. I grasp the container and back into the tunnel, pulling the container behind me, and balance it over the entrance as best I can. Then I sink against the tunnel wall, grateful for the cool darkness that envelops me.

My back throbs. I gently pull a glass shard from my shoulder, and a rush of blood wells up and coats the white sleeve of my uniform in crimson. I unfasten the bib, pull my arms from the sleeves, and shrug the top of the uniform from my torso. The gash across my back burns. I tear off a sleeve, wrap it as tightly as I dare around my shoulder, and tie the ends beneath my armpit. Then I run a hand across my cheek and down my neck. Dried flakes of blood coat my palm. I reach around to the wound on my back. It isn't deep, and already the blood is coagulating. It hurts like hell, though.

I take stock of the rest of my body. My jaw aches where Zady punched me, and I'm covered from head to toe in bits of tile and glass and earth. I lean over to shake the debris from my hair.

The clink of metal on tile draws closer. No more time. I stand, pull the remaining sleeve over my arm, and fasten the bib. Then I tear up the tunnel, listening for any movement behind me, anything that could possibly warn me. Give me a fighting chance, at least.

The tunnel rises, twists a little right, and suddenly it ends at a red metal door. The city is louder here. I catch the *whoosh* of a maglev overhead, as well as voices, foot traffic, people going about their business. I try the door and am surprised that it opens into a dimly lit storeroom crammed with shipping containers. One closest to the door is open, piled high with all sorts of foodstuffs: Protein packets, chalky wafers, dried fruits.

I step into the room and close the door gently behind me. Grabbing a handful of protein packets and stuffing them into my backpack, I slink past containers labeled with symbols for their contents—organic compounds for NutriPrints, nanohardware, medtech equipment. I tear open a medtech container and dig through its contents until I find a nanosuture tool. I unwrap the sleeve from my shoulder and seal the still-bleeding wound. Then I shrug out of the uniform again and seal the gash across my back as best I can. I rummage through a few containers marked for textiles, but they're filled with human clothing, which would certainly draw attention. At last, I find a tunic that looks generic enough. It may get a few looks, but fewer than my bare, bleeding back would. I pull it over my head as I work my way through the storeroom.

Finally, I reach another red metal door. Locked. I pull down on the handle and break it off with a sharp twist. Holding my breath, I push the door open, just a crack, and peek through.

A human man rushes past me, close enough that I can smell synth on his breath. Then another man, a woman, a group of three women. I close the crack, keeping it ajar just enough to peer down the walkway. It's crowded with people. Unsure of what to do next, I watch for several minutes, looking for Dua. I notice only a few, but the humans don't react in a way that suggests they're out of place. I look down at myself. The knees of my uniform are thick with grime. My back is sticky and hot, although the pain has subsided to a dull throb. I squint back through the crack, waiting for a break in the flow. A group of Dua comes my way, four of them. I grip the door, fling it open as the Dua pass, and fall in step behind them, nearly careening into the Dua closest to me.

She doesn't break her stride, but she gives me a wide-eyed look of surprise. Her hair is arranged in neat braids bound together at the nape of her long neck.

"Paix Porteur," I say in a low voice. "Do you know it?"

"Yes."

"Where can I find it?"

The Dua skip-steps to match my stride. "Keep looking forward. Stay with us until I tell you to move. You'll break left to go southeast, toward the port."

"Got it." I keep my arms stiffly at my side and try to keep my head forward. Humans swarm all around us, and I struggle to avoid their eyes.

"You're him, aren't you? The SoAm Dua."

I cut my eyes across to her. *Not all Dua are friends.* "I am from SoAm."

"Authority are turning this city upside down looking for you."

"Just point me in the right direction."

"They're arresting a lot of us. One was killed. Because they're looking for you."

I clench my jaw. "I don't want any harm to come to anyone."

"Then what are you doing here? It's hard enough already—"

"Just tell me where to go."

The Dua frowns. "A few more blocks." A human steps aside for us and stares curiously at me as we pass. Or am I just imagining it? The other Dua pull ahead of us. "This isn't SoAm. Maybe they'll join your movement there, but here—"

"I'm not part of some damn movement."

She cuts a glance toward me. "We don't want it here. You're going to make the next left. Follow the alley until it dead ends, then make a right. The Paix is sandwiched between two metal buildings." She turns her head to meet my eyes. "It would be better if you turned yourself in."

I spin on my left foot and duck into the alley, not daring to stop until I've reached the dead-end. Pressing myself against the wall, I look back toward the main street. The foot traffic continues. A white transport whirs by.

We don't want it here. Do they all feel that way? I take a breath and peek around the corner.

The side street is lined with small residential dwellings. Solar lights line the walkway, and a few homes boast a garden box in front, filled with bright flowers, tomatoes, herbs, or vegetables. Across the street, a Dua woman pauses in her raking to regard me curiously. Otherwise, the street is empty. I glance behind me one last time and listen for the screech of metal on tile. Nothing. I step around the corner and stride down the street, focused on striking a balance between watchfulness and not looking watchful.

Southeast toward the port. Between two metal buildings.

Voices drift toward me from up ahead. The sound grows, and half a minute later I find myself in the middle of an outdoor market, crowded with humans. I jog through, rushing but trying not to rush, avoiding the eyes that turn to follow me. A human child runs across my path, glances briefly in my direction, and continues. A group of humans gather around a kiosk a few meters ahead. Everywhere I look, humans and—

And Dua.

Together.

I slow down. Another kiosk comes up on my left, and the smell of roasting meat emanates from an iron grill set above red-hot coals. Around the kiosk stand more than a dozen humans and Dua; their children—Dua children!—dodge between the adults, their faces brilliant with perspiration. As I pass, a human man and Dua woman glance my way. The Dua smiles broadly and lifts a hand, then stops. Her mouth drops open as she takes in my appearance.

The uniform and the tunic are one thing, but I suddenly realize my face is probably covered in blood and dirt. I speed up, darting through the crowd and leaving the scene behind within the next block. Breathing heavily, I listen for sounds of pursuit, but the chatter subsides until it is gone completely, leaving me in silence.

What is this place? All those humans and Dua. Together. I've never seen anything like it. Never imagined anything like it.

The Paix is at the border between our world and theirs. I'd only half understood what Story meant. But those humans, those Dua. It was like there was no difference.

No separation.

I feel a layer of heaviness peel away, and the beginnings of a smile tug at the corners of my mouth.

Then a bot steps from between two buildings a dozen meters ahead.

I duck into a narrow walkway between neatly manicured hedges. The bot's rotating head whines behind me, and I imagine its sensors boring into my back, my head. I turn behind a dwelling and break into an easy run, zigzagging up and down alleys, making my way southeast to Paix Porteur.

To Peace Bearer.

19

PAIX PORTEUR IS easy enough to find. Ligeia follows a steady bass beat until she's close enough for it to infiltrate her body. Paix Porteur's rhythmic pulse, its steady thump thump, louder, deeper, hypnotic, pulls her forward. The sun begins its descent, and as brilliant as Mombasa is in the light of day, it's mesmerizing in the early evening, as the sunlight fades and the city's nightlife takes hold. Buildings are alight with a multitude of colors, and the air is cool, crisp. The further southeast Ligeia travels, the less brilliant the city is; the illuminated signs and buildings give way to smaller, more modest structures, dwellings perhaps.

She also notices more NiCIes among the human residents. It takes her a while to realize most of them aren't dressed in their usual white coveralls. Everyone she encounters, human and NiCIe alike, wears floaty tunics and loose trousers, much like the garments Sakata wore at the Symposium. Many cast strange looks at her as she passes among them; her ISA insignia and her silver-grey garments stand out here in a way they never have before.

The beat grows louder, and she spies a group ahead. Their laughter echoes against the industrial buildings that characterize Mombasa's far southeast edge. Even from a distance, she can tell they're dressed for a night out. She quickens her pace to catch up with them; they make a right turn and disappear as they round a metallic building. A few seconds later, she turns the corner and jogs straight into an alley where, at the corner of the building on the right, pale light streams across the concrete through an open metal door. The group is just stepping into the dim opening when Ligeia pauses, notes the flashing holographic signage above the door: Paix Porteur.

Unsure, she takes only a few steps into the dark corridor. Story's words come to mind: *Chege. He can help Caen. Tell Kriz I love him.* The only illumination is the pulse of flashing lights several meters away, in rhythm to the steady beat. Her chest thumps in time, and the music seizes her, pulls her into the darkness, sends her head spinning. She stretches her hands out at her sides, feeling for a wall, something to orient her. The light coruscates blue, red, green, purple, orange, blue, the steady bass beat completely envelops her, and suddenly she stumbles into a warehouse, its spaciousness made less so with the throbbing, vibrating beat. Humans and NCIs in strange clothing gyrate under more pulsing lights to a steady *thrum thump thrum*. Ancient vinyl booths and deteriorating tables of all shapes and colors line the walls, push up against wallscreens, and are nestled in dark corners. The regular hum of voices mixes with the music. A NiCIe male, his torso bare above a knee-length piece of white cloth, glides in front of her, a tray filled with beverages held steady above his head. A human female, her torso naked above her knee-length white skirt, passes by in the opposite direction, her tray filled with empty containers.

Ligeia freezes, her mouth agape. A young human female bounces past, her hair dyed a bright red and piled high atop her head. Her eyes are thickly lined in black, and she wears a tight shirt of natural fabric, synthetic black boots that reach to the middle of her thighs, and a black skirt several inches above their tops.

Ligeia glances down at her dull grey suit and realizes she's going to have a little difficulty blending in. A young NiCIe man dressed in tight-fitting blue trousers reaches for the young woman's arm, twirls her around, and pulls her close.

Ligeia is not unfamiliar with places like this one. She was a young person once, although far too serious to be much of a party goer. But this place, human and NCIs together, celebrating a human culture long gone. She's intruding, and she considers leaving for a second.

Do I cross over? Is this the moment when I find out what's on the other side?

She catches the arm of a passing human server.

"Where can I find Chege?"

The woman narrows her eyes. Balancing the tray in her left hand, she points toward a far corner. "Bar!" She turns on her heel without waiting for a reply.

Winnowing her way through the crowd, Ligeia finds the bar behind some barricades, about two meters tall, made of metal and natural fabric to muffle the music and clamor slightly. Mismatched stools, some of them wood with cracked and missing spokes, others made of twisted iron and other metals, wait at the bar. At one end, an NiCIe bartender places drinks neatly on a tray, his bare torso covered in a sort of bib that covers his chest, tied at the neck and around his waist. He gives Ligeia a quick look as she hoists herself onto a cracked leather stool covered with what was probably ostentatious embroidery work. She touches the animal skin gently with her fingertips, marveling at its unfamiliar texture. A few chairs away an NiCIe male sits. He glances at her briefly, then looks away quickly before their eyes meet.

"What can I get you?" The barkeep's blue eyes glint in the pulsing lights.

"I'm looking for Chege."

He raises an eyebrow. "Popular guy tonight." He casts a glance toward the NiCIe a few seats over. He produces a short glass container and fills it with clear liquid from a decanter he retrieves from beneath the bar. "I'll see what I can do, for both of you." He disappears through a door at the far end of the bar into a dimly lit corridor.

Ligeia picks up the glass and sniffs the contents. She reads the words etched into the glass across a large black circle with two smaller circles above it. *"The Happiest Place on Earth,"* she muses.

"Why are you looking for Chege?"

The NiCIe's accent is unusual. Ligeia swivels to get a better look at him. Full mouth, aquiline nose, olive skin, spiky white hair. He wears an ill-fitting tunic over dingy white trousers and boasts several wicked looking cuts across his face. She brings the glass to her lips, swallows, and enjoys the warmth that trickles down her throat and into her stomach. "I have business with him," she says, meeting his eyes.

"What kind of business?"

"My business."

He frowns, leans away. "My apologies. I hope you don't mind that I speak with him first, then. My business is urgent."

He stares unnervingly at her, making her more than a little uncomfortable, particularly when she finds herself unable to wrest her eyes from his. Dark blue, like sapphires, like the ocean. Like the sky at night. The accent—

"Where are you from?"

He eyes her jacket and its insignia. He clenches his jaw. "I think that's my business."

Ligeia leans closer. "I'm just asking because—" She swallows. "Are you—Are you Caen?"

He raises an eyebrow, then slides from the stool to stand beside her. Ligeia cranes her neck to look up at him. *Unusually tall.* "Who's asking?" His voice is soft and deep.

"Ah, well, my name is Ligeia Obumbwe." Her own voice sounds small and squeaky to her ears. He takes a step closer to her.

"And who are you, Ligeia Obumbwe, to know my name? Who are you with?"

He's so close she can feel his breath on her face.

I should be afraid, yet I've never felt safer.

Ligeia clears her throat. "Story sent me. She said her name was Story."

He brightens, glances around the bar area as if Story were hiding somewhere, waiting to surprise him. "Where is she?"

"She sent me here to find you. Her last words were—" Ligeia could bite her tongue off now as his face falls. He clenches his jaw, pounds a fist softly against the bar.

"She's dead."

"I'm sorry." Ligeia takes a breath. *Damn, I'm bad at this.* "We were in a café, and she was hiding. I didn't know why, but the Authority I was with said—"

"You're Authority?" Caen steps away, casts a glance around them.

"No, no, I'm International Science Academy. I'm being escorted by Authority, though, to the moon—"

He grabs her upper arm. Not hard. Urgent. "Please. Tell me everything."

So, she does. She tells him why she's in Mombasa, why she's traveling with the Authority Director herself, and how she ended up cradling a dying NiCIe's head in her lap on the sidewalk outside a café on her last full day on dry earth.

"She told me to find you, to tell you that Chege could help you." She wants to remember the words just right. "She said, 'Tell Kriz I love him.'"

"Her son." Caen sinks onto the barstool next to hers. "My fault. My fault. I never should have gone home with Kriz that evening. I put them all in danger."

You've delivered your message.

Ligeia acknowledges the voice, the one that's always kept her from crossing the line, from going over the edge. She could leave now. She should leave now.

What would Finn want me to do?

An image of her brother flashes in her mind's eye, their last conversation.

We are you. You are we. Unification is the answer.

"You're him, aren't you?" she whispers as she leans in. Caen smells of blood and sweat and earth. "You're the SoAm NiCIe they're looking for."

He sits straight, runs a hand through his hair and across the back of his neck, and glares. "We call ourselves Dua."

You don't get to use that word with me is implied.

Ligeia feels her cheeks flush. "Dua. I apologize."

Some of the hardness disappears from his eyes. Caen puts his palms together at his heart. "Thank you, for delivering her message, Ligeia Obumbwe." Her name sounds exotic on his tongue. The hairs on the back of her neck prickle.

"You're welcome."

They glance at one another. Their eyes meet. They turn away, both chuckling nervously.

"International Science Academy. You're a scientist."

"I am." She is on the verge of grinning, which seems completely inappropriate yet also unavoidable. *What is going on with me?*

"What kind of science?"

Ligeia looks down at the empty shot glass, wishing she had something in it. "I, ah, study Dua. The Dua genome, anyway."

Caen clears his throat. "Interesting. And what do you know about my genome?"

"Well, um, I guess I would say Ni—I mean, Dua have diverged quickly from humans since the initial outbreaks and have become an entirely new species within just a few generations—" She swallows against the lump in her throat. "I never realized how offensive my work is until I said it out loud to you."

Caen smirks. "No. I appreciate the interest. We're different from you in many ways, and you want to know why. What makes us, at the cellular level, *inferior* to you."

Ligeia's nose twitches. "That's not it at all. Maybe for some people, but not me. I don't think you're inferior. I have a brother who became a Ni—Dua, and I love him. I would do anything for him, including going to the damn moon."

Caen cocks his head. "OK, you're different. You cared about Story's death. You even took the time to deliver a message for her. I guess that makes you less of a threat. But you don't see Dua for what they are. You don't see us as beings. We're science to you."

Pressing her lips together, Ligeia nods. "I don't know about Dua culture, no. I should learn."

"You should, because, 'I have a Dua brother' doesn't make you an ally."

That stings a little.

Caen's leg bounces nervously as he stares at the corridor into which the bartender had disappeared.

"I, uh, wonder what's taking so long'" Ligeia begins, when suddenly the music drops.

"Paix Porteur!"

She and Caen both flinch as the voice echoes throughout the crowded warehouse. A roar explodes from the crowd on the other side of the barricade. The lights above the dance floor flash slow and steady, switching from green to red to blue to violet to orange to yellow and back to green.

"What's going on?" Ligeia dares a glance at Caen.

A corner of his mouth turns up. "Peace Bearer. It's a Dua ritual. Interesting it's being performed before humans." He cocks his head, gives her a more appraising stare. Then, holding out his hand, he slides from his chair and covers the distance between them. "Lesson 1."

His hand envelops hers.

"Oh, I can't—" But he pulls her from her barstool, around the barricades, and to the edge of the dance floor. Humans and Dua are squeezed shoulder to shoulder, their faces upturned to a tall human woman with deep brown skin who stands on a low platform. She raises her arms above her head, and the crowd cheers.

"Paix Porteur!" Her voice is amplified by a digital mic implanted in her throat. "I honor your being."

"We honor your being," the crowd repeats.

"Paix Porteur, you arose from the ashes of Ruĝa Morto," the woman chants.

"Out of the one, many have suffered," the crowd responds.

"Unprepared, unaware, innocent. Your difference is a threat, your empathy your downfall. Your children arose from the water of your tears," the woman sings.

"Out of the one, many have suffered."

Ligeia's shoulder brushes against Caen, sending an electric thrill down her spine. "It's fascinating," she murmurs.

"A ritual of binding," he whispers back. "Dua believe that separation is what brings suffering to beings, the idea that we are individuals without connection to one another. The binding ritual is meant to reclaim our bonds. First, there is the Call to Generations. Then, there is the Binding, which is a sort of dance. The third part depends on the occasion."

"Ignored, enslaved, wiser," the woman continues. "Your knowledge is a threat, your apathy, your downfall. Your children arose from the rubble of your expectations."

"Out of the one, many have suffered."

"Awake." She pauses, looks around the crowd. "Aware. Ignorant. Your action is a threat. Your arrogance is your downfall." She brings her hands in front of her, her palms together. "How will you nurture your children?"

A Dua female is lifted onto the platform, and she stands next to the dark woman. Her white hair is loose around her shoulders, and she is dressed in several gauzy layers of thin fabric that cling to her solid frame and accentuate her every move. She too brings her hands before her chest. They both bow to the crowd below.

"Out of the one, many will have hope." The crowd bows as one.

"A binding of human and Dua." Caen bends close, his breath hot against Ligeia's cheek. "I've never seen it used in that way before."

The Dua woman begins to sway. A soft beat begins, punctuated with electronic tones. The lights above the platform match the syncopated rhythm, and the woman throws an arm gracefully to her side, bending at her waist, then she sways to the other side, her arms stretching in elegant arcs, above her head, then down toward her bent knees. The crowd mimics her moves as she strides to the platform's edge, where four humans stand below her. She steps lightly from the platform onto their outstretched arms, and they lower her gently to the floor, where she continues her undulation as she moves through the crowd. As she passes, she touches some of the now-dancing crowd tenderly, caresses their shoulders, their faces.

"What are some of the occasions?" Ligeia asks, unable to take her eyes from the beautiful dancer.

"Births, deaths, coming of age." Caen pauses. "Partnering."

The Dua dancer traces a winding path around the dance floor and stops before Ligeia and Caen, where she holds out both arms. Unable to stop herself, Ligeia takes her hand. Immediately, an electric buzz runs up Ligeia's arm, into her shoulder, and filters down the length of her body. The woman sways with her, runs her open palm across Ligeia's cheek and smooths the wild curls from her eyes. She spins

Ligeia gently around and, as suddenly as she appeared, glides away, leaving a trail of energy in her wake, leaving Ligeia tingling all over and grinning. In fact, she's laughing as she skips back to Caen's side.

"What's funny?" he says, frowning a little.

"Nothing. I think that was a happy laugh."

"You think?"

Ligeia looks up, meets his eyes. In the flashing lights, they're almost black. His lips are curved in a half smile. Her face grows hot. "I, ah, don't think I laugh much." He looks at her in a way that puzzles her. A way that makes her feel like she knows him.

But there's no way I can know him.

"I—" she begins.

He takes her hands in his and swings her around again. Giddy with the gentle snap-wave of electronic tones rippling through her body, Ligeia laughs aloud.

"Follow my movements." He brings her close. He's solid, substantial. He wraps an arm around her shoulder to draw her closer, glides with her in a slow circle. "Listen to the words," he says as the human woman on the stage begins to sing.

"These are the steps we shall take together, so that we may never be alone."

Caen releases Ligeia's shoulder, spins her gently around so that they're standing side by side, hand in hand.

"These are the hands we shall use to work together, so that we may see our dreams."

Caen pulls Ligeia to him, takes her other hand in his. He gazes into her eyes, and the throbbing lights catch a glint of sapphire.

"These are the eyes we shall use to speak together, so that we may see the truth."

Taking a step away, Cane pushes Ligeia at arm's length, their hands still clasped, then pulls her to him, body to body, his arms around her in an embrace.

"These are the bodies we shall honor together, so that we may love one another as ourselves."

They sway together, arms entwined, bodies pressing against one another. Ligeia feels her head buzz in time with the music.

I can lift from the floor. Perhaps I'm already there, floating in the darkness of space, a warm body my only tether.

The music ends as the dancer regains the platform. She stands with her arms outstretched, gazes down at the still swaying crowd below her. "I honor your being." She bows as she touches her palms at her chest.

"We honor your being." The woman allows herself to be lifted from the platform again by two human men, who escort her across the dance floor and back toward the bar.

Caen and Ligeia suddenly realize they're still locked in an embrace. They back away from one another in an embarrassed silence.

"So, that's the ritual of binding." Caen half-smiles.

"It was nice."

"I'm sorry."

Ligeia smiles. "There's no reason to be."

"We need to get to Chege."

"OK. Let's find Chege."

THEY RETURN TO THE BAR, an uncomfortable distance separating them. The bartender seems surprised, maybe a little annoyed, they've returned. Nevertheless, he refills the last two glasses on a serving tray and motions for them as he places the decanter on a shelf behind him. They follow him behind the bar, where colored lights line the hall. Opening a door on the right, he motions them inside. "Here they are."

"I thought you'd lost 'em!"

Ligeia blinks as her eyes adjust to the sudden blinding light. Caen follows behind her, ducking slightly beneath the low door.

"Jesus, you're tall." The man who stands before them is a good thirty centimeters shorter than Ligeia. He has a short beard and wears a long tunic made of natural fibers. Elaborate embroidery decorates the hem, cuffs, and collar. Long, greying hair spills over his shoulders. "And you're human," he says, looking up at Ligeia.

"*You're* human," Caen responds.

"Yes, I know. Weird, right? I gotta lot to do, so, you say you...and you...are friends with Story. And why would she send you to me?"

Ligeia twitches. "I have a message for you."

Chege cocks his head. "Which she can't deliver because?"

"She's dead." Caen's voice is flat.

Chege's face falls. "So, I was right." He looks between them. "I guess there's probably more. Come."

He leads them through a narrow door into a dimly lit interior. The scents of sage and lemongrass fill the air. Rounded cushions are arranged in a neat circle around a low table, and upon one of the cushions lounges the Dua dancer. She's exchanged her gauzy layers for an embroidered robe, featuring abstract patterns in gold, orange, and dark blue, tied around her waist with a large crimson sash.

"Story's dead," Chege says.

The dancer nods solemnly. "I thought so. You were with her?" She directs her question to Caen.

"I was," Ligeia says. The woman's forehead wrinkles. "Authority. She ran, and—"

"Where was this?" Chege says.

"Some café, in uptown. I can't remember the name—"

"Why would she be in uptown?" the Dua woman says.

"We were running from Wylan," Caen says.

Chege and the woman jerk as if they've been struck.

"You're the one they're looking for," Chege says.

"But how did you meet each other?" the woman asks Caen.

"Wait a minute." Ligeia raises her hands. "Too many questions. Maybe we need to tell you what we came here to tell you."

"Fair enough." Chege sinks into the cushion next to the woman, who drapes an elegant arm across his shoulders. "Tell us. Why are you here?"

"I have only the name Chege." Caen stares at the dancer.

The woman bristles. "Riannon is my partner." Chege places a pudgy hand on the Dua's shapely knee. "Whatever you tell me, I will tell her. You may as well tell her in person."

Caen frowns. He casts a look at Ligeia, his brows furrowed.

"I'll go first," she says.

"Please. Sit." Chege indicates the cushions opposite him and his partner. Ligeia gives Caen a smile that he doesn't return. They both sit, stiffly.

"Well, ah. I'm here to catch the next boat to the Vine," Ligeia begins. She tells them the same story she'd told Caen, up to Story's final words.

"She wasn't their target, but she didn't know that. She wanted you to tell Kriz that she loved him."

"The poor boy." Chege shakes his head. "This is bad news. Really bad. And you're the cause of all this trouble?"

Caen shifts under Chege's direct gaze. "Yes, I suppose I am."

"Authority in uptown. So close to the Versteck." Chege frowns. "I don't like the sound of that."

"It only confirms our suspicions," Riannon says. "There are rumors of sentinels in the villages."

"I can confirm that rumor. One attacked me in Story's village." He shrugs under their surprised glances. "I—disassembled it. And we saw several sentinels in a mechtech storefront in the Versteck. Being repaired."

"Sentinels? You mean dogbots?" They all look to Ligeia, the expression on their faces a mixture of pity and disgust.

"Only a human would see them in that way," Caen grumbles.

Ligeia frowns. "That's what they were, originally. One of my professors had one in Paris. She'd found it in an abandoned warehouse, put it back together. Said it must have been overlooked after OnyxCorp recommissioned them for Authority. Hers didn't have the AI-guided weaponry, but it could tear a rat apart in two seconds." She cocks her head to look down her nose at Caen. "I know my history."

"Then you know their presence in Dua villages isn't good news. Wylan's cooking up something, and he has support from OnyxCorp," Riannon says.

"Perhaps." Chege rubs his chin. "Story's loss is grave. She helped many Dua escape Wylan. She introduced me to the love of my life." He clasps Riannon's hand. "That explains your presence, Dr. Obumbwe. Why on Earth did you and Story involve Wylan, Caen?"

Caen clenches his jaw. "Wylan was an unfortunate detour. Story believed that you could help me get to the moon."

Chege's eyes widen. "Impossible. Why would you do that? The moon is death for Dua."

"The future is death for Dua. Unless the future is changed. I believe the moon holds the key."

Riannon scoffs, then laughs as she throws her head back. "You believe you're Vagabonder." Her mouth twists in a smirk. "Oh, that's wonderful. I've seen this before. I'm pretty sure I know how it plays out."

Vagabonder? Ligeia glances at Caen. She's heard the word before, but where? *Wanderer? Moon, in French, perhaps?*

"I don't have any illusions about what I am. I'm just another Dua, trained for a mission that will probably fail. But if I can get to the moon, that's one step further. And whoever follows me may get even closer."

"Send them away, Chege." Riannon eyes Ligeia, who feels the hairs on the back of her neck prickle. "They bring trouble with them."

Caen sighs. "I don't wish to bring harm to anyone else. But if you can't help me, point me to someone who can. I've come this far. I'm not turning back."

Riannon shakes her head. "We're already in danger, Chege—"

"My love, my love!" Chege puts a hand to Riannon's cheek. "You have seen only one part of this equation. Don't you need to see the other side?"

Ligeia can't contain herself any longer. "Wait, what's going on? What's *Vagabonder*? Why are you going to the moon? Why are they looking for you?"

What have I gotten myself into?

Riannon pulls her legs beneath her as she leans against Chege. "The Vagabonders are the original moon dwellers, the first Dua. The original Dua, and their progeny. The humans exiled them, many generations ago, at first to keep both species safe from one another, when it was unclear what Ruĝa Morto was or how it spread. They built their own culture there, had their own system of governance. The moon was theirs."

"When OnyxCorp took ownership of the moon, they forced the Dua into servitude, but the Vagabonders—the moon wanderers—resisted," Chege continued. "There were attempts at negotiation, then demonstrations, then protests, but the Corporation had weapons, where the Vagabonders had none. Most people believe the original colonists were all killed."

"But the legend is that they are still there, waiting for—" Riannon's lips curl in a sneer as she meets Caen's eyes. "Waiting for you? Who's been filling your head with such nonsense?"

Caen stiffens beside Ligeia. "Yes, waiting for me. Or waiting for you. Waiting for someone to do something, other than dance."

Riannon returns his cold stare. "Not all humans are bigoted, Caen. You saw them out there, our allies. We gather more each day. If we're going to win, we need to build a bridge, not wait for a savior."

"And how many more generations will suffer while we wait for dancing to change the world?"

Ligeia waves her hands at them. "Wait, wait! You're going to the moon because you think you're some kind of superhero? Some legend?"

Caen turns his glare on her now. "I'm going to the moon because no one else has tried it. I'm going to the moon because it's what I've been preparing for my entire life. I'm not a superhero, whatever that is. I'm a Dua who can't live this way anymore. I'm a being who won't live this way anymore."

"But, going to the moon," Ligeia says slowly. "For a rumor? A legend?"

"And why are you going?"

Ligeia swallows. "My brother. He's, uh, not safe unless I play ball with OnyxCorp."

"Then let's say I'm going for every Dua who doesn't have a sister with connections to OnyxCorp." Caen shifts away from her, his arms crossed over his chest.

Huffing, Riannon swings her legs out, scoots to the cushion's edge, and gathers the folds of her robe about her. "Fine. I want to read you."

"What?"

"Give me your hands," Riannon holds out her own hands, palms up, toward Caen. He narrows his eyes.

"Why do you need to read me?"

"Because I have already read her, yes?"

Ligeia blinks. "Wait. You *read* me? What does that—"

"When we danced. We touched, I read you. You know Dua can do this, yes? The jolt of energy when you touch us?"

Caen looks askance at Ligeia. "She's not a part of this equation—"

"Give me your hands." Grunting, he places his hands in Riannon's. Riannon breathes deep, exhales in a slow, steady hiss. Three more times she does this, wrinkling her nose at her last breath. "You are of the moon, and of the Earth. Your journey will be perilous. Many stand in your way." She takes in another long breath. Her nose twitches. "You will encounter succor, and you will have everything you have desired. You will lose something you do not know you have." Suddenly she gasps, and she opens her eyes. "You have the energy of Old Earth. But how—"

The top of Ligeia's head buzzes. Riannon's face blurs, then Caen's. Then the room. Ligeia blinks, tries to adjust her vision, but the room, the gentle *thwump* of the music, the heady herbal scent, the colorful cushions all fade. She hovers, weightless, above a grey surface, up, up, into space. She feels the hand in hers, tugging at her. Then she collapses with a soft moan.

When she opens her eyes, Riannon stands over her. She smooths her palm across Ligeia's forehead. "There. There. You're OK now." The rush of blood through Ligeia's ears slows as she takes several long, deep breaths.

"What—What happened?" Ligeia's voice sounds odd, distant in her own ears.

"Is she OK?" Caen's eyes are wide over Riannon's shoulder.

"She transcended too quickly." Riannon places a hand against Ligeia's chest. "You have a very open heart."

"Are you OK?" Caen leans closer to her. *Blue eyes, the bluest she's seen.*

Ligeia blinks, then coughs. "Oddly, I feel fine. I feel—weirdly peaceful."

Caen presses his lips together. "Humans aren't meant to transcend." He faces Riannon. "You should be more careful around them."

"She's fine." Riannon smiles and brushes Ligeia's forehead. "She's going with you."

For a terrifying moment, Ligeia forgets how to speak. Slowly, the edges of the room come back into focus. "Going with who? Where?"

"Are you certain, my love?" Chege's voice is muffled; Ligeia shakes her head to clear it.

"That's not happening." Caen's voice is clear, deep, like the slow, bass beat that vibrates the walls.

"That is not your decision to make," Riannon says. "It is hers."

Ligeia pushes herself up to her elbows. "What decision? What are you talking about?"

"Your fates are intertwined through death. You have an obligation to fulfill to each other. You are human, however, so you are free to choose. You may walk away. He may not."

Ligeia meets Caen's sapphire eyes. Riannon's words are mysterious, yet nothing has ever felt so true to Ligeia. Nothing has seemed as real as this moment. "So, what do I have to decide?"

"Nothing." Caen's voice is sharp, definite. "There's nothing to decide. I need passage to the moon. I don't need an aide—"

"Perhaps I do," Ligeia says, her voice stronger now. "It wouldn't be unusual for me to have a Dua accompanying me."

"That's not a bad idea," Chege breaks in. "A registry for a servant might not even get pinged—"

"I'm not traveling as a human servant."

Chege crosses his arms over his chest. "How were you planning on getting to the moon? I can get you a registry, but it's going to ping. They're already looking for you. As soon as you step foot on the Vine, they'll nab you. The only other option you have, mate, is to smuggle yourself in the cargo from Mombasa and hope you can get a registry past Vine security."

"Can you help me or not?"

Chege and Riannon exchange glances. He clasps her hands in his. "My heart says I must try, my love."

"I know." The squat, awkward human man and the graceful Dua couldn't be more different, yet their love for one another fills the space between them, permeates the room. Ligeia sneaks a look at Caen. His mouth is a straight line, the look in his eyes determined.

"I'll give you a registry," Chege says. "Do with it what you will, although my hope is that you'll do what's sensible and allow this human to help you. You have every reason not to trust us, of course. But Riannon is never wrong. Not about humans. Not about Dua. Come. This will take only a few moments."

He rises, and Caen follows him to a desk in the corner of the dim room. On its surface sits what looks like a NutriPrint, only smaller, more compact. Chege sits behind the desk and begins tapping away at a flexscreen while Caen stands behind him, his head bent to watch the small man's nimble movements.

"How do you feel?" Riannon's question draws Ligeia's attention away from Caen and Chege.

"I'm fine. Just a dizzy spell. I'm just tired."

Riannon cocks her head. "You can help them understand, you know."

Ligeia blinks. "What do you mean?"

Riannon leans forward. "It is your choice, as I said. He," she nods toward Caen, "will fight it, although he knows the bond is unbreakable. It will be your decision to make."

Ligeia swallows. "You said you read me. What did you see?"

"I was drawn to you back there, on the floor. Before I saw you, I was pulled to your energy, your openness. I suspect Story felt the same; it's the only explanation for her trusting you with her message. He feels it, too, but he will fight it. This is a suicide mission for him. He expects to fail. He will never give up, but he tends toward carelessness, to impulse." She sighs. "A very unusual trait for Dua. But then, he's an unusual Dua."

The mechanism in the corner whirrs, and Chege gives a satisfied grunt as he retrieves a thin data chip and holds it up, inspecting it carefully. "Double encrypted. Normally, that would cover you, but since they're looking already—"

The steady beat they've been hearing from the club suddenly stops, followed by muffled screams and the sharp pop of electristic fire.

"Authority," Riannon gasps.

Chege shoves the chip into Caen's hand. "Go!"

Riannon leaps from the cushions, grabs Ligeia's hand, and ushers her to the back of the small room. She presses her hand to the wall, and a hidden panel slides open, revealing a dark corridor. "Follow this to the alley. Then get as far away as you can."

Ligeia looks behind her. Chege is pushing Caen, as best he can, toward the open entry. "Go!" Chege calls. Ligeia ducks into the dark tunnel, glancing back just as Caen's figure is silhouetted against the dim light beyond.

"I honor your being, Ligeia Obumbwe!" Riannon calls, and suddenly Ligeia and Caen are plunged into shadow, their hands barely visible in front of them, as the secret door slides shut. The clamor beyond is muffled, punctuated by sharp pops that seem to grow steadily louder.

"They're getting closer," Ligeia says. "We should go."

Caen's eyes glow in the gloom. "The binding of human and Dua. Are you sure you're ready for this?"

"No." Ligeia orients herself in the tunnel, takes a few steps in the only direction left to them. "I'm not sure at all." Then she follows the tunnel to the alley and into the cool Mombasa night air, pausing only to wait for Caen as he emerges, reluctantly, to join her.

20

"IT'S A TERRIBLE PLAN," Ligeia says for at least the sixth time. "There has to be another way."

We'd stayed the night in the tenebrous warehouse through which I'd made my escape from the Versteck into Mombasa, uncomfortably close to one another regardless of what we'd experienced in the hours before. I tossed and turned all night, waking in response to every whimper, every grunt I heard from the human woman who lay by my side behind a stack of containers. In the twilight of the dawn, she'd sprung to sitting with a sharp cry, "Finn!" As she searched the semidarkness, her eyes met mine, and she looked away.

Who has she left behind? What makes a woman like her make such a journey? For that matter, what are human women like at all? I drift into sleep watching the rise and fall of her waist as she breathes, her scent close, like a garden after a gentle rain. My dreams are filled with memories of her body pressed against mine, our hands clasped at Paix Porteur.

What was I thinking, showing the Ritual of Binding to a human woman? How had I let myself get caught up in the moment? Was it the music? The news of Story's death? In the dim warehouse, I realize I have been careless with others' lives as well as my own.

As the morning light crept beneath the door opening onto the street outside, I awakened her, resolving to send her on her way. When I told her my plan, she insisted on coming with me. As we advanced toward the dock, however, her motives became clear. She has tried everything to talk me out of it.

"Another way, for example, by letting me help you," she continues.

"I've been counting on others to get me where I need to go, and it's only resulted in their getting hurt or killed. I'm doing this alone."

"Look, I'm somebody in the human world, OK? I say you're an assistant."

She has spirit. But she's frustratingly naïve how the world works for Dua. "It's astounding that you think that would work, or that it wouldn't draw even more attention to me."

"Let me help you, Caen. I—"

"Help me make this work or go away."

She snaps her mouth shut, but she doesn't break her stride. We walk in silence to the docks, where we search for the loading section for the *Constellation,* our transport to the Vine platform. She as a passenger. I as cargo.

"The journey from the port to the Vine will take two days. The supply cartons will sit on the elevator platform another few days before they're loaded onto the Vine. I'll have plenty of time to escape from the container and board the Vine as a crewmember."

"If you don't die on the way. If you aren't discovered first."

"Yes, if those things don't happen."

"Without anyone to vouch for you," Ligeia murmurs.

"It won't be necessary." My words come out harsher than I intend. Her eagerness to help is endearing and mystifying, and were I not in a state of constant anxiety about Authority or Wylan or both finding us, I would welcome it. But things have not gone as planned since I arrived in Mombasa.

At last, only a few hours before the transport is scheduled to depart, we make our way through a maze of light metal cartons, outbuildings, and crane equipment to a cordoned-off area, its digital ribbon reading *Constellation.*

"We don't have much time. You start over there. Call out when you find one that's open."

"I state again for the record that this is a terrible plan." Ligeia turns on her heel and heads toward her stack without waiting for my reply.

As I navigate through my stacks, I find most cartons locked. After several minutes, I begrudgingly realize my plan may not work after all. I'm about to tell Ligeia just that when she calls out. I make my way through the maze toward her voice.

"What—" I round a corner to find her inside a large carton, tossing its contents on the ground outside: Human clothing, a few smaller boxes that spill open, revealing a variety of personal items only humans would find important. Ligeia pulls at a large chair, its arms worn through use.

"Someone's going to be upset when all this goes missing," I say.

"No, they won't." She straightens and points a finger at the transport code on the carton's side, followed by a name.

Obumbwe, L.

"All this belongs to you." I shake my head. "I can't let you—"

"My choice, isn't it?"

I swallow. "I'll consider your obligation fulfilled, then."

She grunts as she pulls again at the chair. Stepping inside, I lift it, carry it outside, and stride to the edge of the dock, where I toss the chair into the briny sea. It sinks, slowly, beneath the surface. Behind me, Ligeia carries an armful of what I know are her personal items. She stares into the murky water for several seconds before she opens her arms.

"I hated those clothes anyway." Without another word, she winds back through the stacks to the emptied carton. I catch up with her at the carton's entrance, where we stare into the inky blackness in silence.

"It seems airtight," she says finally, stepping inside. "You won't be able to breathe."

"That can be easily remedied." I glide past her toward the carton's interior, feel the sides, and retrieve a knife from my backpack, one of my remaining possessions aside from the digiscreen. Gripping the handle firmly, I stab into the side of the carton and twist, making a small but serviceable air hole. I turn to face Ligeia, smirking, as I replace the knife in the backpack.

"OK, then there's the question of stability. You're going to move around like a ball in this thing." She puts her hands on her hips. "You're going to end up with a broken leg, a broken neck—"

"It will work. I'll be fine. I promise."

"You can't make that kind of promise."

"Help me keep it."

Frowning, she sighs. "Look, it's just—Of all the plans. You could suffocate. Die of heatstroke. You could be crushed. You could drown." She drops her hands to her sides and meets my eyes. "I can get you to the moon. It might take a little more time—"

"Stop. I—I'm grateful you want to help. But I'm not getting anyone else hurt." *Or killed.* Something tells me I'm only just beginning on that front. "You've done what you can here. If you're that important—" She flinches. "They'll be worried about you, looking for you. You think they'll let me walk away, after kidnapping Dr. Ligeia Obumbwe and forcing her to smuggle me in a container bound for the Vine?"

It's a half-smile, but a smile nonetheless that causes her green eyes to sparkle. She backs away into the opening, where she is silhouetted against the light outside. "Ask for me. The minute you're found, you escape, you get stopped—and the dozens of other things that could go wrong with this ridiculous plan—"

As my eyes adjust to the half-light, she seems already in another world. A world I may never see again.

"I will. I promise." She draws the door closed, slowly, and darkness envelops me. As the opening narrows, our eyes meet, causing my heart to grip.

Suddenly, a flash of light, and a blue stream of electricity connects with Ligeia's shoulder. She stumbles backwards, her hands flailing, and falls from view. I scramble to the still-open entrance and skid to a stop when the door swings wide.

Ligeia, sprawled on the dusty ground, is unconcious. Behind her stands Zady, a stunstic in her good hand. Her other arm is bandaged tightly against her side, and an enormous bruise decorates her temple. Standing to her side is Wylan, his arms crossed over his chest, his mouth stretched in a grim smile.

"You'd better hope she's alive," I growl. Zady levels the stunstic at my chest.

"For now," Wylan says. "It really depends on you."

Then I see Chege on his knees, just behind Wylan, his shoulders hunched over, his face turned away. "What have you done to Chege?"

Wylan smirks. "I knew where she'd take you, who she would contact. Authority wanted their shot, of course. Chege's forgery prowess is one of Mombasa's open secrets. But I knew they'd miss."

"Forgive me." Chege turns to face me. One eye is swollen shut; dark, thick blood oozes from the side of his mouth. "I couldn't...Riannon."

"There's nothing to forgive, Chege. It's I who should be begging forgiveness of you."

"How very NiCIe of you," Wylan says, scoffing. "Where has all that 'I honor your being' bullshit gotten us, huh? That's the problem with you true believers. You really think you can win against humans, that we can 'live together in harmony'. The only way to win with humans is to beat them at their own game. I sell information, at a premium, and humans pay it. The Versteck is just the beginning. I have plans. And you are not going to ruin them. Any of them—OnyxCorp, the EFC, SoAm—would do anything to get their hands on you."

I clench my fists at my sides. "How did you convince anyone you were a Vagabonder? You sound like the humans, speaking only of power and profit. It's never enough, though, not for them, and not for you. Did you resist at all when OnyxCorp asked you to sell Dua in addition to their technology?"

Zady's aim wavers; she lowers her weapon. "What do you mean 'sell Dua'?"

"He's putting sentinels in the villages." Her eyes widen, and she cuts a glance at Wylan. "Sentinels where there are Dua children—"

"Lies!" Wylan scoffs.

"Story knew everything. She confronted Wylan about it, told him he had to confess, but he wouldn't have it, and he kicked her out of the Versteck. He's playing you false, Zady, all of you. He's selling out his own people for a place with the humans."

A meter away, Ligeia groans. Taking my eyes from Zady, I take a step toward Ligeia.

"Don't move, anyone!" I freeze as Zady raises the weapon again. "Why are you doing this? Why are you risking everything to go to the moon, the last place any Dua should go?"

I raise my hands in front of me. "Out of the one, many have suffered. Out of the one, many will have hope."

Zady's arm trembles. She points her weapon at the ground. "One Dua doesn't make a difference. The humans have the power." She jerks her head toward Ligeia, who has rolled to her side with another groan. "Our only hope is to take what we can from them."

"His kind don't want what they can get. They want it all. Equality. Autonomy." Wylan steps closer to Zady, leans in close to her. "That only hurts other Dua. They don't need an excuse to police us more, but challenging them directly like this? It will only lead to more Dua deaths."

I take two more steps toward Ligeia, who struggles, wobbly, to her feet. "Why should we be satisfied with the scraps? With what they're willing to give us, to let go of? You got yours, Wylan. Now you're telling us we have to be content with just survival when everything you've accomplished in the Versteck shows we can do so much more?"

"We must earn our seat at the table," Wylan returns. "The humans see us only as diseased savages. How will you change that perception through threatening the Vine? Through rousing Dua anger on the moon? The only way to make changes is within, as part of the system."

"That will never happen." Ligeia rises unsteadily. Grasping my hand, she faces Wylan. "It doesn't matter how advanced your tech or how much you give to the Corporation. They will never see you as equals. You'll wait generations for equality, and even then it will have to be taken."

Wylan sneers. "Somehow I doubt you can speak for all humans."

"Like you can speak for all Dua?" Zady's voice cuts through Wylan like a knife.

"What did you say?"

Zady holsters her electristic in a smooth motion and meets Wylan's eyes. "I said you don't speak for all Dua. I'm not willing to wait generations for freedom. It's been long enough already. What more do we have to prove, Wylan? Build another Vine? Another TES? I won't be a slave any longer. Not to the humans. And not to you." And with that, she turns her back on us all and strides toward the narrow alley between the stacks.

"They will find him, Zady!" Wylan screams. "And when they do, they'll make it even worse for the rest of us. I won't let him ruin everything we've built!"

Zady doesn't look back or break her stride. For a few poignant seconds, Wylan seems unsure of what to do next. Then he sprints toward Zady and collides with her body with such force that he slams her into the side of a container, crushing her injured arm against the corrugated metal. She lets out a sharp cry as she collapses to her knees, throwing her good arm in front of her to break her fall. Wylan jerks her electristic from its holster. He brings the weapon up and smacks it against the side of her head. She slumps to the ground against the container's side.

Wylan pivots as he brings the weapon around to level it at Ligeia.

"Ligeia!" I leap for her and bring us both crashing to the ground as an energy pulse bursts against a container just above our heads. I scramble up as Wylan advances, holding the weapon out before him, aiming at Ligeia. Suddenly, the ground explodes at Wylan's feet.

"Drop it!" Chege's arm trembles with the weight of the electristic in his hand. "Walk away, Wylan."

Wylan's mouth twists. "Zady's betrayal is complete, then. She said she'd checked you for weapons."

"She did. She's just scared of humans." Chege's arm shakes violently. I know he's weak with pain, that he can't hold up much longer.

Smirking, Wylan says, "I'm not afraid of you."

He fires. Chege jerks back then falls without a sound.

"No!" Before I can think, I spring for Wylan's throat. I catch his arm just as he is swinging it back around to aim the electristic at me. I wrench his arm around and push him to the ground; he drops the weapon with a sharp cry. Pulling his arm behind him, I press my knee into his back, eliciting a stomach-churning crunch. Wylan screams, but he struggles, attempts to get his legs under him.

"Enough," I say. "I don't want to hurt you."

"Fuck you," Wylan says between clenched teeth. "They'll turn on you, too. Just like they've turned on me." He kicks his legs weakly. "Fuck you." He groans, louder this time, as I put more weight into his back. A few seconds later, he lies still, breathing hard. I loosen my grip.

"I'm going to help you up now—"

I feel the shot before I hear it, feel the warm burst of blood spatter my face and hands and torso. The top of Wylan's head explodes across the ground. I drop Wylan's arm to clamp my hands over my ringing ears as I stumble backwards, crashing onto the ground next to Ligeia. Zady stands over Wylan. Her recovered electristic points where the Dua's head used to be.

"I won't be a slave to you." Zady stares at Wylan's body with glazed eyes. "I won't let anyone be a slave again."

I push myself up, my ears still ringing. I hold out a hand toward Ligeia to pull her up. Chege lies a few meters away, his chest a gaping hole, his mouth open and slack.

"I wanted to believe him. Even after Story showed me dozens of manifests. I still wanted it to be true." Zady sticks out a foot and pushes gently at Wylan's body. "I wanted to believe it was all OK, because we were keeping ourselves safe. There's nothing to believe, though. Not him. Not you. Not anyone."

"The Vagabonders—" I begin.

"Won't help us. They abandoned us long ago. Even if you did find them, do you really think they'd help us, after seeing what we've done? Go get yourself killed. Do it quick, before you convince any other lost souls to follow you." Zady kicks the ground, sending bits of rock and dust over Wylan's torso.

"You can make this right," I plead. "You know the truth."

"Sometimes," Zady says, pushing the weapon into her belt, "knowing the truth is worse." She gives Wylan one last glance and sets her shoulders. "I'm not stopping you, and I'm not helping you." She turns her back on us again and disappears into the stacks, leaving me and Ligeia alone again.

. . .

WE FEEL the crane rumble before we hear it whine into life, several rows away. From above us, on the *Constellation's* deck, a black arm swings around and down, catches a large container between its massive clamps, and lifts it high above us. It swings back with a metallic groan and lowers the container onto the ship.

"Time to go." I stride back to the container.

"You aren't still doing this. After all that?"

I inspect the container's interior. "All that convinced me I have to do this alone. If I could close the door behind me, I'd do it. As it turns out, I need you for that."

"I won't do it." Ligeia puts her hands on her hips.

"After you close that door, I don't want to see you again."

"I said I won't do it." The light spills through her mass of curls, creating a halo effect that I know I will never forget. Retrieving my backpack from the container's floor, I secure it over my shoulders and sink against the interior, pushing my legs against the opposite wall for stability. Less than secure. But if my mother could do it—

"I don't give a shit what you say," Ligeia says. "I was gone overnight in Mombasa. Who's to say I didn't pick up a Dua servant? Come with me."

"No."

"I can make sure you get to the moon—"

"No, Ligeia!" Her eyes widen. "Dr. Obumbwe, no. My plan never involved you."

"That doesn't mean—"

"I don't want your help, human!"

She'd be less hurt if I'd struck her. Ligeia stares, open mouthed, and I look away, unable to bear the sadness in her eyes.

"I hope you find what you're looking for." Her voice is barely above a whisper. I don't look after her when she steps through the entrance, although I know she pauses in the door. Then the strip of light across the container's interior grows thinner and thinner. I look up just in time to see the last sliver of light, her hand backlit for only an instant.

Then I am in darkness.

21

"WHERE THE BLOODY hell have you been?"

Erlang stands, alone, arms crossed over her chest, at a kiosk toward the *Constellation's* aft marked PASSENGERS. She seethes, and not without reason. Ligeia quickens her pace slightly, using the distance to compose herself. "They're about to leave. You can guess the reason they've waited."

"I'll be sure to thank the crew."

"You're a piece of work. Let's go." Spinning on her heel, Erlang heads up the gangplank. Ligeia follows, trying to ignore what is going on at the ship's bow. A metal carton hovers far above the deck, borne by a towering crane. The crane lowers the carton down, down, down to finally rest on the ship's deck among dozens of others. She tears her eyes from the scene. Erlang has already crossed the gangplank, so she hurries forward, catching up with Erlang at the steward's station. "We're here," Erlang growls to the Dua steward, jerking her head toward Ligeia. "She's sorry for the delay."

"Dr. Obumbwe, we have been waiting for you."

"I'm terribly sorry. I lost track of the time." Erlang scoffs behind her.

"Here are your quarters." Their RistWaches flash briefly. "We will be departing immediately. Take the corner to your right, and you'll find the lift to reach your deck."

"Thank you."

"It is my pleasure, Dr. Obumbwe," the Dua replies. Ligeia catches the tail-end of Erlang's eye roll as they proceed to the lift. They stand in silence as the car ascends to the VIP deck until Erlang, who's reached the end of her patience, breaks.

"Mind telling me what's going on with you? Where were you all night?"

"I don't think that's any of your business."

Erlang leans against the back of the lift, draws one foot up to rest on the wall, and retrieves a drugstic from her jacket. "Fair enough." She takes a drag. "But Hedges may not take that for an answer." The lift comes to a gentle halt. The doors slide open, and Erlang steps out. "Get some sleep, doc. It's going to be a bumpy ride from here on out." She strides down the hall ahead of Ligeia, opens the door to her cabin, and enters, closing the door without another word.

Sighing, Ligeia finds her own room. Throwing her bag on the floor at the entrance, she crosses to the bed, collapses across it, and passes out before her head hits the pillow.

A WARM, *strong hand grips hers. Oxygen fills her lungs, and she feels herself floating down, slowly, slowly. Her feet brush the ground as the landscape comes into fuzzy view. Grey rock, grey dust, set against an inky black sky with a million twinkling stars.*

The hand pulls her gently. Finn? *she hears herself saying. A tall, thin figure pulls her along. She glides effortlessly behind, squints, and tries to bring the figure into focus. White hair. Olive skin. The horizon suddenly bursts with light. The blue, green, yellow, brown, and white planet blinds her, and she reaches up a hand to shield her eyes. The hand pulls, insistent, toward a steady pulsing rhythm. She feels a tug backwards, then the hand is gone. She floats again, her legs rise behind her. The pulse grows louder, louder, louder...*

Ligeia rises in the darkness with a gasp, recognizing the steady *womp womp womp* for what it is: An alarm. She glances at her RistWach.

Past midnight. She's been asleep for five hours. She throws her legs over the side of the bed; the ship's gentle chug vibrates through her feet. She pads to the lavatory, relieves herself, and pauses to look in the mirror. Her eyes are red and puffy, her hair in more disarray than usual. Putting her hands beneath the faucet, she splashes cold water over her face. The alarm cuts off just as she reaches the window, where she pushes aside the shade to look out over the bow below. Dozens of bright lights cause her to blink and rub her eyes before the scene comes into focus.

Dua and humans are scattered among the maze of cartons on the deck below; the biggest group is gathered outside one of the larger cartons. A few smaller cartons are open, their contents spilled out across the deck, piles of furnishings and textiles and other materials.

Among the contents lies a figure, face down, arms and legs splayed out awkwardly. With spiked white hair.

Ligeia forces down the bile that rises in her throat. Two Authority bots advance through the maze toward the large container; humans and Dua scatter as they approach. The Authority pause, and one points its weapon at the carton's entrance while the other interfaces with the door panel.

Ligeia darts from the window and rummages through her carryon, retrieving an oversized sweater. Pulling it over her head, she leaves her room and goes to Erlang's, where she taps on the door. Several moments pass. No response. Doubling her hand into a fist, she pounds. After a few seconds, she hears shuffling, then the door slides open.

"Doc, just what the fucking hell do you want?" Erlang, wrapped in a silky robe, rubs her eyes.

"There's something going on outside," Ligeia replies, taking in the robe with a curious glance.

"What? Come on—"

"You come on!" Ligeia pushes past Erlang and crosses to the sliding door that leads to a small balcony outside. The pungent scents of salt and brine waft through the state room as Ligeia opens the door and steps outside to lean against the railing. The large carton is open now. Beams of light jerk up and down as the bots step inside. Ligeia strains to hear something, anything, but she can only make out muffled shouts. Then she hears the sharp *pop pop pop* of a weapon being fired.

Erlang grunts beside her and wraps her robe tightly against her as the wind makes it billow about her long legs. The beams of light grow steady, and the Authority reappears. It holds its weapon at the ready, pointing it toward the container.

The first Dua that emerges is filthy. Even from a distance Ligeia can tell he's sick. Five more follow him, stumbling with every step. The last two are a mother and a child. The child clutches his mother's hand and leads her outside gently, slowly. The woman staggers, lets go of the child's hand, and falls.

"What a stupid plan," Erlang mutters. The Dua huddle, their arms around each other, their heads held high. The child lies against his prone mother. A bot picks up the child by his thin arm, then scoops up the mother in another of its subarms. It strides past the frightened Dua with its sad cargo, through the maze of cartons, and to the lurching ship's starboard. It lifts the Dua woman over the railing and drops her into the ocean below.

Ligeia has a last look at the child's blank face before it too disappears over the side of the *Constellation*.

"Fuck," Erlang says softly. Her dark skin stretches tightly over her knuckles as she grips the railing.

"A child." Ligeia barely hears the *pop pop pop* of weapons discharge as the Authority fires into the group of Dua stowaways. They collapse almost as one. Outside a smaller container, two humans lift the limp figure on the deck between them. Its head lolls forward, hiding its face.

Ligeia runs to the lavatory, barely making it to the basin before she vomits. Her stomach heaves until she thinks it is going to come out of her throat.

"You're burning up." Erlang's hands are on Ligeia's shoulder. "Damn it. Here." She presses a cold cloth against the back of Ligeia's neck. "Breathe." Ligeia takes several sharp, gasping breaths as she melts onto the floor.

"I'm fine," she croaks.

"Like hell. Can you stand?"

"I'm fine." Ligeia gathers her feet beneath her and stands, wobbling. She stumbles back to the window, but she can't locate the two humans carrying their grizzly burden. The bots have already cleared the Dua bodies on the deck. Now they enter the carton, and a few moments later they emerge with their main arms loaded with three Dua bodies each. Ligeia chokes down another wave of nausea. "Why?"

"They're still looking for him, the SoAm NiCIe I told you about. I guess they're following up on every tip, no matter how outrageous."

"I mean why are Authority killing them? They're just trying to get to the moon. It's their religion, isn't it? That the moon is their natural home? Why kill them when OnyxCorp wants them there anyway?"

"Not those kinds of NiCIes. The sick. The old. They'd be a burden on the system."

"A child, Erlang. A child!" Ligeia's face is hot, burning. She feels on the verge of hysteria. "What if that had been Zinda? Would you be OK with that?"

Erlang's expression hardens. "I warned you. I'm going to have to ask you to leave, doctor." Erlang crosses the room and stops at the door. "We'll catch up when we board the Vine."

Ligeia stares at her from across the room, open mouthed. "You're a coward."

"Watch it, doc. There are lines that you don't cross with me. You're bumping up against one."

Ligeia strides unsteadily to the door and pauses to glare at Erlang. "I have lines, too. That," she says, pointing to the balcony, "is one of them." She stomps through the open door and reaches her own just as she hears Erlang's door close behind her with a soft click.

LIGEIA STEPS INTO HER ROOM, slams the door closed behind her, and lets out a scream that makes her throat raw.

"What the fuck am I going to the moon for?" She paces the room, kicks at the low table, the cushioned chairs. "To do what they tell me to do? To play the role they want me to play in this sick fucking system!" She pulls the linen from the mattress and throws it on the floor. "He's dead! He had a reason to go to the moon! He was doing something! What are you doing? What are you fucking doing, Ligeia Obumbwe?"

Another burst of weapons fire resounds from the deck outside. Kicking the low table again as she passes, Ligeia steps out onto her balcony. Moonlight spills across the bow and casts an eerie glow over the dark metallic Authority bodies as they move from container to container, their bodies barely squeezing through the tight rows. They open every single container on the ship's bow, eventually discovering another group of Dua, a family perhaps, with a single child. Ligeia forces herself to watch as the bots line them up. The child tries to hide behind the adults, her eyes wide with fear, as the bots open fire. She doesn't turn away as the bots gather the bodies and drop them into the inky waters below.

MINUTES LATER, the Authority are gone, and the deck is clear. Thick clouds dim the moonlight and add a chill to the air. Ligeia shivers and returns to the stateroom.

She lies down on the bed and stares out the open door. The stars bob up and down, up and down, until dawn breaks. She watches the sky turn indigo, then pink and purple, then orange and yellow. She rises only when she catches a glint of sunlight against the man-made structure outside.

She expects an industrial piece of metal, but the Vine platform shimmers with golden sunlight. The elevator cable descends from far above Earth, through wispy white clouds. It's almost beautiful, save for the black letters emblazoned on the side of its central building: *OnyxCorp.*

As the *Constellation* approaches, Ligeia faces a residential section covered with tiny buildings stacked several sections high. Advertisements blaze in the distance. *OnyxVision presents EyEnhance 4.0! OnyxMed's SleepRite IV, now available only for Lunar employees. OnyxCorp Vine Station and Casino: Luxury among the stars!* As the ship rounds the platform, it passes storage units and industrial sites, a downtown section with storefronts and entertainment venues, and a three-story barracks surrounded by a towering wall. *OnyxCorp Lunar Staging Facility. OnyxCorp Space Industries. OnyxCorp Market: Gateway to the Vine. OnyxCorp Support Internment Facility.* Half a dozen cargo ships chug past, heading in the opposite direction, as the *Constellation* approaches the marina. They sit low, their names obscured, then revealed as the ships plunge through the churning waves. *OSS Indomitable. OSS Conqueror. OSS Star Trader.*

Ligeia observes the rest of their approach from the ship's deck. She takes deep, gulping breaths of sea air as she wipes away intermittent tears.

It's not too late.

Dua workers pull the *Constellation* alongside the dock, loosening and tightening the lines with perfect precision. A perfect dance.

I can go back right now. I can refuse to play their game.

And then what? Run away with Finn? There's no place on Earth they could hide.

She glances up at a white building that dominates the dock area. *OnyxCorp Space Elevator Port Authority.*

And do what? Live the rest of their lives watching it all happen over and over and over again?

What kind of life would that be?

Not one I can live with. Not now, after what I've seen. After what I've felt.

The ship sloshes to a gentle stop. Within minutes, the enormous cranes begin lifting one container after the other from the ship's bow and swinging them down to the dock below. Human passengers disembark, laughing, smiling. Unaware of what is happening before their eyes. Or aware and indifferent.

Caen had a purpose. A goal. And now he's dead. He's dead, Story is dead, the Dua woman and her companions at the Gala are dead, those children are dead.

And OnyxCorp is responsible.

"You thought you'd use me." Ligeia glares at the tall, black letters, allows them to fill her mind, to be the ending punctuation to a long, sordid sentence that encapsulates everything true about the Corporation. "You have no idea what's coming."

Because now she *is* interested in toppling OnyxCorp.

She runs her hands through her wild curls. It isn't until the last container is lowered gently among the offloaded cargo that she returns to her room, gathers her belongings, and leaves the *Constellation*.

ERLANG WAITS for her on the dock with Sakata. The old man leans on a polished wooden cane, its pommel an intricate carving of some type of bird. Erlang doesn't say a word about her tardiness. She merely grunts when Ligeia is within range, turns on her heel, and walks through the dock area, past the Port Authority, and onto a tiled pathway that extends both left and right. Sakata follows her, his cane clicking rhythmically with every step, and Ligeia follows still further behind. Dozens of transports swoosh past on an electromagnetic road that runs parallel with the walkway. The pathway itself is busy with humans, often escorted by Dua. Erlang turns right and stops to allow Sakata and Ligeia to catch up.

"You feel OK, doc? You're slower than Sakata."

"I'm fine."

"So many humans," Sakata says as he catches his breath. "Is it always this crowded?"

"Only since they opened the new gambling facility on the Station," Erlang said. "It'll get worse."

She leads them, a bit more slowly, around a group of implant kiosks. Several humans stand at the terminals, thin fibers extending from portals in their arms, their necks, behind their ears.

"How about Dua transport? Has that increased also?" Ligeia asks.

Erlang clears her throat. "I couldn't say."

"Just in general."

"Couldn't say."

They walk for a few more blocks in silence. Ligeia's head swims at the rush of passersby and traffic. Everything seems loud and close and smothering. Perhaps it's the heat? When her vision begins to blur, she stops, drops her bag from her shoulder, and wipes a cold sweat from her brow.

"How much further?" She hears the waver in her voice.

"Are you quite well, Dr. Obumbwe?" Sakata's voice sounds far away. Ligeia sways, prompting Erlang to grab her by the shoulders.

"I—think so." Ligeia's voice echoes now.

"You definitely aren't." Erlang holds her up, and her face comes into Ligeia's view briefly, surrounded by mist. "Hold on, I'm getting a transport." Knees buckling, Ligeia sinks to the walkway, where she closes her eyes and concentrates on breathing in, breathing out.

What's wrong with me?

Her legs feel rubbery, but she doesn't hurt anywhere. Other than feeling as if she might suddenly float away, she's buoyant. Alive. Her head buzzes, her heart pounds. She feels wonderful, even. As if in a dream.

After what seems like several hours, Ligeia feels herself being lifted. She opens her eyes to see Erlang on her right and Sakata on her left.

"I'm fine," Ligeia says, a little too loudly. She jerks against them, struggling to free herself. "Really. Just a little tired." She sinks against the cushion in the back of the transport and closes her eyes as Erlang and Sakata crawl in. Their voices are raised, but what they are arguing about Ligeia cannot tell. The transport travels only a couple of blocks before it halts at a white building with glass doors. *OnyxCorp International Space Elevator Visitor's Barracks* covers the space above the glass entry doors in towering letters.

"I could have made that," Ligeia grumbles as the transport doors lift to allow them to disembark. Erlang leaps out and retrieves Ligeia's bag from the cargo area.

"Take it slow, Dr. Obumbwe." Sakata grabs Ligeia's hand as she crawls from the transport.

"I'm fine." Ligeia waves him off. "In fact, I'm hungry."

Erlang returns with her bag and regards her skeptically. "I can have something sent to your room."

"Does the barracks have a mess?"

Erlang's brow furrows in deep creases. "Yes, but—"

"Good. Let's go."

Erlang shoulders the bag and motions for Ligeia and Sakata to follow her into the barracks. They are less than impressive, and appear to have been military barracks before being converted into housing for human visitors on their way to and from the Vine. A few decorative touches here and there—a painting, a sculpture, some seats with faded, worn cushions—have made the facility more appealing, but otherwise it is plain, industrial. They approach the concierge, where the Dua attendants check them in and scan their RistWaches for entry. Erlang raises an eyebrow when Ligeia asks for the mess again, but the attendant directs them toward the second level.

Ligeia walks briskly in the direction the Dua indicated until she's sure both Erlang and Sakata are well behind her. Gasping, she leans against the wall for support. *What the hell is wrong with me?* Her heart pounds, its steady *whoosh whoosh* fills her ears. Her stomach churns. Hungry. That must be it. She hasn't eaten since the day before, before watching Story murdered in the street, before watching a Dua child—

She shakes her head to clear it just as Erlang and Sakata catch up to her.

"We should get you to your room, doc," Erlang says, real concern in her dark eyes now. "You look terrible."

"I'm just hungry. I'll be fine once I get something to eat."

Erlang takes in a deep breath. "OK," she says, resigned.

THE MESS IS a medium-sized room with several tables and a serving area where rows upon rows of NutriPrints wait for patrons. It is full and noisy, and Ligeia half considers ordering in her room after all. She does not want to be alone, though. Setting her shoulders, she approaches a NutriPrint and orders what the machine calls the American Breakfast: Scrambled generated eggs, a protein cube engineered to taste like crisped meat, and a coffee. She's almost feeling herself when she reaches the table where Erlang and Sakata sit, their faces both wearing expressions of confusion and concern.

"You look like shit," Sakata observes.

"Thanks." Ligeia brings her coffee to her lips and gulps it down.

"Was the journey that bad?"

"On the *Constellation*? Oh, no. It was just wonderful." She casts a glare at Erlang. Her head begins to buzz again. She takes a bite of the eggs, chokes them down as they seem to expand in her mouth.

Sakata frowns. "I heard there was some trouble. With some stowaways."

"No trouble is too big for Authority, right Erlang?" Ligeia looks down at her tray, at the greying eggs and the rubbery cube, and her throat constricts. "I knew one of them—" A mist begins to form over the tray, over Sakata, over Erlang.

"Are you all right, Dr. Obumbwe?" Sakata's voice is remote and thick.

"I—" She gulps. "I—don't feel well."

Then all is darkness.

GREY DUST AND ROCKS. *The sky above is black, dotted with tiny pinpricks of light. There is something behind her. Something important.*

She turns and turns, for hours it seems. It is a tunnel, dark, descending into the moon. She is drawn to it, afraid until she sees the child's face, until his eyes meet hers. He disappears into the tunnel, and she jumps after him; inky blackness gives way to flashing lights that pulse red and green and blue and yellow.

Then she is in her old room in her childhood home. Across the room, far, far away, lies Finn. His skin is red and raw and hot to her touch. His eyes are closed, his mouth is turned up in a smile. He is dying. She shakes him, but he doesn't wake.

Suddenly, he opens his eyes.

Follow him, Geia.

Finn disappears. She stands atop the Eiffel Tower and looks down on the flooded Paris streets. The moon, enormous, blinds her. The tower rises, bringing her closer, closer to the moon. She knows she can jump from the tower to its surface in a single leap, so she does. Again she floats, away from the surface, her feet rise above her.

A hand grasps hers, pulls her down, down toward the grey surface, down to blue eyes.

Come with me.

. . .

LIGEIA LIES ON HER BACK, her head propped up with soft cushions. She's wrapped up in a long, soft tunic. Her hair is wet.

The ceiling, the walls, the bedclothes, even the side table are all unfamiliar. A whistled song draws her attention to where Sakata sits at a small table, a flexscreen spread across it, a few meters away.

Caen is dead.

Funny that is the first thing that comes to mind, but the rest comes flooding back. She sits up slowly, groans as her joints pop and creak. Sakata looks up as she pulls herself into a cross-legged position and rubs her eyes.

"Welcome back." Sakata pushes back from the table and moves to her side. "How do you feel?" He puts a hand against her face. "You're cooled off."

"What was it?" Ligeia says thickly. She tries to swallow, but her tongue feels like it's coated with dust, and she falls into a fit of coughing.

"Ah, let me get you some water." He returns a minute later from the kitchenette with a full glass, which Ligeia gulps down. "Easy. Not too fast." Ligeia takes another long gulp and swirls the liquid around her mouth. She licks her lips.

"What was it?" she repeats. Sakata holds out a hand for the glass, and she gives it to him. He places it on the bedside table and folds his hands in his lap.

"I'm not sure. A virus, that's certain. You were out for only a couple of days, but—"

"Days?" Ligeia straightens. "What do you mean days?"

"You collapsed. At first I thought it was—" He shrugs. "Well, it doesn't matter now. You must have picked up something in Mombasa. Erlang said you disappeared overnight. She's been worried about you. I had to finally send her away so she'd get some rest."

"Did I miss it?"

Sakata narrows his eyes. "Miss what?"

"The Vine."

"No. But you're in no condition—"

"When does it leave?"

Sakata sighs. "In four hours. But you're not well enough."

Ligeia swings her legs over the side of the bed. Her head spins, forcing her to pause for a few deep breaths. "Help me get dressed."

"OnyxCorp knows you took ill. They're going to house you in Mombasa until next month and send you up with the next one."

Ligeia shifts a little weight to her feet, leans a little forward. Then she sinks back onto the bed. "I'm going now." She is surprised by how calm she sounds.

"You can't. I'm the medtech on record for your case, and you can't go unless I approve it."

"Then fucking approve it, Sakata." She tries to stand again. "Approve it and help me."

"A week ago, you didn't even want to go. What's the hurry now?"

"A week ago, I didn't have a reason to go. Now, I do."

Sakata shakes his head. "What happened to you in Mombasa?"

She tells him everything then. About Story. About running into Caen, Paix Porteur, the dockyard. About Wylan and Zady. About the child's face before he was dropped into the roiling waves. About the lifeless body the two humans carried through the maze of shipping cartons.

"You think that was this Caen?"

Ligeia shakes her head. "Maybe. I don't know." She scoots to the bed's edge. "It doesn't matter. He's one of millions. Just like Finn. One of millions who are abused, oppressed, murdered." She runs a hand through the curls at the back of her neck. "But I can stop them. Will you help me?"

Sakata cocks his head to the side. "You said you weren't interested in toppling OnyxCorp."

"Will you help me? I'll do it alone if I have to, Sakata. If you aren't going to help, then stay out of my way."

Sakata sighs. "You'll never make it alone in your condition. Yes, of course I'll help you. Nothing would please me more."

AN HOUR LATER, she leans on Sakata more than she wants as she emerges from the Visitor's Barracks into the brisk salt air. A steady breeze stirs her hair, and after a few deep breaths, she feels strong enough to stand on her own, although Sakata insists she keep a hand on his arm for support. They follow a neat pathway from the visitor's quarters through a small park area. The modified grass and plant life are a far cry from the sophisticated versions found in Maun, but the park is apparently one of the more popular areas of the Vine platform. There are humans everywhere, but no Dua. Not here.

"The gateway to the elevator," Sakata says, taking in the park. "It's terrible, isn't it?"

The ocean breeze whistles through her ears. They pass two humans, drawing on nicostics, on a bench several meters away. A small group of humans rounds the corner ahead to enter the Vine boarding area.

"It certainly makes Earth seem less appealing. And humanity."

Sakata grunts. "You can't give up on us." He rests his hand over hers. "Yes, in general, human beings are — shitty." Ligeia laughs softly. "But we do our shitty best."

As they round the corner, they are confronted by a long line of Dua in white uniforms. Dozens wind their way through a maze of digital roping, its letters flashing "NCI Designated Boarding" and "Departure 2709" and "Time Remaining: 002:39:46." The winding line culminates in a wide opening where the Dua present their credentials, enter the Vine under a green glow, and disappear into the darkness. The Dua give them little more than a glance as Sakata and Ligeia pass by. Authority are scattered throughout the winding line, pushing the Dua as they trudge along, one after the other.

Further along the dock is the human boarding area, where passengers take their turn at scanning their RistWaches and ascend a ramp leading to a spherical elevator car that will carry them to the Vine Station orbiting high above. The passenger area comprises the top three levels of the 10-level car. Ligeia notices passengers standing already at the observation windows, their tiny figures dark against the glass. She tears her eyes from the elevator just in time to see Erlang approach.

"Heads up," Sakata says. Erlang strides purposefully toward them, cuts through the line without stopping to apologize to a squat man who must dodge her. She carries her uniform jacket over her shoulder.

Her undershirt clings to her arms and torso, and she bears an expression that suggests she's not slept in a few days and she's looking for a reason, any reason, to lash out.

"Doctors. I'm glad you're here but confused. Dr. Sakata, you are free to board. The attendant will show you to your seat. You can come with me, Dr. Obumbwe."

"I'll wait for my colleague," Sakata says.

"Get on board, Owen," Erlang drawls.

"What's this about?" Ligeia asks, putting a hand on a hip.

"We have some business to attend to. With the boss."

"What do you mean?"

"I mean Hedges wants to speak with you."

Ligeia's throat tightens. "About what?"

"I guess we'll find out. You," she says, indicating a Dua steward standing a few meters away. "Escort Dr. Sakata to his quarters. This one is with me." Without a word, she pulls Ligeia along with her up the gangplank. Ligeia struggles to keep up with the Director's long strides. They reach a metal door, where Erlang hovers her RistWach above the wallpanel. The door swings open, revealing a room equipped with a wallscreen and a few cushioned chairs. A low table sits before them, covered with flexscreen material. "Have a seat," Erlang says as she taps at the table. The wallscreen flickers.

"You aren't dead." Walter Hedges' plasticized face fills the screen. "But you look bloody awful."

Ligeia coughs lightly, then swallows. "Thanks for your concern."

"Where were you in Mombasa?"

"Pardon?"

"You disappeared for almost twenty-four hours in Mombasa. You interfered with an Authority bot during the official performance of its duties, then you walked away. Twenty-two hours later you showed up, gravely ill. Sakata thought you were dying. So, I'll ask again, Dr. Obumbwe. Where the bloody hell were you in Mombasa?"

Ligeia clenches her jaw. She grips the back of a cushioned chair and leans forward, focusing on one of Hedge's grey eyes beneath a perfectly groomed brow.

"That's none of your business."

"You are OnyxCorp business, Dr. Obumbwe. You and everything you own. Which means you answer to me. You don't answer, you don't get on the Vine."

"And you don't get your vaccine."

"Did you miss the part about everything you own? I don't need you." He blinks. He softens his mouth into a thin smile. "But I want you to be a part of this. I need to know, Dr. Obumbwe. I need to know that you're still on board."

Crossing her arms over her chest, Ligeia paces before the wallscreen, her footfalls in perfect rhythm with her words. "You threatened my brother. You rushed me, forced me to come here with less than a month's notice. I signed your NDA and the rest of the bureaucratic bullshit documents, and I traveled here, without complaint, just to make this Vine launch."

"If you weren't happy with your accommodations, then—"

"Fuck the accommodations, Hedges. I've agreed to turn my life over so you and your cronies can make some enormous bank from my work. MY work." She stops pacing, faces the wallscreen with her hands on her hips. "So, forgive me if I don't feel like what I did during my last twenty-four hours on Earth is any of your goddamn business. I've dedicated my life to my studies. You just bought a piece. You think you can do this without me? Fine. Put me on the next transport home."

Hedges presses his lips together in a barely visible line, clenches his slim jaw. "As I said, I want you to be a part of this. If you can convince me you're still with us—"

"I have an elevator to catch, Hedges. Either I go now, or I don't go. Good luck telling your backers the project is off because you didn't approve of a night out on the town."

Hedges swallows. He reaches a hand up, scratches the side of his nose with an oval fingernail. "Get her on the Vine, Erlang." The wallscreen flickers out.

Ligeia lets out a long breath and rubs the back of her neck. Her head throbs.

"Impressive," Erlang says from a corner of the room, where she leans against the wall, a foot propped up.

Ligeia scoffs. "You heard him. Get me on the Vine. We've wasted enough time." She enters the hall without waiting for her escort, feeling surprisingly steady. Erlang catches up with her as they re-enter the boarding area, where they halt behind a half dozen other passengers.

"He doesn't trust you," Erlang says behind her.

"The feeling's mutual." Ligeia coughs again, then rubs her temples.

"There's a price to be paid there, though. None of my business, I know. Just a friendly warning." She puts a hand on Ligeia's shoulder and pushes her past the Dua attendant. "I'll handle this one."

Ligeia doesn't resist as Erlang guides her to the lift that will take them to the launch area, where they will be restrained as protection against the Vine's acceleration. Ligeia's too drained, too wrought to protest.

"You're over here," Erlang says. Ligeia allows herself to be led to a grouping of cushioned seats separated from the main launch area by a partition. A wallscreen shows a scene of bright sunlight that glimmers off a snow-covered meadow; a few sprigs of yellow peek through the snow. Sakata is already there, sipping a light brown liquid. His face lights up when he spies Ligeia. Erlang leads her to a cushioned seat, into which Ligeia throws herself. Then, Erlang herself sits in the remaining chair.

"We'll stay here until we clear the platform," Erlang says. "Then, I'll show you to your quarters. Let's try not to make any more trouble, at least for today, yes?"

Sakata huffs. Ligeia gazes out a small window at the sunlight casting its glow across the undulating sea. "Going up the Vine," she says aloud. She looks to Erlang. "Just like Jack."

"Who's Jack?" Sakata says absently.

Erlang frowns as she meets Ligeia's eyes. "A giant killer."

22

"I'M SAYING OnyxCorp is completely unprepared for what's coming."

The young exec is midway through his third drink, and with each sip, Madge Erlang observes, he grows more vocal, more belligerent with the four other passengers gathered to her left. Several other small groups of execs and civies meander about the Vine Lounge, enjoying a break from the monotony of the last three days aboard the *Klimmer*, one of two elevator cars. Once the initial excitement of being on the space elevator wears off for first-timers, most of the one hundred human passengers settle into a daily routine of three square meals and nightly entertainment. A few, however, exhibit signs of altitude sickness, including depression and paranoia. The Midway Mixer delivers just the right amount of synth to quell those symptoms.

"The bots are everywhere," an older female executive says. Erlang recognizes her as a long-standing EFC member who recently joined OnyxCorp after her retirement from public service. *Aster something.* "If anything, OnyxCorp is over prepared. There hasn't been one riot in Mombasa, and you literally cannot walk a block without running into a NiCIe. This fear-mongering is the real problem."

"Fear is the great motivator," says a man with an overly sculpted chin. Erlang remembers Chandler Hadar from her days in Senegal as the regional Authority admin. She also remembers his penchant for retaining NiCIe children as his personal household staff.

"An astute observation, Senator Jakkerson," says a man with jet-black hair and a white mustache. *Aster Jakkerson, that's it.* Erlang frowns as she recognizes the man behind the white mustache: Salim Cordev. *A bigger suck-up this world has never seen.* The remaining member of the group is a short woman with light brown skin wearing a purple headdress. Her lapel insignia designates her as a dignitary, but Erlang doesn't need it to know who she is: High Commissioner Uma Quaoar, Ambassador from SoAm.

What a group.

Erlang stands at an observation window a few feet away, a cocktail growing warm in her hand. Below, Earth is a shimmering, multicolored marble beneath puffy white clouds. There, in the green spaces that comprise the African continent, is everything she's left behind to become what she is now. Senegal, home of her birth. Her family. Zinda. *And what am I now? Personal cleaner to Walter Hedges? Medtech babysitter?* Neither Obumbwe nor Sakata are in the Lounge today. Not that Erlang blames them. Nothing worse than a cocktail hour with a bunch of egotistical corporate lackeys. Present company included.

"Bots are a blunt instrument." The young man must be a new exec. Either that or he doesn't have the faintest idea of who he's talking to. "We deliver approximately five hundred NiCIes to the moon each month. Operations is talking about increasing that by 20%. You think the bots are going to be sufficient when the NiCIe populations in places like Mombasa or Buenos Aires decide to stop cooperating?"

"Why would any of those in the general population pose a threat, Reynolds?" Aster Jakkerson's voice is thick with condescension.

Reynolds rolls his eyes. "That's what I've been telling you. We've separated families, killed mothers, fathers, brothers, sisters, children—"

"You make an interesting point, Reynolds," says Cordev. "Let's concede the remote possibility they have emotional attachments." His voice, pinched and nasally, makes Erlang's skin crawl.

"Let's not," Reynolds says disdainfully. "The sublunar tunnels—"

"Christ, again with the tunnels." Hadar brings his glass to his lips and throws back his head.

Reynolds tightens his jaw. "Fine." He downs the rest of his drink. "I'll expect a full apology when they all turn on us, right before they push us out of an airlock."

Jakkerson chuckles. The side of her mouth draws up in a smirk, accentuating the thin lines around her lips. "You shouldn't pay attention to the channels, Reynolds." She brushes a hand across her silver-grey hair to smooth it back into place. "Ever since the Symposium, you've been filling your head with that nonsense. Was Sakata really that impressive?"

"He's the first person I've seen stand up to Hedges and Proxy. I'd call that impressive."

"I'd call it anti-corp," Hadar says. "Sakata is a relic. You hear that bullshit about sending him and that NiCIe researcher up there? What a fucking waste of resources."

"It's good business," says High Commissioner Quaoar, speaking at last in her signature husky voice. "OnyxCorp is losing its public relations with the younger generation."

"Such an important group," Cordev says.

"A bunch of overprivileged crybabies," Hadar replies.

"Who certainly don't appreciate how fortunate they are," Cordev says.

"Who are necessary for the future." The High Commissioner's sharp reply calls them to attention. "They've grown up with NiCIes. They don't see them as we do, as threats. They want them treated humanely. The demonstrations in SoAm started with small groups of NiCIes, easy to put down. But they've become an issue since humans began joining. They're proving rather difficult to—quell."

"Doesn't explain why they're sending up Sakata and Dr. No-Personality Obumbwe," Hadar murmurs.

Erlang chuckles. She feels the group turn, as if one, toward her.

"Erlang, I heard you were aboard," Hadar says. "You're their handler, aren't you? What do you think?"

Their handler. What an ass. Every one of them—save for Reynolds, perhaps—knows exactly who she is. And every one of them recognized her the moment they'd stepped into the lounge.

"About Obumbwe lacking a personality?" She takes a long swig, swallows, and shrugs. "I don't think I'd say that at all."

"Commander Erlang, it's so good to see you," Jakkerson says.

"Yes, indeed," Cordev chimes in. "And congratulations are in order, yes, Director?" He gives her a wide, toothy grin.

"I was hoping Walter would be joining us," the High Commissioner says.

Erlang steps away from the observation window and strides to the circle. "Senator, good to see you too," she says, shaking Jakkerson's hand. "President Hedges will be joining us within a month, High Commissioner." She gives the High Commissioner a low bow. "I'm going ahead of him to ensure our very special guests have everything they need to do what they're going up there to do."

"Which is what, exactly?" Reynolds says.

Erlang gives him a withering look. "Director Madge Erlang, Special Authority Forces."

"Darus Reynolds," the young man replies. "OnyxCorp Engineering. A pleasure to meet you, Director."

"I'd like to be able to tell you, Reynolds," Erlang continues, "but I'd be guessing at best. They're the experts in their fields, though, and that's good enough for me."

"Fortunately, Erlang, you aren't in Accountability," Hadar says. "Knowing they're 'the experts' might be good enough in Special Forces, but it doesn't justify an expenditure on a ledger."

"Why the delay?" High Commissioner Quaoar interrupts.

Erlang shakes her head. "What's that?"

"Why didn't Walter join us this month?" Quaoar puts a hand on a hip. "I've sent three communiques updating him on the riot in Buenos Aires. Where are Authority? At the least, OnyxCorp should be handling its assets. We're doing what we can to manage the human participants."

"I'll pass the message along, High Commissioner," Erlang says.

"Will that do any good?" Quaoar snaps. "Just how much of the Authority's job are we expected to do? I forwarded intel on a known

SoAm dissenter weeks ago, right down to his predicted destination in Mombasa. The only way I could have made it easier was if I'd apprehended him myself."

"I understand, Uma," Erlang says soothingly. "But you know Authority operations are confidential until one hundred- and fifty-days post-closing. I can assure you, however, the intel was actioned. Does that help?"

The High Commissioner sniffs. "Not with the riots."

"That's what I've been saying." Reynolds looks only a little abashed when all eyes turn on him. "No offense to you, Director. I'm sure you're doing all you can with what you have. But you must concede that OnyxCorp is not prepared to deploy the number of Authority required to address these conditions. Demonstrations are cropping up everywhere. I saw it firsthand in Maun." He points a finger at Erlang. "You were there. And so was Hedges."

"Are you talking about the naked NCIs at the Gala?" Erlang chuckles. "I wouldn't call that an uprising."

"It's not just one incident, Director, and you know it. Are you all just going to ignore the facts? There could be NiCIes on board, this very moment, who aren't what they seem."

"Reynolds," Jakkerson begins.

"Putting together a plan to kill us, or blow up the station—"

"That's enough." Erlang takes a single step toward Reynolds, who flinches. "I'm not going to have you panicking the rest of the passengers. The NiCIes are safe and secure in their compartment, just like you like them. They're separate from you, and significantly less comfortable. They're screened and questioned and tracked in ways you'll never be."

"And still Ruĝa Morto spreads," Quaoar says.

Erlang clenches her teeth. *I fucking hate politics.* She downs the last of her drink; the lukewarm liquid races down her throat. "And still it spreads. Finding a vaccine, quelling demonstrations, tracking down errant NiCIes. You can imagine why Hedges wanted to delay his trip a month. And why I must leave you now. Duty calls." She turns on her heel. "Enjoy the rest of your journey."

It's an unspoken part of her job to listen, to be where those types of conversations take place. To know who is saying what, and to whom. It's the part of her job that reminds her every day how she's waited too long to get out. How she should have taken the opportunity before *that* case, immediately after *that* mission.

Maybe there never were opportunities after all.

But there are other matters that need her attention. Now that half the journey to the Vine Station is complete, they'll be losing gravity until they dock with the structure itself. Erlang steps into the lift, leaving behind the murmuring crowd and the angry stares as the door slides closed.

Erlang takes the lift to Levels 7 and 8 and checks in with a few Authority admin passengers in the common area. The human quarters are spacious, airy, and largely empty. Most everyone is in the lounge back on Level 6, downing as much synth as they can tolerate. Erlang takes the lift to Level 9, where the VIPs are quartered.

Obumbwe and Sakata sit together in a luxuriously appointed lounge area. They've found they have a lot in common, Erlang supposes, given the easy friendship they've formed over the last few days. Ligeia sits with her legs under her on the sofa, and Sakata relaxes in a cushioned chair. They both look up when Erlang emerges from the lift.

"Doctors." They regard her warily, just as they'd looked the last few times she'd interrupted their conversation. "Just checking on you. Didn't see you at the Midway Mixer."

Obumbwe makes a face.

"I learned everything I needed to know about our exec passengers at the First Day Fete," Sakata says. "Another such experience would only deepen my disappointment."

Erlang gives a half smile. "Can't say I disagree with you, doc. We'll be arriving in less than thirty-two hours. There's a short layover in the Station, about six hours. I, ah, wanted to ask that you not wander off this time?"

Obumbwe scoffs. "I'll be on your shuttle in time, Erlang."

"I'd appreciate that. Like I said, a short layover. They're trying to make up the time lost back there." She takes a little pleasure in seeing Obumbwe bristle. "I'll check in with you at boarding."

She re-enters the lift without waiting for a response. All quiet on the human front. "Level 4."

Whereas the elevator's upper levels are spacious and brightly lit, its lower levels are meant for cargo, including NiCIes, who are crowded about a large common area. Some of them sit on sparse industrial furnishings and others cross-legged on the floor. They are all young adult males and females. OnyxCorp stopped sending NiCIes over one hundred years of age to the moon a few years ago, and they never accept children, even when they send parents.

The NiCIes closest to the lift look up when Erlang steps out and onto a narrow strip of tile that runs alongside the thick, reinforced glass wall that encloses them. Erlang meets their eyes, gives them a slight nod of acknowledgement. She strides to the comm station a few meters away and taps the flexscreen. Then she waits for one of them to approach. Several NiCIes closest to the comm simply stare at her. A few others walk away.

Erlang waits. At last, an unusually tall NiCIe with a long nose approaches the comm. He meets Erlang's eyes as he interfaces with the comm on his side of the glass.

"How is everyone today?"

The NiCIe cocks his head to the side. "Enslaved."

Erlang frowns. "I meant do you have anyone ill or injured? In need of attention?"

"I know what you meant." His blue eyes are piercing, and Erlang finds herself tempted to look away. *Zinda. This could be Zinda.* "All are healthy on this level. We'll be fit for the work you require." He glances around the room behind him, breaking the eye contact to Erlang's relief. "The rations are sparse."

None of the NiCIes look malnourished, but Erlang knows that a month on the moon will change that. Their reprieve on the Vine is possibly their last opportunity to know how it feels to have a full belly.

"I'll see what I can do. Any other requests?"

"Let us go." The NiCIe stares at Erlang as if he can see straight through her and into her thoughts. Everything about him is disconcerting, from his olive skin to his strange accent.

SoAm. It all snaps together for Erlang in an instant. But what are the chances? Is this the one they're looking for? "Talking like that gets you noticed, NiCIe."

"I meant before we free ourselves."

"I know what you meant." Erlang looks around the enclosure at the hundreds of NiCIes huddled together in the cramped quarters. They're all watching the exchange now, and Erlang becomes suddenly aware of her facial expression, her body language. Look away now and they'll see it. See it and remember it. "I'll see what I can do. About the rations." She taps the flexscreen to cut the comm. The tall NiCIe doesn't move when she backs away and strides casually back to the lift.

She enters Level 3 without hesitation, although she feels shaken. The NiCIes huddle together here as well, their expressions wary. The NiCIe who responds to the comm answers her questions with a careful "We are all well," and "We require nothing further." The other captives don't look her way at all, which Erlang finds even more disconcerting than the exchange with the tall NiCIe.

Defiant or docile. Which is worse? She tries to shake the image of Zinda's face as she takes the lift to the observation deck. "Message to NCI operations." The comm in the lift chirps. "Increase NCI rations by 50% until lunar processing. Authorization Erlang, Madge."

The comm chirps again. "Message received."

She'll get an earful from Hedges once that line item is brought to his attention, but she doesn't care. It's the least she can do.

The very fucking least.

THE LIFT STOPS at the observation deck. This level, exclusively for humans, is surrounded by palladium glass and warmly furnished with benches, cushioned chairs and sofas, and small tables. A few humans are there, engaged in private conversation. A couple sits on a sofa to Erlang's left. Erlang glances about the deck until she spots her target alone, on a bench across the room from the lift. Her head bends over a flexscreen, and orange and cream-colored ringlets of hair obscure her face. Erlang saunters across the observation floor to join her.

She eases herself down next to the young woman and takes out a drugstic. "What a day, huh?" The woman doesn't look up. Erlang blows out the vapor and takes a deep breath. Then she sighs. "Enjoying the view?"

The woman cuts her a glance from beneath the colorful curls. "I'm a newbie. What can I say?"

Erlang takes in another hit. "Sure you're not avoiding something?"

The young woman looks up from her flexscreen. "You got me, Erlang. Yes, I'm avoiding this shitty assignment for as long as I can. I realize that's not OK with you, but I really don't give a damn."

Erlang holds out the drugstic toward her. The young woman stares at it for several seconds before taking it between her fingers and putting it to her mouth.

"Better?" Erlang asks.

The young woman shrugs as vapor pours out from between her full lips. She stands, crosses to the window, and presses her palm flat against it.

"It's down there. My home." She leans her forehead against the reinforced glass. "I'll never see it again."

Erlang shakes her head. "Neither will I. We both made choices, Forsey."

The young woman scoffs. "Violet Forsey. I still don't recognize it as my own name." She meets Erlang's eyes. "I was fifteen when I made that 'choice', Erlang. Why am I still paying for it?"

"Because OnyxCorp doesn't forgive. Or forget. I need you with Obumbwe, keep an eye on her. But first, I need you to do something for me, on the quiet."

Violet pushes herself away from the glass. Her forehead has left a smudge next to her handprint. "OK." She runs her hands over her face, squeezing in at the bridge of her stubby nose. "What is it?"

"Level 4. Unusually tall NiCIe, light skin. Strong accent. Bring him to me, in my quarters."

"You said nothing about dealing with them," Violet says, the corners of her mouth turning down.

"Circumstances change." Erlang stands. Violet holds out the drugstic, but Erlang waves her off. "Keep it. We'll be docking in less than thirty-two hours. After that, I want you on Obumbwe. No more nights on the town for her. Understood?"

Violet takes another long drag. "Loud and clear." Vapor loops around her oval face as she speaks.

Erlang frowns. "Don't fuck this up, Forsey."

Tossing her head, Violet smirks. "Would it really matter if I did, *Director*?"

"Let's stay in the game as long as possible then, shall we?"

Shrugging, Violet turns back to the observation window, putting her back to Erlang. "Whatever you say, Director."

ERLANG TAKES the lift to the tenth level, where Authority headquarters is located, and enters her private quarters. She checks the comm and follows up on a few messages related to the lunar lab preparations. She makes a cup of tea and takes it with her to the low sofa in her quarters. The book she's been carrying with her since Maun, *Moby Dick*, lies on the side table. She opens it up, and within minutes finds herself re-reading the same sentence three, four, five times.

There are certain queer times and occasions in this strange mixed affair we call life when a man takes his whole universe for a vast practical joke, though the wit thereof he but dimly discerns, and more than suspects that the joke is at nobody's expense but his own.

Throwing the book on the sofa, she rises. She reaches a hand into her pocket and remembers she's given the drugstic to Violet. "Now's not the time to give it up, Madge," she grumbles. She opens a cabinet that she knows holds a bottle of twenty-five-year-old scotch, left there by her predecessor, a man who had risen and fallen as so many have done in the past, will do in the future. She pours a finger of golden liquid into a glass and gulps it down. It burns her throat and brings tears to her eyes.

Damn damn damn damn damn.

Why am I still paying for it, she'd asked.

Let us go, he'd said.

A question and a demand of the same entity. The entity that Erlang despises herself, is paying back herself, is slave to herself.

You think you know blackmail, Violet? You don't know the half of what OnyxCorp can make you do. Erlang pours herself two fingers of the scotch and takes a smaller gulp. She takes the glass with her back to the sofa, where she sinks down into the cushion with a soft groan.

It's bad enough Hedges pulls me *in every time.*

She allows her limbs to melt against the cushion as she closes her eyes and relishes the first few moments of alcohol-induced lightness. Her head buzzes. *Like the time I took Zinda to that old-timey amusement park.* One of the rides had been an experiment in weightlessness, back when artificial grav technology was new. To Erlang, who'd made dozens of journeys up the Vine, the effect was unimpressive. But Zinda had laughed and screamed and laughed again.

Has the SoAm NiCIe ever screamed with joy? Have any of them?

As if on cue, a soft chime announces someone at the door. Pushing herself from the sofa with a soft groan, Erlang stands, sets the glass on the side table, and straightens her jacket. "Enter."

Violet looks almost like a child against the tall NiCIe in the open doorway. She steps aside and gestures for the NiCIe to cross the threshold. "Delivered as requested. Will that be all, *Director?*"

Erlang frowns at Violet's sarcastic tone. "Thank you," she replies, dismissing Violet with a wave. The door slides shut as Erlang beckons the NiCIe to join her. "Have a seat." The NiCIe's expression is inscrutable as he eases himself down into a low chair to face her. "You're wondering why I've sent for you."

"Not at all."

Erlang raises an eyebrow. "Indeed? Why don't you enlighten me, then?"

He meets her eyes. Dark blue, darker than most NiCIes. She finds his gaze more than discomfiting. Intimidating. Defiant.

Dangerous.

Leaning forward, Erlang retrieves the scotch, brings it to her lips, gulps it down. They'll be docking soon. She'll be needed to supervise. Getting the NiCIes—and the dozen or so humans who would continue the journey to the moon—to the shuttle is a symphony in chaos, and the addition of the Vine casino recently only makes it worse. The through passengers are the least eager to get to their destination; hanging around the gamers for five days as they ascend the Vine only increases their displeasure.

I don't have the time for an interrogation. Erlang closes her eyes and rubs the bridge of her nose. Better to deal with this one after docking. Besides, she's tired. Tired to her bones.

"All right." She sets the empty glass on the table and rises. "We'll take this up at the station, you and I. " She taps her RistWach, and seconds later the cabin door swooshes open. A bot fills the doorway, its arms and subarms poised above the weapons it houses at its sides. "Take him to 10-4 and stand outside. No one enters but me."

"Affirmative," the bot responds.

Erlang sweeps her arm toward the open door where the bot awaits its prisoner. "Enjoy the private quarters for now." The NiCIe stands, slowly, allows Erlang to observe his full height, the breadth of his shoulders and chest. Erlang forces herself to meet his stare. "You may go." She is relieved when the bot attaches a manacle over the NiCIe's wrist and backs into the corridor. The door closes on a last scathing glance from her prisoner.

She should be pleased. He's almost certainly the SoAm NiCIe they've been squawking about for the last few weeks, the one that's been one step ahead of them the entire time. And she just casually runs into him by sheer luck. But it doesn't feel like a victory. Rather, she can't shake this feeling of impending doom, that something terrible is about to happen.

"Tired," she says aloud. "Worn out. Get some rest, Madge. Tomorrow is going to be one hell of a day." Collapsing on the sofa, she allows the scotch to wash over her as she closes her eyes.

BEFORE WE FREE OURSELVES.

She awakes suddenly when the empty glass gently taps her on the forehead once, twice, three times. They've lost gravity as the elevator slows in its final approach to the Vine Station. Erlang groans. She maneuvers around to orient herself to the floor and pushes herself gently across the room to the wardrobe, where she grabs a pair of magboots, pulls them over her feet, and engages them. They snap to the floor. The glass still floats above the sofa; a few droplets of golden liquid hover just inside its rim. Erlang strides to the sofa, plucks the glass from the air, and carries it to the ReClaimer. Stepping into the corridor, she glances at the bot standing outside Room 10-4. Its bulk practically fills the cramped hallway. "As soon as we dock, escort the prisoner to Boontjie, under my authority. Put him in an interrogation cubicle and don't let anyone near him."

"Affirmative."

Eager to put this business with the NiCle off a bit longer, Erlang follows the circular corridor in the opposite direction toward the Authority admin station.

Ludlow is on duty, a twenty-year Special Authority Forces veteran and one of the few people Erlang trusts. He stands at attention before a wallscreen that spans more than ten meters across, his back to her. Dozens of feeds fill the screen from throughout the elevator car.

Erlang clears her throat. "Morning, Ludlow." He spins around and snaps to attention.

"Good morning, Director."

"How's everything looking?"

Ludlow spins back around to face the wallscreen. "Cargo reports a canister leak that has been contained. Hazard has been notified and will remove and jettison upon arrival." Erlang peers at the two feeds in the upper left corner. "No damage to other cargo is reported. Level 3 has been quiet. Level 4 sent a message, 24 hours ago maybe."

Erlang joins him to get a closer look at the feeds from Level 4. "What's the message?" The NiCles are all strapped into the benches that line the level's walls. Many of them sleep; their limbs float awkwardly up and around.

"*Thank you*? The message said it was specifically for you."

Erlang grunts. "How many bots at the Station?"

"Admin reports a dozen per level." Ludlow gives her a sideways glance. "Permission to speak freely, Director?"

"Always."

"That seems like overkill to me. Is there a threat I should be aware of?"

238

"The High Commissioner from SoAm is here. She's been telling Intel they have a dissident at large with plans on the Station. Guess they took her seriously."

"Should we?"

"I don't know if we could get much more serious than that," she replies, motioning toward the Level 4 feed. "Let Oz and Barda know about the increased Authority at the Station. Who's on Level 7?"

"Macron."

"And Level 8?"

"Lonnagin."

"Good. Send them the list of through passengers and tell them to add a marker to those passengers' RistWaches. I'm not waiting around for them."

"Some of them may object."

"Let them. It's not the NiCIes who cause us delays. Maybe an Authority escort will send the message."

"You want to include Obumbwe and Sakata on that?"

"No. I'll see to them myself." She steps away from the wallscreen. "Good work, Ludlow. Let's report every fifteen until shuttle departure."

"Yes, Director." Ludlow resumes his position as Erlang strides to the lift. She takes it to the Observation Level, where the human passengers will gather shortly to disembark. The deck is empty save for two attendants, who will secure the airlocks. Erlang nods to them as she passes to the other side of the deck to wait for docking. Darkness begins to engulf the planet below as the elevator car slowly, steadily comes to a stop beneath the Station. Erlang listens to the crew's chatter through the comm, hears the heavy metal clamps closing on the sides of the elevator car, feels the grinding jolts that rumble through the deck. After several minutes of knocks and pings and echoes of metal on metal, there is a sudden, empty silence.

"Docking successful," the pilot says through her comm.

"Docking successful, confirm," the Station replies. "Welcome back, *Klimmer*."

"Thank you, Boontjie," the pilot replies. "We alerted you to a canister leak. We'd like to jettison and destroy before disembarking."

The passengers filter into the observation deck now, their footfalls heavy in bulky grav boots. Erlang directs them to the exit, where the two attendants wait.

"Authority says that's a negative, *Klimmer*," the Station replies. "They want the NiCIes now."

Senator Jakkerson enters the deck, followed by the High Commissioner, her headdress now a deep burgundy. Reynolds appears shortly thereafter, followed by Cordev, who chatters, as usual, to the air. Reynolds bears a look of extreme annoyance.

"We didn't get a chance to catch up, Erlang." Chandler Hadar steps away from the slow-moving crowd to stand beside her.

"Maybe next time." Erlang doesn't take her eyes from the growing jumble of human bodies that fill the observation deck.

"All right, Boontjie," comes the pilot's voice in her ear. "It's your party now. Secure airlocks."

"Airlocks secure. Boontjie, prepare for arrivals."

The passengers near the airlocks begin moving forward. They hold out their wrists so the readers can scan their 'Waches as they leave the *Klimmer* and enter the Vine Station.

"There isn't always a next time," Hadar says. Erlang cuts her eyes over at him. His hair is slicked back from his tightly stretched forehead.

"Even better."

"You have a lot of nerve, Erlang. These people, they think you're in charge." Hadar waves a hand around the observation deck. "But we both know you make one mistake, the EFC will space OnyxCorp in a heartbeat."

"That a threat, Hadar?" The deck is almost clear now, and still Erlang hasn't seen Sakata or Obumbwe.

"Not from me," Hadar says. "But if you want some advice—"

"I don't." Erlang looks him square in the face. "The casino awaits. Although I'm afraid you'll find the servers there a little old for your tastes."

Scowling, Hadar takes a step toward her. "Scientists don't pay the bills, Erlang. Hedges has wasted enough time and bank on research. You're likely to go down with the ship."

"Now, that definitely sounds like a threat, Hadar." Behind him, Sakata and Obumbwe finally emerge from the lift. "I'm sorry I don't have time for a witty exchange with you, Hadar. I have other matters to attend to."

Stepping around him, she meets the two scientists as they merge with the remaining passengers. "Not off to a good start," she says as Obumbwe nears.

"I'll make your shuttle, Erlang."

"I'm going to make sure of it. Doctors, if you'll follow me." Erlang falls in next to them.

Sakata narrows his eyes. "What's this about?"

"Making sure the Corporation's special guests are safely delivered to the moon."

"I can find my way across the Station," Obumbwe says tartly.

"Ludlow to Erlang," the comm sounds in Erlang's ear.

What now? "Erlang."

"Director, cargo's reporting another canister leak, maybe two—"

Sakata is two paces ahead of her and Obumbwe. He holds his RistWach to the interface then trudges through the airlock, leaning heavily on his cane.

"Canisters of what?" Erlang asks.

"I—I'm not sure. I can't understand—"

Obumbwe jogs to catch up with Sakata. She passes beneath the reader and into the airlock.

"We have to jettison the entire cargo! Code Red! Jettison the cargo!"

A low rumble moves up through the bottom of the elevator car.

"No, they're still in there!" Ludlow screams. The rumble deepens. Erlang notices Obumbwe turn back, midway through the airlock, a look of confusion on her face.

"Move!" Erlang screams.

She darts for the airlock, stumbles as the entire structure shakes violently. Obumbwe has just enough time to run for the Station entrance before the *Klimmer* shudders and shimmies, and Erlang falls to her knees. Smoke fills the observation deck. Choking, Erlang scrambles to her feet and runs toward the airlock.

"Move goddamn it!" she yells as she glimpses Obumbwe, framed in the Station's entrance. "Boontjie, close the airlock!"

"Repeat that, Director?"

"Fucking close the airlock!" She can't see anything now, can't breathe. An alarm blares. She sees the red flashing light, two meters away, where the door would be. Where she was on the wrong side.

"Move it!" Her voice is barely a squeak above the din of twisting metal and screeching alarms. Her lungs are on fire. She knows she's not going to make it, but she forces herself forward.

Someone grabs her by the front of her uniform and jerks her forward and through the narrowing airlock gate. She falls through, onto the floor, and rolls away.

The airlock snaps shut centimeters from her foot just as the entire station quakes and shudders and groans.

Then the entire station goes dark.

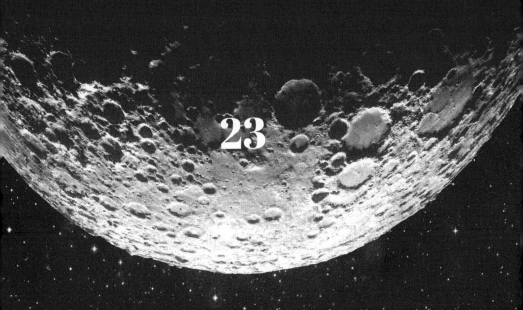

23

THICK, acrid smoke fills the air. Ligeia pushes herself up to sitting, chokes on the fumes, and finds she's pinned. Erlang sprawls across her legs. Sakata lies a few meters to her right, his face covered in blood. Alarms, screams, cries for help echo in the corridor ahead. Ligeia wriggles her legs beneath Erlang.

"Erlang, are you all right?" She squirms again, and Erlang groans as she lifts her head.

"I'm alive." Erlang pushes herself to all fours as Ligeia scrambles to Sakata's side. She checks for a pulse at his throat, finds it.

"Sakata! Owen! Can you hear me?" He flinches as she wipes blood away from his eyes..

"I can't see."

"It's blood. Wait. Let me do it." Ligeia brushes his hands from his face and twists out of her jacket, the second one she's sacrificed to a bloodsoaked victim on this trip. She dabs at Sakata's face with the sleeve.

"Is it bad?" Erlang and Sakata say at the same time.

Ligeia frowns as blood saturates the sleeve. "I can't tell yet—"

The station rumbles again. In the passage ahead, the station's lights flicker. Screams grow louder. Figures, silhouetted against the smoke-

243

filled corridor, lurch toward the lights. Erlang sways, steadies herself with a hand on Ligeia's shoulder.

"We have to go!" Above the din of screams and cries the station creaks and twists. "It's not over!" She hauls Sakata up with a hand beneath his armpit, but Ligeia pulls him back down.

"Give me a minute!" The blood won't stop. A lot of blood. From where, though? Another low rumble vibrates beneath them.

"We don't have a minute!" Erlang lifts Sakata to her shoulder as if he were a small child. "We're going, now!" She strides toward the station's interior. Ligeia jogs after her, trailing the blood-soaked jacket.

Sakata bounces against Erlang's shoulder, wincing in pain. He lets out a violent cough, then a low groan. "Rib," he says weakly. Blood drips from his head to the floor.

Ligeia grabs Erlang's upper arm. "I have to stop the bleeding, Erlang. There's too much—"

"Just a few steps, doctor." Erlang's voice is steady. "Stay with me." They pass a woman lying in a protective fetal position, her burgundy headdress askance. Erlang hesitates for a moment. "It's High Commissioner Quaoar. Doc?"

Ligeia's eyes water. She squats next to the Ambassador and puts a hand against her neck. "Breathing," she says. Erlang lowers Sakata, and Ligeia pulls his arm over her shoulder.

"I'll meet you ahead. Get as far into the Station as you can." Erlang turns to the unconscious woman as Ligeia takes on Sakata's weight.

"Come on, Owen." She lurches forward with her arm around his midsection. "We're close."

THE SMOKE THINS as they exit the corridor into a spacious marketplace. The words *Welcome to the Vine Station: Gateway to the Moon...and Beyond* scroll above them across an arched ceiling. Emergency lights blink in rapid pulses, casting a dim glow that Ligeia follows into the Vine Station.

"What," Sakata gasps, "happened?"

Ligeia spies several shadowy figures ahead. As they draw closer, sobs, cries of pain, and angry words drift their way. She glances behind her. No Erlang.

She spots a small group huddled next to a food kiosk. "Over here." She lowers Sakata into a nearby chair. "Let me take a look." She dabs at his head with her ruined jacket until the source is revealed: A small but deep cut on the top of his head. "It's just a gash. Can you hold this against it while I look for something?" Sakata nods as he presses his hand over Ligeia's. "I'll be right back." She takes two steps away before Erlang emerges, half lifting, half pulling Uma Quaoar Her burgundy headdress sits awkwardly on the side of her head.

"High Commissioner!" A woman Ligeia recognizes as Senator Jakkerson rushes to the woman's other side and lifts her by the arm. "My god, Erlang, what's happening?" They lower the High Commissioner into a chair not far from Sakata. Ligeia doubles back.

"Is she injured?" Ligeia leans over Quaoar, feeling for broken bones or injuries, her hands steady although her heart thumps against her chest.

"I'm fine," High Commissioner Quaoar rests a hand at her heart. "Just got the wind knocked out of me."

Ligeia rises. "No serious injuries. Are there emergency supplies somewhere?"

Erlang nods. "We need to get to admin." She glances around the small group. "Is anyone else injured?"

Ligeia shakes her head. "I haven't che—"

A low, broadening rumble moves through the station. A few people cry out, clasp at each other for support.

"Everyone, listen to me," Erlang says. Her locks are loose and flow around her shoulders. Blood has coagulated at her temple. "We're going to go further into the station, to the administration pod. It's the safest place on the station. Can everyone walk?"

Murmurs of assent are muffled by another low rumble. Erlang hoists the High Commissioner to her feet and steadies her. "Everyone stay close, and I promise you'll be OK."

"Keep pressure on your head," Ligeia says as she pulls Sakata's arm over her shoulder. "We have to keep up."

"I'll do my best," Sakata wheezes.

Erlang's broad back is already obscured by the thick smoke ahead. Ligeia half drags Sakata as she hurries to catch up to the small, scared group. Another low rumble shakes the station, this time less severe. After a few agonizing moments in which Ligeia loses track of Erlang, she spots the High Commissioner's burgundy headdress ahead, silhouetted against an open airway. As they stumble forward into the airlock, Erlang peers into the corridor, waits a few seconds, then closes the door. In the time it takes her to cross the lock to the other door, the lock has pressurized. She waits for the green light, then opens the door that leads into the Vine Station's administration pod, Authority headquarters.

"My god! High Commissioner!" A thin, middle-aged man scrambles to his feet from the floor. "Are you alright? I thought you were—"

"Chandler Hadar. Why am I unsurprised to see you here?" Erlang pushes past the man to deposit Uma Quaoar into a nearby chair. "I'll bet you were the first one here, weren't you?" Erlang growls as she rounds on him.

LIGEIA EASES Sakata onto a cushioned bench several meters away. He holds the ruined jacket against his head. Ligeia pulls his hand and the jacket away gently. The deep gash still bleeds freely, but the pace has slowed.

"Good. Keep putting pressure on it. There has to be a medpack here somewhere."

"I'll go down with the ship, will I?" Ligeia looks up to see Erlang lurch for Hadar and catch his arm at the elbow. She twists it inward, and he falls to his knees with a high-pitched groan. "Chandler Hadar, you're under arrest." Erlang reaches around to the side of her belt and draws out a pair of restraints, then fastens one restraint over the man's wrist.

"Erlang's making a mistake," Sakata says, closing his eyes. He sways a little as Ligeia presses his hand against the gash.

"Yeah, what's new?" Ligeia mumbles.

"Tell her. She doesn't know enough. I mean she's right, but she's making a mistake in saying it now, without—"

"Director, I insist you stop—" says Senator Jakkerson.

Erlang pulls Hadar's free arm behind him with a hard jerk. Hadar groans and doubles over. "I have reason to believe this man is responsible for what just happened, and as Director, I have jurisdiction at this Sta—"

"Erlang, you will release Hadar immediately." Behind Ligeia, the High Commissioner has risen. She leans heavily on Senator Jakkerson's arm. Her headdress, torn and filthy, has been put aright.

"The hell I will." Erlang pulls Hadar to his feet. "This man made a direct threat to me."

"Bullshit," Hadar says in a long groan.

"Director, I insist you release Chandler Hadar." The High Commissioner's gravelly voice stops Erlang short. "It's clear to everyone here what has happened, and I won't allow you to make Hadar a scapegoat for your incompetence."

"As I said," Sakata mumbles, so low only Ligeia catches it.

Hadar's face is slick with sweat, his jaw tight. Erlang jerks him toward her and glares at Quoaor.

"And what is that supposed to mean?" Erlang says.

Quoaor takes an unsteady step away from Jakkerson. "You were warned of the high probability of a terrorist attack somewhere along the Vine. SoAm Intel informed you of a NiCIe dissident weeks ago, yet you did nothing, *nothing* to increase security. I had to call in a favor with Boontjie to get the Authority we needed to supervise the transfer of NiCIes to the shuttle. And now what has happened?" Her mouth twists. "Director Erlang, you allowed a NiCIe terrorist on board the *Klimmer*. Perhaps you did so in ignorance, but that doesn't matter to the people who have lost their lives—"

"That's a lie."

"Is it? I understand Authority found this SoAm escapee as soon as the NiCIes began disembarking. Aren't you charged with vetting the cargo?"

Erlang scoffs. "Figures." She jerks Hadar around, snaps the restraints open and pulls them from his wrists, none too gently, then shoves him away. She fastens the restraints to her belt. "I guess this target was just too tempting without Hedges here. The cat's away, and all that."

"How dare you—" But Erlang has already turned her back to the High Commissioner. "There are questions, Director!"

"Send them to Hedges. I wish I could see the look on his face when he hears about this."

Tearing her eyes from the scene, Ligeia bends toward Sakata. "Come on," she says in a low voice. "We're going with Erlang."

Swaying as he stands, Sakata drapes his arm around her shoulders and staggers alongside her as she marches after Erlang.

"Erlang." The Director doesn't react. "Erlang!" Ligeia calls again. "Wait up!"

"Get to the shuttle, Obumbwe. I'm getting everyone out of here in 15 minutes." Ligeia increases her pace, dragging Sakata with her. They pass four bots posted at each corner of a short airlock and emerge unimpeded in a smaller pod lined with wallscreens. Bots stand at attention at regular intervals, while humans mill about, shouting, their foreheads creased with worry as they scramble to contain the disaster unfolding on the Vine Station. "The docking supervisor on duty," Erlang calls. "Where are they?"

A woman glances at Erlang and, seeing the insignia, snaps to attention. "Director, Special Agent Plano is in command of Boontjie. You'll find him that way, second office on the right."

Sakata limps beside her, but Ligeia doesn't want to risk losing Erlang. When she finally catches up, Sakata wheezes and coughs; his arm slips from Ligeia's shoulder. She struggles to pull him through the door just behind Erlang.

A youngish man looks up from a desk over which a holographic image of the Vine Station hovers. "Seal that level off. I want a forensics crew in there before the half hour." He waves them in. "Tell the Senator that he's not leaving my custody until I get that warrant. I don't answer to the High Commissioner. Director Erlang." He stands. "I heard you were aboard. I'm glad to see you're OK."

"Where's the NiCIe?"

Plano glances at Ligeia and Sakata. "If you're referring to the prisoner you had transferred at docking, we have him in custody."

"I need to see him." Again, the agent cuts his eyes over at Ligeia and Sakata. Erlang looks to Ligeia, her eyes narrowed, but Ligeia merely crosses her arms over her chest and cocks her head. Erlang sighs. "They're with me, Special Agent. That's all you need to know."

The agent clears his throat. "Two doors down. But you have less than a half hour. The High Commissioner's on a rampage, and she's got Jakkerson getting the sign off from the Council to take him back down. They're serious about getting him back to SoAm."

Escapee? SoAm? Ligeia swallows against the sudden tightness in her throat, pushing down the hope that rises in her chest. "What happened?"

Plano gives her a sharp look. So does Erlang.

"What happened, Special Agent?" Erlang repeats. Plano grunts. He holds a hand over the hologram. "As far as we can tell, there was an explosive device here." He points to the *Klimmer's* cargo bay. "We're not done with our investigation yet, but my guess is the canisters were a diversion. Set to make the whole thing look, well, cruder than it was."

"The explosive device?"

"If a NiCIe put that together—Well." He glances again at Ligeia. "I'd be surprised. But they're calling for blood. We lost sixty-three crewmen, and a dozen unaccounted for. Not to mention the three hundred-plus assets."

Ligeia's stomach turns. *Over three hundred dead.*

"Then we better make this fast, Special Agent." Erlang steps aside to gesture toward the corridor outside.

Special Agent Plano stands and straightens his jacket. "Follow me."

TWO DOORS down the curving corridor, two Authority stand outside a closed door. The Special Agent approaches them. "Authorization Plano, Jorge. Special Agent, Vine Station Authority." The doors slide open, and the Authority step aside.

The NiCIe's arms lie atop a metal table; restraints around his wrists make it impossible for him to move. His forehead touches the tabletop, spiky white hair caked with ash, legs secured to the chair. He lifts his head when the door slides open. A badly swollen eye, a deep cut across the bridge of his long nose, a busted lip, and a single glint of sapphire.

Ligeia fights to suppress the cry that rises in her throat. The NiCIe blinks and squints. He scans the group from Plano to Erlang. To Sakata. To Ligeia.

His eyes widen.

No. Ligeia gives a quick jerk of her head. *No, Caen.*

Because Caen it is. Bruised and bleeding, but alive.

Alive!

But how? She presses her lips together, meets his eyes and jerks her head again.

"Leave us, Special Agent," Erlang says. Plano hesitates. "I'm still the Director, Plano. At least for now."

"Fifteen minutes, Director. That's all I can give you."

He ducks outside, and the door slides closed behind him. Erlang crosses to the table, presses her palms flat against its top, and leans forward.

"Right in front of my face." Caen cranes his neck to meet Erlang's stare. "Sixty-three people lost their lives today."

A shadow passes over Caen's face. "That's terrible. But I had nothing to do with—whatever it is that's happened."

"What are you doing here? Who escapes *to* the moon?" Erlang says. "Who did you know already in Mombasa?"

"I know no one in Mombasa."

"Bullshit. Who are you working with?"

"Why would he kill his own people?" Ligeia offers. Erlang glares.

"Kill...*my* people?"

"They lost over three hundred *assets,*" Sakata croaks, then breaks into a coughing fit. He leans heavily against the wall next to the door, his face deathly pale.

"Maybe they see themselves as expendable as the Corporation does," Erlang says, shrugging.

Ligeia puts her hands on her hips. "I think you know that's not true, Director. Three hundred Dua. And why here? If he's some kind of mastermind terrorist like you all seem to think, why would he go to the trouble of coming up here? There are hundreds of places in Mombasa alone that would have been better targets."

Erlang paces a few times as she fumbles around in her jacket pocket, uttering an angry, "Bloody hell," when she doesn't find the drugstic. "Then who?"

"Who gains from a violent attack on the Vine Station?" Caen asks, blinking. "Dua? No Dua would be unaware of the consequences of such an act. This attack will only make conditions harder for our people. So who gains?"

"The EFC, SoAm. Maybe the African Republic," Sakata wheezes, drawing everyone's attention. His eyes are closed, and he looks like he could collapse. "If they discredit OnyxCorp's handling of security, any of them can call for a review of the Vine Agreement."

"Which means they could start cutting away at OnyxCorp's stranglehold on the lunar mines." Ligeia lifts an eyebrow. "They're going to make you take the fall, Erlang."

Erlang grunts. "It'd take months to prove a plot like that. We have less than fifteen minutes."

Ligeia bites her lip. "If you let them take him, you'll never know the truth."

Erlang's jaw flexes. "I know."

Ligeia takes a step toward Caen. "Let us take him."

"Are you crazy? Let a terrorist in custody escape. You think my career's in trouble now—"

"Did you see that mob out there? I did. Sakata did. Kind of mob like that could storm in here and toss him out an airlock before any of us had a chance to stop them."

"He's a suspect in an event of international terrorism," Sakata chimes in. "There's a clear and present danger to his life. Call their bluff. Invoke jurisdiction under the NCI Rights Clause. Worry about whether you're within the law when it comes before the Council."

Encouraged, Ligeia adds, "If they get rid of him, you'll be next. What happens to her then? What happens to Zinda?"

Erlang cuts a glance at her. *You're crossing that line*, her eyes say. But she begins pacing again, slow, thoughtful. "Let's say I invoke jurisdiction and wrestle custody of this NiCIe from the High Commissioner."

"My name is Caen."

Erlang scoffs. "Let's get something straight here, NiCIe. Something doesn't add up, and I'm going to find out what it is. I want justice. But I don't give one damn about *you*."

Caen sticks out the tip of his tongue, running it across his broken lip. "And I don't give a damn about your *justice*."

"Can we quit with the posturing?" Ligeia throws up her hands. "We're running out of time."

Erlang shakes her head. "I can't protect you. You'd be on your own when they find out. And they will find out."

"He'll come with me," Sakata says.

"This was my idea—" Ligeia begins.

"And it's a good idea. But I have considerably less to lose. Don't I, Erlang?"

Erlang wrests her eyes from Caen, her brows furrowed. "This doesn't change the nature of our relationship one bit, doctor."

"I wouldn't dream of it." Sakata pushes himself away from the wall and sways unsteadily. "Shall we?"

Erlang glances around the room. "I can't believe I'm doing this. This thing goes sideways, I'm not going down alone."

"Neither am I," Ligeia replies.

"Nor I." Ligeia dares a glance at Caen, taking note of the trickle of blood over his clenched jaw. He doesn't meet her eyes.

Erlang takes a breath. She opens the door, steps into the corridor, and faces the Authority standing at attention.

"I'm remanding NCI790612 to an undisclosed location. I claim jurisdiction in the matter of NCI790612 under Section 11 Article 3.49 Addendum 1 of the Earth Federation Council Constitution, commonly known as the NCI Rights Clause. I certify I have the right of jurisdiction by virtue of my citizenship in the EFC and my rank as Director of Special Authority Forces, a wholly separate and independent entity serving both the Earth Federation Council and its citizenry and OnyxCorp and its assets. Authorization Erlang. Madge. Special Authorization Code Ishmael."

They wait, breathless. Finally, the bot's electronic response comes: "Action received. Affirmative."

Erlang marches back into the room, reaches for the restraints around Caen's wrists, and snaps them open.

"You'll take this corridor around to the security access to the shuttle," Erlang says. "I'll let them know you're coming. Get to the shuttle and don't come out of your quarters, Sakata, until I come get you. Stay out of sight, all of you, and away from me."

Ligeia notices Caen's head snap up at Sakata's name. He eyes the old doctor curiously as he glides around the table to join them at the door.

Erlang steps back into the corridor, glancing one way, then the other. "Let's go." She points down the corridor, where it gently curves to the left.

"What about you?" Ligeia asks.

"I have some comms to make. Some people to piss off." She takes a few steps in the opposite direction, then looks back at them. "Don't talk to anyone." Then she strides down the hallway toward the main entrance, leaving them to make their way to the shuttle alone.

"We have to go." Sakata's face is drawn and colorless. He looks as if he's aged another ten years in the last hour. Gently, Ligeia lifts his arm to place it over her shoulders.

"I'll carry him." Effortlessly, Caen scoops Sakata into his arms. "Lead the way."

They see no one—human, Dua, or bot—until they emerge from the lift, where a young woman in Authority garb waits. After confirming Sakata and Ligeia's identity, she escorts them to the shuttle. It's crowded with humans. Their faces show confusion and terror, and many bear cuts and scrapes from the chaos that erupted only a few minutes ago.

"Launch is in ten minutes. They want everyone off the station in case of another attack. We must hurry to your cabins."

"Dr. Ligeia Obumbwe!" Ligeia looks behind her to see a young woman, her face surrounded by orange and cream ringlets, maneuvering through the crowd. *Don't talk to anyone? Dammit.* "Dr. Obumbwe, am I glad to see you. I'm Violet Forsey. I've been assigned as your personal assistant. Courtesy of OnyxCorp. I was so worried you'd been harmed."

Ligeia narrows her eyes, glances toward Caen, who cradles Sakata in his arms. "I'm sorry, Ms. Forsey, but we're in a bit of a rush—"

"And I'm here to help!" Violet's full grin bares her teeth a little too much. "I'm responsible for ensuring your safe travel to the lunar facility." She seems to notice Sakata finally when his head lolls back in Caen's arms. "Is that Dr. Sakata? My god, he's hurt—"

"Doctors, please follow me. Director Erlang was quite specific." The officer inserts herself between Violet and Ligeia. A flash of annoyance crosses Violet's face, quickly replaced by a thin smile. "This way."

The officer leads them through the crowd and into another lift that takes them to the shuttle's private quarters, reserved only for dignitaries and other important personnel.

"You won't be bothered here. Dr. Sakata is here," the woman says, touching her RistWach to the panel, "and you are next door, Dr. Obumbwe." The door swooshes open, and Caen ducks inside with Sakata in his arms.

"Thank you, officer," Ligeia says. "We'll take it from here."

"Safe flight, doctor." She leans a little to the side to peer past Ligeia and into the room. "I'll let Erlang know you're safe."

Ligeia takes a sideways step to block her view. "I appreciate that." The officer looks askance at Violet, who waits just at the door's edge, and backs away. Smiling far too brightly, Violet bounces inside just as Ligeia touches the wall panel to close the door between them.

Inside, Caen sits on the edge of a low bed. He holds Sakata's hand between his. The room has little else, just enough to provide comfortable accommodations for a twenty-four hour journey from the Station to the moon: A table, a couple of chairs, a lavatory, a wardrobe, and a single wall covered with wallscreen material.

"May I?" Ligeia takes Sakata's hand in hers. Clammy. She puts her fingers against his neck and feels his pulse, faint but steady. "I know there's a medkit in here somewhere. Can you find it?"

"Yes." He rises and strides to the lavatory.

"You," Ligeia says to Violet. "Keep this pressed against that cut on his head." The strange young woman obeys as Ligeia probes Sakata's side, feeling for the self-diagnosed broken rib.

"What's with the NiCIe?" Violet whispers. "Do you know him? They're saying a NiCIe did this. To kill one of you. Or the High Commissioner. Or both."

"What?" Ligeia narrowed her eyes. "What are you talking about?"

"It's all over the comms. Look." Keeping one hand across Sakata's forehead, Violet reaches for the wallscreen control on the side table and taps it. The panel lights up, and the wall flickers with six different channels, each with a code in the upper right corner so viewers can link their audio sensors.

"Keep pressure on that head wound, please," Ligeia says, annoyed. She notes the channel titles: *OnyxCorpNews, OnyxCorp Trends for Tomorrow, OnyxCorp Presents, OnyxCorp Breakthroughs!,* and *OnyxCorp LunarLinks.* They all feature the same feed: Footage of the cargo bay of the elevator blowing out in an explosion of debris and bodies.

The sixth channel is static. It is the elevator feed.

"Volume up," Ligeia says.

"...tell us that sixty-three brave Citizens were killed in the explosion, which also damaged life support on the Asset Transportation Levels. Reports estimate asset losses at no more than three hundred total. In a statement from OnyxCorp, the Corporation acknowledged the quote 'terrible accident today on the Vine car, resulting in the tragic loss of sixty-three patriots. OnyxCorp remains committed to its lunar mission and assures its patrons they will experience no disruptions in products or services.' More details are forthcoming." The feed switches to show an attractive woman standing at the entrance to the causeway leading from the Station lobby through to the damaged elevator car. Smoke still hangs in the air, giving the scene an otherworldly quality. "Sabryna Bywood reporting from the Vine."

"Thank you, Sabryna." The feed changes to a man seated at an illuminated desk. "While Authority conducts a thorough investigation into the incident, High Commissioner Uma Quaoar of the Republic of SoAm, who was on the Vine at the time of the attack, tells

OnyxCorpNews that SoAm intel uncovered a NiCIe plot to murder two top OnyxCorp scientists several weeks ago."

High Commissioner Quaoar's face fills the wallscreen. "We alerted OnyxCorp that a SoAm NiCIe had gone off the grid several weeks ago, his whereabouts unknown. An interrogation of the NiCIe's only known contacts suggested he had specific targets in two scientists."

"Which scientists, High Commissioner," the interviewer asks.

"I hesitate to say. We learned too late, I'm afraid, of their presence on the Vine, and presently we don't know if they survived the attack."

"They're saying it was an attempt on us," Ligeia says incredulously. Was that the reason for the Authority escort? Then why hadn't Erlang said anything? "But that doesn't make sense."

Behind her, Caen clears his throat, and Ligeia jumps. He pushes past Violet and hands Ligeia a medkit. Violet casts a dark eye on him and flinches as he brushes against her.

"What's he doing here?" Violet asks, a little sharply.

Ligeia opens the medkit and pulls out a thin cylinder. She adjusts its settings and leans over the old man, whose breathing is steady but shallow. She holds the cylinder above the gash on Sakata's head, sterilizing and sealing the wound.

"Where's he from? I don't remember being told a NiCIe would be part of your staff."

Ligeia keeps her eyes on the laser, barely registering the young woman's questions. "You'll have to ask Sakata."

"Or you can just ask me," Caen says. Ligeia clenches her jaw.

"What did you say?" Violet snaps.

"You heard me."

Violet clears her throat. "Dr. Obumbwe, I'm only here to help you—"

"Then help, for fuck's sake!" Ligeia cries, throwing up her hands. "I don't know who you are, or why you're here, and I'm just a little busy, Personal Assistant Violet Forsey. I'll be happy to discuss your concerns about Sakata's NiCIe attendant when he's not in immediate danger. Now, please, will you piss off!"

Violet sets her jaw. Without another word, she marches to the door, opens it, and disappears into the corridor.

"WELL, THAT WENT WELL," Caen murmurs in the silence that follows.

Sakata's body shakes as he struggles not to laugh, then groans in pain. "Ribs. Still ribs," he says, opening his eyes to meet Ligeia's. "I'm not dead yet." A corner of his mouth turns up. Then his eyes widen. He nods to the wallscreen. "Erlang."

Erlang stands before a throng of reporters, dozens of lights trained on her face. She's changed into her dress uniform.

"...in the escape attempt, and subsequently died of his wounds."

"Director, where is the body?"

"The body was jettisoned, as is standard practice with dead assets."

"What documentation can you provide to confirm this was the SoAm NiCIe?"

"We will be releasing those documents once the one hundred and fifty-day waiting period expires."

"What's your answer to the High Commissioner's charge that Authority ignored intel that could have led to this NiCIe's apprehension in Mombasa?"

Ligeia notices Erlang's jaw tighten. "The High Commissioner knows the intel was actioned, but the leads didn't pan out."

"Director Erlang, what about the suggestion that OnyxCorp isn't appropriately staffing security?"

"I don't know what you mean."

"The High Commissioner says SoAm requested increased Authority presence in its provinces to combat the growing unrest, with no response from OnyxCorp."

Erlang smiles thinly. "Again, the High Commissioner knows that her request was received and will be actioned."

"But what about the charge that OnyxCorp is actively withholding Authority to destabilize the SoAm area—"

Erlang puts a hand up. "Thank you. We'll share more as it becomes available."

"Director Erlang, why isn't the president here?"

"When did you know the NiCIe terrorist was aboard?"

Ligeia mutes the sound. She looks to Sakata, then Caen. A curious triangle, brought together by an even more curious set of events. Sakata's breathing comes easier now, and his pulse is steady although still shallow.

"Told you. She made a mistake back there." Sakata's eyes close as he groans softly. "There's so much we don't know yet." His body relaxes against the mattress, and his face grows slack with unconsciousness.

Ligeia and Caen both reach out to smooth the gray hair from Sakata's forehead. Their fingers touch. They linger for a moment before they pull away and face one another.

"I thought you were dead." Ligeia meets Caen's eyes. "On the *Constellation*. I saw so many dead."

"I thought so too, for a while," Caen says slowly. He blinks. "So many. Tossed over the side, like refuse. Children. Dua who were only seeking a better life. A part of me died with them." He reaches across Sakata's body to clutch Ligeia's hands. "Then I saw your face back there and—" He swallows, squeezes her hands. "I knew we had more to do, together."

His hands are warm in hers, comforting. Grounding. Giving her the sense that she is tethered to something, even in the nothingness of space. Tethered to truth. Perhaps even tethered to love.

"What do we do now?"

Sakata coughs and groans a little. "Burn it down." He tosses as if in a dream. Ligeia pulls a coverlet over him.

So many hurt. So many dead.

Finn.

The demonstrators at the gala.

The group on the maglev.

The child right before it disappeared into the black water.

Caen runs his hand through his spiked hair. "We have to stop it." He grasps her hand in his. An electric pulse courses up her arm and into her chest. "It all has to stop."

She knows it does. She doesn't know how, but it must end. She can't see any other way around it.

"Burn it down," she repeats. "Burn it to the fucking ground."

acknowledgments

When I decided I'd try my hand at writing a book in 2012, I had no idea what I was getting myself into. Fresh off a lengthy dissertation process, I felt confident in my writing skills, but it quickly became apparent that academic writing and creative writing were very different animals. I want to thank some of my early beta readers, Angelic Rodgers, Robyn Lane, Tom Coleman, Rick Taverner, and Zak Haynie, for trudging through and being so very kind with feedback and encouragement. I'm glad you weren't completely honest, otherwise I probably wouldn't have kept working.

My mom was kind enough to read a later, better version, in which Ligeia's parents were perfectly horrible people, and I want to assure her that in no way did that reflect on my own parents. They're just about the best people I know, and they've always encouraged me to go for my dreams, even when those dreams might seem a little weird.

I cannot thank my agent, Stephanie Hansen with Metamorphosis Literary Agency, enough for taking me on. I was lucky enough to pitch my book to her at a writing workshop in Kansas City in 2015, and she extended a contract to me even after reading an early version that, in retrospect, seems unreadable today. She coached me through edits, breaking up *Vagabonder* into two smaller books (that's right, Part Two is on its way!), and being patient with publishers until she found the right home in Aurelia Leo.

Finally, none of this would have been possible without the support, feedback, brilliant ideas, and love from my forever partner in life, Joe. Writing a book is very hard, and I wouldn't have gotten through it if he hadn't been there to encourage me. He believed in me as a writer well before I ever believed in myself.

I hope this makes you proud, my love.

about the author

R. T. Coleman grew up in Little Rock, Arkansas, where she nurtured a passion for reading and writing while nestled among blankets and pillows in her bedroom closet. Her love of science fiction was born when she saw Star Wars in the theater in 1977. Imagine her disappointment when she realized she could never actually be Princess Leia. She lives in Springfield, Arkansas, with her partner Joe on their 25-acre farm, where she works as an instructional designer by day and a writer and editor by night. *Vagabonder* is her debut novel. Find out more at www.rt-coleman.com